PRAISE FOR
CATHERINE ANDERSON'S NOVELS

"One of the finest writers of romance."
— #1 *New York Times* bestselling author Debbie Macomber

"Catherine Anderson doesn't shy away from characters who face life's toughest challenges—but she also gifts readers with a romantic tale that celebrates the hope and resilience of the human spirit."
— #1 *New York Times* bestselling author Susan Wiggs

"Catherine Anderson writes with great emotional depth and understanding of complex relationships and family dynamics."
— #1 *New York Times* bestselling author Sherryl Woods

"Catherine Anderson weaves beautiful stories overflowing with emotion and heart. *The Christmas Room* is an absolute keeper, destined to be read again and again."
— *New York Times* bestselling author RaeAnne Thayne

"Master storyteller Anderson has skillfully penned the heart-wrenching story of domestic abuse and its aftermath . . . compelling."   — *Booklist* (starred review)

"The minute you open an Anderson novel, you can immediately feel the vision of humanity and warmth that runs through all her books. No one does heartfelt romance better!"   — RT Book Reviews

STRAWBERRY HILL

A MYSTIC CREEK NOVEL

Catherine Anderson

JOVE
New York

A JOVE BOOK
Published by Berkley
An imprint of Penguin Random House LLC
1745 Broadway, New York, NY 10019

A JOVE BOOK, BERKLEY, and the BERKLEY & B colophon
are registered trademarks of Penguin Random House LLC.

ISBN: 9780399586361

First Edition: December 2018

Printed in the United States of America
1   3   5   7   9   10   8   6   4   2

Cover art: Polar bear cub by Eric Isselee; Strawberries by Lubava

This book is dedicated to my sons, Sidney Jr. and John, who have both been the joys of my life, each in his own way, and to my wonderful grandsons, Joshua, Liam, and Jonas. They carry forward my husband's surname and are doing so in a way that would make him extremely proud.

I also wish to thank my editor, Kerry Donovan, for all that she did to support me during the completion of this novel. I'm also very grateful for others at the publishing house who were supportive of her efforts and of me as a writer.

Prologue

It's too quiet here. Not a peaceful quiet, but the kind that makes the hair stand up on the back of my neck. Slade Wilder drew his horse to a halt. He didn't travel this trail often, only when he rode for pleasure, but he knew the area like the back of his hand. About five feet ahead and off to his left was an avalanche area where rocks, both large and small, precariously blanketed a steep slope. The stones periodically broke loose and rained hell on anything in their way. Slade always practiced caution as he passed over this section of trail, but never in his memory had being here given him the heebie-jeebies. *It's almost as if something terrified is watching me.* Some people would laugh at that notion, but he never had, especially not in a wilderness area. Any woodsman knew that a sixth sense did exist in both animals and humans, and to make light of it was foolhardy.

He studied the path ahead, which had been chiseled into the mountainside by human hands and then worn to a curvy ribbon by countless human and equine feet. Bordered on the north side by rocks, the narrow track gave way on the right to a sharp, boulder-strewn decline where lofty pines, still skirted by a thin crust of snow in mid-April, struggled for purchase to remain upright. One stone about a foot in diameter lay at the trail's center, surrounded by a scatter of smaller rocks. It was due to recent shifting, Slade knew, because the debris hadn't been there when he'd ridden up the mountain earlier. Normally he'd hear squirrels chattering and birds singing, but right now even the wind seemed to be holding its breath.

Slade couldn't recall ever having felt this uneasy here. Acutely aware of everything around him, yes, but never edgy. His family's ranch, which he now operated, rested about a mile away at the base of this peak. As a youngster he had played in these woods with his friends. Later as a teenager he'd pitched a tent under a tree, gathered tubers and berries, cooked his supper over an open fire, and stayed the night alone. This whole mountainside had been an extension of his backyard. Heck, he'd even lost his virginity under one of those pine trees.

Slade released a breath and refocused on the present. The rockslide had apparently frightened all the wildlife in the immediate area, so he assumed it had happened just before he got within earshot. He pictured chipmunks sitting motionless on tree limbs, deer frozen in their tracks, and other creatures hiding in their burrows. While shifting in the saddle, he realized that his Wrangler jeans had gone damp with sweat where his thighs pressed against the leather. All his mental alerts still jangled. With over sixty years of wilderness experience under his belt, he knew better than to ignore his feelings. They had saved his ass more times than he could count, allowing him to live long enough to get arthritis and so much silver in his dark brown hair that he was tempted to dye it.

Even Bogey, Slade's trusted red roan, felt tense beneath him. The gelding didn't like the vibes he was getting, either, Slade guessed. When a woodland went this quiet, both man and beast paid attention.

Keeping his mouth closed, Slade drew in a breath. It was then that he smelled it. *Fresh blood.* It was faint but unmistakable, a metallic scent, and made his skin pebble with goose bumps. Next he caught the almost imperceptible scent of black bear, which he'd always likened to a wet hound that had wallowed in something rotten. Online environmentalists claimed that bears didn't stink, that they smelled like the berries and other things they ate, which might be true at a zoo or rescue site, but it wasn't in the wild. A bear was an opportunistic diner, an omnivore that fed on both vegetation and meat, the latter sometimes carrion that stank to high heaven. The odor clung to them.

He studied the rocks that blanketed the mountainside. *Nothing alarming.* All the boulders looked firmly reseated. Then he saw a glisten of crimson on the side of one slab. He homed in with his gaze. Something blackish brown protruded from under the stone. It was the front paw of a bear.

Just then Slade's dog, Pistol, burst from the forest onto the trail. He'd been off chasing a squirrel or rabbit and still wore a goofy grin. Of undetermined lineage, the canine had the coat of a collie, the coloring of a Rottweiler, and the agile build of an Australian shepherd. He had appeared on the porch six years ago, the scraggliest and skinniest pup Slade had ever seen. He hadn't wanted a dog. In fact, he'd sworn years before that he would never have a dog again, but he hadn't had the heart to call Animal Control. He'd never once regretted the decision. Pistol was the best all-around canine friend that Slade had ever had, adept at herding cows, friendly with horses, smarter than some men, and beautiful now that he received proper care. The dog skidded to a stop by Bogey's left knee, swung around, and bristled.

"Yep," Slade said. "You smell bear. Heel up. Don't get all crazy on me and go into those rocks. You'll get us all killed."

Pistol aligned his shoulder with Bogey's front leg. After swinging out of the saddle, Slade gave the gelding a comforting pat, then snapped his fingers and pointed at the ground to make Pistol sit before he approached the steep bank. Crawling up into that jumble of rock would be foolish. Instead he remained on the trail and moved eastward. Then he turned and saw the hindquarters of the bear. She lay on her side, rear legs sprawled. Definitely a sow. Her teats were swollen with milk. Now he understood the faintness of her scent. Well over half her body was buried.

A full-time rancher and a seasonal outfitter and hunting guide, Slade had been raised on wild game and homegrown beef, so he didn't think of himself as a tenderhearted man, but he hated to see a dead mama sow. Her offspring might not survive without her. Black bears normally bore litters of one to six cubs, typically two, sometimes more, and it was only April. Snow, bluish white in the shadows, still defied the advent of warmer weather. Sows were probably just now emerging with cubs from their dens.

He sighed and turned in a full circle, watching for any sign of movement. Then he studied all the nearby trees. Frightened cubs often shinnied up a trunk and held on until their mother told them it was safe to get down. Sadly he saw no babies. Not that he knew what he'd do for them. He supposed he could call the Oregon Department of Fish and Wildlife. Until cubs grew older, they needed their mother's milk.

He strode back to his horse. Bogey snorted and flung his head. Pistol whined. "Now I know why you didn't spook, Bogey. You smelled the blood before I did and knew she was dead."

Bogey chuffed and flared his nostrils. Slade gave him a scratch along his poll before swinging up into the saddle. The horse didn't like the smell of bear, whether it was alive or not. "Heel, Pistol. Let's circle the area before we head home. See if we come across those babies."

Slade spent the better part of an hour combing the vicinity. Mostly he watched his dog. Pistol had a sharp nose and found some scents that interested him, but nothing was fresh enough to excite him. If the cubs had stayed near their mother's body, Pistol would smell them.

Heading downhill through the forest, Slade picked up Flotsam Trail again about a half mile south of the rock-slide. He was in no particular hurry to reach the ranch, but his pleasure in the ride had diminished. He couldn't get the possible fate of the dead sow's offspring out of his mind. *Damn*. At this time of year, they'd be so little, and by now their tummies would already be panging with hunger. The thought saddened him.

And also made him think of Vickie, his one and only love. Ignoring the advice of nearly everyone in their hometown of Mystic Creek, she had once rescued a cub. Now that Slade was older, it was funny how memories popped into his mind, as shiny as new pennies. Images of her holding that baby on her hip played on his mental screen like a video clip. She'd been a little gal with an unruly mane of curly auburn hair and arresting green eyes. He'd been so besotted that he would have laid down his life for her.

Slade tried to school his thoughts. It was nuts to be thinking about Vickie now. For all he knew, she could be dead. He hadn't seen or heard from her in almost forty years, and good riddance. If she were with him, he'd still be looking for that dead sow's cubs, and then if he found them, he'd be trying to convince her that caring for them was a bad idea. *Nope*. He was better off alone. A woman messed with a man's head, led him down a merry path, and then ran off with a big chunk of his heart.

Screw all of that. He would have been a rotten husband anyway, and probably an even worse father. He'd cared too much about horses, cows, and bull busting in his younger days. He'd probably still be following the rodeo circuit if his body hadn't given out on him. Losing Vickie had left him free to grab life by the tail and hang on for the ride. In his wild days, it had been a rough one.

On a bridle path, Pistol liked to take the lead, and he was three horse lengths ahead of Bogey when a high-pitched shriek rent the afternoon air. Still lost in the past, Slade jolted to awareness and drew back on the reins as he attempted to place the sound. Spooked by the noise, Bogey hopped sideways. Slade almost went one direction while his mount went the other. He grabbed for leather and quickly righted himself.

Pistol let out a bark and pointed like a bird dog. "No!" Slade said. "Heel up. Whatever that is, it doesn't want company."

Black fur rippling as he ran, Pistol circled to stand by Bogey's left front leg. Slade was still trying to determine where the noise had originated when another scream echoed through the trees. His stomach muscles snapped taut. It was like nothing he'd ever heard, the cry laced with terror and what had to be pain. Pulse accelerating, he urged Bogey farther downhill. It had to be an animal, Slade reasoned, only for the first time in his life he couldn't identify a species by the sound it made. He reined Bogey to the right, heading toward a copse of underbrush canopied by pine boughs. Within

seconds he heard another wail and then came the
sound of thrashing in the woodland brush. Slade saw a
flash of yellow about fifty yards down the slope. *Cougar* was his first thought. But as he trained his gaze on
the spot, his stomach felt as if it dropped to the ground
and bounced back up into his throat. *A blond bear
cub.* Just as Slade realized what it was, it flipped head
over heels in the air, slammed back to the earth, and
shrieked again. He also heard the rattling of metal
chain.

"Damn it! Down, Pistol! Down!"

Whining and trembling with eagerness, Pistol lowered his rump to the dirt. Slade dismounted, tied Bogey
to a small tree, and then pushed through the brush to
get closer. The cub was a blur of golden fur, frantically
trying to free its right front foot from the jaws of a coyote trap. Slade's blood boiled. What kind of idiot set a
trap so close to a trail? It was a wonder that Pistol hadn't
stepped in it as they came up the mountain. If the steel
jaws of a leghold trap snapped closed at just the right
angle, bones could be fractured or crushed. The last
thing Slade needed was a crippled dog.

As he drew closer, the baby panicked. Not wanting to
make the cub hurt itself any worse, Slade retreated to a
less threatening distance. He scanned the area, looking
for the tracks of a sow or other cubs. His trained eye saw
nothing. He also sniffed the air, hoping not to catch a
whiff of an adult bear in the vicinity.

He finally concluded that the cub was alone. Otherwise the mother would be facing off with him to protect her trapped offspring, a turn of events that Slade preferred to avoid. Now the question he had to ask himself was, where was the mother? Sows wandered away from their cubs sometimes, and vice versa, but normally a mother and her babies stayed within earshot of each other. This cub was making enough noise to wake drunks on Sunday morning.

Less than a mile up the mountain, a dead sow lay mostly buried in a fall of rocks, and Slade couldn't help but think this had to be her baby. Normally a cub remained near its deceased mother as long as it could, but maybe the rockslide had frightened this one so badly that it ran. The explosion of sound must have been deafening. The hail of huge rocks would have made the ground tremble. This little fellow, being so young, could have gotten so turned around in the forest that he couldn't find his way back. Now he was in trouble. Leghold traps were treacherous. Slade hated the damned things.

He tried to think of some positive outcomes for the cub if he released it, but in reality there was only one, that another sow in the area with nursing cubs would adopt him. That was a long shot. Some sows would accept a nursing baby planted by humans in their birthing dens, but once they took their cubs out into the world, they grew protective and cautious. Even the appearance of a lost cub could get their hackles up. Slade could understand why. Most cubs of nursing age had their own mothers, who might strongly object to the interference of another sow.

After considering his options, Slade walked back to where Bogey and Pistol waited and drew his cell phone from his pocket. He texted his foreman, Wyatt, who kept his phone on him at all times, set to vibrate. *"On Flotsam Trail, about a half mile up. Bear cub in trap. Bring men, blankets, and first aid."* He pressed SEND. Then as an afterthought, he sent a postscript. *"Vet wrap, too."*

Slade questioned his own sanity as he led his horse and dog farther down the trail. If he turned that cub loose, what were the odds that it would find a kind-hearted sow to feed and protect it? Slade knew that was a fairy-tale ending. The baby would probably die out in the wild by itself. Slade stared hard at the rifle he always carried in a saddle sheath when he rode in a wilderness area. No matter how he mentally circled it, he knew a quick death for the baby was far more merciful than starvation. But, damn it, he'd never sighted in on a young creature and pulled the trigger. Newborn animals were helpless. They needed to be protected so their species could thrive for generations to come.

Most humans had an inherent soft spot for babies, he assured himself. He wasn't alone in his feelings. He sighed and resigned himself to the fact that he didn't have it in him to put that cub out of its misery, not when there was a chance, no matter how slight, that it might survive.

While waiting for his men to arrive, Slade felt as if every second lasted an hour. The cub continued to bleat and moan, and every sound made Slade's heart twist. He wished the poor thing would stop trying to get loose. With every jerk, the trap would do more damage to its leg. *But* the cub kept struggling.

In the distance Slade heard the roar of a ranch ATV. By the sound of the engine, he determined that it was the Honda Pioneer side-by-side, which resembled a golf cart but had stouter framework, a higher undercarriage, a lot more power, and tires that could crawl over most woodland obstacles. He was glad Wyatt had decided against using horses. The Honda covered ground faster. The thought no sooner crossed Slade's mind than he saw a blaze of red through the trees.

Despite profound deafness, Wyatt Fitzgerald, Slade's foreman, was nothing if not attuned to the needs of animals. Most men would have held the gas pedal to the floorboard and slid to a stop where Slade stood, stirring up a cloud of dust. The blond foreman, hair presently covered by a brown Stetson, had more sense. Over the years he'd become more conscious of the effects of sound than most hearing individuals. He knew the roar of an engine at full throttle would terrify a trapped cub. The instant he saw Slade, he slowed to a stop and turned off the ignition.

Slade waited for the men to exit the ATV. Wyatt swung out first. He was tall with a body tempered like steel from hard work. In his younger days Slade could have given the younger man a run for his money, but now he counted himself lucky just to be in decent physical condition. Tex, nicknamed after his home state, piled out next. A wiry old fellow in a faded red shirt and dusty Levi's, he carried the first aid case and a roll of vet wrap. Wyatt's younger brother, Kennedy, also a blond, emerged last, one of his cheeks bulging with what Slade guessed was food, his arms cradling a bundle of blankets that Slade suspected had been filched from the trunk at the foot of his bed. It seemed to Slade that Kennedy's main occupation in life was eating. When it was the eighteen-year-old's day to cook, more grub went into his mouth than ever reached a platter.

Wyatt, who appeared to walk slowly with a well-oiled shift of his hips, covered ground faster than the other two men. A talker only when necessary, he merely arched an eyebrow in question when he stopped in front of Slade.

Hooking a thumb over his shoulder, Slade said, "He's over there. I moved off a ways to give him some space."

Tex and Kennedy arrived just then and flanked Wyatt. They looked like two mismatched bookends, Tex measuring in at just over five feet, Kennedy lofty and muscular like Wyatt. The youth's larynx bobbed as he swallowed. The smell of cheese-flavored Doritos drifted to Slade's nostrils.

"How d'ya know that cub's a he?" Tex asked. Half the time the old fart pretended to be senile, but he was sharp as a scythe. He'd obviously caught every word Slade had just said even from a distance. "Kinda hard to tell without lookin', ain't it?"

"Can't see that it matters," Slade replied. "He looks like a boy to me. I could be wrong."

"It matters," Tex insisted. "Girls ain't as feisty."

The cub screamed just then. Everyone but Wyatt flinched.

Slade said, "Tell that to a sow with her dander up, Tex."

"Point taken." Tex, who always wore a green baseball cap to cover his bald head, spit tobacco juice, narrowly missing Bogey's hoof. "And speakin' of which, are we gonna do somethin' damn fool stupid, like try to save that cub? Its mama hears all the racket it's makin'. She's probably off in the woods watchin'. She'll shred us up like party paper if we get too close."

"Confetti," Slade corrected. "And no worries about the mother. She's dead, half-buried in an avalanche farther up the trail." Slade made sure he faced Wyatt as he repeated that and then continued talking. "Her cub probably won't survive without her, but I couldn't bring myself to shoot him. If we can free his foot and doctor him as best we can, at least he'll have a fighting chance."

Wyatt nodded. "If the weather stays warm, he might make it." He enunciated each syllable carefully and paused for an instant between words. Three years ago when Wyatt had first hired on at the ranch, his speech had bugged Slade, but he'd grown accustomed to it now. The foreman pursed his lips. "He may not know what to eat. It depends on how long he's been foraging with his mother."

Tex elbowed Wyatt to get his attention. "He ain't got no chewin' teeth yet. They don't cut 'em 'til later in the spring. And just so you know, cubs may snack with their mamas all summer, but they nurse straight into autumn until they go back to the den. Even with a belly full of forage, that cub will still need his mama's milk."

Wyatt's blond eyebrows snapped together in a scowl. "What's your point, Tex?"

"That rescuing him from a trap is a harebrained idea," Tex retorted. "With his mama gone, he's as good as dead anyhow."

"But he isn't dead yet!" Kennedy protested. "At least we can give him a chance. I know I'd want one."

"We need to put a bullet between his eyes," Tex grumped. "It's the only kind thing to do."

"My rifle's in the boot," Slade replied. "I couldn't do it. I'll leave the dirty work to you, Tex."

"Dad-blame-it!" Tex kicked the dirt with the toe of his riding boot. "You know I can't shoot a baby."

"So who's going to shoot it, then?" Slade asked.

Silence swooped down over the men. Slade let that do the talking. Then he led the way to the cub. As they drew closer, the cries of terror and pain from the small animal intensified. Slade stopped about twenty feet away. The pathetic mewling of the baby made his throat tighten. He looked more closely at the trap, and anger surged within him. "Oh, sweet Jesus."

"What?" Kennedy asked. "Do you see his mother?"

Slade worked his throat to swallow. "No." He turned to make sure Wyatt could read his lips. "That trap has teeth. I didn't get close enough to notice that earlier."

"Teeth?" Wyatt repeated. His blue eyes flared with outrage. "Those are against the law. They don't even make them in this country anymore."

"No, they don't," Slade confirmed, "but that doesn't mean people don't still have them. You can pick them up in antique stores."

Wyatt's jaw muscle rippled. "I'll shove it down that trapper's throat once I get it off that cub."

Slade shook his head. "You'll never find him. No legitimate trapper would risk his license by using an illegal device."

Kennedy, who had apparently seen pictures of traps with teeth, turned as white as a motel room towel. "Why would anybody do something so cruel?"

"For the fun of it. Maybe hoping to get a dog or a deer." Slade made fists and slowly relaxed his hands. "There are sick people in the world, son." He met and held Wyatt's gaze. "You have a way with animals that I lack. Never thought I'd say that, but it's true. I hope you have a plan, because I sure as hell don't."

Wyatt turned to study the frantic cub. He didn't move for so long that Slade almost nudged his shoulder. The cub needed help now, not sometime next week.

"He's terrified of us," the foreman said. "The less he

sees of us, the better. Kennedy, go with Tex. Use the trees for cover and circle around. Stay close, because I'll need you both. Make sure you've got the first aid kit and vet wrap with you, Tex. Stand ready." Wyatt swept off his hat and tossed it on the ground. Then he turned and grabbed a Pendleton blanket from the stack in his brother's arms. "Get going, both of you. Be as quiet as possible."

Kennedy and Tex left with a shuffle of feet, circling away from the cub before they turned back into the trees. Wyatt pivoted to face Slade. "I need you to walk right behind me. I mean almost at my heels, and don't talk unless you have to."

Slade rarely talked unless he had to. It was a waste of breath.

Wyatt unfolded the blanket and gave it a snap. Then, still gripping the wool, he turned toward the cub, stretched his arms out to his sides, and lifted the upper edge of the cover to just below his eyes.

"That's your plan?" Slade asked. "To hide behind a blanket? Shit. It'll only make you look bigger and scare him more."

Wyatt didn't argue the point, which gave Slade pause. Then he realized the foreman hadn't heard a word he said. He sometimes forgot about Wyatt's deafness. That was easy to do, because Wyatt compensated for his hearing loss so well. He spoke differently, but then so did Tex, and Slade probably did, too, at times.

Slade fell in behind the younger man. They moved

toward the cub as slowly as snails, and with every step, Slade wanted to say, *This is ridiculous.* But he just thought it instead. Without warning, Wyatt stopped, Slade didn't, and their bodies bumped together. Then, with a thrust of his arms, Wyatt threw the blanket. It caught air. The tiny cub, no longer lunging against the chain, stared up at it as if the sky had just busted loose from heaven and was about to fall on him. *Innocence,* Slade thought. Babies were born possessing it, and then brutal reality robbed them of it.

The broad expanse of wool landed on the tiny bear like a deflated parachute silk. During that one instant of stillness while the cub tried to figure out what had happened, Wyatt sprinted forward and made a tackle dive, landing on his belly and wrapping his arms around the wriggling lump under the wool. Moving with the same impressive speed that he exhibited during branding season, the foreman wound the blanket around the baby and then held him fast to the ground.

"Boss, come get his foot out!" he ordered. "Tex, Kennedy—*now!*"

Slade jumped in without hesitation. Through the thick weave, he groped to find the trap. When he located it, he lifted that section of blanket so he could see to open the jaws. Only he saw no levers. "Damn it!"

The other two men ran up.

"Kennedy!" Wyatt yelled. "Grab his trapped leg! Hold it as still as you can!"

The youth knelt beside Slade and got a firm hold on

the baby's spindly appendage. Slade had never used traps, but until that moment, he'd believed he at least knew how they worked. The new leghold traps had a tab at each side of the jaws that released the hinges with simultaneous pressure, but this old contraption had nothing. Slade knew there had to be a release mechanism, but he didn't have time to search for it. "Hold on tight, Kennedy. I have to pry it open."

That proved to be harder than Slade thought. The cub mewled and struggled, wiggling so much that Slade couldn't get a good grip on the steel jaws. A prong pricked his finger, and pain shot to his wrist.

"Get ready, Tex. The second I get this off, you'll have to doctor the foot as fast as you can."

Tex dropped to his knees and opened the white case. Slade cut another finger. Blood smeared his hands, some of it his own, some the bear's. Finally the trap gave way. The cub shrieked with the release of pressure. The awful sound rang in Slade's ears and crawled like cold fingers down his spine.

"Help me hold him!" Kennedy cried.

Slade dropped the trap and grabbed for the baby's leg. Wyatt readjusted the blanket to keep the bear from scrambling free. Tex captured the injured foot. "God help us. One of his toes is cut almost off."

"Remove it," Wyatt ordered. "Quick and clean. Hurry, Tex. I'm losing my hold on him."

Tex, who'd once worked with horses at a Kentucky racetrack, jerked out his pocketknife, sterilized it, and did as he was told. Then he grabbed a squeeze bottle and squirted antiseptic into the open wounds to clean them.

"Hurry," Wyatt said again. "Wrap it up to stop the bleeding."

"Just hold fast." Tex grabbed a bottle of something else and dribbled the creamy contents over the cub's foot. "Numbin' agent. It'll take the edge off." He pressed a large gauze pad around the foot and then grabbed the vet wrap, sticky and stretchy bandaging used on horses that normally held fast to an animal's leg for at least a couple of days. He finished by cutting the material and tucking the end under a fold. "There!" he said. "Turn him loose and get back. Those little claws are razor sharp."

Wyatt released his hold on the wriggling lump. The cub hobbled around under the wool, unable to find his way out. Kennedy surged forward to grab a corner of the blanket and flip it off the tiny animal. When the cub glimpsed daylight again, he tried to run and tumbled head over heels into a bush. Then he wheeled around to face them. Slade couldn't help but admire his spunk. He was so tiny that his mama could have still carried him in her mouth, but he was ready to fight for his life.

"He's pretty as a gold nugget," Tex observed.

"He's the cutest thing I've ever clapped eyes on," Slade agreed. "You think he'll ever grow into those ears?"

Wyatt, who'd sprung gingerly to his feet, spoke directly to the cub, which had shrunk back against the foliage. "Remember what your mother ate, little bear, and go home to the den at night so you can stay warm."

Slade hated to think of all that the cub might face. "We've done all we can," he said, mostly to comfort himself. "It's time we get out of here so the poor little guy can recover from the fright and get his bearings."

"I've never seen a yellar black bear," Tex said. "He's gonna be a sight to see when he grows up. I like them dark markin's on his back and face."

"Yes, he'll be gorgeous," Slade agreed. "If he makes it."

Kennedy stared solemnly at the baby. "He's so itty-bitty. Why can't we give him puppy formula or something?"

Gaze fixed on his brother, Wyatt said, "It is illegal to feed black bears, Kennedy."

Kennedy gave Wyatt an imploring look. "But he might die."

"I know, but it isn't for us to decide what's best," Wyatt replied. "If he survives, he'll grow huge. He could weigh two hundred and fifty pounds, possibly more. And if he's been fed by humans, he won't be afraid of them when he's hungry. That would be big trouble for him and dangerous for people."

Kennedy sighed. "It just seems so wrong to leave him out here with nothing to eat."

Slade agreed. "I'll call ODF and W," he said. "Maybe they'll come get him and take him to a shelter."

"But even if they decide to help, he'll be long gone

by the time anyone gets here!" Kennedy argued. "And how the fuck will they catch him?"

"Watch your mouth," Wyatt said. "You know how Mom feels about language like that."

"Everybody my age says it!" Kennedy argued. "Hell, Wyatt! Everyone *your* age says it, too."

Wyatt grinned. "I have never heard a single person my age say that word."

Kennedy rolled his eyes. "Very funny."

The cub bleated and limped away into the underbrush. All of them watched until he vanished.

"If he lives, we'll recognize his tracks if he ever comes on the ranch," Kennedy observed. "He only has four toes on his right front foot."

"There's a good name for him, Four Toes," Tex said. Then he whacked at the dust on his jeans and added, "I guess that's it, then. We done our good deed for the day. I got a nice wrap on the foot. He lost some blood, but he ain't gonna die from that."

Slade wondered if it wouldn't have been kinder to shoot the cub, but he kept the thought to himself. It had been his decision to call Wyatt for help. At the time it had seemed like the only thing to do. Now, what was done was done, and there was no point in second-guessing himself.

"You boys go ahead and take off," he said. "I'll be slower getting back down the mountain on horseback."

Wyatt shook out the blanket, refolded it, and fetched his hat. "See you there, boss."

* * *

Slade got back to the ranch by four in the afternoon. Kennedy unsaddled Bogey and promised to rub him down so Slade could call the Department of Fish and Wildlife before the offices closed. Slade walked away, thinking that the boy was starting to come around, no longer acting sullen all the time and griping when he had to work. After sitting on the porch steps, Slade placed the call on his cell phone. He got straight through to a man named Wilson, which he took as a good sign, but things went downhill from there.

Wilson listened to the story and said Slade couldn't be sure that the cub he found belonged to the sow killed in the avalanche. Slade hadn't seen the blond cub with the sow prior to the rockslide, and the baby in the trap was nearly a mile from the accident site.

"I searched the area around the avalanche," Slade said again. "My dog's got a good nose. There were no cubs anywhere near the carcass."

"I understand your frustration," the man said.

"No, I don't think you do. I'm no stranger to bears. I'm certain it's orphaned. It's injured and too young to survive on its own."

"I know you believe that, sir, and I commend you for helping the cub and treating its wounds. Normally I would advise against that, but it sounds as if your man did a great job. A trap with teeth would have done a lot more damage by the time we got someone out there."

"It did enough damage as it was."

"I'm sure it was awful," Wilson commiserated. "And now you have a vested interest in the cub's survival. You have to see our side of this, though. People rescue newborn animals from the wild all the time when it isn't necessary. And just because you didn't see the mother doesn't mean she's dead or not in the vicinity."

"The mother is buried under a pile of rocks," Slade said flatly. "I saw her. I looked for cubs. I found none. The only cub in the area was the blond one."

"You don't know that for a fact. Black bear sows will share their territory with other female bears, especially daughters. They don't hang out together, but they encounter each other. It's possible for two sows with cubs to be in the same area, and it would be tragic if we took a cub away from its mother. Black bear rescue shelters have made great strides in releasing orphaned cubs back into the wild, but the attempts aren't always successful, and the failures end sadly. The cubs either die or are returned to a shelter. If possible they're then placed in zoos or wildlife observatories. If not, they remain in shelters for the rest of their lives. Do you think that makes for happy bears?"

Slade rested the back of his head against the porch post and closed his eyes. The punctured tips of his fingers still ached, which made him wonder how badly the cub's foot must hurt. "Ideally all bears would live in their natural habitat. But looking at the flip side, bears don't have it so bad in zoos, and their presence educates children and adults about their species."

"Zoos and observatories are fabulous alternatives,

but there are twenty-five to thirty thousand black bears in Oregon alone, Mr. Wilder. How many rescue facilities do you think there are in the continental United States?"

"I don't know, but I'm sure you'll tell me."

Wilson sighed. "I don't know the exact number, but I do know there are black bears presently in custody that haven't found homes yet, and their numbers continue to grow."

Slade could see where this was going. Four Toes wasn't going to be rescued, and nothing he said would change that. He wished he had seen the baby with its mother prior to her death, but he hadn't, and he couldn't blame the state for refusing to remove a cub from its natural environment without absolute proof it was necessary.

By the end of the conversation, Slade believed Wilson was a good man who had a very difficult job. Feeling heavy of heart, he wasn't happy to see Kennedy, blond hair ruffled by the breeze, walking from the stable to the house. He knew the kid was hoping to hear good news.

"What did they say about Four Toes?" Kennedy asked when he was still twenty feet from where Slade sat. "Are they going to rescue him?"

Wishing he were a gifted liar, Slade found himself searching for a way to sugarcoat the facts. Only that wasn't possible, so he gave it to Kennedy straight, and the kid walked away with slumped shoulders. After a few minutes Slade followed him. There were evening chores to be done, and sitting around feeling frustrated would accomplish nothing.

Two hours later as Slade forked hay over a back pasture fence into feeding troughs for his horses, he caught a flash of gold at the edge of the woods. He froze with the handle of the pitchfork gripped so tightly in his hands that his knuckles ached. *The cub.* The ranch proper was bordered by fenced pastures that stretched on all sides to the surrounding forestland. About a half mile into the trees, Slade's land merged with state or federal holdings. How in the hell had that baby found its way through all that rugged terrain to reach the ranch?

Pistol, always Slade's companion, growled low in his throat. Slade let go of the pitchfork to fondle the canine's silken ears, which stood up halfway and then curled over. "Don't be a tough guy, Pistol. He's only a baby."

The cub mewled. It was probably the way he would call to his mama, only she wasn't around. Only Slade could hear him.

"Damn it, Four Toes, don't do this to me," Slade murmured. The heart-wrenching sounds that drifted through the twilight rang with urgency. "Go away."

Slade nearly parted company with his skin when Wyatt spoke from behind him. "He's been out there a couple of hours, boss. He must have followed you back."

Slade turned to meet Wyatt's gaze. "Why would he do that?"

Slade's question went unanswered for a long moment. Then Wyatt stepped forward to rest his arms on the top fence rail. The green background of a forested hillside contrasted vividly with his blue eyes and blond hair, which wisped over his collar in the evening breeze. He kept his gaze trained on Slade's face. "We all helped him, but you were the last to leave. He probably watched you from a hiding place."

"He was terrified of us."

"Maybe we seem less scary to him than being out there alone." Wyatt shrugged, the flex of his shoulder muscles visible through his shirt. "I don't have answers, boss. All I can say for sure is that he's here. He's little, hurt, all alone, and hungry. Do you really think it's so strange that he sees us as his only hope?"

"Don't say that."

"Whether I say it or not, it's the only explanation." Wyatt shifted his weight from one leg to the other. "Kennedy told me what the state guy said. The man had some good points. You couldn't be sure Four Toes was the dead sow's cub. Not then, anyway. Now it's a different story. If Four Toes had a mama out there, he wouldn't be here."

Sometimes Slade didn't like to have another man studying his face. His feelings were private, and he was afraid his expressions might reveal too much. He broke eye contact with Wyatt and stared across the field.

"I didn't come out here to push you into doing something you feel is wrong," Wyatt went on. "I just want you to know I'll support you in any decision you make."

"That's a comfort."

"What?"

Slade released a rush of breath and turned so Wyatt could read his lips again. "I said you're a pain in the ass."

A grin slanted over the younger man's mouth. "You're going to help him. Aren't you?"

"If I don't, he'll just come closer and keep me up all night. Sounds like he's saying, 'huh, huh, huh?' So innocent, so bewildered. Makes me want to cuddle him up and rock him to sleep. He's such a cute little guy. In pain. Probably scared. Definitely hungry. It'd take a harder man than me to ignore him."

"You could wear earplugs. Now that we know for sure his mother's dead, you can call the state again in the morning."

Slade shook his head. "I still have no actual proof that he's orphaned. It'll be the same answer tomorrow as it was today, and for good reason. The state has to draw the line somewhere."

Wyatt sighed. "If you don't feed him, I'll have to. Otherwise Kennedy will, and with him on probation, I can't let him get in trouble again. I promised my folks."

Slade held up a hand. "I clean up my own messes. I just don't know what to feed him."

Wyatt smiled. "I found a recipe online for cub formula at a black bear rescue site. Kennedy drove to town to get all the stuff."

Slade shook his head and chuckled. "How did you know I'd decide to feed him?"

Wyatt lifted his shoulders again. "I didn't. Like I said, if you don't, I'll have to. If my brother breaks the law, *any* law right now, and gets caught, he'll go to prison for ten years."

"We won't get caught, not way out here." Slade rubbed the back of his neck. "Not now, anyway. Three years from now maybe, but Kennedy's probation will have ended by then, and I'll never say he had anything to do with it."

With a frown Wyatt asked, "What will happen in three years?"

Slade peered through the gloom that heralded nightfall. "That bear out there will be a big boy by then, and he might lumber into town to take a nap on someone's porch."

Chapter One

Three and a half years later

What the hell am I doing up here? Erin De Laney had asked herself that question at least two dozen times over the last hour, and the only answer she could think of was, *Shit happens.* Only she wasn't really certain she would survive this to laugh about it later. She was all alone in the middle of a montane forest and on a horse, for Pete's sake. Given the fact that she'd never ridden a horse and her idea of a wilderness foray was a trip to Seattle's Woodland Park Zoo, she was completely unqualified for this assignment. When she'd been five, her uncle Slade had put her on the back of an old mare and led it in a circle around a corral, but that was the grand total of her experience with equines. She knew even less about remote, high-elevation woodlands. And, damn it, the gelding she rode had no digital compass like the dashboards of patrol vehicles did. What if she got lost out here? Most of the time, she could tell her direction by studying the sky, but in this jungle of towering old-growth trees, she couldn't find so much as a sliver of blue without nearly breaking her neck to look up.

Hands clenched on the reins, Erin stared hard at the open space between her mount's ears. His name was Butterscotch, probably because of his color, a mottled-caramel body with a mane and tail the off-white of whipped cream. Sheriff Adams, his owner, said the gelding was a red roan. Not that Erin cared. What mattered to her right now was being on top of a four-legged giant when her cell phone and portable radio might not have reception to call for help if she fell off. A thirty-minute predawn riding lesson hadn't prepared her for this, and, emergency or not, she didn't appreciate being asked to do something when there were other deputies far more qualified. How was she supposed to check hay for noxious weeds with only a skimpy pocket manual as a reference? While tending the flower gardens that bordered the front lawn of her rental cottage, she'd pulled more actual plants than she had weeds, and her landlady had nearly fainted when she saw the damage. In Erin's parents' neighborhood, most people hired all the gardening done, and Erin's mother reviled practically everything that came in contact with dirt. As a result, Erin had never learned anything about plants or the weeds that invaded flower beds.

Calm down, she lectured herself. *Being a deputy in this laid-back county is so much better than working in a crime-ridden metropolitan area, and you don't want to lose the job because you're a whiner. Focus on your surroundings. Take a deep breath of the pure mountain air. Watch for deer. Notice the ferns and wildflowers. This is why you left the Greater Seattle area, remember? You wanted a slower lifestyle and to be surrounded by nature. Instead of being such a grump, why don't you try to enjoy this?*

She straightened her spine and filled her lungs. It was silly of her to be so tense. Horses were just larger versions of dogs. Right? And she loved dogs. Well, she liked them from afar, anyway. She'd never actually had one. Her mother had forbidden it, afraid that Erin would sneak it inside her spotless house.

The trail ahead crawled ever upward through a stand of old-growth ponderosa pines. Massive tree trunks the color of cinnamon sticks peppered the terrain. Drooping lazily under their own weight, pine boughs formed an overhead canopy of interlaced green and shielded the forest floor from the late September sunlight, allowing only splashes of butter yellow to spill through. On a light, capricious breeze, the smells of evergreen, fern, moss, manzanita, and wildflowers created a heady perfume unlike anything she had ever experienced. *This* was why she'd pulled up stakes over a year ago and moved to Mystic Creek, Oregon. *This* was why she'd abandoned a promising career as a law enforcement officer in King County to become a deputy in a country setting. For her, this place should be like a dream come true. Except for the man-made trail ahead of her, there were no obvious signs that humans had ever been here. No buildings. No litter. No city sounds. It was so different from where she'd grown up.

If she hadn't been on a horse, the majesty of this place would have made her want to linger. She'd find a comfortable place to sit at the base of a tree and just absorb the peacefulness, reconnecting with the basics of life and pondering the fact that she was only a tiny speck on a gigantic canvas painted by a divine artist. Just ahead, the terrain grew steep on one side of the path. Huge slabs of shale and lumps of lava rock, trimmed with clumps of fern, composed much of the hillside. *So beautiful and serene*. She could almost imagine woodland fairies living here, momentarily hiding so they wouldn't be seen. Somewhere up ahead, she even heard the rush of what sounded like a stream. If she quit making noise, she'd be sure to see animals. Maybe even a deer or elk. But she'd be happy just to study the squirrels and birds that would surely show themselves.

With a mental jerk, Erin snapped back to the moment and, with a lurch of sick dread, realized that the gelding had stopped walking. It was almost as if he'd sensed that her mind had wandered off, and he'd been uncertain what to do. The rhythmic clomp of his hooves had ceased. The rocking motion of his gait no longer shifted her from side to side on the saddle to make her thighs burn.

"Butterscotch?" She leaned forward to pat his neck. "We aren't where we need to go yet, buddy. You need to keep moving."

With a flick of his ears, he snorted and then blew air out his nostrils. Erin's heart caught. What did that mean? Sheriff Adams, her boss, had given her very few tips during her riding lesson that morning. *"There's nothing to it,"* he'd told her. *"He knows what to do. Your only job is to stay in the saddle."*

As Adams had directed, Erin tapped the gelding's sides with her feet. In response, he chuffed, snorted again, and angled his head around to look at her. She didn't like that she could see the whites of his eyes. Surely that wasn't a good sign. She could only hope he wasn't thinking about different ways he might get her off his back. The thought stripped her of the magical feeling that had come over her moments before. *Fact-check.* She'd been trained how to fall so as not to injure herself, but during those sessions, she'd been on a gym mat. The dangerous hooves of a slightly overweight male quarter horse and countless jagged rocks hadn't been factored into the equation. If she got hurt out here in a wilderness area, her goose might be cooked.

"Okay, Butterscotch." Who in his right mind named a male horse Butterscotch? "Maybe I'm forgetting part of the go signal." He'd started fine for her down at the trailhead. She nudged him with her heels again, then clicked her tongue. At the sound, he flicked his ears but didn't budge. "Let's go!" she tried. "Giddyup!" Still nothing. Finally she nudged him and made the clicking noise both at once, and the gelding moseyed forward into a walk again. "Awesome!" she said, uncertain of whom she felt prouder, herself or the equine. "You're such a good boy. I think I heard the sound of a creek while we were stopped. Maybe when I find a place to set up my checkpoint, it'll be where you can drink *and* graze. Sheriff Adams said to make sure you have grass to eat. He didn't mention water, but if I'm thirsty, you must be, too. You're the one doing all the work."

Only Erin didn't feel as if the animal had been doing all the work. Being on a horse made her nervous, and she'd been vising her legs around his belly all the way up the mountain to make sure she didn't fall. She tried to stay in shape, working out five days a week without fail and jogging six miles each weekend morning. But apparently she needed to focus more on her legs. Her inner thighs and glutes hurt. As in, *ouch*. What was that all about? She'd been convinced as recently as yesterday that she had thigh muscles of iron, but they were sorely disappointing her now.

The trail suddenly grew steep, and without warning, Butterscotch decided to do the horse version of a jog to scale the incline. Erin's butt parted company with the saddle and slammed back down, not once but repeatedly, each landing hurting so much that it nearly took her breath away. Only she was so scared, she couldn't focus on the pain. The saddle seat was slick, and no matter how firmly she tried to grip with her knees, she could barely stay on. Her right boot came out of the stirrup, which started flapping without her foot to anchor it, and Butterscotch seemed to think she wanted him to shift from fast to jet speed.

"No, Butterscotch! Whoa! Are you trying to kill me?"

The horse only increased his pace, and in her panic,

Erin couldn't think how to make him stop. The lunging motion threw her backward, and she almost went flying off over the gelding's rump. It flashed through her mind that she could mortally injure herself if she fell and hit her head on the rocks. Realizing that she'd completely lost control of the situation, she turned loose of the reins and threw her arms around the horse's neck to stay on him. That decision resulted in breath-robbing punches from the saddle horn to her belly.

When they reached the top of the hill, Butterscotch settled back into a walk, and Erin sent up prayers of thanks, silent ones because she felt as if her lungs had collapsed. As the horse moseyed forward, she finally caught her breath and dimly registered that the reins were dangling from the roan's nose. Now what? Butterscotch was still moving, and she'd lost her grip on her only way to steer him. She got both feet back in the stirrups and leaned as far forward over his neck as she dared, trying to grab the long strips of leather. He stopped and raised his head, bringing the reins closer so she was able to catch hold, one in each hand.

"Thank you, Butterscotch! Thank you!" She was so grateful that she wanted to hug him. As she got herself situated in the saddle again, she said, "Maybe you don't like it any better than I do when I have no control."

The horse chuffed, and Erin smiled shakily. She could have sworn he was saying, "Of course I don't, you idiot."

Erin sighed, took a moment to collect her composure, and then realized Butterscotch had stopped again. This time, she knew to click her tongue and nudge him with her heels simultaneously, and he moved back into a walk. She scanned the grassy flat that stretched to another tree line about a quarter mile away. Just ahead of them was a trail that intersected with the one they were on. At the junction was the large wooden box with a rickety, hinged lid that her boss had told her about. A drop station, he'd called it. When outfitters who provided guided hunts ran out of things at their base camps, they could find a hilltop that got cell phone service and text someone in town to bring what they needed to the drop station. It saved them from having to ride clear back down to the trailhead for a trip into Mystic Creek, and the people who delivered the goods were tipped handsomely for their trouble.

"We made it, Butterscotch! Sheriff Adams said there's only one uphill trail that flows into this one, so that has to be it. We can set up a checkpoint right on the other side, and nobody will be able to get past us without me seeing them." Erin couldn't help but feel proud of herself. She'd made it, and for a born-and-bred city girl, that was no small victory. The sound of rushing water that she'd heard earlier came from just ahead of them, too. That would be ideal. She'd brought water for herself, but it would be nice if Butterscotch could get a drink as well. "Yay! Now if I can just find some shade, we'll have a reasonably comfortable place to set up shop. I don't know about you, but I'm more than ready for a break."

They didn't go far before Erin saw the stream off to her left. It wasn't very wide, and due to the rocks, brush, and trees that peppered its banks, the water was almost inaccessible. But she did see one reasonably level place where she thought Butterscotch could slake his thirst. She also saw a big boulder partially shaded by trees, which would offer a comfortable spot for her to sit and watch the trail. She'd be a little way off the beaten path, but she saw no problem with that. If anyone pulling a string of packhorses appeared, she could just holler out and check their hay before they went any deeper into the wilderness. *Perfect.*

The crown of her brown Stetson, which was as much a part of her uniform as the tan britches and dark chocolate shirt, absorbed heat from the sunlight that bathed the clearing. As she steered Butterscotch toward the boulder, she realized that her head felt sweaty, and a hank of her dark brown hair had worked loose from the twist at her nape to tickle her neck. It felt like a bug was crawling on her. She'd be so glad for some shade, and a drink of water would be welcome, too.

Butterscotch quickened his pace and whinnied softly, indicating to Erin that he was as eager for a rest and some lunch as she was. She leaned slightly forward to pat the animal's neck, which was as sweaty as she felt.

"You okay, buddy?"

The gelding snorted and then blew air out his nose. That didn't sound like a positive reply.

"We'll get to rest in a minute," she assured him. "I'll take you over to the stream to wet your whistle first. How does that sound? And just look at all that grass! Sheriff Adams stressed that you'd be happiest if I could find a place where you can graze. This will be awesome for both of us."

The sky, now visible since they'd entered the clearing, was incredibly blue and wisped with fluffy white clouds. Erin could barely wait to get down, stretch her legs, and take off her hat. As they drew near the large rock, she pulled back on the reins to halt the gelding. Grabbing the saddle horn in both hands, she lifted her right leg back over the cantle and shifted her weight onto her left foot still in the stirrup. The next thing she knew, she hit the ground with such force that it nearly knocked the breath out of her. Stunned, she pushed up on her elbows and looked at Butterscotch, who'd turned his head to study her. He looked bewildered. That made two of them. She couldn't feel her legs. *What the heck?* Even her butt felt numb. What if she couldn't get up? The horse might step on her.

She wiggled her feet, hoping to get her circulation going. The prickly feeling shot to her thighs. "Ouch!" she said loudly. Then to the horse, she added, "You are sworn to secrecy. If the guys at the department hear about this, they'll razz me again about staying home where I belong and making cookies." Her hat lay about four feet away. It looked undamaged, and for that she was grateful. She'd have to replace it herself if it got ruined. She sighed and decided to wait for the numbness in her legs to go away before she tried to stand. "The last time they made cracks like that, I almost made the jerks laxative cookies when I got home that night. Chocolate chip, my specialty."

Butterscotch snorted and looked as if he nodded. Erin grinned and decided they might become good friends before her stint as a hay inspector was over. According to the sheriff, she had to do it for only a few days. A group of U.S. Forest Service agents—or were they called rangers?—had been on the way to an educational conference in Albany the previous day when the bus carrying them had plowed into the back of a stalled SUV on Interstate 5. A few people had been badly hurt, and as a result, the normally well-staffed department was faced with a temporary shortage of personnel. Late in the afternoon, the USFS had called Sheriff Adams to request emergency help. That was a big deal to Blake Adams. At a county level, he rarely dealt with the feds, and he acted as if working informally with the Forest Service was the equivalent of joining forces with the CIA.

The first of the autumn hunting seasons began in a little over a week. From now until opening day, outfitters and their employees would be entering wilderness areas to set up their base camps for paying guests. It had fallen to Erin to man a checkpoint on Strawberry Hill to check their hay for weeds. Why this mountain was called Strawberry Hill, she hadn't a clue. She hadn't seen a strawberry yet, and referring to a peak as a hill was an understatement.

She worked her way slowly to her feet and then took some tentative steps to make sure her legs would hold her up. Her inner thighs screamed with every movement. Riding a horse should have been easy for her, as religiously as she exercised.

"I'll get up to speed," she assured Butterscotch as she dusted off her pants. Determination welled within her. She hated when a new activity got the better of her. It made her go all wonky in the head about having to master it or die trying. She suspected she'd gotten that trait from her father, also a law officer and fitness freak. At fifty-five, he prided himself on still having the body of a thirty-year-old and worked out every day to keep it that way. "By next week, if this stupid assignment even lasts that long, I'll be jumping off your back like a gymnast on steroids."

Butterscotch snorted again. Erin had decided that was something horses just did and wasn't a sign that they were unhappy about anything. She grabbed the gelding's reins and set off for the stream. The grassy spot along the bank was level enough, and although tiny pine trees poked up here and there, the way was clear for the animal to reach water. Curious about how horses drank, Erin watched Butterscotch closely and decided he must suck it up, much as she did from a straw.

When the animal had slaked his thirst, Erin led him

back to the boulder. *Problem*. She saw nowhere to tie his reins off so he couldn't run away. The ponderosa pines grew tall and nearly straight with no low branches. The moment she stopped, Butterscotch began eating grass. He seemed content and totally focused on grazing. She let the reins slip from her grasp to puddle on the ground. The equine seemed oblivious and didn't attempt to go anywhere. She determined that he'd probably stay put as long as he had grass to munch.

Tipping her head back to gaze at the sky while the midday breeze wafted over her hot cheeks, she sighed. She'd come to Mystic Creek with the hope that she would take frequent hikes into the wilderness areas, but she'd been too busy so far to hit a trail even once. As the newest deputy, she got assigned the shit details more often than not. If someone called in sick, she was expected to fill in. While people went on vacation, she worked double shifts to help take up the slack. She'd found precious little time for hiking—or for having a social life. The latter bothered her immensely, mainly because she really hoped to meet a nice guy. So far, that hadn't happened. Men who were about to receive a citation for illegal parking, speeding, or driving under the influence had no romantic notions about the woman who'd collared them. It was more like hate at first sight.

While Butterscotch continued to graze, Erin stroked his neck. His hair, which looked silky, felt coarse under her palm. He didn't act interested in going anywhere.

She stopped petting him to open the saddlebags and retrieve her lunch case and water bottle. The shady area around the boulder called to her. She could sit on the grass with her back braced against the rock and be fairly comfortable. After she ate, she would have time to skim through the pocket manual her boss had given her and learn mostly everything she needed to know about weed-infested hay and how to recognize it.

As she settled on the ground, Erin glanced at Butterscotch, wishing her uncle Slade could see her now. He'd laugh, she felt sure. All summer long, he'd been after her to visit the ranch and go trail riding with him. The Wilder Ranch, which he had inherited in its totality because Erin's mother wanted no part of it, adjoined public lands that were a gateway to seemingly endless outdoor recreation, horseback paths included. Erin had wanted to go on a ride with her uncle, but her work schedule had been too crazy. As often as possible, he met her in town for a meal at one of the eateries. She loved seeing him, even though he always pestered her about coming out to visit. Erin didn't blame him for that. He wanted her to familiarize herself with the lifestyle that her mother had rejected. He had never married, so he had no kids of his own to take over when he retired or died. She was the only possible heir.

Erin wished she could develop a love of ranching. She would change professions in a heartbeat. In the Seattle area, she'd gotten burned out on law enforcement. The ugliness of street crime, drug busts, and domestic violence had taken a toll, changing her in ways she regretted and might never be able to undo. She'd once been tenderhearted and sometimes moved to tears by sad stories about battered women, abused children, abandoned pets, and homeless people. The first time she'd been called to the scene of a shooting, she'd been so horrified by the sight of the dead man's wounds that she had embarrassed herself by losing her lunch all over the sidewalk. Her partner, Clyde, had clamped a hand on her shoulder and assured her that she'd get used to the blood and gore that came with the job, and eventually she had, but she couldn't be sure she was a better person for it. Where her feelings had once resided, she now felt hollowed out, and even when she searched within herself, she couldn't find the compassion she'd once had. Her job was much easier in Mystic Creek, but if it hadn't been for her parents, who'd financed her education, she would happily take off the badge and never look back. Her father loved being a cop, but she didn't. That was the long and short of it. Her heart just wasn't in it anymore. While still at school, she'd had her head in the clouds, imagining that she would help people in a significant way, the equivalent of Mother Teresa in a deputy uniform. Now she had no such illusions. She hadn't made a difference in Seattle, and she wouldn't make a difference here.

Feeling sad, Erin forced herself to open her lunch case. It seemed as if a lifetime had passed since three o'clock that morning when she'd staggered around the cottage kitchen to make a sandwich and toss crunchy vegetables into snack bags. She couldn't even remember what she'd packed. Carrots. Broccoli. An apple and an orange. The sandwich, made with low-fat deli chicken, had been slapped together while she was still half-asleep, and now light mayo and mustard oozed out over the edges of the bread. Not wishing to soil her uniform shirt, she worked the zippered edge of the baggie down, grabbed a section of paper towel, and let the plastic serve double duty as a drip catcher as she took the first bite. Then, holding her main course in one hand, she fished the pocket manual from her hip pocket, hoping to familiarize herself with the particulars of this assignment as she ate.

Three bites later, Erin was frustrated. The booklet opened with illustrations of and captions about all the noxious weeds that existed and what havoc they might wreak on the flora in a wilderness area. Hello? How would she ever remember what each species looked like or the effect it might have on the health of a forest floor? What had Sheriff Adams been thinking to send her up here to perform duties for which she was completely unprepared?

Feeling a little panicked, Erin set aside her half-eaten sandwich and leafed farther back in the book, searching in vain for any information that might leap out from the tiny print. Nope. It was page after page of small-font gibberish, and she'd have to read every word to learn anything useful. Why couldn't the federal government publish stuff in plain English and leave all the reference sources out of the text?

Just then she heard an odd clanking sound. Snapping her head up, she stared at the trail. It couldn't be an outfitter. Not *yet*! She'd look like a complete idiot if she had to inspect hay right now. Only she heard the clanking again and then the sound of clomping horses' hooves reached her. She shoved the manual back in her pocket, pushed aside her lunch, and sprang to her feet.

Just then a rider came into view at the crest of the hill that Butterscotch had ascended earlier at a brisk jog. At first all she could see was the bobbing crown of a brown western hat a shade lighter than her own. Then the horse's golden head and the upper body of the human on its back came into view. The horse, a palomino with a flowing platinum mane, was beautiful. And so was the man. Normally Erin wasn't into the cowboy look, possibly because very few guys had the right build to pull it off, but this one did. He was twisted at the waist to monitor a string of pack animals behind him, so she couldn't see his face, only a drift of straight blond hair that fell forward to touch the center front of his faded blue chambray shirt. Equally washed-out Wrangler jeans, a hand-tooled belt with a large silver buckle, and dusty riding boots completed the ensemble. He nudged his mount with his heels to increase the pace and kept his attention fixed on the horses and mules that were spilling over the rise behind him.

As Erin moved toward the trail, she thumbed the corners of her mouth and licked her lips to be sure no mustard was on her face. "Hello!" she called, trying for a cheerful, friendly tone. "I'm Deputy De Laney, and if you don't mind stopping for a moment, I need to inspect your hay." The guy gave no indication that he'd heard her, and he didn't slow down when all six pack-horses had made the ascent. Erin raised her voice and repeated herself at a higher volume. When the man still didn't glance her way and just kept going, she yelled, "Hey! I'm a county deputy! You can't just pretend you don't hear me and keep going!"

But that was precisely what he did. Erin waved her arms. Yelled again. And the only reaction she got was from Butterscotch, who snorted, whirled, and ran off into the trees. Caught between two choices, chasing the horse or the man, Erin allowed her sense of survival to be the deciding factor and dashed into the woods after the equine. She'd run only about a hundred yards when she saw the flash of Butterscotch's rump disappear over a hill. Her common sense reasserted itself. Aside from the saddle, the horse bore no weight on his back and could easily outrun her. She probably wouldn't catch up with him until he reached the trailhead.

She cut back through the undergrowth to the trail. The cowboy with the string of pack animals had reached the edge of the clearing. Erin sprang into a run. "Police! King County Sheriff's Office! Halt! Stop where you are!" She winced even as she increased speed. *King County?* Old habits died hard, she guessed, especially in stressful situations. She hadn't been a King County deputy in well over a year. "Evading a police officer is against the law!"

The cowboy pressed forward, never even glancing over his shoulder. His dog, black and white with a collie-like coat, circled back to bark at her, but the man just kept going. Well, that wasn't going to fly. Not with her. There was no way, absolutely no *way*, that he couldn't hear her. By the time she reached the edge of the forest, he and the pack train had vanished, and all she could see was trees. She'd dealt with people like him in the Seattle area. They had no respect for the law or the officers whose job it was to enforce it.

She drew to a stop to analyze the situation and decide whether she should pursue the guy on foot. After being in the saddle for well over three hours, she was hot, tired, and in no mood for a run. On the other hand, Sheriff Adams had put his faith in her to do this job, and her father, once a marine and now a gung ho cop, hadn't raised her to be a sissy. Just the opposite. He'd wanted a boy, gotten a girl, and refused to change her diapers so he could pretend she had the right equipment. Now as an adult, she was competitive, and being the winner in almost any situation was inordinately important to her. She'd long since realized that and worked hard to correct the character flaw. Winning remained important to her, though, and it didn't seem to matter what she was doing—playing pinochle, practicing self-defense, or engaging in aggressive takedowns on a mat with a man twice her size. When doing her job, she still felt a rush of outrage and an underlying sense of inadequacy when she lost control of a situation.

Okay, Erin. What's it going to be? You going to roll over and show your belly? Or will you fight back? She hated when she heard her dad's voice inside her head. It was a sound bite from the past, one that she needed to ignore, but her compulsion to measure up in Gordon De Laney's eyes had never diminished. Besides, she hadn't been for a run in two days, and it wouldn't hurt her to pit herself against a mountain trail with more inclines than declines. It also stuck in her craw to be bested by a cowboy with rocks for brains. Only a dim-witted man thought that he could ignore a cop and get away with it.

She bent her knees, straightened, flexed her legs, and then stretched to plant her palms on the ground. Then she jogged in circles to do a halfhearted warm-up. *Ready, set, go!* That dingledorf probably thought she would walk back to the trailhead and just call in for help, that when and if another deputy found him, he'd be able to lie his way out of trouble. *Not happening.* Back in Washington, she'd run marathons, not the sissy kind where they shaved off miles for participant glory, but actual marathons of twenty-six miles. She'd also completed the Ironman Triathlon twice, not to win but just to prove she could do it. She'd placed ninth in her category once and sixth the second time, earning the right to be called an Ironman. They were brutal events. She'd trained for a year prior to each one, and she'd always feel proud that she'd done it. Mostly because her dad was impressed, she supposed, but she didn't want to think about that.

Erin set a running pace she knew she could maintain. The cowboy had a head start, but she felt confident that she was going at a faster clip than those horses, which were undoubtedly carrying maximum loads. She'd catch up, and the incredulous expression on his face would be all the reward she needed. He probably had her pegged as a city slicker who'd get lost out here if she left the trail, someone soft and terrified of all the big predators that lived in a wilderness area. In a way, that was true. It was difficult for her to get her bearings when she couldn't see the sky, and going nose to nose with a cougar or bear wasn't high on her list. But she was armed, an expert shot, and it wasn't in her character to back down from a challenge.

She'd gone about a mile when her boots started to rub blisters on her toes and heels. When she'd started this run, she hadn't thought about her footwear. Riding boots weren't made for long-distance jogging. When she stepped on loose rocks, the heels tended to wrench sideways, and apparently she'd chosen too loose a fit, because her feet were slopping around in them. *Damn. Oh, well, I've endured worse and won't let blisters stop me. I've got a cowboy to catch.*

Erin fell and did a face-plant going down one hill. Aside from eating a little dirt, she would have been fine if not for the belt-clip radio that dug into her hip bone with crushing force and left her hobbling along until she ran her way past the pain. The experience spiked her temper, and she was fuming when she finally spilled out of the woods into another clearing.

The cowboy had stopped at a creek to water and rest his horses. While the horses drank, he stood off to one side with his back to her. His stance indicated that he was taking a leak. For some reason that irked her even more, possibly because she needed to go herself and hadn't taken the time to stop.

Blistered feet screaming with every step she took, she strode across the grassy flat. "Hey, you!" she yelled. "I issued you a lawful order to halt! This may be a wilderness area, but you can't ignore a law enforcement officer and get away with it!"

It infuriated Erin that he didn't so much as flinch at the sound of her voice. She was finished with this game. His dog came running across the grass toward her, which alarmed her. What if it was vicious? Equal parts black and white, it was a beautiful canine, and when it reached her, it only ran in circles around her moving feet.

As she walked up behind the man, she was too pissed off to care if a certain part of his male anatomy was protruding from the fly of his Wranglers. She moved in close and thumped him on the back with the heel of her right hand. *That* got his attention.

He whirled around and decked her.

Erin never saw his fist coming, but upon impact, the blow sent her flying backward, and she landed on her back with a *whoosh* as all the air rushed from her lungs. Everything went black, and then she saw bright spots—little orbs of sparkly iridescence that bounced around like night stars doing a ballet.

"Oh, God!" she heard him say. "I'm sorry. Are you okay?"

Erin was okay enough to take him apart with her bare hands the moment she could see again. She blinked. Tried to focus. His sun-burnished face swam in and out. Eyes as blue as laser beams. Chiseled features. A square jaw. Rocks for Brains was handsome.

She lay there, still too stunned to move. Finally her lungs hitched and grabbed for air.

"I didn't hear you walk up behind me," he said. "I thought I was alone out here. When you shoved me, I swung around and caught you with my elbow."

Your elbow, *my* ass. *No elbow on earth carries that much of a wallop.* Erin worked her mouth, swallowed, and managed to push out one word. "Bullshit."

Sheriff Adams would scowl about her city-cop language being used in his backwoods county, where he insisted most people were still old-fashioned and wouldn't say *shit* if they had a mouthful, but she was beyond caring at the moment about the virgin ears of little old ladies in polyester slacks. Her face hurt so much she couldn't tell where he'd nailed her. Lifting a hand that felt disembodied, she touched the spot that throbbed the most. *Cheekbone.* She'd have a shiner for a couple of weeks that not even sunglasses would hide. And the other deputies, all but one of them male, would never let her hear the end of it.

Erin rolled toward him to get an elbow wedged underneath herself. *Never turn your back on a suspect.* As she struggled to sit up, he curled an arm around her shoulders to help her. She wanted to knock it away, but it was all she could do not to flop over backward.

"I'm sure you know it's not okay to touch a police officer," she said.

He withdrew his support, and she nearly toppled. He shot out his arm to brace it against her shoulder blades again. "If you charge me with assault for trying to steady you, you're not a very nice cop."

At the moment, she didn't feel like being nice. She squinted against the stabbing pain to meet his penetrating gaze. And then, after really looking at him again, she steeled herself against a purely feminine jolt of awareness. He wasn't merely handsome. She'd had girlfriends in Seattle who'd described incredibly hot men as "sex on a stick," but this guy was—well, she couldn't think how to describe him. Completely unexpected, that was for sure. There were some really good-looking guys in Mystic Creek, but their numbers were limited, and this cowboy had them so outclassed with rugged masculinity that they weren't even in the same league. Maybe he was from another area. After working in Mystic Creek for nearly a year, she had at least seen most of the residents from a distance and didn't think he was a hometown boy. Hair the light, golden color of a wheat field. Strong, carved features overlaid with skin darkened to caramel by the sun. A full mouth that still managed to look firm. Even the way he wore his Gus-style Stetson, tipped slightly forward to shade his eyes, was sexier than all get-out.

"I'll pass on charging you with assault, because you

may not have meant to hit me, but you're going down for evading a police officer."

His lips twitched, and his eyes crinkled at the corners as if he were suppressing a smile. "For *what*?"

"You heard me." Erin straightened her spine to put some distance between the brace of his arm and her back. Her head had cleared, and she felt almost ready to stand up. "I yelled for you to halt, and you ignored me."

With a fluid motion, he pushed to his feet, and then he began unbuttoning his worn, light blue shirt. When the front plackets had parted to reveal a large V of his chest, which glistened with a shimmer of sweat and gold hair, she started to feel nervous. He was a tall and well-muscled man. Normally she would feel confident in her ability to hold her own against him, but nothing about this situation was normal. She reminded herself that she was armed, with both a nine-millimeter Glock and a Taser on her belt, but her head felt so swimmy she wasn't sure she could even stand up. The dog whined and moved in to sniff her shirt and then her cheek.

Upper torso now bare, the cowboy strode back to the stream and pushed the horses aside as he hunkered to plunge the shirt into the water. When he stood, the garment streamed water. Without wringing it out, he walked back to her. With every shift of his narrow hips, she felt her heartbeat flutter. He stopped a few feet from her, gathered the blue cloth in his fists, and squeezed a stream of water from its folds.

"For your cheek," he said as he dropped to one

knee beside her. Before Erin could protest, he pressed the drippy folds of cloth to the side of her face. The icy coldness felt so good that she forgot why she'd nearly objected. "I really am sorry," he told her. "I startle easily."

He spoke softly and slowly—the flow of his words deliberate with slight pauses in between. Erin held the makeshift compress against her throbbing face. "I can only assume you knew my horse took off and you didn't think I'd be able to catch you on foot. Your mistake. If I startled you, it was your own fault for ignoring a law enforcement officer."

She expected him to deny the charge, but he said nothing. She angled a glance at him. He studied her with what appeared to be unruffled calm.

"You *will* be cited for that," she added.

He finally reacted by arching only one eyebrow, a feat that Erin had never been able to master. "I'm sorry. I didn't catch everything you said."

Erin bristled. She'd had enough of his innocent act. "Just like you didn't catch it when I chased you on foot and screamed at the top of my lungs for you to stop?"

He nudged up the brim of his Stetson. "I didn't hear you," he told her.

"Are you stone deaf?" she popped back.

At the question, his eyes went deadpan and his jaw muscle began to tic. Erin removed the wad of cloth from her cheek and plopped it on his upraised knee. Then she struggled to gain her feet, jerking her arm away when he tried to help her. The meadow around her undulated like a gigantic green lake for a moment. She could only pray she didn't lose her balance, because her legs felt as insubstantial as overcooked rice noodles.

"Let's get this show on the road," she said with as much authority as she could manage.

"What show would that be?" he asked.

"I have to check your hay. As if you don't know that. And that's another count against you. Any experienced outfitter is aware that it's against the law to enter a wilderness area with hay that contains toxic weeds."

He did the eyebrow thing again, arching only one like a golden wing. "You mean *noxious* weeds? Yes, I'm aware of the law. But most wardens set up a checkpoint along the trail, which you did not."

"Oh, yes, I did."

"Where? I saw no one out here until you sneaked up behind me and punched my shoulder."

Erin narrowed her eyes. "I did *not* punch you. I *tapped* your shoulder." He was trying to turn the tables and make all of this *her* fault. Well, she wasn't about to play that game. She had left the trail to water Butterscotch and sit in the shade, but even if he hadn't seen her, he should have heard her yelling. She turned and set off walking toward the horses, praying her legs wouldn't buckle. She heard him fall in behind her, the impact of his boots on the grass creating a slower cadence than her own. The packhorses were milling about now and happily grazing. She stopped beside a white equine that looked as if it had been splattered with black paint. Turning toward the cowboy, she placed a hand against a huge, rectangular shape wrapped in canvas that was strapped to a frame on the animal's back. "Hay bale. Correct?"

"Yes. I manty them up to make sure they don't get wet."

"I'll need you to remove this one and unwrap it so I can have a look."

He shrugged and stepped over to do as she asked. Erin, standing beside him, was taken off guard when he loosened the knots with a few quick tugs and the manty fell toward them. She staggered backward to avoid getting knocked off her feet. She wondered if he'd done it on purpose.

He bent to unfurl the canvas, which sent the hay bale rolling and forced her to dance out of its path again. "Please, sir, cut the twine so I can examine the forage."

His piercing blue eyes widened. "Why do I have to cut the twine?"

"So I can check the hay for weeds."

He settled his fists on his hips, shifted his weight to one long leg, and bent his opposite knee. It didn't escape her notice that his stance was one that frustrated males had been assuming with women since the beginning of time. His expression conveyed exasperation and incredulity. "You're kidding. Right? Just look at the twine. It's clearly certified."

Erin cast a glance at the hay. She saw no tags or anything.

As if guessing her thoughts, he said, "Look at the twine color."

"What about it?"

His gaze grew intense. "In Oregon, special purple and yellow twine is issued to weed-free hay producers to mark their bales as being certified weed free. Who sent you out here to do this job, anyway?"

Sheriff Adams had said nothing about looking at the baling twine. And even though she'd had almost no time to read the manual that now felt as if it were burning through her uniform pants, she'd seen no mention of different colors of twine being used to mark safe hay. No way was she going to look at the book now. He'd think she was a complete idiot, and it was her responsibility to maintain an air of professionalism at all times while she performed her job. She straightened her shoulders.

"Please, cut the twine, sir." She kept her voice even as she issued that order a second time.

"If I cut that twine, the hay is going to fall apart. Once that happens, I can't transport it to the base camp. That means it'll go to waste, and it isn't exactly cheap. In addition to that, it means that we'll be a bale short on feed. My boss is not going to be happy."

"It isn't my job to please your boss."

"Fair enough. I'll be sure to relay that message to him." He reached for the knife that rode in a scabbard attached to his belt. "Don't shoot me. I'm just going to cut the twine and then put the weapon away."

Erin bit down hard on her back teeth. Did he really think she was a trigger-happy rookie, or was he just being sarcastic to piss her off? As she'd requested, he cut the binding, and then, just as he had predicted, the hay popped free and spilled in sections over the grass. Erin stepped back, caught her balance, and then leaned forward.

"Where's your weed detector?" he asked.

Weed detector? Erin wanted to cuss, and not in a ladylike way. She wanted to let fly like a dyed-in-the-wool city cop who'd been trained by and worked with male officers who thought the *F* word was a perfectly acceptable sentence enhancer. As one of the few female officers in her Washington district, she'd learned to talk like the men in order to fit in, and now it was difficult for her to break the habit.

She straightened, met the cowboy's smoldering gaze, and said, "Sheriff Adams said nothing to me about a weed detector."

His expression stony, he replied, "To be absolutely certain there are no noxious weeds in that hay, you'll need a detector. What do you think, that they'll wave hello at you?"

Erin wanted to kick something. From start to finish, this unexpected assignment had been a shit show. She'd had no time to read the manual. She'd never been on a horse. She didn't know one kind of hay from another. It was bad enough that the sheriff had sent her up here to do a job she hadn't been trained to perform, but learning now that he'd failed to provide her with a necessary piece of equipment irked her even more.

"I'll have to make do. I have no detector." As she spoke, she noticed that the corner of his mouth twitched, much as if he were struggling not to laugh. Her stomach knotted. "There's no such thing. Is there?"

He lifted one well-padded and sun-bronzed shoulder. "No, but you bought into it for a second, which tells me you don't know jack shit about doing this job."

Erin felt heat inch up her neck. When it pooled in her cheeks, the bruise below her eye started to throb again. She bent over to examine the hay. The cowboy was right; no weeds waved hello. She glimpsed stuff that might be dried weeds, but she was no expert, and she wouldn't pretend she was in order to save face. Instead she straightened, pulled out her citation tablet, and began filling out the form.

"You're writing me up?"

At the question, Erin met his gaze. "Absolutely. I'll let the hay pass, but you ignored a lawful order from a law officer to halt."

"I said I didn't hear you."

"And I don't believe you." As she held his gaze, she studiously tried to ignore how beautifully sculpted his upper torso was. She saw bare chests a lot when she worked out at the local gym and was no stranger to striated abdomens, well-roped shoulders, and impressively pumped biceps. But this guy—well, he definitely had a gorgeous physique. Well muscled, but lean and streamlined, with none of the overblown, rubbery look common to bodybuilders. "As I said earlier, you'd have to be stone deaf not to have heard me yelling."

"And what if I am?"

She'd gone back to filling out the citation and lifted her head again to give him a querulous look. "What if you are *what*?"

"Stone deaf."

Erin almost laughed—not with genuine amusement, but with a snort of disgust. "Sorry. I worked with deaf children for three years in Seattle. That was prior to my becoming a cop. You don't have the speech patterns of a deaf person. And if you've been reading my lips ever since I *tapped* you on the shoulder, you're a walking phenomenon." She shook her head. "Nope. You're a lot of things, but deaf isn't one of them."

"Can you read ASL?"

Erin gave him a long study. "I can."

His firm mouth tipped into a grin that flashed strong white teeth. It was a smile laced with anger, emphasizing the glint of fury in his eyes. "Good! Then you'll have no problem understanding *this*."

His hands began to move so swiftly that Erin struggled to keep up, partly because she was rusty, but mostly because her stomach felt as if it had taken a sickening plunge to somewhere around her knees. He paused in his gesturing to say his name, "Wyatt Fitzgerald," and then resumed signing, telling her his age, which was thirty-two. His hands moved so fast that her vision blurred and she missed his date of birth. Then he got to the good part, telling her to take the citation and shove it up her ass. He'd done nothing wrong unless not being able to hear was suddenly a crime.

Stunned, she watched as he wheeled away and began taking the pack off the horse, his movements jerky with anger. Even so, he was gentle with the animal. He met her gaze over the gelding's back. "It'll take me at least an hour to rebalance all this stuff. Of course, you know nothing about horses and packs, because you're a city slicker. So much so that you never visit your uncle's ranch for fear you'll get cow shit on your boots."

Erin was still marveling at the speed with which he'd spoken in sign. But that didn't mean he was deaf, she assured herself. She had learned ASL, and she had no problems with her hearing. He definitely didn't speak like any deaf person she had ever encountered, either. This guy spoke with inflection and nearly perfect pronunciation. The only particular thing she'd noticed was that he spoke slowly.

She realized he was watching her as if to gauge her reaction to what he'd said. "If you're stone deaf, I'll kiss your bare ass on the courthouse steps during rush hour," she told him. "You picked the wrong deputy to bamboozle."

His blue eyes danced with amusement. "You're on. Name a date and time. I've never had a cop kiss my ass. I'll sell tickets for the show and make a killing."

Erin resumed writing the citation, a task normally made easier by entering the information on an electronic tablet and then printing it out.

"If you cite me, ma'am, you are going to regret it. Sheriff Adams knows me. I truly am deaf."

"If that's true, you took your own sweet time to inform me of it!" she shot back.

"I do not make a habit of informing everyone I meet that I have a disability. Would you? I've worked hard to overcome it."

"I'm not just anyone, sir. I'm a law officer."

"A law officer who goes strictly by the book, no exceptions. I get it. But given that I am deaf, I am not guilty of evading a police officer. You were not on the trail where I could see you, which is where you *should* have been. Maybe you yelled. It does not matter. A wilderness checkpoint should be clearly visible. I could have witnessed the bombing of Hiroshima and not heard the explosion. How could I hear someone yelling at me to stop?"

He had quit using contractions and his pauses between words were now more pronounced. She wondered if he was growing weary of engaging verbally. The hearing-impaired kids she'd worked with had tired easily during speech therapy. *Stop,* she told herself. *If he was deaf, he wouldn't be able to speak so clearly.*

"If I have to appear in court," he said, jerking her back to the conversation, "it will be a waste of my time, but worse than that, you will be a laughingstock."

Erin's fingers clamped tighter on the pen. "That's a chance I'll have to take."

"Come again? I can't read your lips when you don't look at me."

Erin didn't believe for a moment that he'd been reading her lips. The last she'd seen, the average accuracy of lip-reading was thirty percent. Some incredibly accomplished individuals tested to be as high in accuracy as fifty-two percent, but this cowboy seemed to comprehend nearly everything. She jerked his copy of the citation from her tablet and extended it to him.

"Last chance," he said. "You can still tear it up, and we can both pretend this never happened."

Erin imagined him laughing and slapping his knee as he told *that* story to his buddies. In her experience, people loved to brag about how they had talked their way out of a ticket. *I told her I was deaf,* he'd say. *She actually fell for it, ha-ha-ha.* If she was going to be a laughingstock, she preferred to have the sheriff be the one to do the guffawing, not the general public. Law officers had to guard their reputations. A rumor about her buying into a cock-and-bull story would damage her credibility.

He folded the citation and stuffed it into his front pants pocket. Then without another word to her, he turned toward the horse to resume his work on the packs. Erin didn't appreciate being dismissed with so little ceremony, but given that their business was concluded, she couldn't quibble about his attitude. People were required to abide by the law, but nowhere was it written that they had to like the individuals who enforced it.

She turned to walk away, only to stop when he asked, "Where's your horse?"

She angled him a look over her shoulder. "He ran off."

"When?"

"When I yelled at you to stop at the checkpoint."

He sighed and removed his hat to slap it against his leg. He had gorgeous hair, the color of spun gold and as straight as a ruler. It slid over his shoulders like threads of silk. "You didn't tie him off?" He held up his free hand. "Forget I asked. Of course you didn't."

She flung her arm to indicate the pack animals. "You've tied off none of these horses."

"They are carrying heavy loads." His burnished brows snapped together in a scowl as he settled the Stetson back on his head. "How did you follow me? On foot? Where is that checkpoint? How far from here?"

Erin had to give him credit for sticking to his story, namely, that he hadn't seen or heard her at the checkpoint. "Three, maybe four miles," she replied.

"And you walked all that way up the mountain?"

"No. I ran."

"Uphill, for four miles?" Incredulity darkened his gaze. Then he rested his hands on his hips. "So what is your plan to get back to the trailhead?"

Erin didn't look forward to the walk. She was bone tired, she was hungry, and her face ached. "The two feet God gave me are in fine working order."

He held up his hand again. "I will take you down. Just give me a few minutes to run a high line."

Erin had no clue what a high line was, and she had

no interest in hanging around to find out. "Thanks for the offer, but I'll pass."

As she retreated across the meadow, she ignored the blisters on her heels and didn't allow herself to limp as long as she was in his line of sight. That changed when she entered the bordering forest. She groaned and sat on a rock to pull off her boots and check her feet. Her heels were bloody raw and stung as though doused with rubbing alcohol. She drew her socks back on and decided to carry the boots. Not the best plan, given that the trail was rocky in places, but she could pick her way to avoid bruising the soles of her feet.

And walking, even if it hurt every step of the way, was better than feeling helpless.

Chapter Two

Erin had walked about a mile when she heard a horse on the trail behind her. When she turned, she wasn't surprised to see Wyatt Fitzgerald. As far as she knew, he was the only other person on the mountain today. He reined the animal to a stop when he reached her and swung out of the saddle with enviable ease, his every movement attesting that he'd spent most of his life riding. Watching him, she felt as if she'd wandered into the filming location of an Old West movie. His penetrating blue gaze shifted to the boots she carried in one hand, and his mouth thinned to a grim line.

"How bad are your feet?"

She sighed, hating that he'd circled back to find and help her. That was her role to play, not his. And she sucked at being a damsel in distress. Her father had made sure of that. For a horrible moment, she felt tears sting her eyes. She *never* cried. She just wasn't herself. The throbbing pain in her cheekbone now radiated to her temple. Her inner thighs ached from the long ride that morning. Pain pulsated in her hip from being crushed against the radio. Her feet burned like those of a Salem witch tied to a stake with flames licking at her ankles.

"Nothing to write home about," she replied.

"Open sores?" he asked.

"What difference does it make? It is what it is." She lifted the boots. "These stupid things aren't made for jogging long distances."

He glanced around and then pointed at a fallen log. "Sit over there. I carry a first aid kit."

Erin shook her head. "I don't need your help."

"It's ten miles to the trailhead." He showed her his back as he opened one of his saddlebags. "You can't walk that far on blistered feet."

Erin blinked, because she'd just now noticed that he wore a fresh shirt, this one a faded red and worn thin at the elbows. "Watch me."

He made no reply. When he turned to face her again, she contemplated the possibility that he actually might be deaf. Years had passed since she'd worked in that field, and many changes had occurred.

"Please, sit down," he said. "The boss I mentioned who'll be angry over the loss of hay will be even madder if I let you walk out of here. I'm helping you whether you want me to or not."

He was once again using contractions when he spoke. Erin removed her hat to finger-comb her sweat-dampened hair. She'd tied it into a tidy knot at the nape of her neck that morning, but the band had long since lost its grip. Limp shanks puddled at her collar and lay like a damp minishawl over her shoulders. She yearned for a drink and wished now that she'd dropped to her belly by the stream to quench her thirst. At this point, she was willing to risk an *E. coli* infection.

"Do you have water?" She didn't want to ask, but the words rushed out anyway. "I think I'm getting dehydrated."

He reached over the horse to grab a bota bag hanging from the pommel. She dropped her boots to take it from his outstretched hand. With a twist of her wrist, she removed the cap and then wasn't sure how to drink from the bag. Those blue eyes were intent on her face. She had a feeling he missed very little.

"It's all right to drink straight from the bag," he said. "If you don't mind my germs, that is. Some people hold it high and aim the stream at their mouths. I don't. Good way to get wet and waste water."

Erin was so parched that she was beyond caring about any germs he possibly had. According to her dad, what didn't kill her would make her stronger. She sucked water straight from the bag and gasped when she came up for air.

"Have all you want. Just don't get sick." He moved past her toward the log. "I carry iodine tablets. I can purify more if I run out."

"Thank you."

He didn't reply. After drinking all that she safely could, Erin capped the bag, looped the braided leather strap back over the saddle horn, and hobbled toward the log, leaving her boots lying in the dirt next to his horse. As she sat down, bark jabbed her rump, which was already sore from bouncing around on a saddle that morning. Wyatt saw her wince and arched a brow in question.

"Saddle sore," she said by way of explanation.

"Not used to riding?"

She considered the question and debated the wisdom of exaggerating her experience with equines. At this point, she was too exhausted to be prideful, and she was a lousy liar. "Before dawn I received a thirty-minute riding lesson from Sheriff Adams. That was my first time on a horse. Well, when I was five my uncle put me on the back of an old mare and led her around a corral. I don't think that really counts."

His eyebrow arched again. "Adams sent an inexperienced rider up the mountain alone?"

Erin heard the ring of disapproval in his voice and said, "Butterscotch—that's his horse—is bulletproof, according to him."

"No horse is bulletproof." He jabbed a thumb over his shoulder at the equine behind him. "That is Shanghai. Wonderful mount. I put my faith in him because I have to, but I'm always watchful. Horses are just like people. They get startled. They panic. Shanghai is pretty solid, but I never forget that he might do something unexpected."

Listening to him talk, Erin got a sinking sensation in her chest. At the meadow, she'd been angry. Now she was too tired for her adrenaline to spike and she detected a definite pause between each word he spoke.

Maybe she'd been too quick to decide he couldn't possibly be deaf.

"Are you truly hearing impaired?" The question was out before she had a chance to cut it off. "No BS, Mr. Fitzgerald. I just—well, if I made a bad call on that, I'm sorry."

His mouth curved up at one corner to flash a dimple, which was boyishly attractive in a face so relentlessly masculine. "Why would I lie about being hearing impaired?"

"To get off scot-free for evading a law enforcement officer?"

He shook his head. "Not my style. If I had seen or heard you, I would have stopped. No reason not to. The boss is a stickler about weed-free hay for his horses. Even as rarely as you visit the ranch, you should know that much about him. He's so careful about it that he feeds his stock weed-free hay and grain for four solid days before taking them into a wilderness area. Most people do that for only three."

Erin frowned in bewilderment. "Who is your boss?"

He studied her face. "You don't know? All the pack animals at Elk Meadow carry his brand. You surely noticed that."

"Looking at brands isn't something I think to do." She searched his gaze. "Are you talking about my uncle Slade?"

"Bull's-eye."

"You work for my *uncle*? Why didn't you just say so? When I've visited the ranch, I've never seen you there."

"If you had come more than twice and stayed long enough to let the dust settle, you would have seen me."

"I've been to the ranch more than *twice*." She searched her memory and could clearly recall only two visits to the ranch after her initial stay of two weeks. Both times she'd received a call from the sheriff's office and had to leave before she could finish a cup of coffee. "And the only reason my time there was short was because all hell broke loose in town."

He pushed up the brim of his hat, presumably to better watch her lips. "The crime rate is terrible, I know. Murder on the streets in broad daylight. Armed robberies right and left. Prostitution. Drug deals. Gang wars."

Physical exhaustion had robbed Erin of her ability to laugh. The absence of all those things he'd just mentioned had been the lure that had drawn her to Mystic Creek. "I'm the junior deputy, Mr. Fitzgerald. When a cat gets stuck in a tree and the fire department can't handle it, I get the call. When a senior officer gets the sniffles and can't come to work, I get the call."

"So you're busy." He held her gaze, and in that moment, she knew she'd never seen more beautiful eyes, not simply a startling blue in contrast to his sun-darkened face, but almost electrical in their intensity. "So busy you can't drive ten miles out of town and park your butt on Slade's porch to have a mug of his black sludge every once in a while?"

Uncle Slade's coffee was the worst Erin had ever tasted, and because this man knew it, she reluctantly accepted that he worked on the Wilder Ranch and knew her uncle well. It followed that he wouldn't have lied about being deaf. An out-of-towner might get away with such a deception, but a local would be found out almost immediately. The Mystic Creek grapevine rivaled the transmission speed of underground fiber optics.

"Please, don't judge me," she said, holding his gaze just as relentlessly as he held hers. "I love my uncle. I'd like to spend more time with him. It's just—" She broke off to give herself a mental scold. This man deserved no explanation from her. She didn't have to defend herself simply because his eyes compelled her to do so. Only she heard the words spilling from her mouth anyway. "I'm new, and I'm a woman. If you think the glass ceiling doesn't exist in this good-old-boy county, think again."

He gestured at her feet. "You want to pull those socks off, or should I?"

Erin leaned over to do it herself. "No, thanks. You'd peel off hide and all." She glanced up, realized that he hadn't been able to see her lips move, and repeated herself. "These blisters already sting like the very devil." After she got both socks off, she met his gaze again. "If you're thinking about getting your revenge by hurting me, remember I'm armed."

He chuckled. "I'll bear that in mind."

He slipped a hand under one leg of her trousers, his broad palm leathery with calluses against her skin. She likened the sensation to the grainy underside of silk sliding over her nerve endings. A jolt of physical awareness shot from just below her knee to the pit of her stomach and then zinged up to her nipples. She didn't appreciate her body's reaction. She wrote it off to the fact that she hadn't been in a relationship in over three years. Being touched by warm, capable hands sparked physical yearnings she normally didn't have.

The first aid kit lay open on the ground beside him. He hunched his broad shoulders to bend over her foot. The crown of his hat nearly grazed her nose. The smell of it tantalized her, a masculine blend of dust, sweat, horses, male musk, and a dozen other scents she couldn't identify.

"Good thing I followed you," he muttered, and she finally heard traces of the throaty tones she'd come to associate with a deaf person. Then, putting more effort into his enunciation, he said, "These need attention. Otherwise infection will set in. That's no fun. Shoes are breeding grounds for bacteria and fungus."

When he looked up at her, she said, "You really are deaf."

"And you have a shiner. It is only red right now, but it'll be purple tomorrow and black in three days. I guess none of us is perfect."

"Give me that citation," she said. "I'll tear it up."

"Never. I may be deaf, but I'm not stupid. You're new. Without any training, you came up here to check hay and believed me when I said you needed a weed detector. My guess is, you're skating on thin ice with Sheriff Adams and fighting to keep your job."

Erin bristled. "I am *not* skating on thin ice with my boss," she protested. "I held the rank of sergeant when I left Washington. It takes many people years longer to earn those stripes. I'm a good cop. I bring a lot of valuable experience and knowledge to the table."

"But you're still a woman competing against male colleagues. Men who probably know how to ride a horse and check hay. Men who may resent your presence at the department. You can't afford to look foolish in their eyes. If pressed, you might tell your boss whatever it takes to cast yourself in a good light, which would, by necessity, shine a bad light on me."

Erin tried to jerk her foot free, but he tightened his grip on her ankle. "You're questioning my integrity, and I don't appreciate it."

"I'm not going to risk doing time behind bars to spare your feelings," he retorted. "I never meant to strike you. You sneaked up behind me and whopped me on the back when I thought I was alone in a wilderness area."

Erin narrowed her eyes. "How will the citation prove you didn't deliberately strike me?"

He grinned. It was only a flash of white teeth, but the crooked shift of his lips transformed his face. "It says I refused to stop for a hay check and evaded a law enforcement officer who was yelling at me from behind. Anyone who knows me is aware that I'm profoundly deaf. The citation proves you didn't realize that when you wrote me up. The eruption of hay in the meadow also proves you know nothing about weed-free hay or the color of the twine that identifies it. In short, you came up here to do a job you're unqualified to do. Sling dirt my way, Deputy De Laney, and I'll bury you with a return volley."

Hands braced on the log, she dug her fingernails into the bark. "I'm not given to lying, Mr. Fitzgerald, not even to save face."

"And I'm not fond of the idea that I could do time for assaulting a cop. You're Slade's niece. For that reason, I'll get you off this mountain, but that doesn't mean I trust you—or that I've seen much about you that I like."

Erin appreciated his honesty, if not his attitude, and she couldn't say, even to herself, that she'd put her best foot forward with him. She'd been exhausted and angry when she walked up behind him in the meadow, and she probably had put more force behind her hand than she had intended when she touched his shoulder. She'd also believed he was lying when he claimed he hadn't heard her yelling, and she hadn't bothered to pretend otherwise. He probably didn't appreciate being called a liar any more than she did. In short, she'd screwed up big-time with him, and there might be no way she'd ever undo it. Which was a shame, because as little as he might like her, she was coming to respect him. He didn't mince words. He didn't back down. And, as much as she hated to admit it, she didn't blame him for trying to cover his ass.

"I would never say or do anything that would put an innocent man behind bars."

His unflinching gaze offered her no quarter. "And I would never strike a woman, let alone a police officer, but I did."

"I know now that you didn't mean to."

His jaw muscle rippled. "I'll keep the citation, just the same."

As he worked over her foot, flushing the open sore and then dabbing it dry, he was gentle. Incredibly so for such a rough and rugged man who had undoubtedly pitted himself against the fury of Mother Nature on a frequent basis and wrestled huge animals into submission almost daily. Earlier, bare from his waist up, he'd revealed a body to her that was honed to be nearly as strong as forged iron. Yet he touched her lightly and with caution. The contact warmed her in places she hadn't realized felt cold.

"I'm sorry about the hay debacle," she said to his hat brim. He didn't hear her, didn't look up. She tapped his shoulder with a fingertip. When he lifted his head, she repeated herself and then added, "A bunch of federal employees were in a bus wreck on Interstate 5 yesterday. On the way to a seminar, I think, where they would have been briefed on setting up hay checkpoints. Several people were injured in the accident, which caused a shortage of manpower. As the new man on the county totem pole, I was assigned to take up some of the slack. Other deputies were called upon as well, but Sheriff Adams could spare only a few to help out. He probably didn't want to send an inexperienced rider and hay inspector like me up here, but he didn't have much choice."

His jaw muscle rippled again. "In the past, the U.S. Forest Service patrolled the outfitter camps after they were set up. Certified weed-free hay is more expensive. Some people bring in only certified on the first trip and then have regular hay brought up after a ranger checks their camp."

Erin knew next to nothing about how hay inspections were normally done. "Maybe Sheriff Adams is doing it differently." She couldn't help but smile. "He may not know much more than I do about the procedures for checking hay. I don't think the department has ever been called upon to help out before."

He bent back over her foot. "I've been setting up base camps for Slade for years. I've heard of hay checkpoints, but I've never happened upon one. In the past a ranger rode by our camp, saw the colors of our baling twine, and called it good."

Erin frowned. It had never occurred to her that her boss might be as clueless about weed control procedures as she was. "The sheriff's department is county level," she settled for saying. "And the wreck on Interstate 5 was totally unexpected. I'm sure the Forest Service will send more of its own people in as soon as possible."

"We can hope." He bent back over her foot again. "I'm sorry I got you with my elbow. Normally I am not so jumpy in the wilderness, but Slade's been having trouble with his bear."

"*His* bear?"

An odd expression flitted across his face, giving her the impression that he regretted sharing that information, but it came and went so fast that she couldn't be sure.

"*A* bear," he rectified. "Not really *his* bear. It's been bedeviling him and everyone else on the ranch. I was thinking about the bear when you punched my shoulder. You scared the sand out of me."

He bent his head again. Within seconds he applied something to her heel that felt wonderfully cool, which he topped with a wide bandage. When he lowered that foot to the ground, Erin kept her heel elevated so the wrap wouldn't get dirty. He grasped her right leg then and propped it on his bent knee. Without her interrupting him, he worked faster, and she was soon able to put her socks back on. Glancing at her boots where she'd dropped them, she dreaded having to wear them again.

"I'll put them in my saddlebags," he told her. "Riding double, you won't need footwear."

Erin really, *really* didn't want to get on another horse. Butterscotch had turned out to be gentle and mostly unflappable, but Shanghai might be just the opposite. And her inner thighs were already so sore that it would take days for her to recover. "I can just walk."

"In your stocking feet?"

"I'm tougher than I look. If I were a man, you wouldn't object."

"As much as you may wish differently, you are not a man."

Erin couldn't argue the point.

"And, even if you were," he continued, "it is a long hike without shoes to protect your feet. I wouldn't do it if given a choice. The bottoms of those socks will wear away to nothing. You'll have dirt and spores and God only knows what else in those open sores by the time you reach your vehicle. Then, if I'm guessing right, you'll have to load Adams' horse into the transport trailer. Mark my words. That is where the horse headed, straight back to your starting point. Even wearing boots, you can get a foot smashed if a horse starts dancing on a ramp."

Erin knew he was right. Walking out of here was a stupid idea. The bottoms of her feet would be in sorrier shape than her blistered heels. She just hated needing help. *Hated* it. She'd been seeing her therapist, Jonas Sterling, for nearly six months in an attempt to overcome her personality quirks, traits that had been carved into her psyche during childhood by her father. One was her need to not only compete physically with men, but also to outdo them. She refused to accept that being a female made her physically weaker than a male. Refused to accept that any man could best her. Rationally, she knew that was nuts, but the child within her still felt compelled to meet the goals her father had always presented.

"Given that I'm no expert with horses and my feet

have withstood enough damage for the day, I suppose you're right." So she wouldn't block his view of her lips, she stopped talking as she bent to don her socks. "Thank you, Mr. Fitzgerald. My heels feel much better."

He closed the first aid kit, grabbed it in one large hand, and stood, all in one smooth motion. "I will get your boots packed. I need to get going. When I get back to the meadow, I have to reach base camp before dark even though I won't have time to start unpacking. At least the horses will be settled in."

Hating that she was taking so much time out of his day, Erin pushed up from the log. She wanted to say he didn't need to take her back to the trailhead, but the bottoms of her feet panged from the abuse they had already endured. "I've delayed you. I'm sorry." She cringed inwardly when she recalled their confrontation in the meadow. She'd all but called him a liar. Her insistence on examining the hay made her feel foolish beyond words. He probably would never forgive her—or like her—and she honestly couldn't blame him. It was just her luck that he worked for Uncle Slade. Today's encounter with him would come back to bite her every time she visited the ranch.

As she followed him to the palomino, she asked, "What kind of work do you do for my uncle? Are you a ranch hand or do you only work seasonally when he guides?"

No answer. She stared at his back, and the purely female part of her that she'd never been able to completely squelch was fascinated by the play of muscle under his shirt as he shifted his shoulders. *Deaf,* she reminded herself. She needed to make sure he could see her face when she addressed him. That would be difficult to remember, because he didn't speak like any deaf person she'd ever met.

He stepped around the horse to stow her boots in the opposite saddlebag. She caught his gaze and asked the question again. Expression stony, he replied, "I am the foreman. I do a little of everything."

Erin had heard Uncle Slade speak fondly of his foreman. For some reason, she'd pictured a much older man who'd lived enough years to acquire all the know-how that her uncle raved about and claimed was amazing. Supposedly Wyatt was the best horseman that Slade Wilder had ever known, and that was saying something. Slade wasn't too shabby with equines himself.

"Do you like the job?"

He searched her gaze as if he wondered what her game was. "Do you like to breathe? That is what ranching is to me—like the air I breathe. I would never be happy doing anything else."

Erin wished she could say that about her own chosen profession. "Uncle Slade would like to leave me his ranch."

Wyatt's mouth drew tight, a grim set of his lips that conveyed his disgust of her. "I know that. Everyone within a mile of him knows that. He was so excited when you applied for a job in Mystic Creek. All he talked about was how you would fall in love with his spread and want to take over for him when he retires.

Then you arrived." He bent slightly to mess with the saddle cinch. She guessed that he was adjusting its tightness because they would be riding double down the mountain. "Now he never talks about it. He knows it was only his dream and never yours."

Erin clenched her teeth to keep from defending herself. In many ways, he was right. She hadn't carved out time to spend on her uncle's ranch, and she knew how that looked to everyone, even her uncle. "Do you have bills to pay, Mr. Fitzgerald?"

"Not many."

"Well, I do. Lots of bills. Rent, food, utilities, a car payment, car insurance, and that isn't to mention that I'm paying off my folks for all the money they spent on my college education." She stopped when she reached the horse and held Wyatt's gaze over the saddle seat. "Judge me if you must, but at least be fair. I don't know if I'll like ranching. I'm a city slicker. Remember? I have a good job right now that covers my expenses, but my work schedule is crazy. If I slack off as a deputy, I could lose that job and leave myself high and dry without an income. In short, I have to work, and I have to be the best deputy I can be. That's my sure thing. The ranch—well, at this point in time, it's anyone's guess if I'll like that lifestyle. My mother walked away from it, and she's never looked back. She won't even visit my uncle at the ranch. She says the stench makes her stomach roll."

"The smell of exhaust in a city makes mine roll."

With a final jerk on the cinch, he motioned for her to circle the horse and come to stand beside him. "You can have the front seat. I don't get saddle sore, so sitting back on the cantle won't bother me."

Erin almost protested, but she managed to squelch the urge. Her butt was already screaming from the punishment of her morning ride, and if she pretended otherwise, she'd only look foolish. A horsewoman, she definitely wasn't. "That's thoughtful of you."

"Practical," he corrected. "If you're behind me, I won't know you're having problems unless you *tap* me on the shoulder again."

Erin wished he would turn loose of all that and press a restart button. She'd been furious because he had ignored her shouts. And even now that she felt fairly certain of his deafness, he still defied all the stereotypes of nonhearing individuals. Then, to top it all off, he'd decked her when she touched him. Couldn't he take a step back and understand that she'd had no valid reason to believe his story?

"So how long will you hold this morning against me?" she asked when he glanced at her.

He propped a bent arm on the saddle seat and assumed a hip-out stance that was so sexy her mouth went dry. She'd never found the whole cowboy thing attractive, only this man lent it a whole new definition.

"Why do you care?" he volleyed back. "I will take you back down the mountain, catch your horse, get him loaded in the trailer, and off you'll go. If you visit your uncle sometime over the next six months, I will be surprised, but if you do, I will keep busy elsewhere. No skin off your nose and none off mine."

"Is that why I never saw you when I visited my uncle, because you were keeping busy elsewhere?"

His gaze sliced at her like lasers. "Have you ever seen hope vanish from an old man's eyes, Deputy De Laney? I watched your uncle lose all hope after you came to town. He is a good man. One of the best I've ever met. It doesn't seem right that his own niece doesn't love him. I sure do."

"I love him! I've always loved him."

"You have a really odd way of showing it." He straightened away from the palomino and bent over to lace his fingers together. "Up you go."

Erin didn't want help mounting. But she put her foot in the cradle of his hands anyway. He stared up at her from under the brim of his hat. "Wrong foot."

Heat rushed to her face, making her bruised cheek and eye pang. "Silly me." She stuck her left foot into the stirrup created by his hands and hopped to get a grip on the saddle horn. The next instant, he propelled her upward with such strength that she nearly went over the horse and off the other side. When she'd narrowly avoided that disaster, she darted a fulminous glare at him. "You did that on purpose."

"I'm sorry. Judging by looks, I expected you to be a lot heavier."

Erin almost laughed. She had her share of hang-ups, but feeling self-conscious about her weight wasn't one of them. She worked too hard to stay trim. "What if I'd gone off the other side and broken a leg?"

"If you'd gone off the other side, you would have landed on your feet."

"Was that a backhanded compliment?"

"No."

He said nothing more as he swung up behind her. The next instant, her rump was wedged between his hard thighs and his left arm was locked around her middle. Every rational thought in her head leaked out her ears. His hand, which he splayed over her ribs, felt as large as an oversize dessert plate, and his fingertips grazed the underside of her right breast. The heat of his touch electrified parts of her body that she hadn't acknowledged she had for over three years. Her physical reaction to his potent maleness drove home to her that she needed to stop living like a nun and waiting to meet Mr. Right before she dated again. At the rate she was going, she might never find him. As Wyatt had pointed out, she didn't have time in her crazy work schedule to visit her uncle, so how could she hope to socialize and meet men?

Not wishing to think about her sex life, or the lack thereof, she searched for something to say to her chauffeur. "So, how long have you worked for my uncle?" she asked.

No answer. She suspected that he'd felt the vibration of her voice against his chest, but for whatever reason, he didn't wish to engage. That suited her just fine. The last thing she needed was to get involved with a cowboy who had his name engraved on the back of his belt so he could remember who he was when he put his pants on in the morning. Did he have his name on his belt? She hadn't thought to check. She'd been too busy admiring his butt.

Okay, fine. She found him attractive. But that was purely aesthetical appreciation, not a serious desire to get to know him better. She knew his kind. No ambition to own a ranch of his own. Content to have only three pairs of Wrangler jeans, two pairs of boots, a few shirts, a horse, and a saddle. By his own admission, he had few bills. He probably drove a battered old pickup with only liability insurance on it. If he thought about his future, which she doubted, he probably pictured himself hiring on at another ranch after Slade Wilder retired. Or maybe he hoped that her uncle would start to think of him as the son he'd never had and leave the place to him. That would happen over Erin's dead body. Things at work would settle down. She'd find the time to go out to her uncle's place. Maybe work with him. If she hated the ranch, fine. But if she loved it, as her uncle had once hoped she might, she sure wasn't going to stand aside while Wyatt Fitzgerald stole her birthright.

Wyatt felt an immeasurable sense of relief mixed with anxiety when he was finally able to leave Deputy De Laney at the Strawberry Hill trailhead. Her horse had been waiting there, just as Wyatt had predicted, and he'd made fast work of getting the gelding loaded into the trailer. Then he'd made even faster work of getting out of there. Everything about the woman made him uneasy. Extremely so, and what bothered him most was that he couldn't figure out why. He only knew that Erin De Laney sent out mixed signals, and he'd found it nearly impossible to get a read on her. That rarely happened to him.

Being deaf had forced Wyatt to sharpen his other four senses and perfect them to a point that he had what others considered to be an uncanny ability to understand both people and animals. Some individuals who watched him interact with a terrified or difficult horse grew convinced that he was telepathic, because he appeared to communicate his thoughts to an equine without words or gestures. And, in truth, he did, but he possessed no superhuman power. It was a learned ability. Some kids developed incredible balance by walking on logs and later became champion gymnasts. Others became gifted musicians simply because they had a good ear and practiced hour after hour to perfect their talent. For Wyatt, honing what he thought of as a fifth sense to compensate for the one he'd lost in utero hadn't been a choice. He'd been forced to practice those skills every waking moment. If asked to explain how he had accomplished what he had, he'd be at a loss, and yet it was actually so simple it needed no explanation.

As a young child, he'd been expected to feed, water, and clean up after the horses, so he'd been within striking distance of them every day. Except for being adept at American Sign Language, he'd been unable to talk yet, so he'd found other ways to let horses know what he wanted them to do. He'd also learned to sense their presence, because they were large and sometimes unpredictable creatures, which put him in constant peril. His mother had heatedly objected to putting her deaf child in harm's way, but Wyatt's grandfather had overruled his daughter-in-law's wishes by insisting that Wyatt would learn to compensate for his handicap only if he was forced to do so. Looking back, Wyatt was glad of his grandfather's wisdom, because he had learned. It hadn't been easy, and he'd been scared more times than not, but he'd learned. By the age of ten, he'd developed the ability to feel something or someone staring at him and could sense the nearness of another being. He couldn't pinpoint how he had cultivated that ability. He only knew he had. It was an all-over feeling that made his skin tingle and his hair stand on end. A different scent would flood into his nostrils. A trill of alarm would electrify his nerve endings. In short, he didn't *hear* the world around him; he'd learned to *feel* it. And he had come to depend on that ability as surely as others counted on their ears.

Yet Erin De Laney, while beside herself with anger, had approached him from behind and gotten close enough to touch him without him sensing she was there. The realization had rattled him then and still upset him now. If a bear or a cougar had gotten that close, he'd be either dead or seriously injured. His fifth sense—or what he'd come to think of as his fifth sense—had come to him only with hard work and years of practice. He needed it. For him, it was crucial to survival. And now he was no longer certain he could trust in it.

What was it about Erin De Laney that was different from every other person and animal? Not even Kennedy, his beloved younger brother, could walk up behind Wyatt without setting off Wyatt's alarms. Yet that woman had. Weird thoughts had been circling in Wyatt's mind ever since. Was it some kind of sign that Erin was somebody special and would become an important individual in his life?

God help me. He didn't even like the woman. In all fairness, he'd disliked her before he ever met her, so maybe he hadn't given her a fair chance. But even when he tried to cut her some slack, he couldn't. Slade Wilder was a good man, and he deserved a niece who cared about him. Wyatt didn't expect Erin to fall in love with the ranch or even pretend she did. Every person had his or her own path to walk in life, and horses and cows might never fit into Erin's vision of her future. But this wasn't about only the ranch and who would run it one day. It was about a man who faced the winter of his life and had no family—unless one counted a sister who refused to come see him and a niece who couldn't be bothered. The least Erin could do was carve out one hour a week for her uncle. Maybe her story about working long hours was true. Maybe, as low man on the totem pole at the sheriff's department, she got all the emergency calls and rarely had time off. But she surely got some downtime, and when she did, a certain amount of it should be slotted for visits with Slade.

In Wyatt's opinion, she'd failed miserably to do that. And no matter how nice she might seem otherwise, he'd never be able to overlook it. Actions spoke louder than words. If she cared about her uncle, she didn't care enough, and that reflected badly on her. Slade had a heart of gold, which was apparent in his ranching practices. Wyatt had grown up around ranchers, and a substantial percentage of them grew callous toward animals over time. For some, it was undoubtedly a result of starting out with a tender heart that got in the way of their ability to do what had to be done. Sometimes a person had to take an emotional step back, and for some, that step distanced them so much from feeling compassion that they never regained the ability to care. Slade had never done that, and Wyatt deeply admired him for it. He supplied beef to the marketplace. The steers he raised from calves to adulthood were destined from the moment they were born to become a steak on someone's plate. Yet he still cared for them in a personal way, giving them a scratch behind the ears when he could spare the time and never allowing a hired hand to mistreat them. Any man on Slade's payroll who stepped over the line was terminated without notice. Slade wouldn't tolerate cruelty and told every new hire exactly where he stood on that issue.

How a man like Slade Wilder had never found a

woman who loved him was a mystery to Wyatt. The older man had spoken a few times of a gal he referred to as the love of his life, but he'd never gone into detail. Wyatt's impression was that Slade had been quite young at the time, and now so many years had passed that the girl had become little more than a fond memory. What had happened to ruin the relationship? Where was she now? Slade had been born on the Wilder Ranch. He would be an easy person to find, given that he'd always been based here. Maybe she was married and couldn't reach out to him.

Wyatt patted Shanghai on the shoulder and sighed. Now that Slade's niece was living in Mystic Creek, he had to hope that Erin's presence wouldn't cause her uncle further emotional pain.

Chapter Three

Holding the photograph by one corner between thumb and forefinger, Vickie Brown stared down at the baby picture of her firstborn son. A musty odor drifted up from the box of keepsakes she'd taken from her closet and now sat beside her on the bed, reminding her how old the snapshot was and how ancient that made *her*. She'd be sixty-three in December, and suddenly her life seemed to have rushed past her. When had she become someone who'd borrowed against her house to get her hands on money, then lost her job due to an economic downturn, and now had a mortgage payment she couldn't afford? An old lady who couldn't get hired on at any decent restaurant within a reasonable driving distance along the Oregon coast? An old lady who might be forced to work for minimum wage in order to survive, like an inexperienced line cook?

And what the hell was going on in her brain that had her thinking about Slade Wilder and wishing there was still a chance for them to be together again as a couple? Over forty-one years had passed since she'd last clapped eyes on the man. Brody, the result of their relationship, was going to celebrate his forty-second birthday next May. It was imbecilic of her to go waltzing down memory lane. Maybe she had early-onset dementia. Only was it even *early* at her age? The thought terrified Vickie. Her memory definitely wasn't as sharp as it had once been. How many times a day did she walk into a room to do something and then couldn't remember why she was even there? And looking frantically for her cell phone when she was talking to someone on it. She'd done that, too.

Only her yearning to remember those days with Slade still burned within her. Needing to go back in time, she dug deeper to find images taken in her late teens and early twenties, which she hadn't looked at in years. Her hand came up filled with slippery, four-by-six photos, some black-and-white, others in color, and as if guided upward by her aching heart, a likeness of Slade Wilder sat at the top. Her stomach knotted, and her throat went tight. He'd been so handsome. Tall, well muscled, and wearing that teasing grin that had always made her knees feel weak, he stood beneath a ponderosa pine. Sunshine filtered down through its boughs to surround him with a nimbus of light. Skin burnished by exposure to the elements. Shoulders and arms strengthened by hard work. He wore the red shirt she'd given him for his twentieth birthday. At his waist, a championship rodeo buckle flashed silver and gold. With a quivering finger, she traced his outline, and remembered how wonderful it had been to be held in his arms. She'd loved him so much.

She had fooled herself into believing her feelings for

him were gone, but the rush of excitement that she'd felt when she saw his Craigslist ad for a camp cook had brought it all back. She'd loved him practically all her life, and she guessed she always would. She could mentally berate herself for being an idiot, but her foolish heart wouldn't listen to reason. She lifted that picture from the pile on her palm, let the others slide off into the box, and retrieved the likeness of Brody to hold both images side by side. And there it was, an astounding resemblance that Slade couldn't have ignored. But, for whatever reason, he had refused to acknowledge that she'd borne him a son.

As always, anger surged through Vickie's veins with such force that every beat of her heart thrummed in her ears. And then the tears came, filling her eyes and blurring her vision so that the two photographs swam together. She felt her body begin to tremble. The salty wetness that spilled over her lashes and trickled down her cheeks burned her skin and made her nose itch.

She felt so tired. So awfully, horribly exhausted. She couldn't walk back into Slade's life without warning after all these years. She must have gone momentarily crazy to even toy with the idea.

"Mom? What are you doing? You don't have time to look at keepsakes! You're supposed to be packing your duffel bag and making a list of things we need to go buy."

Vickie jerked so violently that she almost tipped over the box. She tossed the picture back into the cardboard container and glanced up, hoping that the tears on her face weren't obvious. *No such luck.* Her daughter's green eyes, so very like Vickie's own, widened with dismay. After studying Vickie for a moment, Nancy pushed a hank of curly, brilliantly auburn hair from her cheek and took a slow step toward the bed.

"What's wrong? Why are you crying? I thought you were excited about the job."

Excited. If Vickie took that job as a camp cook, she would have to face her past, and nothing about that would be easy or pleasant. She wanted to explain that to her daughter, only when she considered the magnitude of the secret she'd kept for the last forty-one years, she could think of no excuses that would absolve her. She'd lied to her oldest child—to all three of her children—and life didn't come with an eraser. A person had to live with her mistakes, and oh, how she regretted this particular one.

Please don't look in that box, Vickie thought. She had no idea if the photo of Slade had landed with the face up or down, and if she dared to check, Nancy's attention would be drawn to it. "I'm, uh, reconsidering my decision to take the job in central Oregon," Vickie settled for saying. It had seemed like fate earlier that morning when she'd seen Slade Wilder named as the outfitter who needed a camp cook in the Mystic Creek, Oregon, area. She'd been unable to shake the feeling that it was divine intervention, with God orchestrating things so she would finally gather the courage to face the man who had almost destroyed her. "I think I'll be happier working for the fellow out of Ontario."

Nancy sat on the bed. "Mom, Ontario is so much farther away! Plus it has a population of only about twelve thousand, and that man guides hunts clear across the Oregon state line in *Idaho*."

Vickie battled her urge to grab the box flaps and fold them over. Nancy was too observant for anything like that to get past her. "Nevertheless, I've decided against the Mystic Creek job."

"I don't get it. Thirty minutes ago, you couldn't wait to get packed and hit the road. Now you've put on the brakes." Nancy pushed at her hair again. Shoulder-length strands of it had come loose from the ponytail and sprung out around her heart-shaped face like coppery Christmas ribbons that had been curled on the sharp edge of a scissor blade. She glanced into the box, stared blankly for a moment, and then smiled. "What a great picture of Brody! That's one I've never seen." She reached for the snapshot. Vickie clenched her hands into fists to stop herself from grabbing her daughter's wrist. "Hot damn, he was handsome back then." She grimaced. "God, I'm getting old. He probably looks at me and sees the mileage on me, too." She lifted the image and continued to admire it with a wistful expression. "So young and ready to take on the world. It's sad that things have turned out so badly for him."

Vickie wanted to slap the photo from her daughter's hand. Brody bore a marked resemblance to Slade, no question about it, but there were subtle differences, and Nancy would notice them if she continued to study it. The younger woman sighed and started to put the likeness back in the box, only her gaze snagged on something and her forehead creased in a frown.

"Wait a minute. This isn't Brody. This guy's wearing a prize buckle. Brody won a few himself, but not until he was older than this." She peered at the silver and gold design. "It's for roping, I think." Filled with bewilderment, her gaze shot to Vickie's. "Who is this man, Mom? He has to be a relative to look so much like Brody, but I don't remember ever seeing him."

Vickie thought quickly. "My uncle, Mama's brother. He, um . . . he was killed in Vietnam. No, I'm sorry. I'm getting my wars confused. It must have been World War Two—or maybe the Korean conflict."

"Oh, how sad!" Nancy stared at the image. "I didn't think people had cameras that took color pictures way back then."

"Color photography existed, but it was very expensive, so most people's cameras used black-and-white film. I had that snapshot tinted. A gift for Grandma." Vickie remembered lecturing her kids about the pitfalls of lying. Once you told one untruth, you found yourself lying again and again to back up your story. Boy, had she ever been right about that. "She thought the world of him."

Nancy's frown deepened. "If it's a special gift, why doesn't she still have it?"

Oh, how Vickie hated this. For one, she was a lousy liar, and for another, it filled her with guilt to be untruthful with her daughter. "Seeing it made her sad. She gave it back to me and asked me to keep it safe."

"Oh, how awful. She's never mentioned losing her brother to me. What was his name?"

Vickie had started to sweat. "She never talks about him. Hasn't in years. I can't really remember now. Ben? Glen, maybe. Something like that." She didn't dare say Slade, because they'd both been on the computer earlier, reading about Slade Wilder and his outfitting business. "I don't bring it up anymore. Remembering his death upsets her, and I worry about her heart." *Stop, Vickie. You're chattering. Saying more than necessary. Shut up while you're ahead.* "If she thinks of him, she no longer brings it up."

"I thought Grandma grew up in Portland and was such a greenhorn when Grandpa took her to his farm that she didn't know the difference between a bull, a cow, or a steer. But her brother was a champion roper?"

Vickie laughed, a forced, shrill twitter. "Yes, well. Her brother was older and left the city to find work. He ended up at a ranch. Got interested in rodeo competition. Then he joined the service when the war broke out."

"Sad," Nancy mused as she put the snapshot back. "So young, with his whole life ahead of him, and it was over just that fast." She sighed, and Vickie followed suit. "You have to show Brody that picture, though. When you're not around, he jokes that his father must have been a mailman. Once he sees that, he'll know where he got his looks. The resemblance is uncanny. For a minute, I actually thought it was my brother!"

Vickie couldn't wait to close the box and did so with

lightning speed. If other pictures of Slade were lying on the surface, faceup, the web of lies she'd just woven would be blown wide open. "Please don't mention to Grandma that you saw his picture. It might upset her, and she's fragile."

"Yet another reason you should take the job in central Oregon. In case of an emergency with Grandma or Grandpa, you can get home a lot faster."

Vickie wished Nancy would stop pressing her to take the Mystic Creek position. "You act as if Idaho is in a different country, Nancy."

"It may as well be. It's well over a five-hour drive from here just to Ontario near the Idaho border. If I left right now, I could be in Bend in only two hours and forty minutes. Ontario is twice that. And that Ontario man may meet his clients at a base camp that's another couple hundred miles over the Idaho state line. On your first job as a camp cook, I want you closer to us than that. Mystic Creek isn't that far south of Bend. If anything goes wrong, we kids can reach you quickly."

Vickie remembered when she'd come to Coos Bay, alone and with very little money. She didn't need her children to watch out for her now. "I'll be fine, sweetie." She wiped the wetness from her cheeks. "Maybe I won't even take a camp cook job. I could easily sell the house, get rid of all my debt, and start drawing on my social security. I'm old enough to do that now."

Nancy shifted, the jerkiness of her movements indicating her agitation. "Sell everything you've ever worked for? Where would you live? I mean, you'd be welcome to live with us, but you're so independent, you'd go nuts within a week. And your social security checks won't cover all your monthly expenses, Mom. You probably won't receive that much money."

"I could get a small apartment, maybe in a retirement community."

"With a money tree in the backyard, of course, because those rentals don't come cheap." Nancy pushed to her feet and turned to face Vickie. Dressed in jeans and a black checkered blouse with the tails tied at her slender waist, she didn't look like the professional she actually was. Hands spread wide, she cried, "I have a better idea. How about telling my nephew to forget going to Harvard and come home? Marcus should get his degree here in Oregon at a *regular* college like most kids do! The money you gave him can be returned to your bank account! You can pay off that stupid home equity loan, which you never should have gotten in the first place, and you won't *need* to take some crazy out-of-town job to stay afloat. A part-time position here at minimum wage would cover your monthly outlay until tourism picks back up along the coast and you can work again as a chef for better wages."

"Are we back to that *again*? Marcus going to Harvard, I mean." Vickie anchored the box flaps down with the palm of her hand, half-afraid Nancy might open them again. "I think you're just jealous because I helped Marcus. How many times must I tell you that I'd do the same for your kids and Randall's as well?"

"Our kids don't *need* your help. Randall and I both

started college funds for our children right after they were born. We both have spouses who are as successful in their careers as we are in our own. Brody, on the other hand, is borrowing from Peter to pay Paul right now, and with Marissa being so sick, I don't see that changing. His life is a screwed-up mess, and damn it, Mom, his son knows that. But did he let his father's money problems stand in his way? No."

"It's not Brody's fault that Marissa's got rheumatoid arthritis and can no longer work as a nurse, Nancy. And it's not Brody's fault Marissa's health issues have created a mountain of debt for him."

"It *is* his fault that Marcus is a spoiled brat who expects everything he wants to be served to him on a silver platter."

There. Nancy had finally spit it out. Vickie knew this had been eating at Nancy since the spring. Now they could at least discuss it. "Marcus worked hard to pull the grades he did! Nobody served those to him on a platter."

"My kids work hard to pull good grades, too!" Nancy's auburn brows arched. In Vickie's younger years, she had possessed eyebrows that color. Now she was getting silver in her hair, which made her look as faded as an old pair of blue jeans. "Randall's kids work hard as well," Nancy continued. "But they won't expect to be sent to Harvard or Yale or Princeton or Brown to get their degrees! They'll never even apply at those schools, because *they* understand the financial limitations. But Marcus *did* apply! And he turned down a partial scholarship at Oregon State. Kissed that money goodbye as if it were nothing! He knew you would cough up what he needed to chase his dream of being a big-time Harvard grad."

Vickie struggled to remain calm. "It was such an honor for him to be accepted at Harvard. And even though you claim that a degree from a college here in Oregon is just as good as one from Harvard, I disagree."

"I'm a teacher, Mom. I guess I know more about it than you do. A pigskin from an Ivy League school draws attention, and it's impressive for a moment. But in the end, people are hired on the merits of their accomplishments. Marcus can graduate summa cum laude at any college he chooses."

"Having the name of that university on his résumé will open doors for him. I'm sure of it. And he'll pay me back someday. He understood from the start that it was only a loan, not a gift."

"He has *years* of college ahead of him. Then he'll have to find a position and work his way up. By the time he can start paying you back, you may be six feet under!"

"Then the money can revert into my trust account and will be evenly divided between my heirs. You'll receive your share, and you can spend that portion on your kids. It'll all come even in the end. I'm sorry you feel that I've played favorites with my grandchildren. That wasn't the case. I love each of them equally. It's just that Brody—" Vickie broke off. She'd almost said too much. "This whole conversation is ridiculous. I've always been fair to my grandchildren. I don't have to prove that to them or *you*."

"It's just that Brody . . . what?" Nancy jutted her chin, which was a replica of Vickie's, right down to the deep cleft. "You almost said something more and stopped yourself. Do you know how many times you've done that over my lifetime? And it's *always* when you talk about Brody! There's something you're not telling me. You were all hot to take that job in central Oregon the instant you saw it on Craigslist. And now you've suddenly changed your mind and want to hare off for Ontario and possibly the wilds of Idaho. It makes no sense."

Oh, if only you knew, Vickie thought. But she had to keep her mouth shut. It was better to let sleeping dogs lie. She'd made choices years ago that she couldn't undo now. Not at this late date. The truth would only harm those she loved the most, and no matter how hard it was to carry the burden of her secrets alone, she had no choice.

"Who is Slade Wilder?" Nancy demanded. "When you saw his name—*that* was when you got all hot to trot over that cooking job. And he's located in Mystic Creek, where you grew up. You know him. Don't you?"

Vickie needed space. Her chest felt as if it might explode from swallowing back words she could never utter. She veered around her daughter to escape the suffocating confines of the bedroom. Once in the hallway, she heard Nancy following behind her. The floors of the old house creaked under their feet. At least she knew for certain that the box of pictures was now safe from her daughter's prying eyes.

"I'm thirty-nine years old, Mom. Not a baby you have to coddle. Why can't you be honest with me? Just once. Why can't you trust me the way I've always trusted you?"

"Because some things are better left buried!" Vickie turned at the archway and entered the farmhouse kitchen. *Tea*. She needed a soothing blend. Something to calm her down. She shouldn't have said that last bit. Nancy would sink her teeth into it and hold on like a pit bull with its jaws locked. "I'm not taking the job in central Oregon, end of conversation. I'd rather work out of Ontario."

"Those commercial cooking pots are huge and weigh a ton when they're filled with food. What if you hurt your back? It's different in an actual kitchen, less risk of injury than there is in a tent. You could trip and hurt yourself. Scald yourself with boiling liquid. Or, God forbid, have an issue with your heart! As far as I can tell online, the nearest state-of-the-art cardiac center for Ontario is in Boise! They'd have to medevac you there."

"My heart is fine."

"You're not a young woman anymore, Mom. You need to think about the things that might go wrong and at least *try* to be close to good medical care."

"I realize that Bend has great medical care, but I've decided against taking the job outside Mystic Creek. I grew up there, and I have bad memories of the place. I'm not going back."

"Because you don't want to see Slade Wilder."

Vickie foraged in a cupboard for a tea that soothed the nerves. When she found nothing, she grabbed a half-full whiskey bottle from another cupboard. She rarely drank alcohol, especially not during the day, but her stomach was tied in knots and her hands were shaking so badly that she felt as if she might fall apart and burst into tears.

"Who is he, Mom?" Nancy stepped closer. "You and I should be best friends. I've always felt as if I could tell you anything without worrying that you'd hold it against me. Won't you afford me the same favor? You've erected some kind of wall between us. We're close, and you share your concerns with me, but only up to a point. Slade Wilder is clearly someone notable from your past."

Vickie sloshed whiskey over the side of the glass. She set the bottle aside with a *thunk* and gripped the counter's edge, head bent above her braced arms.

"Trust me, Mom. Please? You were crying when I walked into the bedroom. I've hardly *ever* seen you cry. Who is this man? You seemed excited about the job with him, and now you're suddenly not. Are you afraid of him or something? Is he a violent jerk, like my father was?"

"No," Vickie finally replied with a release of breath that signaled defeat. "He's Brody's father."

The kitchen went so quiet that the hum of the

refrigerator suddenly seemed as loud as a diesel truck engine. Seconds ticked by, and with every beat of her heart, Vickie regretted the words that had just left her mouth. That was the deepest and darkest secret of her life, one that she'd only ever shared with her ex-husband, Matt, when he'd begged her to marry him. Not even her parents knew that Brody was Slade's child.

"Holy shit," Nancy said. Her voice trembled like an aspen leaf in a brisk wind. "Oh, dear God. The man in that picture." She laughed, but there was no humor in the sound. "He's not your uncle! Not Grandma's dead brother. You were lying your ass off! Weren't you?"

Vickie felt as if her legs had turned to water. "Yes, and I hope God forgives you if you blab it to Brody, because I won't." Dimly, Vickie realized what she'd just said. "I don't mean that. I'd forgive you if you murdered someone and help you bury the body. But, *please*, Nancy, don't break my confidence, not about this."

"So Brody doesn't know."

"No." The pressure in Vickie's chest had eased with the admission. Maybe she'd been wanting to blurt out the truth for over forty years. Even though she regretted finally saying it, her body felt relieved to be rid of the burden. "Matt—your father—didn't want Brody to know he wasn't his. He said it would make him feel like the odd child out when we began our own family. Since he said he loved me and would love Brody like his own, I honored his wishes. As bad as it may sound, Matt wasn't just my best bet; he was my only bet. And at that point in our relationship, I had very little bargaining power. I did what he wanted, because I felt trapped, had a baby coming, and didn't see how I had any choice. Maybe that was wrong. No, I *know* it was wrong not to tell Brody. But it's sure as hell too late to correct the mistake now."

She heard Nancy cross to the table and draw back a chair. "Don't be selfish with that whiskey. Now I need a drink, too."

Vickie got another glass, poured a measure in each one, and joined her daughter, taking a seat across the table from her. She slid Nancy's portion toward her.

"You can scream at me," Vickie said, her voice sounding hollow, as if she spoke from the bottom of a wine barrel. "You can hate me. I did the best I could as a mother. The best I knew how to do, at any rate. By the time I left Matt Brown, it seemed like the lie about Brody's origins was set in cement. He was only five, and I hadn't told him the truth in a matter-of-fact way and reminded him of it often. Hadn't read him stories about other little boys with fathers who didn't want to be dads. How do you spring something like that on a little boy?"

"I'm not going to scream at you, Mom, and I definitely don't hate you. You've been a fabulous mother, the best of the best. Naturally, I think you should have told Brody the truth about his father, but I can understand how hard it must have been to broach that subject and how a mother could put it off for so long that before she knew it, it seemed too late."

"The moment never seemed right," Vickie told her. "Not when he was five, not when he was ten, and definitely not when he was a teenager, yearning for things I couldn't afford to provide for him. If he'd found out then, he might have looked his father up. I didn't want him to go through any more pain than Matt had already subjected him to. Slade refused to acknowledge Brody's existence, you see. Any attempt on Brody's part to get in touch with his real father would have ended with rejection. Or I was afraid it would, anyway."

Nancy tipped back her glass and took a slug of whiskey that would have curled the toes of most women. The bottom of the tumbler clicked loudly on the table when she set it back down. A whistling noise came up her throat as she tried to catch her breath. "Matthew Brown treated Brody like a second-class citizen while you were working nights. No, it was way worse than that. He acted as if he detested him. Spanked him for things he didn't do. Yelled at him, called him names. And in the end, when he bruised Brody up so badly that he couldn't hide it from you any longer and you left him, that was the worst night of my whole life."

"I'm sorry," Vickie pushed out. "So sorry. I swear to you, Nancy, I had no idea what was happening."

"Stop saying you're sorry!" Nancy cried. "It was my *father's* doing, never yours. The instant you saw the marks on Brody, you left the bastard. I was so scared for you that night, Mom. All of us were. You grabbed us up and hustled us out to the car. Locked all the doors so he couldn't reach us. I was too little to realize our father was a drunk. I only knew he was mean and might pummel you with his fists like he'd done to Brody earlier."

Vickie's heart squeezed. "I didn't know he was being abusive until I got home that night. He always oversaw your baths, so I rarely saw Brody without clothes on. And because alcohol seemed to be the catalyst that sent your dad into a rage, I'd made him promise he wouldn't drink while I was working. If I smelled scotch on his breath when I walked in, he always swore that he'd just poured himself the first drink. He said he saw no harm in that since all of you were asleep and I was going to be there in only a few minutes." Tears burned in Vickie's eyes again. "We had nowhere to go. Grandma and Grandpa hadn't sold out in Mystic Creek and moved here yet. I had very little money on me. We slept in the car that night. Do you remember that?"

Nancy smiled slightly. "I wasn't quite three, but, yes, I remember. Not so much the good stuff, but most of the bad stuff. It's what imprints on a child's mind, I guess. What really stands out in my memory is seeing my tiny mother grab up a yard rake to stand toe-to-toe with a violently angry man twice her size. I remember Brody trying to climb over me to get out and help you. He was in the middle, with his arms around me and Randall because we'd been bawling. He kept saying, 'He's going to hit our mama.' But Randall grabbed the back of his pajama top and wouldn't let go. And by the time Brody got loose, you were getting in the car. Dad tried to jerk open the passenger door. But it was locked. He beat on the window with his fist."

Memories swirled through Vickie's mind. "I got the car started, shifted into reverse, and gunned the accelerator. I ran over his foot with a front tire."

Nancy's eyes widened. "Is that why he jumped down the driveway after us on one leg?"

Vickie giggled. Nancy snorted and cupped a hand over her nose. Voice muffled, she said, "Oh, dear Lord, that's *priceless*."

Vickie knew it wasn't really funny, but both of them couldn't seem to stop laughing. Between giggles, Vickie pushed out, "I hoped it broke every bone in his foot. But it didn't. I think it only fractured a couple of his toes."

Hand over her side, which apparently ached from laughing so hard, Nancy took a deep breath and released it. "Oh, Mom, the memories. You've always been such a spitfire. I'm surprised you didn't kill him with that rake. If Brad did such a thing to one of my kids, I'd be sorely tempted." She turned her glass and circled a fingertip around the rim. "You drove us to the beach. Tried to make it seem fun by telling us we were going to camp out."

"I had only a few bucks in my purse. I couldn't get a motel room."

"You told us not to get out of the car, and you went traipsing out through the sand. Brody thought you had to pee. But when you came back, you were carrying a big piece of driftwood."

Vickie closed her eyes, remembering how terrified she'd been. "I thought he might drive around town until he found us. I needed a weapon. Back then, people still collected driftwood for beach fires, so the pickings were scarce. It took me forever to find something I could swing like a bat."

Nancy giggled again, but it was only a ghostly echo of actual laughter. "Death by driftwood?"

"A stay in the hospital, at least."

"What I remember most about that night—at least at a gut-deep level—is how safe I felt as you backed out of that driveway. It was far less frightening to sleep in our car at the beach, even though it was dark and scary there, than it had been to sleep at home in our beds that night. I knew you wouldn't let him hurt Brody again. That you wouldn't let him hurt any of us." Her cheek dimpled in a lopsided smile, and her eyes shimmered with tears, making them look almost forest green. "As a mother, I've remembered that night many times. You've been my template, the person I've always tried to emulate. You truly were the best mom ever."

Vickie closed her eyes. "Thank you for telling me that. I should never have married your father. I never loved him. I was honest with him about that. He said he loved me enough for both of us and that I'd get over Slade in time. He promised to take care of me and the baby. Said Brody never needed to know his real father didn't want him. I was still young enough to believe in fairy tales, I guess. And I was desperate. It was a rough pregnancy. I got too sick to work. Couldn't pay my bills. Marrying Matthew Brown seemed like a better option than running home to my parents and facing the shame of being pregnant with Slade Wilder's unwanted child."

"Tell me about him. What makes you believe he wanted nothing to do with his son? No foul, no blame, Mom. Just tell me the truth."

"Slade didn't know I was pregnant when I left Mystic Creek. I didn't know it myself. But I notified him by letter when I realized I was carrying his child. That was before I even knew the sex of my baby. Back then, ultrasounds to determine the gender of the fetus were not commonly used everywhere. All I knew for sure was that I was knocked up and scared to death." She held her daughter's gaze for a prolonged moment. "Before I knew I was with child, I'd gotten a job cooking in a little greasy spoon, and I was skating by. So sick that I spent half the breakfast rush in the bathroom, puking. I had no clue what was wrong with me until the boss's wife finally asked if I might be pregnant. I don't know when home pregnancy tests came available, but if they were around then, I didn't know about them. I went straight to a doctor, and sure enough, I was PG. Within a week, my boss canned me. He needed a fry cook, and as good as I was at my job, I burned more stuff than I managed to serve because I was upchucking so much of the time. Just the *smell* of the food made me gag. It was awful. So there I suddenly was without a job. The morning sickness got better of an afternoon. I was looking for a night shift position somewhere when I met Matt. He was a rough-and-tumble logger. He never drank in front of me until after we got married."

"And you thought he was your knight in shining armor?"

"I couldn't even afford groceries, and I was behind on my rent. I knew I'd soon be out on the street. I was inches away from going back home to face the music when Matt proposed to me. He *wanted* to be my knight in shining armor, and I definitely needed rescuing." Vickie spread her hands. "I was naive. I look back and wonder how I could have thought Matt was everything he pretended to be. Within six months, I was heavy with child and married to a drunk with a horrible temper."

"Did he ever beat you up, Mom?"

"Once. It was shortly after Brody was born. He came home and found me writing a fourth letter to Slade, that time with a picture of Brody to send with it so Slade could see with his own eyes that he truly was his son. Matt thought I wanted to get back together with Slade. That wasn't the case at all. But I did feel obligated to make sure he knew he had a child. Not so much because I felt I owed it to Slade, but I definitely thought I owed it to Brody."

"How badly did he beat you up?"

"Bad enough that I could barely walk the next day, but I swore to him that I would leave if he ever struck me again and he took me at my word. He was never violent with me again. Until he went after Brody, that is. And then I left him, got him arrested for child abuse, and filed for divorce."

Nancy finished off her whiskey, grabbed both their glasses, and stepped over to the counter to get them each a refill. "We're having a spur-of-the-moment girls' day. Mother and daughter, getting drunk on their butts."

"Before I get drunk, V. L. Brown needs to email Slade Wilder and tell him she's changed her mind about taking that job. I'm supposed to be at the Strawberry Hill trailhead tomorrow afternoon to help get camp set up."

"Give it a few minutes and one more drink. Let's talk about it first."

Vickie couldn't see what else there was to talk about, but the small amount of liquor that she'd gotten down hadn't stopped her hands from shaking yet, and she'd never gotten tipsy with her daughter. Maybe it would be therapeutic. "Okay. Bring the bottle."

Nancy tucked the whiskey jug under her arm in order to carry both partially filled glasses. As she served Vickie and resumed her seat, she said, "I've never sipped straight whiskey. It's not bad."

"You're a Granger. Most of us like our whiskey straight." Vickie felt such a sense of relief to have that huge secret off her chest. She'd carried it around for so long that it felt liberating to have at least told her daughter. "It's funny with kids. Brody took after Slade. He's a Wilder to the marrow of his bones, that boy. Then Randall came along, and he took after the Browns. They're good people, and I got Randall away from Matt before any of his bad traits could rub off on him. You popped out with my auburn hair. You grew to look more like me with every passing day. Now when I look at you, it's like seeing a younger version of myself in a mirror. You're slightly built, just like me, all red hair, big green eyes, and stubborn chin."

"You loved Slade Wilder," Nancy said softly. "I see it in your eyes every time you say his name."

"Oh, yes, I loved him. In that deep, trusting, and all-encompassing way that only young girls and foolish women can love. He meant everything to me."

"So tell me about him."

Vickie drew up her shoulders and then relaxed. "We rode the same school bus, and I met him the day I entered first grade. In Mystic Creek, mothers didn't go with children on the first day of school. Everybody knew everybody, or almost." The memories made her smile. "My hair was wildly curly, just like yours, so Mama braided it into pigtails, and of course Slade, being a second-grade boy, couldn't resist tugging on them, never hard enough to hurt, just enough to irritate me. But somehow I knew he was flirting with me, even though I had no idea what flirting was at that age. Inborn feminine wisdom, I guess. He liked me, and I thought he was the cutest boy in school."

"Apparently you still thought so years later."

"Oh, yeah. The older he got, the better-looking he got. But you asked to hear the story."

"Yes. Do tell."

"On picture day in the first grade, I had to wear a dress. Mama went all out making it. Lots of frills and lace. The only time I ever had to wear dresses—we lived on a farm, remember—was to church on Sunday. I hated going to school in that stupid dress that day. The lace on my collar and sleeves made me itch. When I tried to run on the playground, the skirt snaked around my legs. I was a tomboy, probably because Daddy had no other kids and let me ride shotgun with him all over the farm. Anyway, I got on the swings with my little girlfriends. It never occurred to me that my dress might flutter up in a rush of wind. A boy named Sammy Suitor saw my panties and yelled what color they were to all the other boys. The next thing I knew, Slade was on him, arms whirling like windmill blades in a high wind. Before a teacher could get there, Sammy was crying and Slade was making him eat dirt. From that day on, he became my protector and my friend."

"Aw."

Vickie savored a sip of the liquor. "I'm not sure when our feelings for each other started to run deeper. Definitely by the time I was in junior high, but Slade didn't take things to a romantic level with me even then. I think he was waiting for me to grow up. I was a sophomore the first time he really kissed me. When I say *really*, I mean more than a peck." Vickie sighed. "I swear, I heard bells ringing and fireworks going off."

"Uh-oh. And you managed to avoid pregnancy until you were, what, twenty-one? That's a miracle."

Vickie shook her head. "We didn't go all the way. Back then, and in a small town like Mystic Creek, nice girls didn't put out. Slade respected my parents. He knew my father trusted him. He always drew back before either of us reached a point of no return. Until he asked me to marry him, that is. The moment I said yes and he put that diamond on my finger, all his restraint went out the window. He never got off his knees. He got the ring on my finger and then pulled me down beside him. I lost my virginity under a pine tree."

"Was it the first time for him, too?"

Vickie shook her head. "He didn't ask me to go steady until I was a junior. He was a senior. He'd had girlfriends along the way, and though I never asked, I know he'd been with others that way before he made love to me." She shrugged. "He wasn't clumsy or uncertain. I'll put it that way."

"My first time was horrible. Steve Sharp. Remember him?" Nancy grinned and rolled her eyes. "Talk about clumsy and awkward. I thought I'd die from the pain and never be the same. And that night after I got home—well, you'll never know how close you came to rushing me to the ER. I was bleeding and thought I had internal injuries."

Vickie cringed. "You were only fourteen when you liked Steve! I had no idea!"

Nancy took another sip of whiskey. "I stayed away from boys for a while after that. And then I met Brad.

I was so terrified to have sex again that I wouldn't even kiss him on our first few dates. When Brad finally convinced me to trust him, he made sure I was ready and it didn't hurt."

"Well, I'm glad he was careful with you," Vickie said. "When I kill him for touching my daughter that way, I'll make it quick and merciful to show my appreciation."

Nancy didn't laugh. She didn't even smile. "I got a happy ending with my first love. I wish you'd been as lucky."

Vickie shrugged again. "They say women never forget their first love. Slade was my *only* love. I tried to love your father. I truly did, even though he didn't make that easy. But what began as fondness for him and a fervent hope that we'd be happy together deteriorated day by day, until all I felt for him was disgust." Passing a hand over her eyes, Vickie shook her head. "I can't believe I just said that. I've tried so hard never to talk badly about your dad. Now I'm bad-mouthing him like no tomorrow."

"*Mom*, let it go. There's nothing *bad* you can say about that man that we don't already think ourselves. Besides, the man is dead and gone. He alone is responsible for the legacy of dislike that he left his children. He never once called on our birthdays or sent us a token gift. Christmas after Christmas went by without a word from him. Never tried to see us. Didn't care whether you were managing to keep the wolves away from our door. Never showed up when the boys had games or competitions or for my dance recitals. We meant nothing to him. You can't make a derogatory statement about our father that he didn't make himself with his actions." Nancy grabbed the bottle and sloshed more booze into their glasses. "And enough about him. Judging by what you've told me about Slade Wilder, I think he thought you were pretty special, too. What happened to break you up? It's such a romantic story. It reminds me of that George Strait song, 'Check Yes or No.' Two little kids, falling in love. Granted, an immature love back then, but it lasted, and eventually it became the real deal. Real enough for him to ask you to marry him. How did everything go south?"

"He was unfaithful." Vickie's heart ached again, just from saying it aloud. "It was a week before our wedding. Only a week! Mama had made my gown. She'd worked for weeks on the table decorations. Daddy had been fitted for a suit. You know all the folderol that takes place right before a wedding. Parties, too. Slade competed in a lot of rodeos and had cowboy friends. They decided to throw him a bachelor party. I didn't go. I didn't think girls went to bachelor parties. Slade got drunk. At least that's what I've always surmised. He had sex with a girl named April Pierce."

"How did you find out?"

"She couldn't wait to tell me. She'd had a crush on him forever. She figured I'd break up with him when I found out. She was right. I may have been young and naive, but I wasn't stupid enough to marry a man who couldn't keep his Wranglers zipped when he was around other women."

"Did you confront him?"

"Of course I confronted him. And of course he denied it. He said he danced with her one time, nothing more."

"Maybe nothing more happened. If that April gal had the hots for him, she might have lied."

Vickie shook her head. "Nope. He has a birthmark on one buttock, a birthmark she couldn't have known existed unless his britches were down around his knees. When she described the mark, down to a T, I knew she had to be telling the truth. He'd been with her that night. Even worse, he'd come directly from that party to me. We made love. Can you imagine how degraded and humiliated I felt when I found out I was his second lay of the evening?"

"What did he say in his own defense?"

"That he never touched her that way. He got huffy with me, said I was questioning his word, calling him a liar." Vickie made finger quotation marks. "He said 'my word is my honor' and expected me to just believe him."

"What did he say when you told him she described his birthmark?"

"I never brought that up. I was devastated. Sobbing. I could barely talk, and he was clearly guilty. She'd seen his bare ass, after all." Vickie tipped her glass, staring into the amber liquid that angled sharply inside the tumbler. "I might have forgiven him. If only he'd confessed. Said he was drunk. That it would never happen again. But he never said any of that. He stuck to his story that he'd only danced with her, and when I kept asking him to please tell me the truth, he just got madder and madder." Vickie met her daughter's gaze. "How can you forgive someone if they refuse to ask for forgiveness?"

"Oh, Mom." Nancy looked as if she were about to cry. "I'm so sorry he hurt you so deeply."

"He didn't just hurt me. I felt as if he'd gutted me and ripped my heart out. I ended it between us that night. He accepted it. His expression was—well, *stony* is the only way to describe it. *Unrelenting* as well. Like *he* was the injured party. He just let me walk away! No following me. No trying to talk me out of it. He just stood there and watched me go. If he truly loved me, I mean *really* loved me, wouldn't he have fought harder than that to convince me he was innocent? Or changed his story and begged me to give him another chance?"

Nancy took her turn staring into the liquor. "And then when you notified him twice of Brody's existence, he just didn't respond? At that point, I would have been calling him a dozen times a day."

"Actually, I notified him by letter four times, but I couldn't call him. People didn't have cell phones back then. Long-distance calls were charged by the minute. People without much money said their piece as fast as they could to get off the line. One second over a minute, and you got charged for two, and so forth. I didn't have as much as a nickel to call him from a phone booth. Calling collect would have meant asking one of his parents to accept the charges. I was afraid they'd say no. Just buying stamps was difficult for me to afford. After I was with Matt, things got better, but not by much. He handled the money and, unbeknownst to me then, spent a goodly share of his paychecks on alcohol. He drove me to the store and let me buy groceries. And we could pay the rent and utilities. We didn't get a phone at our house for well over a year."

"So Slade had every opportunity to acknowledge his son. You're certain of that."

"Well, yes, pretty darned certain. How could four letters to him get lost in the mail?"

"Good point. Once, maybe, but not four times." Nancy fussed with her hair, trying to gather it back into a ponytail. "I'm sorry, Mom, but even if that April gal lied about him screwing her, his failure to acknowledge the existence of his own son doesn't speak highly of his character."

"Nope." Vickie finished off her whiskey. "I think I'm getting drunk."

"Do you care?"

"Not really."

"Me, either. It's not every day I have such a revealing heart-to-heart with my mother. I'll drink all I want and call Brad to take me home. I've held his head enough times while he worshiped the porcelain god. It's his turn."

Vickie smiled. "You've got a good man in Brad.

I'm so thankful for that. Maybe I raised you to be a better judge of character than I am. A two-time loser, that's me."

Nancy spent a moment making invisible doodles on the table with her fingertip. "So, just so I understand all of this clearly, why did you jump on the idea of taking a job with Slade this morning?"

Vickie wasn't sure she could explain what she didn't completely understand herself. "I wanted to do it for Brody."

"How would your seeing Slade again make any difference for Brody? Is he rich or something?"

Vickie shook her head. "Not rich, exactly. But he's got to be well-heeled. The ranch alone has to be worth several million now. It's a big spread, all of it prime ranchland. But it doesn't boil down to just money, Nancy. From the time Brody was little, he loved horses. For his second birthday, I got him one of those little broom-handle ponies, and he rode that silly thing everywhere. He was still galloping around the house on it when he turned five. All he ever wanted was to have his own horse and be involved in western-style equestrian sports. I couldn't afford that. Brody was born to be a horseman. I think it's in his blood. But there was no way I could help him pursue that dream. I saved back as much as I could for each of you to attend college. Brody took his tuition money and put a down payment on that dilapidated farm he has now. Bought a horse. To this day, it's all about the land and the horses. He's so much like his father that it's sometimes difficult for me to believe that he's never even met Slade Randall Wilder."

Nancy's gaze sharpened. "Slade *Randall*? Good grief, Mother. Please don't tell me you named my younger brother after your first love."

"Guilty." Vickie stared past her daughter through the window that looked out on the side yard. "I was obsessed with Slade. I admit it. I couldn't name Brody after him. Matt would have gone ballistic. But he didn't know Slade's middle name. I sort of sneaked it in on him. I was older than you are before I ever stopped hoping for a happy ending with Slade. I kept thinking that he'd sow his wild oats. Have all the women he wanted. Drink, party, and get it out of his system. You know? And then he'd realize that the only woman he'd ever really loved was me. It never happened. He never showed up on my doorstep. Never looked me up on Facebook. I know he didn't, because my page is listed under Vickie Granger Brown. Lots of women use their maiden names so old friends can find them, but I did it so one particular person could find me. He never even tried."

"So this morning, when you saw the job listing, you couldn't help but hope that by taking the position, you might be able to open the door for Brody to meet his father."

"Yes. And for nearly an hour, I deluded myself into thinking that Slade might leap at a second chance to have a relationship with his son. Stupid, I know. But there it is. I'm a romantic at heart."

"I don't think it's stupid, exactly. But it is hoping for a lot."

Vickie puffed air into her cheeks and emptied what remained of the whiskey into their glasses. "Of all you kids, I feel like I failed Brody the most."

"You didn't fail any of us, Mom."

"I did fail Brody. I listened to Matt. Chose to keep the identity of Brody's real father a big secret. It was the worst decision I could have made. Even back then, the state went after fathers for child support. I could have forced Slade to step up to the plate. If I had, I could have done more for Brody."

"Slade's support check would have gone to make it better for all of us, not only Brody. It wouldn't have stretched far enough to cover frivolous extras like a horse."

"You're right, I suppose," Vickie replied. "It's just—well, this sounds mercenary, but Brody should have been a rich kid like Slade was. Not *rich* rich, like we read about in magazines. His folks didn't own a yacht or a jet or have servants. But Slade's financial situation was a huge step up from ordinary kids in Mystic Creek. Brody would have had so many more opportunities if Slade had acknowledged him, and it would have been better for you and Randall, too. I could have spent the lion's share of my income on the two of you."

The green of Nancy's eyes darkened again, making Vickie wonder if her own irises changed shades with her shifting emotions. "Oh, Mom. I think I just got a glimmer of why you felt compelled to help Marcus attend Harvard. You feel guilty for breaking up with Slade, because that deprived Brody of his birthrights, and you saw a chance to make sure that Brody's son got at least one chance at something better."

Vickie nodded. "I loved Slade. Despite his infidelity, he was a good person. When I broke up with him, I did it out of hurt and a sense of betrayal, thinking I couldn't be with a man who was unfaithful to me. And look how that turned out. I ended up with another man who was even worse and had two kids with him that he refused to even help support. Looking back on it, I can't help but think how it would have played out if I had married Slade instead. All three of you kids would have been his. All of you would have had a better childhood and far more opportunities. Marcus was my chance to help at least one grandchild move up in the world."

"Loving a man who can't be faithful would be an endless heartbreak for a woman like you. Your choice to end the engagement wasn't a frivolous decision." Nancy pursed her lips. "And money and opportunity don't give other kids a better childhood than we had. Once you got rid of my father, our home was a happy place. None of us went without anything important. That said, I can finally understand what drove you to get a home equity loan on this house. And what drove you to help Marcus realize his dream of attending an Ivy League school. You could never offer Brody what you felt he had coming to him, so you couldn't resist trying to do it for his son."

Vickie felt tears welling in her eyes again. "Thank you for trying to understand. I know how it looks on the surface—that I'm partial to Marcus. But that isn't the case at all. It's just that seeing Brody in the fix he's in now, watching him struggle to make ends meet and take care of his wife, I'm reminded on a daily basis that a decision I made years ago put him in this situation. If I had stayed with Slade, Brody would have grown up on the Wilder Ranch. He would be able to afford Marissa's medication and all the physical therapy. His kids wouldn't be approaching college age with no money available for their educations."

"I get it, Mom. Finally." Nancy let her eyes fall closed for a moment. "I said some rotten stuff in the bedroom. But I didn't know all this yet. And I did feel jealous. Not for myself, but for your other grandkids. I couldn't understand why you'd go so far for Brody's son with no thought for mine or Randall's."

"When Marcus pays me back, I'll help my other grandkids. Maybe not quite as much, but I'll be there with my checkbook open."

"It's unnecessary to be even-steven with your grand-children." She lifted her hands, palms turned upward. "I didn't understand and felt that you were doing more for Marcus than you should."

"Even what I did doesn't really balance the scale," Vickie observed. "I will never regret marrying Matthew Brown. As bad as the marriage was, I got you and Randall out of the deal, and I'd never wish to change that. But sometimes in the dark of night when I try to fall asleep, I do wish that I'd married Slade and had my family with him. Money and opportunity aside, Slade would have been a much better dad." She studied Nancy's face. "He would have loved you like no tomorrow and tugged on your ponytail every chance he got."

Nancy caught a drip of condensation on her glass with her thumb. "I'm over my jealous snit. I hope Marcus excels at Harvard, and maybe, if you go to Mystic Creek to take that job, I'll get to meet Slade Wilder someday."

"If I go, it'll be the equivalent of taking a baseball bat to a hornet's nest. It'll all come out. Brody will hate me for never telling him the truth. Slade will hate me for screwing up his life by forcing our adult son down his throat. When I think of Slade, he hasn't aged in my mind, but the truth is that he's almost sixty-four. He's too old for the drama of dealing with an angry, bitter, illegitimate son. I wanted to bust it all wide open when I first saw his ad, but then I realized I might only succeed in hurting all the people I love most. And for what? Slade may refuse to acknowledge Brody even now."

"There are paternity tests now. He can deny it all he likes—if he's so blind that he can ignore how much Brody looks like him—but he can't deny a DNA match. You've got him by the balls, Mom. All you have to do is squeeze."

Vickie laughed. It wasn't funny, but she couldn't help herself. "But will Brody even *want* to know his father? He's a proud man, my Brody. He'd never refuse to acknowledge one of his children. He'll hold that against Slade. In the end, I could blow our lives to smithereens and no good may come of it."

"You'll never know until you face Slade," Nancy replied. "You have to tell Brody now, regardless. And trust me, he'll hunt down his real father, if only to tell him he's a rotten, low-down, deadbeat jerk! So everything will be blown to smithereens anyway." A grin tipped Nancy's lips into a mischievous smirk. "You may as well see him again yourself. If nothing else, Mom, you can put it all to rest in your own mind and turn loose of the past."

Chapter Four

Using the key-fob remote, Erin locked the county vehicle as she angled across the Flagg's Market parking lot. She appreciated the toot-toot of the horn, which assured her that everything was secured. That feature had malfunctioned on the old pickup she'd been assigned, and she'd wasted a lot of time walking around to check all the doors every time she parked. Getting a new rig had been the highlight of the past week for her.

She tried to take normal strides as she reached the sidewalk, but every muscle in her butt and legs protested. *Saddle sore.* Erin had never imagined it hurting this much. In addition to the tenderness in all her body parts that had touched the saddle, she was sore in places that hadn't touched it, such as her calves. And because she didn't want people laughing behind her back any more than they already were, she refused to ask anyone how long it took for the soreness to go away. Days, possibly? Normally Erin worked out muscle soreness by forcing herself to do the exercises that had caused it, but just the thought of getting back on a horse made her want to groan.

She hurried as fast as she could up the walkway, hoping she would encounter no one. The bruises on the left side her face, which were now red, deep purple, and charcoal gray, seemed to flash like neon lights at people and prompt them to ask questions. Rather than tell the true story, which would mean mentioning Wyatt Fitzgerald's involvement, Erin had been saying that she'd had a riding accident. That wasn't *really* a lie. She'd ridden a horse up Strawberry Hill, met an incredibly attractive cowboy, and, bang, now she had a shiner that not even her new, oversize sunglasses could hide.

The display windows of the Morning Grind offered a welcoming glow inside the cavernous, round building. Purchased by the city council, the massive structure had been remodeled and named the Mystic Creek Menagerie. Various shops and a restaurant called Dizzy's lined the perimeter of the circular common area, which housed at its center a gigantic, revolving dining area for the restaurant's patrons. So far, Erin had never eaten at Dizzy's, so she didn't know if people who sat on the turning platform actually felt woozy after they finished a meal. But the name was catchy, and those seeking gourmet fare either came here to eat or went to Peck's Red Rooster, which had a booming business of its own. The revolving dining area made Erin think of the SkyCity Restaurant at the Space Needle, where she'd dined with her parents countless times to celebrate special occasions.

Her attention snagged by a colorful spray of autumn

leaves in the window, which was dotted with artfully arranged gourds, Erin reminded herself to at least take a stab at fixing up her cottage for Halloween. Maybe she could steal some ideas from Julie, the shop owner who had a knack for decorating that Erin envied. Pushing open the glass door, embellished with the shop's name in gold lettering, Erin called, "Good morning! Look what the cat dragged in!"

"Like all bad pennies, you just keep turning up!" Julie tossed back, laughter lacing her tone. "And you're standing up straight. What an improvement over the shape you were in yesterday."

Erin had been so sore the day before that she'd barely been able to walk, let alone straighten her spine. "I used some of that liniment you gave me, which you forgot to mention burns and won't wash off your skin. It absorbed into my pores, and I think it permanently destroyed all my hair follicles. I may never have to shave my legs again."

"If that's the case, I'll give myself the equivalent of a Brazilian wax job with the liniment and be done with that torture, once and for all."

Erin winced at the thought. "Don't do that. It'll set you afire, and I'm not yet positive that all my hair follicles are dead."

"Now you tell me. I was imagining the millions I could make selling hair-killing liniment to women. Imagine never needing a wax job again!"

Erin shared the sentiment. "I can't believe there are women out there who put themselves through that just to turn guys on. What's up with that? Do men really find bald va-jay-jays *attractive*?"

Julie giggled. "You call yours a *va-jay-jay*? New one on me. Mine's a *hoo-hoo*."

"I worked with a deputy up north who called hers *the princess*. When the guys got wind of that, she never heard the end of it."

Julie's hazel eyes danced with laughter. "Are you the one who leaked the information?"

"Heck, no." Glancing at Julie's hair, she added, "Look how long I've refrained from telling anyone the story behind your blue streak."

The swath of bleached and tinted strands in Julie's dark hair shone like a laser beam in the overhead fluorescent lighting. "And that story better remain untold," she warned. "Unless, of course, you want everyone in town to know exactly how your face got messed up."

Erin smiled. "I guess our best bet is to remain friends so our secrets stay safe."

"Yep." Manipulating a large metal tray to balance precariously on the counter edge, Julie bent to add more bakery items to the display, both glazed and powdered doughnuts, maple bars with filling, and apple fritters, her only four offerings for breakfast. For lunch she featured a soup of the day and oven-fresh croissants. "I'm stuck with you, I guess. You know too much."

Erin had never had a friend she trusted as much as she did Julie, and she felt fairly sure Julie felt the same way about her. They had become fast friends a little over a year ago—almost as if they'd recognized a kindred soul. There had been none of the cautious circling that normally took place between two strangers, and neither of them had felt hesitant about sharing confidences. They'd both just understood without discussion that nothing either of them said would ever be repeated.

Pushing back the brim of her Stetson to peruse the wall menu behind the register, Erin rocked on her boot heels.

"You do this every blessed morning," Julie commented with a chuckle. "Look and drool, look and drool. But in the end you always order a latte, double shot, skim. Don't you ever want to rebel with half-and-half and real syrup instead of that artificially sweetened crap? And the world won't end if you splurge on a maple bar once in a while."

"A law enforcement officer has to stay in shape."

"Tell that to Deputy Bentley. I bet Hank's put on twenty pounds over the summer with all those iced lattes and glazed doughnuts for breakfast."

"And he'll lose all twenty by cutting back the sugar in his coffee at home. It takes me ten minutes to gain ten pounds and a month to lose them."

"If you gained ten pounds, nobody would notice. At your last counseling session, I thought Jonas suggested that you back off the dieting. I don't see you doing it."

Erin leaned her elbows on the checkout counter and jutted out one hip. "Just make me my regular and get off my case."

Julie turned toward the stainless-steel lineup of machines to make Erin's coffee. "You're too controlled, Erin. You stifle every frivolous urge you get. How will you ever learn to relax and turn loose if you don't practice?" She glanced over her shoulder. "That's a masculine stance, by the way."

Erin straightened her hip. "I shouldn't have told you about that. Now you'll be watching every little thing I do."

"Luckily for you I'm willing to help you change. When you meet a man, you probably turn an introductory handshake into a power grip that makes a man worry that you can beat him at arm wrestling."

Erin released a sigh. "If their egos are so fragile they can't handle being beaten at arm wrestling by a woman, they have a problem."

"The male ego is fragile. Men are all about image. Take Derek, for instance. He must have known he was gay when he married me. I was his cover-up so his family would never find out if he was happily married with two-point-five kids and a minivan. He didn't think about what the deception would do to me. He wanted to have his boyfriends, but he couldn't face letting the truth come out. He thought it would have destroyed his image."

Erin knew that Julie's whole world had come to an end when she'd caught her husband sleeping with another man. In many ways, it had been worse for her than if he'd been unfaithful with another woman. A wife couldn't compete with a man. She just had to accept and move on. The blue streak in Julie's hair was symbolic, an outward sign of her broken heart. When she finally got over her husband's betrayal, she said the blue streak would become sunshine yellow, because she'd be happy again.

Coming to the counter with Erin's coffee, Julie said, "Subject change. My nightmare marriage is a depressing topic."

"For me, my obsession with being the son my father wants is just as depressing. And, just so you know, allowing myself to show vulnerability is really hard. You forget that I've had a lifetime of practice at putting up walls."

"I'll pick just one habit a week, and you can work on breaking it," Julie suggested. "Picture each mannerism as an iron shackle, placed upon a part of your body by your father." Julie pressed the insides of her wrists together as if she wore handcuffs and then, pretending to use all her strength, broke free from the invisible clasps. "Have an imaginary conversation with your dad. 'Bye-bye, Father Dearest! I'm a girl. Get used to it, Daddy-O.' "

"You make it sound so easy."

"I have every confidence that you *can* and *will* do this."

With a laugh, Erin said, "Yes, ma'am. Shackles. I got it. Now would you earn your profit by running my credit card?"

Julie took the piece of plastic and slid it through the

scanner. She wore blue jeans and a red plaid flannel shirt, the tails tied at her slender waist to show off an expanse of her flat belly. It was an ultracasual look, but Julie was one of those women who could make a fashion statement wearing a burlap sack. Erin had already promised that she would let Julie dress her when she finally went out on a date. Julie was afraid Erin would pair a sexy dress with commando boots.

As Erin added a touch more artificial sweetener to her latte and stirred industriously with an ineffective red stick, Julie rested her folded arms on the counter again. "Can I give you a well-intended critique of your camouflage glasses?"

Erin angled her a look through the large tinted lenses. "Let me guess. They don't flatter the shape of my face."

"Worse. They make you look like a bug-eyed grasshopper wearing a hat. You'd be better off wearing the aviator-style ones. At least the lenses on those don't cover half your face."

"I aimed for covering half my face when I bought these damned things."

"You cussed." Julie reached under the counter and plopped a pint-size Mason jar on the counter. "Put a five-spot into our vacation fund, girlfriend. That takes us over our first goal. We've got fifty bucks."

"Mostly out of *my* wallet," Erin grumbled as she withdrew a bill from the slender fold of leather that she carried in her hip pocket. She and Julie were saving for a cruise with a company that owned one of the more popular online dating sites and whose advertising slogan promised, *"No one leaves the ship alone."* Erin doubted that the onboard matchmaking was quite that successful, but it would be fun to hang out with Julie for a week. Sunning on deck lounges sounded good, umbrella drinks even better. "You hardly ever slip up and pay the fine."

"I wasn't taught to cuss by my father and a bunch of lawmen. You watched any reality cop shows lately? I swear, practically all the dialogue is bleeped out. Those boys have filthy mouths on them."

"Those boys get shot at," Erin retorted. "Show me a cop who says 'shucks' when bullets are flying, and I'll show you a cop who needs a nice, long psych leave to get his head back on straight."

"Yes, but a certain friend of mine who's hoping to find her soul mate will never be successful if she continues to meet strange men and asks them, 'How's it hangin'?' "

Erin laughed in spite of the ache that radiated over her cheek when she curved her lips. "I'm not *that* bad."

"Almost!" Julie pushed back her hair where it had dipped forward over her eyes. She sighed and met Erin's gaze. "We make quite a pair, both of us messed up by men, but in totally different ways. There's a light at the end of the tunnel, though. If we keep pushing forward, we'll start to see it soon."

Erin nodded. "And sooner rather than later would

suit me just fine. In twelve days, five hours, sixteen minutes, and thirty-seven seconds, it will be three very long years since I've been on a date. Trust me, honey, that's a long dry spell."

"Why do I get the feeling that you had sex on that last date?"

"Because I did, and it wasn't like you're thinking. I was with Todd, my almost fiancé."

"*What?* I thought you dated a lot after the two of you broke up."

"I did date," Erin confirmed. "A lot! That doesn't mean I slept with any of the men. Online dating sucks. I always met new guys for coffee at this café I knew that was always fairly busy. Meet 'em in a public place, never give them your phone number or address, and then run like hell."

"Not all of them could have been weird."

"You'd think not, but most of them were." Erin took a test sip of her latte. "I got kind of excited over one. He was so handsome, and he was a great conversationalist. Nice suit. Italian, I think. He was the one who asked me to sign an exclusivity contract. Can you imagine that, after chatting over only one cup of coffee? I was to date only him from that moment forward."

"Possessive. Possibly obsessive about it. No matter how handsome a man is, that spells trouble."

Erin was about to agree when the portable radio on her belt suddenly chattered. "Oh, duty calls."

Julie rolled her eyes when she saw the caller ID. "It's

the sheriff's department, and another latte bites the dust. Seriously, girlfriend, you need some time off."

Erin capped her drink, considered taking it with her, and then discarded the idea. If she spilled coffee in the brand-new patrol truck, she'd never hear the end of it. "See ya," she told her friend. "Tomorrow, same time, same station."

Waving goodbye over her shoulder, she stepped outside the shop, circled the revolving dining area, and made her way out onto the sidewalk. With a glance to her left, she took in East Main, a street lined on both sides by connected, two-story buildings, with architecture reminiscent of the late nineteenth century. Steep, pitched roofs. Gingerbread trim. Cheerful window boxes, which still sported cascading bunches of Wave petunias that hadn't yet succumbed to the approach of winter and the cold nights that accompanied it. To Erin, accustomed to the sprawl of the Greater Seattle area, it was a town straight out of a storybook, and she couldn't imagine that she'd ever regret moving here. At least it was cute and nostalgic in Mystic Creek, and she could feast her eyes on something besides graffiti.

Keying the mike on the radio, she said, "Adam eleven, code seven. Break."

An all-too-familiar feminine voice came over the air. "Don't start with me, Erin. My day isn't going well."

Erin grimaced. Noreen Garrison was her least favorite dispatcher. "What happened? I thought you had the day off. Break."

"I did have the day off until Patty Molt got sick and

couldn't finish her shift. I'm next up the totem pole from her, seniority-wise, so I'm the lucky person who got called in."

Erin preferred to communicate with Patty, who had at least memorized the police codes and maintained a professional manner while on the air. Noreen knew none of the codes and chewed bubble gum at work. Erin kept expecting Sheriff Adams to fire the woman, but so far, he hadn't, and she was starting to doubt he ever would. Maybe Noreen was related to him somehow. It was difficult to let a family member go without causing hard feelings, and the situation might be even stickier for the sheriff if Noreen was related to his wife.

"Sorry about your day off getting ruined." Erin fleetingly wondered how many townspeople had police scanners and were listening to them talk. "So . . . you called. What's up? Break."

"We've got a runaway horse out at the fairgrounds. Big blowup on a trailer ramp when its owner tried to load it. Owner got hurt. No report on the extent of his injuries. I only know things went from bad to worse when the Turek boys tried to catch the horse."

Erin had heard of the Turek boys, but she had never dealt with them. They were twin brothers, about thirteen or fourteen, and always in trouble of some kind. Never anything serious. "Were they hurt? Break."

"Not that I was told, but the horse went from just being upset to scared half to death. Nobody can get anywhere near him now. A couple of grown men tried and almost got trampled for their trouble."

Erin did *not* like the sound of that. "Noreen, I know next to nothing about horses. Can't you call in somebody else? Barney's good with horses. I think Hank owns a couple. Break."

"Barney's at his daughter's soccer game and has his phone turned off. Hank Bentley has highway patrol today. That quilting show at the fairgrounds is bringing in lookers from all over the state. He's at least an hour out."

"What about Sheriff Adams? He's good with horses. Break."

"Right now he's being good with his wife. It's their anniversary, and he took the whole day off."

"Well, it'd be better to interrupt his day than to send me in. Break."

"Yeah, well, you can call him, then. I happen to like my job and need to keep it."

Erin puffed air into her cheeks and winced at the discomfort. "All right, I'll go. But as the dispatcher, you're supposed to handle stuff like this and send in somebody qualified. If I get hurt, it'll be on your head. Break."

"I wish you'd quit saying *break* every time you stop talking. It sounds corny."

"If you would study the code, you'd see that the FAA requires that we break after every exchange. It's one of those corny things called a *law*." Erin broke into a stiff jog toward the pickup. When she reached it, she keyed her radio again. "I'm en route. Break."

The interior of the pickup had soaked up heat from the late September sunlight beating against the windows. The smells of brand-new leather, carpet, and molded plastic surrounded her as she pressed the start button and fastened her safety belt. As she took a left onto East Main, she appreciated the lack of traffic, which would pick up shortly when people who worked in town began taking a lunch break. Some drove home to eat. Others grabbed a bite at one of the many eateries. She'd missed the first rush by only about twenty minutes.

"At least I don't have to go code three," she said aloud. Although she'd now been working here for over a year, she'd only ever had to use the lights and siren five times. That was Mystic Creek, in a nutshell. Very little crime. Only an occasional fender bender or drunk driving offense. Law enforcement saw plenty of action during Rodeo Days in August, she'd learned, and high school graduation night had kept her and all the other deputies hopping. But mostly, the community was quiet. It had seemed strange to Erin at first, but now that she was getting used to it, she liked the sameness of her shifts. She rarely had to worry about violent suspects. The only time her weapon left its holster was when she cleaned it. Nicest of all, she hadn't clapped eyes on a dead body since she'd moved here. "Now if God will just keep me in one piece while I try to catch a frightened horse."

Thinking of the little old ladies who were probably

being escorted around the quilt show by equally old and fragile men, Erin itched to press the accelerator clear to the floorboard. An escaped and upset horse was a loose cannon. Totally unpredictable. What if an elderly person got trampled? But as badly as she needed to hurry, her training, drilled into her at the academy, kicked in. One cardinal rule stressed repeatedly by her instructor was that every law officer needed to drive responsibly no matter how grave the emergency. Ponderosa Lane, a curvy gravel road, was peppered along each side by houses on small acreages. Dogs and kids, kids and dogs. Erin couldn't imagine anything worse than taking a turn at a high rate of speed, coming upon a child, and being unable to stop.

She settled back on the seat and tried to enjoy the scenery while she held the vehicle at fifty, which was a fast clip when the tires hit more potholes than smooth ground. Ponderosa pines added lofty regality to the area, some of them three feet in diameter with crusty, cinnamon red trunks. She liked that clusters of high-end, cookie-cutter residences didn't exist here. Each home was distinctly different, some circa 1970, others a bit newer, with a smattering of recent construction. Most of those homes were modeled after the Victorian era, all painted in pastels, with touches of gingerbread trim, ornate dormers, and spacious, wraparound verandas. She thought about rolling down the windows to get some fresh air, but she didn't want the new smell of the vehicle to dissipate too soon. It might be years before she could afford to trade in her Honda, which she'd bought secondhand, and she wouldn't enjoy the scent of "new" again until that happened.

As she went around a curve, Erin finally saw the fairground fencing to her right. Six feet tall and hurricane in style, it was a barrier that had been built to last. She drove another quarter mile before she saw the main entrance, its double swing gate hanging open for the public to come and go at will. She slowed down to execute the turn and saw a small crowd gathered in a semicircle near a newer-model blue pickup that was hitched to an old horse trailer.

"Showtime." She grabbed the car radio microphone. "Adam eleven, code eleven. Break."

Noreen immediately sounded off at her end. "Plain English, please. You know I hate all that crap."

Erin rolled her eyes. "I'm in car eleven, Noreen. Adam eleven. Get it? Code eleven means I've arrived at the scene. Break."

"Yeah, so just say that. See how much easier it is?"

The way Erin saw it, easy wasn't their aim. Communicating back and forth with as few words as possible was. "What if I had a code eight, Noreen? Break."

"What's a code eight?"

"Officer calling for help. Break."

"Two words versus four words. I don't see how that's any more efficient."

Erin keyed her mike. "Break! You have to say that. Whether you like it or not, whether it makes sense to you or not, we'll get slapped on the wrist, sooner or later, if we don't."

"Break, break, break," Noreen replied, sounding bored with the whole situation. "Like the FAA listens in on our frequency?"

"I'm assuming you've called Jack Palmer and sent him out here. Break."

"Why would I call the vet? So far as I know, the horse isn't hurt."

Erin was sorely tempted to raise her voice. "Horses can be dangerous. This particular horse is frightened. Jack Palmer can sedate it, if necessary. Get him out here, ASAP. Break."

"If nobody can catch the horse, how will Jack sedate it?" Noreen asked.

"A dart gun, possibly." Erin had an emergency on her hands and no time for arguing. "I'm going code six. I'll report when I can. Break."

Tossing off her seat belt, she cut the truck engine, pushed open the driver's door, and swung down from the vehicle. The crowd parted in the middle to create a path for her, and she saw an older man sitting on the edge of the dusty trailer's loading ramp. He held what looked like a disposable ice pack to his temple. His blue western shirt and faded jeans sported streaks of dirt. A red mark on his forehead and the bandlike depressions in his hair told her that he'd recently been wearing a hat, but she saw no other evidence of it now. She guessed that he'd taken a fall, possibly from the ramp, and was too shaken up to worry about his personal effects yet.

"Hi, Deputy De Laney," a woman called out. Then a man said, "Good afternoon, Erin."

Erin recognized only a few people in the crowd and they weren't the ones who'd spoken. She could only assume that the front-page article about her swearing-in, accompanied by pictures, had stuck in people's memories. She inclined her head to acknowledge each greeting, tried to smile, and was reminded by the pain in her cheek that her face was a complete mess.

Tension knotted the muscles in her back as she walked toward the man. Without removing the compress from his temple, he met her gaze and nodded by way of hello.

"Hello, sir. I'm Deputy De Laney. I understand that you had a problem with your horse."

"Yes. I don't know what the blue blazes got into him. He acted all funny when we got here, but he got over it at the arena and never gave me another lick of trouble until I tried to load him back in the trailer to go home. Went nuts on me. Rearing. Striking the air. That's totally unlike him."

Erin glanced around, hoping to see the horse, but there was no sign of him. "Are you badly hurt, sir?"

"Naw. I'd go get him myself, but I whacked my head pretty hard and still feel woozy when I stand up."

The man met Erin's gaze, and she took advantage of the eye contact to determine if his pupils looked dilated. "You may have a concussion," she observed. "Those are nothing to mess around with. You should have one of these good people take you to urgent care. The clinic is open for walk-ins until six. One of the doctors can check you out."

"I'm not leaving Espresso. He's my best friend in the whole world."

Erin refrained from pointing out that this man's best friend could have killed him. And the thought did nothing to embolden her. Even if she couldn't convince this gentleman to seek medical attention, which was his call to make since he seemed perfectly lucid, she still had to catch the horse.

"You experienced with horses?" the man asked.

Erin nearly said no, but, in front of all these people, she didn't want to come off as a city woman who knew next to nothing about country living. "Some," she settled for saying. And that wasn't a lie. She'd ridden a horse up and down Strawberry Hill. That qualified as *some* experience. Not a lot, but at times like this, just acting confident could go a long way.

Turning to face the audience, she noted that the onlookers had edged closer. She searched the sea of faces until her gaze caught on that of a slender, dark-haired man with a soul patch on his chin that looked like a smear of axle grease. Something about him, apart from the carefully trimmed black hair beneath his lower lip, inspired confidence in her. "Sir," she said, lacing her tone with question. "May I assign you the responsibility of watching this man for signs of concussion while I go to find his horse?"

The man who'd recently joined the gathering stepped forward. "I'm a licensed RN. I'll be fine with that."

Erin wished he were a licensed buckaroo. That would have solved all her problems. "Thank you. If he has a concussion, we really should get him to urgent care."

The man inclined his head. "I'm on it."

Erin glanced at the crowd. At a quick count, she estimated that around twenty people were present. "You have plenty of help, should you need it."

"How about you?" the nurse asked. "A couple of us men could go with you as backup. That horse is pretty wound up. The Turek boys tried to herd him back by swinging ropes at him. Not the best way to calm down a frightened equine."

Erin nodded in agreement, even though she wanted to ask, *And what is a good way to calm a horse down?* Only she couldn't voice the question. Public safety always had to be her primary concern, and soliciting help from these people would put them in the direct path of danger. Instead she struck off through the throng of people, which parted again to give her walking room. "He's over there," someone offered, pointing toward a large exhibit building. "Out behind," someone else added.

Erin put up a hand to indicate the crowd should remain where they were and she kept walking. Her heart bumped loudly in her chest. Her arms and legs felt disembodied. Sweat filmed her skin. She'd tipped the gym scales at one twenty-seven that morning. Now she was about to face a twelve-hundred-pound animal that could kill her with one strike of its hoof. As she put distance between herself and at least forty curious eyes, she struggled to breathe evenly, and for the first time in over a year, she regretted that she'd left her job in Washington. At least there, she'd known what she was doing and she'd always had proper procedure to fall back on. What to do if a suspect grew physically combative. What to do if a crowd grew violent. What to do if someone pulled out a weapon. She'd pored over the manual. Memorized every passage. Even now, she could recite scanner codes in her sleep. But nothing in Washington had prepared her for this.

Eating up the distance between her and the horse, her traitorous feet carried her to the back corner of the building. Erin stopped, took a deep breath, and executed the turn, half expecting the horse to be right there, almost on top of her. She was so scared her knees quivered. In her mind, her father's voice mocked her for being a coward. *It's only a stupid horse. Use the brains God gave you. No daughter of mine can be such a coward.* Anger welled within Erin. No, not anger, she realized. Instead she felt frustrated. *Never quite good enough.* She'd been trying all her life to make the grade. Fighting to be what she never could be to earn her father's approval. The need was always there within her. There when she woke up of a morning and punished her body doing perfect planks, not ten, not twenty, but a hundred times—until her muscles screamed to quit and her arms would no longer hold her up. Why did she do that to herself when all she really wanted was to be happy in her own skin?

I don't even carry a stupid purse. The thought ricocheted into her mind and bounced around like the singsong voice of a first grade bully on a playground. As irrational as Erin knew it was, her brain got stuck on that, and suddenly it felt as if everything that was wrong with her life centered on the fact that she had never owned a handbag. And if she died today, she never would. That couldn't happen. Before she cashed in her chips, she wanted to buy herself a handbag. A great big handbag. Huge. One that she could stuff full of all the crap women carried. A brush. Tampons. Ibuprofen tablets. Band-Aids. Hard candy. Chewing gum. Cosmetics. A wallet filled with photos of people she loved. And, damn it, she would carry it while she was in uniform! Why not? She was a woman, after all, and she knew not a single adult female who went anywhere without taking her purse.

The horse stood about a hundred yards away from her, and judging by its agitation, it also saw her. Erin tried to swallow spit she didn't have in her mouth. Her throat, as dry as parchment paper, felt as if its walls touched and stuck together. She stood still. Stared. *Espresso.* She could see where the animal had gotten its name. Despite the saddle on his back, he glimmered in the September sunlight, his coat as dark as a cup of Julie's triple-shot coffee. And he was beautiful, muscles bunching in his shoulders and haunches, a magnificent play of raw power.

Erin forced herself to move forward. *Don't be a coward,* her father's voice taunted. *Just walk out there. Use your brains. Outsmart him.* Only how could she use her intellect to maneuver an animal who could run at any given moment? Possibly straight at her? Would she be able to dive out of the way fast enough? And if she executed a roll over the ground, might he not turn on her before she could regain her feet? It occurred to her in that moment that she didn't belong in this place. That she'd never belonged anywhere, not even in Washington. She shouldn't even be a law enforcement officer. Instead of following her heart into a career of speech therapy, she'd followed her father's heart and chased his dreams. He'd yearned for a son, a chip off the old block, and she'd spent her whole life trying to be something she wasn't.

Erin stopped walking. At the edges of her mind, she knew it was insane to have the most revealing epiphany of her life when she faced a dangerous animal. But for the very first time, she *felt* the words that Jonas Sterling repeated to her at every counseling session. *You are who you are. You've tried pleasing your father, but look where that's taken you. Can you see how you've been trapped by someone else's expectations for you?* Rationally, Erin had always understood what Jonas tried to convey to her. But until now, this very moment, she had never been able to internalize the concepts. She wanted to announce to the world that she was a woman with all the wants and needs all women had.

As she forced herself to take another step toward

the horse, Erin made a vow to herself. If she survived this, she would go shopping this afternoon. She'd buy sexy underthings and perfume. Maybe she'd even get her ears pierced so she could start wearing matched sets of jewelry. And she would find a purse, not just any purse, but *the* purse. She'd even carry it into the department. If the male deputies made fun of her, she wouldn't allow that to upset her. From now on, she was living her life according to her own terms.

When Erin took another step, the horse reared up on his hind legs and thrashed the air with his front feet. His scream, laced with panic, sent trills of fear coursing through her body, and she knew she'd be a dead woman if she went any closer.

She knotted her hands into fists at her sides, pivoted on one heel, and walked away from the horse. Her father's voice went off in her head again, but she refused to listen. Instead, she focused on basic facts. She was not a horseman. Correction, not a horsewoman. It wouldn't be fair if she pressed forward. Not fair to her, and definitely not fair to the horse. He needed someone who understood him. Someone who knew how to approach him in a nonthreatening way. Someone whose posture conveyed no harmful intent. She wasn't that someone, and for once in her misbegotten life, she wouldn't try to be something she wasn't.

She saw surprise etched upon the faces of people in the crowd, which appeared to have doubled in number. Erin strode toward them, *strode* being the telling word, because she didn't know how to walk in a way that emphasized her femininity. But she was determined to change that. *Shackles*, Julie had said. And in a very real way, all of Erin's learned behaviors were just that, iron-like restraints that had held her captive far too long.

"Sorry, everyone," she called out as she drew close enough to the onlookers for her voice to be heard. "I don't have quite enough experience with horses to deal with that fellow. He's very upset."

The nurse said, "Those fool boys made a bad situation worse by swinging ropes at him. Kids see stuff on TV. Using a rope as a whip looks really cool unless you're the horse at the wrong end of the swing."

Erin moved toward the older man who still sat on the ramp. "Espresso is a gorgeous animal, sir. I didn't want to push him into going berserk."

The man, still holding the ice pack to his temple, gave her a grateful look. "Until he blew up on this ramp, I've never seen him go berserk. He's a fabulous horse. I appreciate you giving him some space. Pretty soon, maybe I can go get him. Until then, we'd better just leave him alone."

Erin wasn't certain in which part of the fairgrounds the quilt show was being held, but she thought of the people attending it and hoped their paths wouldn't lead them near the gelding. Unfortunately, hoping for the best was all she could do. She considered calling her uncle Slade, but he'd told her the previous day that he'd be heading up the mountain to base camp this afternoon. Even if she got lucky and he answered his cell, he might be too far away to help with this situation.

"Excuse me for a moment." Erin loped toward the county truck to call the department on the in-cab radio where people wouldn't overhear the conversation. Once she climbed inside and closed the door, she spoke into the microphone. "Adam eleven," she said to clarify her identity. Then, remembering that Noreen refused to use code, she added, "This is Deputy De Laney. Do you copy? Break."

Noreen came over the air. "You catch the horse?"

Erin closed her eyes. "No, Noreen. I'm not experienced with horses. I'm not the ma—*woman* for the job, and it would make the situation more dangerous for me to attempt something I'm unqualified to do. The horse's life could hang in the balance, not to mention my own. You should have called every deputy we have on the force to find someone who *is* qualified, which I will bring up at the next staff meeting. But for now, we'll focus on Jack Palmer. I hope you at least called him. Break."

"Break, break, break-break-break-break-*break*! You drive me nuts saying that. And who are you to tell me how to do my job?"

"Someone needs to," Erin shot back. "It's your duty to do everything within your power to protect all officers in the field. Did you call the vet? Break."

"Yes. Had to call his cell. He was delivering a calf. Coming breech. He said he couldn't leave until that was over."

Erin wanted to groan. "All right. So who else have you contacted? I need help out here! Break."

"I haven't called anyone," Noreen replied. "*You* are on duty. *You* are the only deputy in the vicinity. *You* are the only person I'm *obligated* to call. If you can't do your job, that isn't my problem." She hesitated an instant and then said, in a loud, obnoxious voice, "*Break!*"

Erin was glad not to be in the same room with Noreen. She feared that she might lose her temper and lash out at her. "So *your* take on your job is to do only what you're *obligated* to do? It's not your problem if I get hurt trying? Not your job to worry, right? You have better things to do, like chew bubble gum and make obnoxious noises with it while talking on the radio. Break."

"You'd like to see me lose my job, wouldn't you?"

Erin wondered how many civilians with police scanners were listening to this conversation, and suddenly she didn't care. "I'd even help you out the door. But the truth is, Noreen, you don't need anyone's help to lose that job. You're heading that way all by yourself. Break."

"Or so you hope! Ever since you came here, you've been on my back. *Memorize the codes, Noreen. Don't chew gum at work, Noreen. Don't talk about anything but department business over the radio, Noreen.* Do you think I don't know that you've complained about me to anyone who'd listen, even to the sheriff, who has the power to fire me at a moment's notice?"

Erin had complained about this woman to only Julie, who had nothing to do with department politics and wouldn't interfere even if she did. Julie was a live-and-let-live person and embraced the philosophy that all individuals eventually got what they asked for. In other words, Noreen would get what was coming to her. If she worked hard, good things would come. If not, bad things would rain on her head. Nobody else could make choices for her or direct her along another path. Erin had been foolish to try.

"I haven't spoken to Sheriff Adams," she confessed out loud. But she would do so at first opportunity. If she lost her own job, so be it. She didn't want another deputy to be abandoned in the field by this woman. "I haven't complained to anyone. Yet. Break."

"But now you will. That's the threat, isn't it? I didn't call the boss and risk pissing him off, so now you're going to make me pay."

Erin heard a vehicle pull through the front gates and looked into the rearview mirror to see a red pickup parking behind her. When the driver door opened, she saw CARING HANDS painted in white on the panel over a pink heart with paw prints dotting its center. *Jack Palmer*. The cavalry had arrived.

"The vet's here," she told Noreen. "I have to go. Break."

"Oh, good. The poor little deputy who's scared to do her job has a big, strong man to do it for her."

Erin refused to key the mike and respond to that. For once in her life, she didn't care what people thought. She felt like a poor little deputy who was afraid to do her job. She wasn't qualified to deal with this situation. Her training had not touched upon dealing with horses, cows, goats, or any other animal with hooves.

"Hey!" Jack Palmer called when Erin exited the county truck. "Sorry it took so long. Breech birth. I had to stay or lose both the cow and calf."

"I understand." Erin swallowed, hard. What she had to say next wouldn't come easily. "I've never been around horses, Jack. Well, I've been around them, but not enough. I'm pretty much useless in a situation like this, and to be honest, that horse scares the shit out of me."

Jack let loose with a from-the-gut laugh. "I understand. Horses make me just a little nervous, too. And that's *before* I'm standing by one."

Erin hoped her bewilderment didn't show on her face. "But you're a vet."

His gray eyes dancing with mischief, he winked at her. "And you're a deputy. You should be able to handle anything that comes your way. Right? So, here we stand, two buffoons who have a healthy respect for horses. I suppose I have a leg up on you. My coursework in veterinary medicine did cover equine care, and I doubt your training did—unless you planned to be a mounted cop."

The tension eased from Erin's shoulders. "Nope. The only thing I ever imagined I might have to ride was a motorcycle. Give 'em gas and oil, and they're ready to roll. Any accidents from that point forward are due to operator error."

Jack came to stand abreast of her. He was tall—not extraordinarily so, for a man—but he loomed over Erin. Only she felt no desire to straighten her spine and lift her chin. She didn't have to measure up. She was what she was, a female deputy whose gender made her shorter than most of the adult males around her.

"Well, this operator knows his limitations. Upset horses are like kegs of dynamite. A smart man doesn't shake them up."

"So what's our plan? Did you bring a dart gun to sedate him? I didn't go too close. He was in no mood for company. But he gave me the distinct impression that he's spoiling for a fight."

"Which he would win." Jack smiled down at her. He was an attractive guy, slim yet muscular, with light brown hair cut short, attractive features, and teeth white enough for a toothpaste commercial. "I left the dart gun at home. I tried using it once on a bull that went nuts."

"Did it work?"

"No. I missed."

Erin wondered if she'd misunderstood him, but when she searched his face, she saw self-derision in his expression.

"Lousy with horses, lousy with guns," he added. "And I don't really have a plan."

"Dear God. We're in trouble, then, because I don't have one, either. Do horses sleep? Maybe we can wait for Espresso to nod off and sneak up on him."

Jack guffawed. "I had a better idea. I called a friend who just happens to be amazing with horses. And, as luck would have it, he was in town. He should be here any second."

"What's his name?"

"You probably don't know him. He doesn't go to town much. A little on the quiet side."

Scanning the faces in the crowd, Erin saw proof many times over that she didn't know all the locals yet. As small as Mystic Creek seemed, the community didn't end at the city limits. The populace spilled over the surrounding countryside. If she stood on a street corner every day for the next year, she still wouldn't meet every citizen who hailed from Mystic Creek.

"How good is he with frightened horses?"

"Better than I am with a dart gun."

She laughed. "Can I comfort myself with the thought that you brought what you need to sedate the horse?"

"Everything but courage. I left that with the dart gun."

Erin rarely followed one laugh with another, but she did now. "I forgot to bring mine, too. Courage is over-rated, anyway. It leads people to do stupid stuff that they shouldn't."

"Amen."

Jack struck off through the crowd. Erin followed him to where the older man still sat on the edge of the loading ramp. "You okay, Ralph?" Jack asked.

"I will be. Hit my noggin pretty hard. Feeling swimmy headed."

"Could be you rattled what's left of your brains," Jack ventured. "Concussions are nothing to ignore. Maybe you should go to urgent care."

"Urgent care, my ass," Ralph popped back. "Not until I'm sure Espresso is safe, and if you're the only cavalry sent to his rescue, it'll be a while."

Jack nodded. "Nobody can be good at everything. I'm great at doctoring horses, but I suck at handling them."

Attending the exchange, Erin couldn't help but admire Jack Palmer's easy acceptance of his own shortcomings. She needed to tear a page out of his book and cultivate that ability in regards to her own inadequacies.

"You call that horse-whispering guy?" Ralph asked.

"Yep." Jack shoved his hands into his pockets. "Don't worry. I'll get my bag when he gets here. Once he has Espresso under control, I'll be there with a sedative if it's needed."

Just then Erin heard another vehicle pull in. She turned to see a late-model silver Dodge Ram with a full cab and a long bed park behind Jack's truck. A moment later as the clearance lights blinked out, Wyatt Fitzgerald swung out of the vehicle. Erin was startled to see him. She knew her uncle would be heading up the mountain to base camp that afternoon, and she had assumed that Wyatt would go with him. Only, now, here he was, and she had to think fast on how to best handle saying hello to him. They hadn't parted company on the best of terms. He'd been eager to get away from her, and she'd been wholeheartedly relieved to see him leave.

"Jack," he said as he cleared the throng of people gathered around the trailer. He spoke with that same thoughtful slowness that she remembered, and he didn't glance her way. "Sorry I took so long. I was shopping for supplies. That's usually the cook's job, but since we don't yet have a cook here, I got rail-roaded. Took all the frozen goods back into Flagg's and asked them to keep them in a freezer for me."

Jack extended his right hand and the two men shook. Then, and only then, did Wyatt turn his gaze on Erin. "Deputy De Laney. Good to see you." His eyes were the same incredible blue that she remembered. His sharply carved countenance was just as handsome. But it was his air of confidence that set him apart from other men in her estimation. He seemed so self-sufficient and completely comfortable in his own skin. She envied him that. "I'm sorry about the cheek. I'm guessing that the eye looks even worse."

Erin wanted to say something, anything to perpet-uate her riding-accident story, which had taken him off the hook. She'd torn up her copy of the citation she'd issued him. As far as she was concerned, what had ac-tually happened on the mountain could stay on the mountain. But he seemed to have a different plan. "It's a little sore, but I'm fine."

He nodded and looked at Jack. "Where's the horse?"

Jack looked to Erin for an answer. She said, "He's behind that building, or he was a bit ago when I went to find him." Erin indicated the structure by pointing. "He's very upset. Scared, angry, maybe both. Apparently two teenage boys tried using ropes as whips to round him up. They may have hit him a few times. I only know he nearly ran down two grown men afterward, and he made it clear he'd do the same again if I went anywhere near him."

"He's a nice horse," the owner said, but Erin knew Wyatt didn't realize he'd spoken. She gestured with a jerk of her chin so Wyatt would look that way. "I don't know what got into him," Ralph continued. "He was acting weird when we got here. Kicking out with his hinds. Whinnying. Almost ran me over to get out of the trailer. He calmed down at the arena and seemed fine again. It wasn't until I brought him back here that he went ballistic again."

Wyatt stepped up onto the ramp from off to the side, easily lifting his weight on only one bent leg. He stepped inside the trailer, toeing aside the carpet of straw to examine the floor and then taking a close look at the walls. He glanced out at Erin. "Would you start the truck for me?"

Erin glanced at the owner. "Do you mind if I start your vehicle, sir?"

The older man looked bewildered. "I don't reckon so." He turned to look over his shoulder at Wyatt. "You thinking there's something wrong with the trailer?"

Wyatt grinned. Erin remembered that slow, slightly off-center tilt of his mouth. The first time she'd seen it, she'd been too angry to appreciate its high voltage, but she wasn't left unaffected by it now. Barring none, he was the sexiest guy she'd ever met, and that purely feminine part of her that she'd tried so hard to deny, responded.

"It's just a hunch," he told the man. "So rare that I've only seen it once. So I'm probably wrong. But according to what you've told me, the horse was beside himself when you got here. Then he calmed down in the arena and was fine until you tried to return him to this trailer." He reached out and bumped one of the doors that angled out like a bird's wing. "My gut tells me the trailer is the problem." He glanced at Erin. "Start the truck, please. Let's see if I'm right."

Erin got the keys from Espresso's master and ran to do Wyatt's bidding. The instant the engine started to purr, she hopped out of the cab and raced to the back of the trailer again, hoping to see what Wyatt did next. To her bewilderment, he just stood there in the doorway for what seemed forever. Then he slowly paced off the distance to the interior's front end.

"Nothing," he announced. "I guessed wrong."

Erin still wasn't following. "What did you expect?"

"To get the sand shocked out of me. Faulty wiring will do that." He shrugged. "Like I said, I've seen it only once. A vintage trailer, like this one. Wires shifting and pulling for years. Those wires can get worn. Go bare." He sighed and leaned his shoulder against the door frame. Then he jumped away, saying, "Holy hell! I wasn't wrong! This old tin can just lit me up!"

Ralph pushed to his feet. "You mean it shocked you?"

Wyatt nodded.

"But it didn't shock me!" the older man protested. "The ramp is metal, a good conductor."

Wyatt toed the rubber pads on the upper end of the ramp. "The current stops there. And I forgot I've got on my mountain boots. Rubberized soles for grip."

"So the trailer was shocking my poor Espresso the whole time I drove him here?"

"That's my guess." Wyatt stepped down the ramp. Looking at Jack, he said, "I'll go talk it over with the horse and get him calmed down. While I'm gone, can you arrange for another trailer to be brought out? Even if we can get someone out here to fix this one, I doubt that the horse will ever trust it again."

"Dear God." Ralph sank back down on the ramp. He'd dropped the compress and it now lay near his feet. "Poor Espresso. I got mad at him when he wouldn't load up. He hasn't been difficult to load since he was a foal. It never occurred to me that the trailer was causing a problem."

"Hopefully not through his feet." Wyatt stood sideways to the ramp and leaned inside the trailer opening to place the flat of his hand on the enclosure floor, which was rectangles of plywood set inside steel framework. When his hand slid over onto metal, he jumped. "Yep, through his feet. At least when he stepped on steel." He glanced at Ralph. "Is he shod?"

Ralph nodded, his expression stricken. "That must have hurt like blue blazes."

Wyatt nodded, too. "Yes. You can get this trailer

fixed, but your horse may never forget what happened today. I'd have this one repaired, sell it, and buy one that your friend won't hate."

Erin stared after Wyatt as he left them and started toward the building. Remembering her mounting fear as she'd followed that path, she watched him for any hint that he was experiencing the same trepidation. If so, he concealed it well. He looked so relaxed that he might have been out for a Sunday stroll.

Jack made several calls on his cell phone. Within minutes, Barney Sterling arrived in his new Ford F-250, pulling what appeared to be a brand-new horse trailer. Jack, using hand signals, helped him get the trailer backed in beside the old one. When Barney finally joined everyone at the end of the trailer with faulty wiring, he smiled at Erin. "Hi, there. How's the face?"

"Sore." Erin scowled up at him. "Last I heard, you were at your daughter's soccer game with your cell turned off. Yet you answered Jack's call."

His grin broadened. "Is Noreen telling whoppers about me again? I *was* at my daughter's game, but I *never* turn off my phone. Well, almost never, anyway. She guards my time off like a mother hen. Doesn't like to call me in unless it's an emergency."

"It was. An emergency, I mean. I'm out of my element with horses and told her I wasn't the right person to send out here."

Barney bent his head. The brim of his Stetson, a black one instead of county-issue brown, shielded his expression from her view. When he looked back up, his eyes were carefully blank. Voice pitched low, he said, "We'll have to closet Blake in his office and have a talk with him, I reckon. I've heard rumors that things aren't what they should be between the two of you, that Noreen calls you in when she doesn't have to instead of bothering anyone else."

Anger tried to well within Erin, but she tamped it down. Acutely conscious of the muted conversations going on all around them, she said in a modulated voice, "I get very little time off."

"I've heard that. Been meaning to mention it to Blake, but things get busy and I always forget. Being the boss, most of the scuttle doesn't come up in his presence. I don't think he realizes what she's doing."

Erin couldn't quite believe her ears. For nearly a year, she'd blamed her hectic work schedule on her lack of seniority. Being a newly hired person was never easy. She'd known that and hadn't expected this job to be any different. But at some point, even she had started to feel that not even a newbie should be expected to work both night and day.

"She doesn't like me, so she's been running me ragged on purpose." She didn't phrase it as a question. And now that Barney had put it out there, she thought back to all the times she'd had to leave most of a meal uneaten at an eatery because she'd been called while off duty. It had always been when Noreen was at the desk. "What did she hope? That I'd get fed up with working such long hours and quit?"

"Maybe so." Barney glanced around to make sure he wouldn't be overheard. "We've all had our issues with Noreen, Erin. You aren't the only one she drives crazy."

"But I needle her about her performance, and I get the feeling the rest of you don't."

"I did at first. Everyone did at first. But Blake didn't can her, and we finally gave up."

"Because you realized she wasn't going to change?"

"Yep. And reminding her a dozen or more times a shift to use code and to never give out people's names over the radio—well, it gets old. And it's a waste of breath. She isn't going to change. I got so frustrated that I actually hoped someone would turn us in for using improper airway protocol and the FAA would come down on us. The sheriff would have to do something about her then. Or so I thought. But once I started asking around I found out that Noreen is Marietta's niece. A single mother of three. If Blake lets her go, she and her kids will be in hurt city, and his marriage won't be in much better shape."

"I *knew* it. That she had to be related to him, I mean." Erin considered the implications. "Before we talk to our boss, though, maybe I should try speaking with Noreen to see if we can't push a reset button."

"Noreen doesn't reset easily," Barney warned. "She honestly thinks we're all high on ourselves because we're deputies, and that our airway protocol is stuff we created to make ourselves feel more important."

Erin frowned. "How can she think that? Doesn't

she ever watch cop shows? Granted, cops don't use as much code now, but they still use it at least half the time. Does she think all cops, everywhere, just make it up, kind of like kids fascinated by pig Latin?"

Barney chuckled. "You just said something." He held up a finger. "Does she *think*? Forget the rest. Focus on the thinking part."

Erin grinned. "You really don't like the lady."

"What's there to like? The bubble gum, maybe?"

Chapter Five

Worried about Wyatt possibly needing her help to catch Espresso, Erin, who fervently hoped her assistance would *not* be required, trudged across the fairgrounds to the enclosed metal exhibit building. She wasn't as frightened this time, because she knew Wyatt was there, but she was uneasy. Horses just weren't her thing, and she'd be perfectly happy never to have another close encounter with one. But this *was* her job, and whether Noreen had been giving her the shaft by shoving all the crap off on her or not, she'd been sent on this call today, and she owed it to the citizens who paid her wages to perform her duties to the best of her ability.

She expected to hear the horse screaming, plus the resounding *thunk*s that only a horse's hooves, impacting with force upon the ground, could make. Instead no sound drifted to her. Well, she could hear the whimsical whispering of the wind, distant traffic sounds from Ponderosa Lane, and the faint drone of voices from the crowd that had gathered by the old horse trailer. But other than that, she heard nothing except the faint rustling sound of her clothing as she moved and the crunch of gravel under her boots. *Strange.* Espresso had snorted, reared, and stomped when she'd tried to approach him.

Easing her head around the corner of the building, she directed her gaze to where Espresso had been when she'd walked out here earlier. She saw no horse and couldn't pick up on any telling noises to indicate where he might have gone. She was about to start walking again when she saw him about fifty yards to the right of where he'd been when she'd tried to get near him. He stood with his regal head up. The whites of his eyes still rimmed his dark irises. Beneath his coat, which shimmered like a freshly poured cup of coffee, it appeared that all the muscles in his huge body were clenched. He was definitely still a very upset equine.

Only where was Wyatt? Ralph had referred to him as "that horse-whispering guy," so Erin expected to witness the extraordinary. Instead she couldn't see the deliciously handsome cowboy anywhere. So why was Espresso so perturbed?

A slight movement caught Erin's eye, and she lowered her gaze toward the ground in front of the animal. *Wyatt.* He was crouched down and using the heel of one boot as a rump rest. Head bent, with the brim of his Stetson casting his profile into shadow, he just hunkered there doing nothing, his well-muscled arms loosely crisscrossed over one bent knee, his big hands relaxed and dangling at the wrists. Only his straight golden hair moved, the silky strands shifting slightly in the breeze to skim back and forth over the shoulder seams of his red shirt. *What the heck?* She'd hoped to see something a little more remarkable.

Slipping quietly around the corner, she relaxed against the building and crossed her arms, determined to watch someone truly knowledgeable about horses use all his tricks. If the last week was any indication, she would occasionally be required in the line of duty to deal with equines, so the more she learned now, the better off she'd be.

Only Wyatt just crouched there, appearing to search the ground for the answer to a mysterious question she couldn't fathom. *This is it? That's all you've got for me?* She was already slightly bored. All she'd learn by watching this was how to hunker long enough to make her knees freeze in a bent position.

The horse smacked the ground with both front feet. Then he lunged forward at Wyatt, which made Erin's heart almost stop. Wyatt didn't so much as flinch. In fact, she wondered if he even knew the horse was threatening him. He couldn't hear the animal's hooves striking the earth or its grunts of warning, after all. She straightened away from the metal siding, groped for what little courage she had when it came to a horse, and tensed to spring forward into a run to alert Wyatt that he was in imminent danger.

Only just as she was about to push off, Espresso whickered and pranced away from Wyatt in a half circle. The horse had been bluffing, she realized. He was trying to let Wyatt know that he was prepared to fight for his life. Feeling as if all the air in her lungs leaked out, Erin went limp against the building again. Espresso came to a stop, once again facing the man. Then he lunged again, drew up short of his target, and pranced back around to resume his prior position. The horse was definitely issuing a challenge and a warning. Wyatt seemed to be oblivious, which was dangerous. But what if this was some kind of game, similar to teenagers playing chicken in automobiles by driving head-on at each other until one person lost his nerve at the last possible second? She watched Wyatt more closely the third time Espresso sprang toward him. She believed she glimpsed a tensing of the muscles across his back. Clearly, he knew the horse was trying to frighten him away, and this *was* some weird game. Erin just couldn't figure out what the point was or who was winning.

Espresso let loose with a shrill whinny. Then he grunted and stepped cautiously forward with his head lowered and his neck extended. *One step. Two. Three steps. Four.* Then the equine stopped, stretched his neck even farther, and sniffed the crown of Wyatt's hat. Wyatt didn't move, didn't look up. The horse whinnied again and whirled away, coming to stand face forward again. Still Wyatt didn't acknowledge that the animal was even there.

It seemed to Erin that the game lasted for hours, when in reality she knew only minutes had passed. Then, as if Espresso was getting as bored with it as she was, he once again approached Wyatt, this time sniffing not only his hat, but also his shirt. Then his hands. At that point, Wyatt flicked his wrist to turn up his palm, and the horse nuzzled his loosely curled fingers before getting spooked again for no apparent reason.

There followed one of the most fascinating thirty minutes of Erin's career as a law enforcement officer. Wyatt won the horse over without lifting a finger. Espresso, apparently tired of the feinting and circling, finally nudged Wyatt's shoulder with enough force to push him off his feet. The cowboy caught his balance, got his boots positioned underneath himself again, and resumed staring at the ground. Espresso bumped him again. Wyatt recovered his position. This went on until Espresso decided enough was enough and tucked his nose under Wyatt's right arm. Erin's heart caught when the cowboy slowly raised his left hand and began stroking Espresso's forehead.

Erin hadn't heard any horse whispering, but she felt certain that she had just witnessed the phenomenon. Espresso was definitely talking now, snorting, blowing, and making soft, grunting sounds. Erin tried to imagine what the animal was trying to say, and she decided his one-sided dialogue went something like, *I got shocked, man. Dang near cooked me extra done. Then my human tried to make me go back into that torture chamber, and I got really scared.* Erin's mind stopped short when Wyatt stood, stepped close to the horse's shoulder, and curled an arm around his neck. More petting and stroking ensued. Espresso's grumbling description of his trials continued. Wyatt appeared to be just listening, but Erin knew now that he truly was deaf and couldn't hear a sound the horse made.

It didn't seem to matter to Espresso. He'd found a friend in Wyatt, someone who understood his fear and knew how to work around it. She was reminded of watching a love scene in a film, only all the sexiness had taken a backseat to emotions far more elemental and difficult to understand. A horse and a man, communicating without words. A burning sensation washed over her eyes, because she'd never seen anything quite so touching or beautiful.

Wyatt gave the horse a final scratch behind the ears and then walked toward Erin. She straightened away from the building to greet him. "Hi. I didn't think you knew I was here." She made sure he could see her lips as she spoke, which was a huge improvement over the last time she'd seen this man. "I just wanted to make sure you didn't need help." She smiled. "Obviously, you didn't." She glanced past him. "Uh-oh. Company is coming. Will he go after me?"

Wyatt held her gaze with those incredible eyes that rivaled the blue of the sky. "Just pretend you don't notice him."

Erin darted a glance at the horse. "Right. I'll just ignore a twelve-hundred-pound beast who could mince me up like ground beef."

The corner of his mouth twitched. "He's not a mean horse, Deputy De Laney. He's just been through an ordeal, and he has to work his way past it."

"It sounded like he was telling you all about it."

"Did you catch anything I may have missed?"

Erin couldn't break eye contact. Something about this man made her toes curl inside her boots. And it wasn't just his looks, which were clear off the chart in sex appeal. Strength emanated from him. And he projected a soothing, rock-solid feeling of steady calmness, as if nothing unexpected or startling could rattle his composure. "He tried to talk to you. Unfortunately you couldn't hear him and I don't know horse-speak."

The twitch teased his full yet firm lips into a slight smile. "Oh, but I did *hear* him. Not in the same way you can, but I still got the gist." He reached back to rest a hand on Espresso's shoulder. The horse huffed in response. "I hope those boys get the licking of their young lives when they get home. They beat him with the ropes."

"Oh, *no*. Espresso *told* you that?"

He narrowed one eye to study her as he might a rare insect pinned to black velvet. "No. I saw the lash marks. I'm not certain what kind of ropes they had, but they were abrasive, and they put a lot of force behind the swings, because he has cuts."

Erin's heart squeezed again. She could be fairly accepting of violence and its outcome between two adults evenly matched, but hearing about a child or animal being abused always hit her hard. "Why would they *do* that? I know the horse needed to be caught. Somewhere on the grounds, a quilt show has drawn in hundreds of visitors, and a frightened horse at large is a threat to public safety. But it wasn't a situation so urgent that the end justified any measures necessary to corner him."

Wyatt was still studying her. The intensity of his gaze made her feel as if her skin was being turned inside out. "You're really upset."

Erin didn't get the point he was trying to make. The horse had been shocked, God only knew how many times. Then two ornery teens had made sport of hitting him with ropes. Of *course* she was upset. "Wouldn't most people be?"

"No." A muscle in his lean cheek twitched. "As sad as that is, a lot of people feel no compassion for animals."

Erin straightened her shoulders. "I'm no bleeding heart, if that's your implication. I just hate when people do cruel things to animals—or kids."

"You're afraid of this animal, though."

Erin's first impulse was to deny her fear, but her sudden determination to break free of all the shackles her father had pushed upon her once again rose up within her. One of those shackles was her inability to admit she was afraid—of *anything*. Gordon De Laney believed that all scaredy-cats were losers, and she'd grown up abhorring the thought of having to wear that handle. "I *am* afraid of him," she agreed. "I hope to get over that in time, but it will take a lot more exposure to horses to get me there."

"Going to visit your uncle would give you some exposure."

Erin bit down hard on her molars. "Jeez, this is like

a rerun. Maybe you can think of something else about me that you don't like, Mr. Fitzgerald, and bitch me out about that instead."

The horse swung his head, and Wyatt was pulled off balance. After regaining his footing, he said, "It was a suggestion, not a criticism. And I have a reason for bringing it up. Slade is putting up extra tents at base camp for guests from town to stay in. For a minimum fee, people can go up and enjoy a campout, no fuss, no muss, with tents, bedding, and food provided. I thought you might be interested. And just in case the new cook he hired doesn't show up, he'll need all the help he can get in the cookshack."

Concern welled within Erin. "A new cook? What happened to the young woman who always went up the mountain with him?"

"She's expecting a baby. Her doctor ordered complete bed rest recently and no lifting or horseback riding. Slade got word only the day before yesterday. Someone who sounds qualified accepted the camp cook position, but you never know with people you negotiate with online. She may not show up. If not, he'll be in an awful mess. Individuals who can afford guided hunts are dis-discerning in their tastes when it comes to their grub."

Erin had never heard him fumble a word until now. But *discerning* was a confusing word, the *s* not followed by a hard *c*. "I'll try to come up. I really will."

He touched the brim of his Stetson. "My hat will be

off to you if you show up. It would mean the world to Slade."

Swallowing her pride, which this man had a talent for injuring, she said, "I'll be there if it's possible. And just for the record, I'm really not the uncaring niece you believe me to be. I haven't had an easy time of it with scheduling. I hope to correct that problem, but it remains to be seen if I can."

"Most of the time, I don't enjoy being proved wrong," he said. "But I'll be delighted if you can ever say, 'I told you so.'" He continued to stroke the horse, calming Espresso with light, comforting passes of his palm. "For now, though, let's focus on this fellow. I need you to clear the way for me. Get all those people away from the trailer that Sterling delivered. Way back. The horse has hooked onto me for the moment, but he's scared, and the way he sees it, he can't even trust his owner right now."

Erin directed her gaze to the equine. He had soulful eyes, and the expression in those liquid brown depths was mournful. As crazy as she knew it might sound, she said, "When I watched you with him, I got the weird feeling that the two of you were communicating, only I never heard you say anything."

He inclined his head, an affirmation that her take on the situation had been correct. Then he cocked one eyebrow and asked, "Did you get that?"

Bewildered, she searched his expression. "Did I get what?"

He said nothing. Mind racing, she regrouped. "The nod, you mean? That you and the horse were communicating in some way?"

He dipped his squared chin again. Erin almost laughed.

"So what you're *not* saying but are trying to impart to me is that communication can occur without words."

"And that's especially true with animals. They talk to others of their species. To a degree, they can even communicate with animals not of their species. They recognize some words that humans use, but their vocabulary is limited. It's natural for them to communicate without words."

"And you somehow figured out *how* they do that?" She heard skepticism in the way she had worded that sentence and wished she'd put it differently. She didn't want to antagonize him, but at the same time, she found it difficult to believe that this singularly attractive man was the only human on earth who'd figured out all the mysteries of the animal kingdom. "And you can engage in silent conversation with a horse."

His eyes darkened slightly, reminding her of a blue sky growing gray with the threat of an incoming storm. He said nothing, and yet she knew she'd just pissed him off. She had also offended him in some way, which, practically speaking, was absurd. When a person said he could *talk* to animals, he had to expect others to react with skepticism and doubt. Did he think he was Doctor Dolittle or something?

He turned away to center his attention on the gelding. "Crowd control, please. I need to get Espresso loaded into the new trailer and finish my business in town so I can get up the mountain before dark."

Erin stared at his back, watching the tension drain from the muscles that padded his shoulder blades. *Mood swing.* He'd gone from angry to relaxed, from potentially explosive to gentle. The way he stood, the way he touched the horse—kindness emanated from him. He *was* communicating with the horse. Even she was getting the message. *I won't hurt you. It's going to be okay. You can trust me.* She tried to give herself a brisk mental shake, tried to blanket her imagination with cold, hard reality. Only this wasn't a telepathic exchange. It was absolutely physical and just as discernible as verbal communication.

It hit her then. At some point in his life, the world must have seemed so frightening to him. As a young child, he wouldn't have been able to talk. Learning how was incredibly difficult for a deaf child who'd never heard any sound, let alone how words were pronounced. Was it really beyond the realm of possibility that a deaf boy had discovered how to communicate *without* words? Now that she'd had time to think about it, Erin knew that was more probable than it was unlikely. A child had needs an adult couldn't fulfill unless the child could somehow ask for things. It made perfect sense that Wyatt had learned how to request a drink of water or food to fill his belly. How to let his parents know when he was afraid or tired or cold.

"I'm sorry," she pushed out. "Of *course* you can

communicate without words. It was stupid of me to question that."

He didn't react, didn't turn to look at her. Between them was a thick wall of absolute silence, and she kept forgetting it was there.

"I'm sorry," she whispered, and then she walked away.

Erin had herded the crowd to stand behind the three parked pickups, which created a physical barrier but didn't obstruct everyone's view if they stood near the lower sections of each vehicle. Everyone seemed eager to watch a horse whisperer in action, a measure of attention that Erin felt sure Wyatt would resent. There was little she could do to change the situation, though. This was public land. She could order the onlookers to stand well back, but she couldn't make them vacate the entire area. She had requested silence, however, which didn't normally work with crowds, but in this instance, it did. Nobody wished to frighten Espresso, and everyone wanted to see for themselves why Jack Palmer, a fabulous vet, seemed to think Wyatt Fitzgerald was such an extraordinary horseman.

When Wyatt and the gelding finally emerged from behind the building, no one made a sound. Erin stood with Jack and Barney behind the pickups, which seemed all wrong to her. She and Barney were the only law enforcement officers present, and if the horse panicked as Wyatt tried to lead it up the loading ramp, she wouldn't be close enough to lend her assistance. Jack, however, insisted that Wyatt would need no help and told Erin, "Just watch and learn."

The first thing Erin noticed was that Wyatt wasn't leading the horse, not in any physical way. The reins dangled loosely from Espresso's halter. Yet the horse followed closely behind the man as if they were attached by invisible strings. When Wyatt drew near the trailers, Espresso stopped and whinnied. Next to the front bumper of Erin's vehicle, Ralph, the horse's owner, now sat on a folding lawn chair that someone had found for him.

"He's gonna blow up again," he predicted.

Someone who stood nearby shushed him. Apparently embarrassed, Ralph bent his head. Erin moved closer to the older man and rested a hand on his shoulder. In a whisper, she said, "I know you're worried, but Wyatt knows what he's doing. He'll get Espresso inside the trailer without a fuss."

"How?" Ralph asked, also keeping his voice low.

Erin had no idea how Wyatt would manage. Espresso was a powerful animal. He'd suffered a lot of pain in the other trailer. He wouldn't willingly go back for seconds. Borrowing Jack's line, she said, "Just watch and learn."

She expected Wyatt to be assertive with the horse now, but instead of grabbing the reins and trying to force the animal forward, he just kept walking. For an awful moment, his nonchalant air convinced Erin that he wasn't aware the horse had stopped. But on some level she knew he was attuned to the horse in a way she couldn't understand, in a way nobody watching could understand. When he kept walking, Espresso whinnied and slashed at the earth with a front hoof. Then a shrill cry erupted from him. Wyatt never missed a step.

"He'll bolt," Ralph observed. "Sure as rain's wet."

Only the horse didn't. Clearly distressed about Wyatt leaving him behind, he kept whinnying to call him back and moved restively in place, but he didn't run.

Wyatt bypassed the trailers to approach his truck. Hooking a hand over a sidewall of the bed, he vaulted into the back, bent to grab a hay bale, and pitched it out onto the ground. During her brief stay at Uncle Slade's ranch, Erin had lifted rectangular bales and knew how heavy they were to pick up, let alone toss, but Wyatt made it look easy. After jumping back out of the vehicle, he swung the hay up onto his shoulder and started toward the trailer that Barney had delivered.

"Deputy De Laney, will you try to find a five-gallon bucket in the livestock building and bring it to the trailer filled with water?" he called back to her.

Erin tensed. She had no idea where the livestock building was. Jack stepped over and cupped her elbow with his hand. "I'll get it. You're needed here to keep these people quiet."

Erin nodded and resumed watching Wyatt. He threw the bale of hay into the transport trailer and then jumped inside after it to cut both strands of twine with a knife he carried on his hip. For such a tall and strong man, he moved with incredibly fluid grace, reminding her of a cougar she'd once observed at the

Seattle zoo. Like Wyatt, it had moved slowly and with well-oiled precision, but the unleashed power of its body had been apparent in every flex of lean muscle.

Jack returned, walking with a lopsided slant of his shoulders from the weight of the bucket he carried. At the sight of him, Espresso shrieked, reared, and then lashed out with his back hooves. Jack was well away from the animal and gave no sign that he even noticed. With a dip of his chin, Wyatt indicated that Jack should put the water on the ground next to the ramp. Erin couldn't help but smile. Wyatt could definitely communicate without speaking.

Curious about how Wyatt intended to get the horse into the trailer, Erin tried to think how she would go about it. Using the hay and water as lures was a good idea, but she didn't think Espresso was hungry or thirsty enough to fall for it. Sooner or later, Wyatt would have to force the horse up that ramp.

Only, of course, that wasn't what Wyatt did at all. Instead he dropped a small amount of hay on the ground so Espresso could see it and then just hunkered on the ramp in the same relaxed position she'd observed earlier—rump balanced on a boot heel, arms resting on an upraised knee, and head bent. It was about as exciting as watching a pastoral painting on a wall and waiting for the grass to grow. Person by person, the crowd dwindled until only Espresso's owner, Jack Palmer, and Barney Sterling remained to keep the vigil with Erin.

Espresso crept toward the ramp, often moving back

two steps for every step he took forward. Eventually he reached the ramp, whickered at Wyatt, and then began nudging him with his nose. Erin didn't blame the poor animal. Wyatt appeared to be asleep. When Espresso kept nudging him for what seemed like a small eternity, Wyatt finally stirred, extending a limp hand toward the horse. Espresso let loose with an excited rumble of pleasure when Wyatt began to pet him.

Before the equine could get any of the hay or water, Wyatt swung over the side of the sloped loading extension to lift the bucket and a small amount of hay onto the ramp just below where he'd been crouching. Then he resumed his former position, once again looking as if he'd dozed off. Erin shifted her weight from one foot to the other. Ralph, still ensconced on the lawn chair, sat with his shoulders slumped forward and his bald head hanging. Erin hoped that the poor man didn't have a concussion. If he slept, there was a chance that he might slip into a coma. She'd tried to convince him to see a physician, though, and because he seemed to be tracking okay, there was nothing more that she could do.

Espresso eventually went up onto the ramp to reach the water. Wyatt allowed the horse to take a few sips and then moved the bucket inside the trailer. The quarter horse danced on the ramp, striking the metal with such force that an earsplitting cacophony erupted, filling the early afternoon air with a maniacal rhythm that snapped Ralph awake.

Wyatt took up squatting rights inside the trailer. It

took another half hour for Espresso to work up the gumption to set a foot inside the enclosure. Muscles all over the horse's body twitched beneath his glossy, dark coat, giving measure of the poor creature's trepidation. When nothing happened, Espresso whickered softly to Wyatt with a note of unmistakable inquiry. Wyatt offered no verbal response, but he did lower himself to the floor, making visible physical contact with wood and steel.

Come on, Espresso. Just go in, pretty boy. It's safe. Erin wanted to say those words aloud. Wished that Wyatt would at least say them, but he remained silent. Minutes passed. Erin glanced at her Fitbit to check the time. If Wyatt still had supplies that he needed to get in town, he'd never make it up the mountain to Uncle Slade's base camp before dark.

When Espresso finally decided that his yearning for water outweighed his fear of getting shocked, he moseyed into the enclosure and thrust his nose into the bucket. Wyatt stroked the animal's neck and finger-combed his mane while the animal drank his fill.

Ralph released a taut breath. "That man has the patience of a saint. Most people would've just tried to muscle Espresso up the ramp."

"Not this guy," Jack said with a smile. "When it comes to horses, the clock stops for him. To Wyatt, it isn't about how long it takes. It's about the animal and only the animal. Doing it this way, he has convinced Espresso that there's nothing to fear in that trailer, and chances are that the horse will remember this and happily enter other ones." He winked at Ralph. "Unfortunately for you, though, even if you get the wiring fixed in that old tin can of yours, Espresso will probably never trust it again. You'll have to get another horse trailer."

Ralph nodded. "I'm overdue to make that decision, anyway. I'll get that one fixed and sell it. I won't ever try to make Espresso go into it again."

Erin kept her gaze on Wyatt. He seemed completely focused on the horse, and though never a word passed his lips, she could almost hear what he was conveying to Espresso with only his demeanor and his touch. *It's okay in here. It isn't hurting me, and it won't hurt you.* With only patience and a deep understanding of horses, he had turned what must have been a night-marish experience for the horse into a positive lesson that would hopefully prevent Espresso from balking in the future on trailer ramps.

He was an incredible human being, and Erin could only wish he'd heard her say she was sorry earlier. There had been nothing paranormal about what she'd just seen transpire. Yes, Wyatt had an amazing talent for conveying messages with his body language. And he was, without question, more attuned to horses than anyone she'd ever seen. But with the same measures of patience, unfailing kindness, and empathy, almost any-one could have gotten the equine into that trailer. Sadly, not many people understood horses well enough to have thought of it, and given the time it had taken, most handlers would opt for a quicker solution, which might have cemented in Espresso's mind for the rest of his life that trailers were to be feared.

After Barney drove away with Espresso safely inside the trailer and Ralph on the passenger seat of the new Ford, Erin could finally leave the fairgrounds to grab something to eat. Thinking of the double-shot latte that she'd left sitting on Julie's counter that morning, she drove back to Flagg's, left the county truck in the market parking lot, and returned to the Morning Grind, eager to try her friend's soup du jour and possibly even splurge on a maple bar. Given that she had missed both breakfast and lunch, she figured she could afford the extra calories.

Several people sat at the small round lunch tables that Julie always placed in front of her shop during the afternoon. Embarrassed to be seen with a bruised face, Erin forced herself to nod and smile at the patrons whether she recognized them or not. Just outside the doorway alcove, a redhead in her midsixties sat with a tall, robust man with a thick mane of snow-white hair. Erin drew to a stop. "Tim! Lynda! I'm surprised to see you guys. I thought you only ate at the Cauldron."

Tim had a grin that could light up East Main on a foggy night. Behind gleaming eyeglass lenses, his merry blue eyes twinkled just as brightly. "Our favorite traffic ticket giver," he said with a laugh. "I'm always glad to be sitting at a table or booth when I see you, not behind the wheel of a car."

Erin laughed. "Nah. My specialty is parking tickets. I stand by the meters that are almost ready to click off, and the instant the time runs out, I gleefully slap a citation on the windshield."

"What do you do for fun in Mystic Creek? They jerked out all the meters a few years back." He snapped his fingers. "I've got it. You patrol the parking lots and ticket all the people who wrongfully use spaces for the handicapped."

"I could actually get into that," Erin admitted. "It's frustrating when someone really needs an accessible parking spot and other, able-bodied people have taken all of them."

"What's the penalty in Oregon for doing that?" Tim asked.

"Last time I checked, the fine for a first offense was around two hundred dollars and repeat offenders could be fined a minimum of four hundred and fifty."

"Whew! That's pretty steep." He winked at her. "Do you get a kickback?"

Lynda elbowed her husband. "Don't listen to him, Erin. He's not happy unless he's giving someone a hard time."

Tim pretended to be offended. "Erin knows I'm only kidding around."

"He's terrible at parallel parking," Lynda inserted. "Nail him if he leaves the back end of our car sticking out in the street."

Tim angled an appalled look at his wife. "I'm *great* at parallel parking. You've never complained before."

Lynda spooned some soup into her mouth. After swallowing, she winked at Erin. "I'm so glad we gave this place a whirl. These croissants are *incredible*, and the Harvest Stew is so good I'm going to blackmail Julie for the recipe."

Erin's stomach rumbled. "Harvest Stew, huh? What's in it?"

"It's a puree, with pumpkin and ginger, I think. Definitely a hint of nutmeg and allspice. Savory, with only a trace of sweetness. It reminds me of a mild curry." She took another bite. "I hear your stomach growling. Go get some. And a croissant, too. Hot with lots of whipped butter. Yummy."

Erin waggled her fingers at Tim, who'd resumed eating his meal, and then entered the shop. The bell above the door chimed. No patrons sat at the six indoor tables, positioned in groups of three near each of the front windows. Julie, who stood behind the counter cleaning coffee appliances, glanced up and smiled. "Voilà! The starving law enforcement officer returns!"

"And the law officer *is* starving." Erin reached the counter just as she drew her wallet from her hip pocket. "Harvest Soup, a hot croissant, and two of your maple bars."

Julie chortled. "My words sank home! Way to break free of the shackles, girlfriend. Splurging on croissants and maple bars will be liberating."

Erin tugged at her credit card, which always got stuck in its slot. "Yep, and I'll enjoy every bite." She slanted an upward glance at her friend. "I had an epiphany today. From this point forward, I'm going to be shedding shackles like an escaped con with a pack of hounds on his heels."

"Good for you!" Julie ladled rich-looking puree into a deep ceramic bowl, its teal glaze hand-painted with colorful autumn leaves. "Tell me about your epiphany."

"I realized that I've never carried a handbag, and I'm going to correct that immediately."

Julie gave her a startled look. "*Never?* How have you survived without a purse? I keep almost everything but a change of clothes in mine."

Erin laughed. "I've gotten along quite nicely, thank you. But I'm tired of just surviving, and I'm going purse shopping when my shift is over. I'm not buying a teeny-weeny one, either. I want a great big one with zipper pockets inside, and I'm going to fill it with everything known to womankind. I'll be a walking first aid kit."

Julie set a latte on the counter. "Another splurge, half-and-half instead of skim, and *real* sea salt caramel syrup. If you're going to indulge, you may as well go whole hog."

A wave of apprehension washed over Erin. The calorie count for a lunch like this would probably be astronomical.

"*Don't,*" Julie said in a firm voice. "You're letting him into your head again. I can see it all over your face."

Erin pushed her card across the butcher-block

surface. "I don't *let* him in. He just barges in. But I'm not going to listen anymore. I'm getting a purse. And I'm going to *carry* that purse."

"To work?" Julie giggled. "I don't think I've ever seen anyone in uniform carrying a handbag. What a sight you'll be. I can't wait. I want pictures."

From the corner of her eye, Erin caught movement off to her right. She turned to see a man standing with his back to her. He was looking at the different blends of bagged coffee beans that Julie offered for sale. He wore a red shirt and brown Stetson, but Erin would have recognized him no matter what he had on. She'd spent a good deal of time staring at those broad shoulders in the past couple of hours.

"Excuse me," she told Julie.

As Erin closed in on Wyatt, she tried to think of what she might say to him. He was a really nice man, and she still wanted to apologize for offending him, this time while he was facing her and could read her lips.

Drawing up behind him, she marveled at the height and breadth of him, which made her feel small by comparison and want to stand taller. *Shackles*, she reminded herself. She didn't have to measure up physically to men, and she couldn't happily live the rest of her life trying. Feeling silly, she tapped Wyatt's arm. He jerked at her touch and whirled to face her, his right elbow almost catching her on the cheek. Erin fell back a step.

"Whoa! It's only me," she said.

"I'm sorry. I almost nailed you again." In the

fluorescent light, his eyes had taken on a hint of turquoise. "How do you sneak up on me like that?"

"Sorry. I didn't sneak. You were deep in thought about the coffee, I guess."

He studied her with a wondering expression. "Doesn't matter. I normally feel it when anyone or anything gets near me."

Erin almost said, *You feel it?* But she managed to bite back the words. She had already ticked him off once today by questioning his ability with the horse, and even though she couldn't imagine how he could possibly sense the nearness of others, she needed to take it on faith that he might have an awareness that other people didn't have. Looking up at his sun-bronzed face, she tried to think how she might best express her regret for upsetting him earlier. Then an idea came to her.

Using American Sign Language, she said, *"I am so sorry about this morning. I didn't mean to offend you, and I apologized right away, but you turned away and didn't realize I was talking to you."*

His gaze moved slowly over her face. Then he signed back, *"Once I had time to think about it, I got over being upset. What seems ordinary to me can strike others as being extraordinary. I tend to forget that."*

From the corner of her eye, Erin saw Julie staring at them as if she were transfixed. *"You were amazing with Espresso. I'm so glad Jack Palmer called you."*

"He texted me. I can't have conversations over the phone, and I never bothered to get a voice-to-text app."

Always interested in innovative solutions for the hearing impaired, Erin had read the reviews on some of the apps, and even those with the highest ratings were still less than ideal. She signed, *"I don't blame you. They aren't very good yet. Speech recognition technology is improving every day, though."*

She enjoyed communicating with him this way. It offered her a chance to practice using sign, and he seemed to be more at ease. She hadn't considered how exhausting it might be for him to carry on a conversation. He had to translate his thoughts into words and then enunciate them correctly.

He shrugged and signed back, *"I get by all right with texting. I keep my phone on vibrate."*

"What do you do when telemarketers call? I've been getting hit hard by them recently."

"I just reject all calls," he told her.

He glanced at the bags of coffee again. Following his gaze, Erin got what she hoped was a great idea. Only in order to carry through with it, she'd need his cell phone number. *"I really hope to get my scheduling problems at work ironed out soon so I can go up to my uncle's base camp. It'd be nice if I had your cell number so I can check to see if there's a tent available for me before I head up. If I call my uncle, he'll know I'm coming, and it won't be a surprise."*

"The reception up there is poor," he gestured. *"We can receive only texts, and sometimes not even those come through."*

"It would be worth a try. Wouldn't it?"

He plucked his phone from his breast pocket, thumbed it on, and turned the screen toward her so she could see his number. Erin quickly entered him into her contacts. Then she flashed him a smile. *"Thank you. I won't keep you from your shopping. You still have a long ride ahead of you to get up that mountain before dark."*

He nodded, but for a long moment, he held her gaze. His expression made her wonder if he was about to say something more, but then his shoulders relaxed and he returned the smile, a quick slant of his firm mouth that deepened the crease in one of his cheeks. *"Be careful coming up the mountain,"* he said with an upward undulation of his hand. *"Do you plan to come up on a horse?"*

Erin bit back a grin. *"Don't I look like a horse person to you?"*

A twinkle slipped into his eyes. *"No. So text me before you head up so I'll be expecting you. If you don't get there, I'll know something went wrong and send someone to find you."*

Erin wished that he would come to find her himself, and then she scolded herself for allowing such a thought to enter her mind. He wasn't her type, and she wasn't his. She did think he was extremely attractive, though.

She signed back, *"Thank you. If something goes wrong, I'll know the cavalry is coming."* Then she added, *"You were a miracle worker with Espresso. If not for you, his owner might never have gotten him into a trailer again without a huge fight."*

"He'll load up fine now. He knows all trailers aren't bad."

Erin nodded and walked away. Julie had her lunch order waiting on a tray. As Erin was paying her tab, Wyatt left the shop without making a purchase. Erin gazed after him, then smiled at her friend. "That's Wyatt Fitzgerald, my uncle's foreman."

"I know who he is. He's become a regular of mine."

"I got off to a really bad start with him," Erin revealed, "and I'm bound to see him a lot if I can start getting a little time off to visit Uncle Slade at the ranch. I noticed that he seems to be into gourmet coffee. Would it be too crazy if I got him a gift, nothing big, just a little something as a peace offering?"

"I don't see why it'd be crazy." Julie thought for a moment and shook her head. "No, not crazy at all, as long as it's nothing too personal or expensive." She glanced at her coffee selection, bright foil bags filled with different blends that she displayed on the shelves of a bookcase. "He does enjoy his coffee. How about two small bags of his favorite roasts and a really awesome bean grinder?"

"That would be perfect. Just a nice little something to tell him I hope we can be friends."

Julie selected two different kinds of coffee and slipped the bags into a white box emblazoned with espresso brown lettering that read, THE MORNING

GRIND. While she went to get a grinder, Erin munched on the croissant and decided she would need to write an explanatory note to Wyatt and put it inside the box. She'd get a nice greeting card, she thought. Something simple, maybe a little funny. She still felt badly about their first encounter. Believing that he had ignored her shouts, she'd been really angry. And she honestly hadn't believed him when he finally came right out and said he was deaf. There was nothing she could do now to change that, but if Wyatt was willing, maybe they could back up and start over fresh. If not, it would be uncomfortable for both of them when she visited the ranch.

As briefly as she could, Erin told her friend what Barney Sterling had related to her about Noreen Garrison. "If she keeps calling me in like she has been, I'm not sure how I'll get this box up the mountain to Wyatt. I'd love to hike up, but that would take almost a full day. Right now, I'm lucky to have enough time to finish a cup of coffee."

"So, let me get this straight. That woman has been calling you in when you're off duty because she doesn't *like* you?"

"According to Barney, yes. The other deputies have been enjoying all the slack time, but they also realize it's an unfair situation for me."

"What'd you do to make her have it in for you?"

Erin spooned some soup into her mouth, considered the question, and then shook her head in bewilderment. "I'm not really sure. She annoys the hell out of me, but until this morning, we've never really had words." She shrugged. "Maybe she just senses that I don't care for her."

Julie's dark brows drew together in a frown. "And the other deputies have just looked the other way. Amazing. She's been doing this to you for months."

Erin shrugged. "We're all on a salary. We don't get paid more for working longer hours. You can't really blame people for not saying anything when they have to work less."

"True. But if Noreen is Marietta Adams' niece, who's going to lose her job if push comes to shove, you or her?"

"I'm sure it would probably be me, and I honestly don't know what I'd do. Financially, I'd be in real trouble." She took another bite of croissant. "That said, though, Noreen is a single mom. She's got kids to support. At least all I have to worry about is myself. I'm hoping I can just talk with her. Come to a meeting of the minds, you know? I don't want to lose my job, but I don't want her to lose hers, either."

Julie shook her head and smiled. "Ah, Erin, you're such an enigma, crispy on the outside and soft at the center."

"You make me sound like an overroasted marshmallow."

Chapter Six

Vickie couldn't believe her bad luck. The drive from Coos Bay had taken less time than she anticipated. She had arrived at the Strawberry Hill trailhead twenty minutes before, a full hour ahead of schedule, and there wasn't another soul in sight. She stared through the dirt-streaked windshield of her Nissan Versa Note, which had never been this filthy in the two years she'd owned it. She'd forgotten that Mystic Creek had only one paved street. All the roads branching out from Main were gravel. No matter how slowly a person drove, dust billowed up around a vehicle. Even her skin felt a bit gritty, despite the closed windows. *No matter.* If Slade was desperate enough not to fire her the instant he recognized her, she'd be a lot grimier than this in short order. She just hoped he would set up camp showers. Roughing it didn't bother her, but she did like to bathe daily.

Trying to calm her nerves, which tingled like tiny live wires beneath her skin, she gazed at the wooden holding area for horses off to one side of the parking lot. It looked exactly the same as she remembered, square in shape and large enough to accommodate a half dozen equines, but realistically, she knew it couldn't be the same one that had been there over forty years ago. It had probably been torn down and rebuilt countless times since she'd last been here. The air smelled the same, though—crisp, clean, and scented with evergreen. She shifted her gaze to the gentle incline directly behind the horse pen and studied the ponderosa pines that peppered the slope. Some had grown to have massive trunks. Off the top of her head, she couldn't recall how long that particular species of pine lived, but she felt fairly confident that they had stood there since before she was born. If trees had ears, they had overheard her and Slade talking the first time they'd ever confessed their feelings for each other, and if they had eyes, they would have witnessed their first real kiss, which had left both of them shaken and yearning for more.

Ah, the memories. Being here again brought them all back to her and filled her with an ache of sadness for the young, idealistic, and absurdly hopeful girl she'd been all those years ago. Never once when she'd lain in Slade's arms and surrendered her body to him had she believed that he'd ever even look at another woman, let alone be unfaithful. Never had she pictured herself running away from Mystic Creek, either. It was her home. How had it happened that she'd grown old living on the Oregon coast without Slade at her side? The young woman she'd been then couldn't have imagined hating his guts someday. That was for sure.

But now she did.

In one way, she could scarcely wait to see him again, her mind spinning with different scenarios. That maybe he'd be glad to see her. That he might be old, bald, and overweight. She couldn't picture him old, though. In her memories, he was still tall, strapped with muscle, and handsomer than any guy had a right to be. Would he be stooped at the shoulders now? Would his mesmerizing gray eyes have turned blood-shot and rheumy? Had arthritis twisted and knotted his hands? The thought deepened her sense of sadness, because coming back to this place and seeing it through mature eyes had stripped it of all the magic. She'd heard people say that a person could never go back to their childhood home and reclaim the past. Now she knew that was absolutely true. Everything was familiar, but nothing was the same.

Her cell phone blasted its ringtone and lighted up the inside of her purse. Startled, she fished around in the interior pocket for the device and answered the call, which was from Nancy. "Hi, sweetie. I got here safe and sound."

"You were supposed to let me know," Nancy complained. "And I'm dying at this end. Did he go ballistic when he saw you?"

Vickie rested her head against the seat. "Haven't seen him yet. I got here an hour early. Nobody here but little old me."

"Oh, no. So now you have to just sit and wait? You must be even more nervous than I am."

Vickie turned the steering wheel from side to side with her free hand. "I am feeling a tad jumpy, for sure. But, oh, well. If he's nasty, I'll just head back into town. Look up the two old friends I've kept in touch with. I haven't seen Mary Alice or Marilyn in forever. We talk on the phone. Marilyn sent me a picture of herself in a Christmas card last year, and she's aged so much. She'll undoubtedly think the same about me."

"You've never talked to me about her."

Vickie sighed. "I left this place and everyone in it behind, honey. To me, it seemed like the less I said, the better. I didn't want you kids asking questions about where I grew up. I made a point to get in the habit of having your grandparents visit us instead of us going there."

A rattling sound came over the air. Nancy grumbled under her breath. "I just spilled my coffee." More rattling and then the sound of running water. "So did you stop to buy all the practical joke stuff?"

"I did. Remembered to hit Walmart before I left Bend. The rubber snakes and glow sticks were displayed on an end cap. A clerk finally helped me find them."

Nancy laughed. "I want daily texts! I hope he's still terrified of spiders, too. Did you get all the stuff hidden in your duffel?"

"Yes, and I even remembered to get a spare bottle of ketchup."

A loud giggle from her daughter prompted Vickie to draw the phone away from her ear for a moment. "I almost hope he acts like an ass," Nancy said. "It'll be so fun to hear how you make him pay. Just remember, Mom. If he lets you stay on as the cook, hold your cards close to your chest for a while. Once you confront him about Brody, he may cut you a check and tell you to leave, and you may not find another job right away. Make as much money as you can before you shake him all up."

Vickie's smile faded and a tingle of panic came up the back of her throat. "I don't think I should have come, Nance. I must have gone temporarily out of my mind."

"Mom, *Mom*," Nancy hurried to say. "You're forty years *late* going back! Don't talk; just listen. He sired a son and then refused to even acknowledge his existence. He never shouldered one iota of the responsibility of raising him! Never sent you a dime! When you start to think you shouldn't be there, that you shouldn't do this, just think about Brody riding a broom-handle horse until he was almost six! And remember when he volunteered at the fairgrounds during every rodeo that came to town? He shoveled shit. Carried water. He did anything and everything, no matter how hard, just to be around those horses."

Vickie closed her eyes. Nancy was so right. It was all too easy to bypass all the bad memories and focus instead on the wondrous moments of her youth. And in the process, she forgot all that Brody had endured as a child and still did as an adult. It wasn't *fair*, and she couldn't lose sight of that no matter how much she'd once loved the man who sired him. Brody was a Wilder. Slade's big, prosperous ranch should become his someday. Vickie had come back here to at least look Slade straight in the eye and try to set matters right. And failing in that, what was wrong with playing a few mean pranks on him and taking the cooking job only to quit right when Slade needed her the most? One good turn deserved another. Slade had abandoned her when she'd needed him the most, and then, even worse and more unforgivable, he had turned his back on his own flesh and blood.

"I'm sorry." Vickie released the words with a slow breath. "You're absolutely right, Nance. I'm chickening out, and I can't let myself do that."

"No, you can't," Nancy agreed. "Bide your time. Then blow it wide open and rub that man's nose in it. What he did was unconscionable, and whatever he gets, he deserves. It may not do Brody one bit of good, but at least you'll know that you did your best to settle the score. Cock both barrels and let that old fart have it."

Just then Vickie heard the rumble of a diesel pickup. "Somebody's here, Nance. I gotta go."

"Text me!" Nancy cried. "I want play-by-play accounts! Scare the shit out of him with the rubber snake first."

Vickie broke the connection and lifted a buttock to shove the phone in her hip pocket. A newer-model red

Dodge, pulling a long horse trailer, parked across the clearing from her Nissan. The trailer was gigantic, large enough to accommodate at least eight horses, but it was the pickup she studied with a measuring eye. The paint was filmed with dust. The long bed had several dings on the side facing her. Piles of camping paraphernalia poked up from the cargo area in front of the gooseneck.

And she knew it was Slade's truck; she would have bet money on it. His favorite color had once been red, and the vehicle had "rancher" written all over it. It had been used hard and rarely been washed. Dried globs of clay dotted the rear mud flap that she could see. The frayed end of a rope dangled over the tailgate. Her dad had once driven a pickup similar to it, a rig purchased for grueling work. Ranchers who ran their own spreads had no use for frivolous vehicles. They needed trucks with lots of muscle and high clearance.

Vickie's lungs hitched when the driver's door opened and a long, denim-clad leg swung out. She noted the dusty and well-worn riding boot, the frayed hem of the pant leg, and the bony shape of a man's bent knee. She stared at that knee, wondering why God had decided to make that particular human joint a gender identifier. Most women had soft, rounded knees with blurred definition of the bones. Men had big, square, knobby knees that pushed against denim and reshaped it. That knee poking out of the pickup screamed "man." Even worse, it shouted "Slade Wilder." All these years later,

Vickie couldn't remember being particularly fascinated by his legs. But in a lineup of two hundred knobby knees, she would have recognized Slade's instantly.

The thought was so stupid—so obsessive and sappy— that it alarmed her. Feelings. Yearnings. Needs. They rose within her like a mushroom cloud after an atomic blast, obliterating her sense of self. And suddenly she was terrified to see the entire length of him again. Frightened in a way she'd never been, not even the night Matt had beaten the hell out of her and she'd believed he might kill her. That commission of violence had been an attack on only her body, the blows inflicting physical injury but lacking the power to touch her inner self. Afterward, she'd crawled into the bathroom and locked the door, not to hide but to regroup and go back out swinging. She'd still known exactly who she was, what she held dear, and what she needed to do to shift her teetering world back onto its axis.

Slade's tactical strategies weren't and would never be physical. She also understood that his power over her was far more dangerous.

Rather than look at him, she searched the interior of her car for just one thing that might ground her and keep her focused on who she was, what she was, and why she had returned to this place and the man who had almost destroyed her. Her gaze caught on the rearview mirror ornament that Brody had made for her in fifth grade by cutting a horseshoe shape from cardboard and covering it with glued-on beads. Over the years, she had replaced bits of glass that fell off, coated it with quick-drying resin to protect it, and replaced the ribbon from which it hung at least a half dozen times. *"Open end up, Mom,"* Brody had told her. *"That way you can catch lots and lots of good luck."* It was the perfect thing to remind Vickie of her reasons for being here, which wasn't to resurrect a relationship that had ended years ago, but to hopefully set things right for her older son, who had never caught any good luck from the moment he'd been born.

Seeing that horseshoe, staring at it, helped to center her as nothing else could. A gift of love from the son Slade Wilder had sired. Coming here was like climbing inside a time capsule and locking the lid behind her. If she allowed it, she could get lost in this place. Become so intoxicated by romantic fantasies that reason held no sway. The line between the present and her past might blur until she could no longer see it. This place that she'd once loved so dearly wasn't her reality now. She had to remember that. Her home, her life, her loved ones, and everything she had struggled to build over the last forty years lay over the mountains in Coos Bay. She couldn't let herself sink into what might have been, could have been, or should have been. She was no longer Vickie Granger; she was Victoria Lynn Brown.

Determined not to let this moment send her reeling, she turned her head to take her first good look at Slade. Over forty years had passed since their last encounter. That was two-thirds of her lifetime. It was silly to think of him in a romantic way. Absurd to think he might be glad to see her. Foolish to wish that what they'd once felt for each other might somehow be re-kindled.

He was leaning against the bed of the truck now, one leg braced in front of him to hold his weight, the other bent. The stance, so classically cowboy, had been duplicated in silhouettes by artists all over the country. She wanted him to have a potbelly. She wanted the strength of his lofty frame to have been diminished by age. She *needed* to see a man who'd become all but a stranger to her.

Only he hadn't. The blue plaid of his western shirt showcased his flat abdomen. Faded Wrangler jeans skimmed his narrow hips and sheathed his long legs, delineating the bunched tendons and muscles in his thighs. Head bent, he studied information on a clip-board he held in his left hand, which didn't appear to be misshapen by arthritis yet. The sleeves of the shirt had been folded back, neatly and precisely, revealing his forearms, which displayed even more of the iron-like hardness that tempered his frame. Had his body always been so steely? Recalling how it had felt to be held close in his arms, she decided it had been. Only then she'd been young and madly in love. Feeling the relentless strength of him had turned her on and made her feel feminine in a way that no other man had ever matched.

And there had been a few men. She'd divorced Matt when she was twenty-six, almost twenty-seven. She'd been too young to be alone, without anyone to hold her close at night and satisfy the needs of her body, so she'd set out to find a life partner. Male patrons at the restaurant had asked her out, and she'd started accepting. She'd learned the hard way that none of them were looking for a lasting relationship, and just getting through the boring dinners had been a trial.

Much later in life, she'd tried online dating. That had been a disaster as well, and she'd eventually given up on ever finding anyone. Slade Wilder had ruined her for all other men.

She stared out the dusty window at his chisel-cut features. Let her gaze linger on his firm mouth. Remembered touching her fingertip to the cleft in his square chin. And suddenly she felt as if her lungs imploded, pushing out all the oxygen so it erupted from her mouth in what sounded like a tremulous sigh. She realized how long she'd been sitting there. How long she'd been stalling, staring, wishing, and dreading. She had two choices. She could get out of the car and face him, or she could drive away and never look back. The latter option smacked of cowardice, and even though life had beaten her down and kicked her in the teeth more times than she could count, she was still and always would be a Granger. Grangers never backed down from anybody.

She reached for the handle of the door, pushed it open, and got out. Slade didn't look over at her. But a dog she hadn't noticed came bounding out from under the pickup and ran toward her. He was a beautiful creature, with long, thick fur that glistened like polished onyx. He had the look of a Rottweiler in coloring, his manner was friendly, and as he skidded to a stop in front of her, she extended her hand so he could smell it.

"Aren't you a beauty," she murmured. "Yes, you are." As far back as she could remember, she'd always loved animals, but dogs were her favorite. Unlike people, canines were always honest and genuine. This fellow was happy, his tongue lolling out one side of his mouth to accentuate his smile. She ran her fingers over his head and knew Slade brushed him frequently. Fur didn't feel so silky without regular grooming. "You're a good dog, aren't you?" As a very young man, Slade had lost an old dog he loved, and he'd sworn he would never get another one. Apparently he'd changed his mind, and Vickie was glad of that. Too many dogs and cats never found good homes. "You're a lucky boy. He's a lot better dog owner than he was a boyfriend."

Giving the dog a final pat, she straightened, hoping Slade might look her way as she took a few more steps toward him. Waiting for him to notice her was agony. Instead he turned to study the camping gear in the bed of his truck and then jotted something down on the paper atop the clipboard. She dimly realized that he was taking inventory. She remembered helping her father do the same thing. An outfitter couldn't afford to go up a mountain without every single thing he needed.

Preparing for such a venture took weeks of planning and making lists, followed by checking items off as they were packed. She remembered one year when her dad had gotten all set up and realized that he'd forgotten to bring salt. The oversight had sent Vickie's mother into a panic, for she was the camp cook, and flavorless food didn't go over well with guests who paid top dollar to enjoy their meals. Even though it was turning dark, Vickie had ridden her trusty horse back down the mountain to get salt and had returned before her mom entered the cookshack to start breakfast the next morning.

Coming to a stop several feet away from the pickup and trailer, Vickie gathered her courage and said, "Hello."

Slade did glance up, but he gave her a dismissive look and resumed his task. She took a deep breath and resumed her advance on him. Only before she could think what else to say, three pickups came around the curve of the road and turned into the trailhead parking area, horse trailers angling sharply behind them. Slade set his clipboard atop a pile of gear and strode toward the vehicles as they stopped side by side near the opposite tree line. Horse hooves drummed on the trailer floors. The animals whinnied, the sounds laced with eagerness and excitement.

Vickie quickly decided that now wasn't the time to make her identity known. Slade obviously hadn't recognized her. And, oh, how it hurt to know that. He clearly thought she was just another city person who'd

come here for a hike and was waiting for friends to join
her. Most women from out of the area didn't venture
into a wilderness area alone.

She wanted to feel angry because he hadn't recognized her instantly. But she knew how much she had
changed. Her mirror told her that. She'd borne three
children. Age and gravity had taken their toll on her
face and body. Her shoulder-length mane of impossi-
bly curly hair, once auburn with coppery highlights,
was now threaded with silver and had lost its gloss. It
was a shame that time changed a person's appearance
so drastically, because she still felt the same on the inside, the girl who loved Slade Wilder.

Her stomach knotted and cramped as that realization sank in. She still loved him. How that could be,
she didn't know. She'd been telling herself that she
hated him for so long that she could barely wrap her
mind around it.

Slade felt shell-shocked. *Vickie.* When he'd looked up
and seen her, his knees had almost buckled. It was like
someone had shoved a liquid nitrogen nozzle into his
ear and pulled the trigger to fill his cranial cavity with
cell-destroying coldness. He couldn't think, couldn't
register his own feelings. He wanted to pinch himself
to make sure he wasn't dreaming. Or having a nightmare.

He greeted his six seasonal hired hands, half of
them men who'd gone up the mountain with him
during seasons past. He'd hoped to take inventory of

their gear to make sure they hadn't forgotten anything, but that was impossible now. All he could think was, *Dear God, it's really her.* Until this moment, he'd sometimes wondered if she was even still alive. A certain percentage of people didn't live into their sixties. Heart attacks, cancer, and strokes took them out. A few years ago Marilyn Fears, who owned and operated the Mystic One-Stop Market at the end of West Main, had slipped up and told Slade that Vickie had borne three children and had lived over on the coast somewhere for a while. When Slade had tried to press her for more information, she'd said that Vickie had stopped contacting her. Marilyn hadn't mentioned a husband, but Slade believed there must be one. The Vickie he'd known wouldn't have slept with a man without a ring on her finger.

Now, after forty-one years, here she was. It made no sense. If she'd intended to shake him up, she'd done a good job of it. If he'd seen her at the ranch, maybe it wouldn't have startled him so badly, because that was the most likely place where she would go to find him. The trailhead at Strawberry Hill was another matter entirely. How had she known to wait for him here? Her car had been parked at the edge of the clearing when he'd pulled in.

Slade went through the motions of getting his men lined out. Per his request, they'd each brought two of their own horses. It appeared that all their gear was in order. Slade had planned to ride up the mountain with them once the cook arrived, but V. L. Brown hadn't made an appearance yet. He didn't know what the hell he'd do if she didn't show up, and right now he was too upset by Vickie's appearance to even think about it.

While the men unloaded their livestock and began the saddling process, Slade stood aside, feeling like a fence post that had been planted in the ground and never had any rails attached to it. *Useless. Inanimate. Frozen.* He could feel Vickie staring at him and knew he had to face her, but his pride waged war with his emotions. He didn't want her to know how unnerved he was. Didn't want her to know that he'd dreamed of seeing her again and thought he never would. She'd become a beautiful memory, something he had tucked away in a separate corner of his heart and only brought out into the light of day when he had a weak moment.

When he finally turned to face her, he had decided to play it casual. He forced himself to smile. "When you first got out of the car, I thought I was seeing a ghost," he said, following the words with a laugh that sounded fake even to him. "What the hell brought you to the trailhead? You waiting for friends to go on a hike?"

She lifted her chin—a small, stubborn chin with a dainty indentation at its center. He'd traced its shape with a fingertip at least a thousand times. Memorized it. Loved it. She'd always been small—a delicately made child who'd grown into a delicately made woman. But despite her diminutive stature, she'd been a force to be reckoned with, ready to double her fists and take on the world. He had once admired that about her. It had also made him fiercely protective of her. When Vickie got her dander up, she was hell on wheels, but like a Chihuahua challenging a pit bull, sometimes she needed backup. As a young man, he'd felt honored to take on that job.

"I thought you'd be expecting me." She glanced at the trail, which began about twenty-five yards behind him. "If I were here to go hiking, I'd already be gone. I don't need a gaggle of friends to hold my hand."

Hearing her voice again was like something straight out of a dream for Slade. Seeing her hair sparkle like fire in the sunlight only added to his sense of surrealism. Trying not to be obvious, he took measure of her tidy figure. He'd always known she would age well, but he hadn't expected her to look so much the same. In the harsh light of day, he could detect wrinkles on her sweet face, a little crepe skin on her slender neck, and some liver spots on her forearms and the backs of her hands. A few more freckles had been sprinkled across her nose as well. But in most ways, she looked like the girl he remembered. She wore jeans, a tank top, and a flannel overshirt, an ensemble well suited to the rugged terrain. She'd chosen sturdy, square-toed boots with two-inch heels as footwear, a wise choice for both walking and horseback riding. *Weird.* She looked ready to step right back into his world. But he wasn't a big enough fool to believe that was her intent, and he wasn't about to let her know that he wished it were.

"So," he said, letting a note of question trail behind the word. "If you aren't here to hike, what *are* you doing here?"

"In your email, you instructed me to be here at one o'clock. I got here an hour early, so I just parked and waited."

Slade got that brain-freeze feeling again. He stared down at her for a long moment. Then he blinked. "My email?" He let that hang there between them like a comic bubble. He hadn't sent her an email. He hadn't even been sure she was still alive until ten minutes ago. "I'm afraid I don't understand."

Her green eyes locked with his. He'd almost forgotten how beautiful their color was. "You advertised on Craigslist for a camp cook. I applied for the job. You hired me and said to meet you here."

The cold sensation inside his head increased, and pain knifed from his left temple to his right one. "*What?* I hired a woman named V. L. Brown."

She nodded. "Victoria Lynn Brown. That's me."

"*You're* V. L. Brown?" Slade knew he sounded like a dumb cluck, but he was so startled and bewildered he couldn't collect his thoughts. "What the hell were you thinking not to identify yourself in our correspondence?"

She shoved her hands into the pockets of her jeans and hunched her narrow shoulders. "You want the truth or a story I can make up really fast?"

"The truth!"

She took what appeared to be a bracing breath. "Well," she said on an exhale, "I was afraid you wouldn't hire me if you knew who I was, and I need this job."

"There are a lot of camp jack jobs on Craigslist. Why pick on me?"

Her eyes turned a brilliant mossy green. Even after all these years, he knew what that meant. She was getting pissed off. "Simple. The chef jobs dried up where I live. An economic downturn, they call it. A huge drop in tourism. I was faced with working locally as a fry cook for piddling wages or working through the hunting season as a camp cook and making enough to pad my pockets until spring. For me, that choice was a no-brainer. But, given that it's been years since I've done any outfitting, I wanted to get back up to speed in an area I know like the back of my hand. This happens to be it."

"Did it occur to you that we didn't part company on the best of terms, and that maybe, just maybe, I wouldn't want you on my payroll?"

"It's been a long time, Slade. I've long since buried that particular hatchet, and I figured you probably had, too."

Slade felt backed into a corner. If he admitted that he still hadn't buried that hatchet, he'd sound like a lovesick fool. But the truth was, he hadn't. He'd trusted her with his heart, and she'd walked all over it. Questioned his word. Called him a liar. Left him without so much as a goodbye and disappeared. Maybe she'd moved on with her life, but he hadn't. He'd never found another woman he could love the way he'd loved her. So here he stood, still unmarried at almost sixty-four. He'd never had children. When he died, a multimillion-dollar ranch that had been in his family for four generations would probably go to the state. In short, she'd ruined his life. He hadn't been able to just put that behind him. *Hell, no.*

"I'm afraid you've made a long drive for nothing," he said. "I try to avoid having friction of any kind in my camp. I get enough of that with paying guests who come in from different parts of the country and have personality clashes."

"So you anticipate that there would be friction between us? It's all water under the bridge now. Right?"

He didn't know what bridge she was standing on, but from his vantage point, all he saw were Class VI rapids, the kind that either pulled a man under and drowned him or threw him against the rocks until he was beaten to death. "I'm sorry, Vickie. There's too much history between us."

"So you're sending me away."

She didn't pose it as a question, so he felt no obligation to respond with an answer.

Shoulders straight and head held high, she just stared at him for a moment. Then she said, "All right, Slade. I'll go. But first we have some old business to settle."

He glanced over his shoulder at his men. "Not today. I'm pressed for time." He met and held her gaze. "I wish you the best of luck. I hope you find another position as a camp jack. Your folks trained you well. You should be a good one."

"I *will* be a good one. And I don't care how pressed for time you may be. I'm not leaving until we've hashed things out. And when I say *things*, you know very well what I mean."

Slade could only wonder what things she was referring to. If she thought for a second that he was going to discuss his alleged fall from grace with April Pierce again, she had another think coming. One of his men shouted his name. He turned his back on her. "I guess you can hold up a tree to pass the time," he said over his shoulder. "I've got a business to run."

He'd almost reached the horse trailers when something struck him dead center on the back. He whirled to see a pinecone ricochet off him and then bounce across the ground. Even with the evidence of his own eyes, he couldn't quite believe that she'd dared to throw something at him. *Vickie.* He doubted she tipped the scales at much over a hundred and ten, but she had a huge attitude to compensate for her lack of size. He gave her a long study. Her eyes flashed at him like green traffic lights.

"Did you just throw that pinecone at me?" he asked, incredulity welling up within him.

"Hell, no. If I'd been trying to hit you, I would have knocked that hat off your head. Or is it glued down so it won't get snatched off by the wind to reveal your bald pate?"

Slade had no clue what a pate was, but he got the

gist, and now *he* was getting pissed off. She wasn't exactly a spring chicken herself, and there were plenty of mean shots he could take at her. Throwing stones when you lived in a glass house was dangerous.

"Hey, boss?" one of the seasonal workers called again. "Do you think we need both of these, or should we leave one behind?"

Slade reached the men. "I don't know if we'll need two." They were quarreling over come-alongs, handheld winches with ratchets that helped a man pull or lift things he couldn't otherwise handle alone. "And they're heavy. The less extra weight we carry up that mountain, the better." Slade's mind was still on Vickie, the pinecone projectile, and her crack about his bald head. The woman always had been able to frustrate the hell out of him. "But come-alongs are also extremely handy. I say take both of them. I may have room in my packs if none of you do."

John, a stout young fellow with dark hair who'd been with Slade the longest, cast a curious glance at Vickie. Slade refused to let his gaze drift that way. He didn't want to encourage her by seeming to notice that she was still hanging around. "Who is that, boss?"

Slade sighed. "She was going to be our cook. Applied for the job online, getting creative with her name so I didn't realize who she was until I actually saw her."

"Our cook, and you're using past tense?" John's eyebrows arched in question. "Does that mean you gave her the boot?"

Slade nodded. "We have a history, and not a pretty

one. I don't want to spend the next month trying to tiptoe around her."

Rex, the youngest of Slade's seasonal workers, dropped the come-along he held and said, "Does that mean you're taking over as the cook? Because that'll be a freaking disaster. Us guys can make do with sandwiches, even if we have to make them ourselves. But the paying guests expect fancier grub than that."

Slade sighed and rubbed beside his nose. "I stay way too busy to be the cook, son. But we have another six days before the guests start showing up. That gives me time to find someone else."

"It sure is too bad Cheyenne is pregnant," Dale inserted. "I mean, I'm glad she is. I know she and her husband want a baby like no tomorrow. It just sucks that she can't be here to cook for us this season."

Slade nodded in agreement. "Chances are she'll retire from outfitting now. A mother can't be gone for a solid month every year. I'll need another cook anyway."

John shot a second look at Vickie. "Six days doesn't give you much time. A thousand things could go wrong. You could hire someone else online, and then that person may get a better offer and never show up."

"Yeah," Rex inserted. "Craigslist is rip-off central. All kinds of scammers are on there, too. If an applicant asks you for money to travel here, don't fall for it."

"I wasn't born yesterday," Slade assured him. "I won't be sending money to some total stranger."

Dale, a wiry blond who got sunburned easily, gave Vickie a slow once-over. "She any good?"

For a moment Slade thought the kid was asking about Vickie's talents in bed, and his temper started to flare. Then he realized that Dale rarely talked smack about women and wasn't likely to start now. "As a cook, you mean?" When Dale nodded, Slade said, "Vickie was born and raised in Mystic Creek. Her father used to be an outfitter, and her mother worked for years as his camp jack."

"You talking about Old Man Granger?" Rex asked. At Slade's nod, he added, "Oh, wow. My dad took me on a guided hunt with Granger one year, and the food his wife put on the table was second to none. If your friend—or whatever she is—can cook half as well as her mother could, she'd be one hell of an asset."

Slade couldn't argue the point. Vickie was perfect for the job. Unfortunately, deep down where reason held no sway, Slade still loved her. Always had and always would. She'd nearly destroyed him forty-one years ago by running away and never looking back. Over time, he'd healed, at least after a fashion. He'd stopped dreaming of her in his arms. He'd stopped searching the streets of Mystic Creek for her. He'd finally accepted that she was gone for good and was never coming back.

"Yes," Slade admitted. "In some ways, she would be an invaluable asset. But in other ways, she might bring unpleasantness into camp, and I can't take that risk."

John shook his head. "Unpleasantness is when a rich man gets your coffee served to him over a breakfast that your dog won't even eat."

Everyone laughed but Slade. "I know I don't make the best coffee."

"Your food sucks, too," Rex observed.

"Yep. Half-raw fried potatoes, rubbery eggs, and burned bacon half the time," Dale added.

Slade sighed again. "Don't worry about my feelings. Just say what's on your mind."

John laughed and said, "We just did. You're a horrible cook. If you can't find someone else, we're going to be up shit creek without a paddle, so I think sending that woman away is a mistake. A bird in the hand is worth two in the bush." He inclined his head in Vickie's direction. "You said yourself that she's probably a great cook. You can keep looking for someone else, but if you're smart, you'll keep her on the hook until you can reel somebody else in."

"Are you saying I should let her think she has the job until I find someone to replace her?" Slade shook his head. "I can't do that. If I send her packing now, she still has time to find another position before the season starts. If I fire her after the kickoff date, all the positions may be filled."

John shrugged. "It's your outfitting business, and if you end up without a cook, it'll be your funeral."

Slade wanted to say words he rarely used. Vile words. Not because he disagreed with his men, but because the thought of letting Vickie stay on scared him. She held some kind of power over him that no other female ever had, and no matter how he circled it, he knew being around her, day in and day out for an entire month, could take him on a return trip to heartbreak. He'd been young the last time she'd walked away from him. He'd dealt with the pain and disillusionment by putting all his energy, hopes, and dreams into rodeo competition. It had kept him on the road a good portion of the year. He'd slept with so many buckle bunnies that he couldn't remember their faces from one night to the next. It had been the worst period of his life, and he wasn't proud of the way he'd handled any of it, but at least he had survived. He was too damned old for that kind of nonsense now, though. Too worn out. Too close to the finish line. If he let Vickie back into his life and she left him again, he might never recover.

He finally turned to look at her, and what he saw turned his blood as hot as a solder iron. Pistol was at her feet. No, not just at her feet. The damned dog was wiggling around on his back, begging for a tummy rub. Pistol bared his belly to no one, absolutely *no one*, except Slade. In canine language, it was a sign of surrender and absolute trust. Pistol was fond of Wyatt, Tex, and Kennedy, and the dog was a love hog when it came to petting, but he had never assumed that position with any of them.

"Damn it," Slade said under his breath. "She's trying to steal my dog!"

* * *

Hips resting against the front fender of her Nissan, Vickie stood in the shade of a pine tree. Slade's dog had decided to curl up on her feet to take a nap, and her right ankle was going numb. She was texting back and forth with Nancy, who was beside herself with anger. Even her typed words looked pissed off, with capitals and quotation marks to accentuate them. Vickie had the absurd feeling that they might morph from mere letters into shouts that exploded into the mountain air. She kept wanting to warn Nancy to keep her voice down.

"If he won't set aside a few minutes to talk with you, just yell the truth at the top of your lungs. Embarrass the hell out of him! DEADBEAT DAD!"

Vickie clenched her teeth. It was always so easy for people on the sidelines to coach the actual players. Nancy wasn't present, and she hadn't seen the deadly calm in Slade's expression. He was a proud man, and a stubborn one. Vickie wasn't certain how to handle him, but she *was* certain that embarrassing him wasn't the wisest tactic.

"I won't leave without confronting him about Brody," she messaged back. *"I promise you that. But he's talking with his employees now. I'll wait for the right moment."*

After pressing send, Vickie pictured her daughter tapping her cell phone keyboard at the speed of light. Then her phone pinged, and Nancy's reply popped up. *"The right moment was forty-one years ago when you sent him four letters to tell him about Brody. HE'S the* one who blew it, the one who never replied. You owe him NOTHING. He deserves to be embarrassed."

Vickie thought for a moment before typing a reply. *"I got a weird feeling while talking to him. Like maybe he doesn't know about Brody. I don't know how that could be. But what if those letters never reached him?"*

It seemed to Vickie that she'd no sooner sent her text than her phone pinged again. *"FOUR letters, Mom? Give me a break."*

"Maybe I made a mistake on the address," Vickie wrote.

"It's a small town. He grew up there. Everyone knows him, and everyone knows where he lives. He got the letters unless you had a total brain fart and sent them to the wrong town."

Vickie knew she hadn't messed up on the address. She'd known it by heart then and still did now. And she was absolutely certain that she had sent all four letters to the correct town. Mystic Creek was her *home*, the place where she'd been born, where she'd grown up. She'd never lived anywhere else except for Coos Bay. *"No brain fart."*

"Then he got the letters!"

Vickie agreed with her daughter. She believed that Slade had received the letters and had chosen to ignore Brody's existence. What other reasonable explanation was there? She was about to message Nancy back when she heard footsteps approaching. The dog pushed up on its front legs and whacked its plumed tail on the ground, sending pine needles and reddish dust airborne. She glanced up to see Slade walking toward her. She powered down her phone and pushed it into her pocket. Then she tried to collect herself. Seeing Slade again was difficult. Meeting his gaze was even harder. His gray eyes seemed to penetrate more deeply than that of other men. He made her feel naked and vulnerable.

"Have you carved out some time to talk to me about that unfinished business?" she asked as he drew up about three feet away from her.

"The only unfinished business you and I have is at the top of that mountain," he retorted. "We've got a camp to set up."

Vickie ran his words through her mind twice, half-convinced she'd misunderstood him. "You mean you've changed your mind about letting me work for you?"

He hooked his thumbs over his hand-tooled belt, which sported an elaborate championship buckle, a common accessory in Mystic Creek among men who were or once had been rodeo stars. "I need a cook, Vickie. And it's a little late in the game for me to find someone else."

His change of heart had Vickie scrambling to regroup. If she was going up to base camp, she'd have plenty of time later to confront him about Brody. "All right." That was all she could think to say. "I'm in."

"Then hop to. We've got horses to unload. Packs to balance. Last-minute inventory to take." He pivoted on one heel and struck off toward his horse trailer. Over his shoulder, he said, "You know the drill." Then he stopped, shot a smoldering look over his shoulder at the dog, whose butt now anchored Vickie's left foot to the ground, and said, "What the hell, Pistol? Get your sorry ass over here!"

The dog whined, gave Vickie a worshipful look, and then loped over to his master. Slade settled a big hand on the top of the animal's black head, administered one pat, and then turned to keep walking.

"Just one question!" Vickie called after him. "What made you change your mind about hiring me?"

He halted midstride and swung around to look at her again. "I'm desperate." He slid his gaze slowly downward, his look lingering on parts of her body during the descent. "You're a little long in the tooth for the job. Men who pay top dollar for a guided hunt enjoy having a beautiful young woman prepare their food. But that's the breaks. The only young and pretty applicant looked like a motorcycle mama. Tattoos. A nose ring. Safety pins in her eyebrows." His firm mouth twisted into a half grin. "She looked damned good in black leather, though."

Vickie felt as if he'd slugged her in the solar plexus, but she popped back with, "I'm like fine wine. I get better and better with age."

"We'll see how you hold up. It's a lot of heavy work, and you're no spring chicken anymore."

Vickie was more than willing to work. She just couldn't believe he'd taken a jab at her about her age, or that he'd changed his mind so suddenly about hiring her. As she recalled, Slade had never been a waffler. Once he made a decision, he rarely second-guessed himself. Fortunately for her, his sudden change of heart would certainly facilitate her purposes better. She could earn good wages until midway through the last week of the season and then confront him about Brody. All hell would break loose then, but she wouldn't care. She'd cull what she could out of her duffel, sling it over her shoulder, and walk back to the trailhead, grinning every step of the way because she'd be leaving him in a terrible bind without a cook.

Chapter Seven

Wyatt normally enjoyed shopping for base camp supplies. All perishables had to be purchased and stowed away in collapsible coolers to be transported up the mountain, where they would then be kept chilled with blocks of ice taken in that day by the pack train. But he was running too far behind this evening to take any pleasure in the process. He just wanted to get done, transport his horses to the trailhead, and take off. As it stood, he wouldn't reach camp until well after dark, and then he'd have to unload the groceries. At least his tent was already up, and his bed awaited him. He wouldn't be stumbling around in the dark trying to erect a shelter.

At checkout, he had the misfortune of getting in line at Bernice Kaley's register. Most of the younger guys in Mystic Creek laughed at her behind her back, because she flirted outrageously with them and seemed to hope she'd get lucky sooner or later. She was pushing seventy, but she still dyed her hair as black as a raven wing and wore it on top of her head in a weird, cone-shaped thing. Little sparkly things decorated it, and during the Christmas season, she wore flashers, which made her look as if she wore a discolored tree as her crowning glory. He wished he could stare at those hair doodads instead of her face, which was buried under so much makeup it cracked when she smiled. She seemed like a nice lady with a good heart, but that didn't mean he could picture himself in bed with her, and she didn't leave him with any doubt in his mind that that was what she wanted. He no longer engaged in physical intimacy, not even with women close to his own age. Nohow, no way.

"Hello, Wyatt!" she said in greeting. "My, my, but you're a handsome one!"

Wyatt read her lips and wished he hadn't. She wasn't just coming on to him. He felt like a bowling pin in the path of a wrecking ball. How did a guy give an old lady the brush-off? He'd been raised to respect his elders, and there was no polite way to tell a female you weren't interested. "Good to see you, Bernice. Only I thought you worked at Charlie's Sporting Goods."

"Your memory is spot-on. I did work at Charlie's." Her smile blinked out and then came back on again. She shrugged and added, "Charlie had to let me go."

"Didn't you work there a long time? Like, for years?"

She nodded and batted her eyelashes, which were fake and reminded him of little black hearth brooms. His eyelids felt droopy just from looking at them. "Yes," she lamented. "It was sad to leave."

He wondered if Charlie had been forced to fire her because she couldn't leave the male patrons alone. She redefined the term *cougar*. Maybe she had an over-abundance of female hormones. All he knew was that he couldn't wait to get away from her, so he helped bag his purchases and put them in the cart.

"So . . . what are your plans for tonight?" she asked. "I'm going to watch college football. Are you a U of O fan?"

Wyatt shook his head. "I'm not into football."

"Oh, well, we could always watch a movie . . . or find some other way to enjoy the evening."

"I won't even be in town. I'm heading up Strawberry Hill to Slade Wilder's base camp. Won't be around much for the next month." And, oh, how glad he was to have a legitimate reason to decline. He sensed that she was lonely—and he didn't want to hurt her feelings. "Maybe you should go to one of the bars. A lot of them have televisions, and people go there to watch Monday night games." With any luck, maybe she'd meet someone. "It's a fun way to enjoy college sports, and most times everyone in the room is a U of O fan. Not always, though. Sometimes Beavers fans invade and try to start trouble. But that only makes it more interesting."

She offered him a smile, which was no longer syrupy with flirtatiousness. "Maybe I will. My husband's been gone for over five years now, but the silence of the house still gets to me. It's hard when you lose your other half. Not so bad during the day, but at night you feel lost."

Wyatt hadn't known about her husband, but it explained her apparent loneliness. It also made him feel even worse for her. He thought of Tex, who was about her age, maybe a little older. He still had a fire in his oven. He might think Bernie was a hot commodity. If Wyatt could remember, he would mention to Tex that he might find some female company if he started shopping at Flagg's Market regularly.

Eager to put as much distance between himself and Bernie as possible, Wyatt paid the tab, grabbed the full cart, and almost ran for the door. Just as he got outside, his phone vibrated in his shirt pocket. He suspected that Slade had sent him a text to pick up something he'd forgotten to put on the shopping list. So he parked his cart against the front of the building, grabbed his cell, and swiped the screen.

"Hi. This may sound a little crazy, but we got off to such a bad start that I got you a little gift as a peace offering. Still don't have my work schedule ironed out, so I can't deliver it to you. But I spoke to Blackie at the pawn shop, and he's hiking the mountain tomorrow. He's going to put the package—just a small one—in the supply box where the two trails intersect. If you can't pick it up right away, no worries. Not perishable."

Wyatt frowned. Who in the hell was this? Deputy De Laney, possibly? She claimed to have scheduling problems at work. The number couldn't be in his contacts, because the name of the sender didn't show on his screen. Just then his phone vibrated again. He read the next message. *"Oops! Sorry. This is Erin."*

Wyatt smiled slightly. They'd gotten off to a bad start, all right. Because of the way she'd treated her uncle, he'd been determined not to like her. But something about her was starting to grow on him. That said, he would have very little spare time over the next few days, and going six miles back down the mountain to get a package might never happen.

He texted back. *"Glad it's not perishable. It may be days before I ride back down the trail. But thanks for thinking of me."*

His phone hummed again. *"Fresh start?"*

His smile deepened. *"You're the one with a messed-up face. If you're game, I am."*

By the time Vickie was able to dismount at Slade's base camp, it was almost dark, and she was exhausted and saddle sore. The men swung off their horses and immediately set to work, removing bundles from the backs of the pack animals, tethering equines to the high lines, hauling buckets of water up from the nearby creek to fill water troughs, and then sorting through the loads to carry one thing here and another thing there. Without any direction, she found the cookshack, which was a gigantic wall tent into which a wooden floor had been inserted. Although dusk hadn't yet surrendered completely to darkness, the interior of the shelter was filled with shadows.

Using a penlight she carried in her pocket, she took stock of what would soon be her kitchen. To one side sat a long plank table with individual folding camp stools arranged around it. Then she spotted a few over-size cans of chili sitting on makeshift shelving, but other than that, all the open storage space was bare. Against another wall, large plastic totes were stacked higher than her head. At the rear of the tent she saw a six-burner propane stove, a fiberglass sink with legs, a long, rectangular table which she assumed would be her workstation, and a lidded trash can with nothing in it, not even a liner.

She resisted the urge to groan, find a seat, and hold her head in her hands. What if Slade expected her to cook tonight? And if he did, how in the world would she manage without a halfway organized kitchen? She whirled to leave the enclosure, only to run face-first into a rock-hard surface. With an *umph* of expelled breath, she planted her palms against the barrier and simultaneously felt a man's hands curl over her shoulders. *Slade's hands.* She recognized the breadth of them, the strength in them, and the warmth that radiated from them through her flannel overshirt, which had proven to be pathetically inadequate to ward off the chill of the mountain air.

"You okay? I should have said something when I started to come in."

Vickie wanted to tell him she *wasn't* okay, that his camp was a jumbled mess, and that he was dreaming if he thought she could cook a meal tonight. But mostly she just wanted to kick him for having said earlier that she was too long in the tooth to be eye candy for his male guests. "I'm fine," she pushed out. "But I can't say the same for this cookshack."

He sighed and cast his gaze over the interior behind her. "I'm sorry about this. My foreman, Wyatt, was supposed to get it all set up this afternoon, but he got held up by an urgent situation in town. He's still riding up the mountain."

Setting her away from him, he removed his hands from her shoulders. "Don't worry about cooking tonight or in the morning. We'll heat that chili up over an open fire for dinner and breakfast, be happy with sandwiches tomorrow for lunch, and maybe we'll have all of this shipshape by late afternoon so you can put a meal on the table tomorrow night."

Relieved that he didn't expect her to cook right away on a stove that wasn't even hooked up to propane yet, she relaxed her shoulders. "Mama used to stay at camp at least two days to get her kitchen organized. While she did that, Daddy scouted for wild game and then went back to be with her at night."

She saw his lips curve into a sad smile. "How are your folks? Are they still with us?"

"Oh, yes. Getting up there, but aside from a few little things, they have no serious health issues yet. My dad turns eighty-four next month. My mom is only two years younger."

"Good people," he said softly. "They sure know how to circle the wagons, though."

She cocked her head to see his face, wishing he'd

take that darned hat off. Maybe he really had gotten thin on top, and he was embarrassed to be seen without it on. "What do you mean, circle the wagons?"

"In the olden days on wagon trains, men circled the wagons to protect the women and children from Indian attacks. It's just a saying now, and metaphorically speaking, your parents circled the wagons to protect *you*." He stepped past her to grab three of the huge cans of chili. "When you left, they wouldn't breathe a word to me of your whereabouts. I remembered that you had an uncle who lived in—was it Grants Pass?— and got his phone number from information, but he wouldn't tell me anything, either."

Her heart gave a painful twist. "You tried to find me?" She hated the incredulous note that laced her voice. "I never knew."

He turned toward her, his arms locked around what would soon be dinner for everyone in camp. "Of course I tried to find you." The hat brim concealed his upper face with shadow. "I know now that it was only puppy love, but at the time, I was still young and foolish enough to believe what we felt was the real deal. About six months later, I ran up a huge phone bill, calling information in different towns to see if you had a phone number listed. My father was so pissed."

Vickie barely heard the last of what he said. *Puppy love.* Those two words cut into her like a well-honed butcher knife. She was older and wiser now, and she *still* loved him. What the hell would he call that, geriatric love? Only she didn't have the courage to ask.

Didn't want him to know, or even suspect, that she still had feelings for him. "Yeah," she said. "I thought it was the real deal, too. But it wasn't. We both moved on, grew up, and"—she broke off, nibbled her bottom lip, and finished with—"lived our separate lives." She hugged her waist, mainly because she felt as if her insides were shattering like fragile glass, but she shivered to make him think she was reacting to the chilly temperatures. "You did both of us a favor that night at your bachelor party." She forced out a laugh. "You weren't ready to settle down, and neither was I. Your infidelity with April Pierce was a wake-up call for both of us."

With that, Vickie left the tent.

Slade swallowed back the denial that tried to spring to his lips. He wanted to yell, "I never slept with that girl!" But, hey, she'd already buried that hatchet, and it would be madness for him to try to defend himself again. She hadn't believed him then, and she wouldn't now. At the time, he'd believed that Vickie would come to her senses and realize he would never lie to her about something so serious. They'd been painfully honest with each other about everything else. He'd shared his deepest and darkest secrets with her, and she had shared hers with him. He'd confessed to her his wrongdoings of the past, and she had confessed hers. They'd laughed together and cried together. The night that his beloved old dog died, he'd wept in her arms like a child, and she'd held him as spasms of grief rocked his whole body. There had been no pretense between them. No holding back parts of themselves. She'd been his everything, and until she'd thrown her engagement ring at his feet, he'd believed he was her everything, too.

"Son of a bitch," he whispered. "Some things never change. After all this time, she's still pissed because she thinks I screwed April Pierce." He shifted the cans in his arms to get a better hold before he followed Vickie from the tent. Then he nearly did a face-plant because he tripped over Pistol, who had decided to lie just outside the tent flap. As he staggered around in the dark to catch his balance, he grumbled, "I didn't even *like* April. She was a twit then, she's still a twit now, and she'll always be a twit. The least Vickie could do is give me credit for having halfway decent taste."

Slade headed toward the area where they normally built the central fire. He found Rex and Dale repairing the rock ring that they'd left intact last autumn when they broke camp. John and another man were hauling over armloads of firewood, which Wyatt had cut, split, and stacked when he'd been on the mountain alone a few days back.

"Glad you boys are on top of this." Slade deposited the cans of chili on the ground near the rocks. "It's going to get nippy tonight, and we don't have the tin-can stoves set up in any of the tents yet. We can warm ourselves toasty by the fire before we head for our bed-rolls."

Using his fingers, Rex dug a shallow depression in

the dirt to seat a rock. Apparently Pistol thought that looked like fun, because he began to dig nearby, making the men chuckle. "We might should get a tin-can stove set up in the lady's tent, though, boss," Rex mused aloud. "Along about midnight, it'll be cold enough to frost our whiskers. We can handle it, but she's not as tough as we are."

Slade could have argued that point. Vickie looked delicate, but she could rough it with the best of them. On the other hand, she didn't have much meat on her bones, and a banked fire in a tin-can stove would keep her tent warm and cozy all night. "Good idea, Rex." He glanced down at Dale. "Maybe you can take care of that."

Dale lifted his blond head. "I don't mind doing it, but what the hell's a tin-can stove?"

John laughed. "You were here last year. They're those little woodstoves Slade bought to go in all the tents. You made a fire in yours as many times as I did."

Dale shrugged. "Those look like regular woodstoves, except they're a lot smaller. Don't look anything like a can."

"Yeah, well," John tossed back. "They're little, they're flimsy, and we just call them tin cans."

"That supper?" Dale asked, glancing at the chili.

"And breakfast," Slade confirmed. "There's more. I figured this would do us for tonight. Does anybody know what tote the paper plates and plastic spoons are in?"

Rex stood and brushed his hands clean on his jeans.

"Nope, but I'll go find them. I sure as hell don't want to be hauling more water to do dishes before we can turn in."

Slade looked around for Vickie. "Where's our cook?"

John gestured over his shoulder. "She went that way."

Slade peered through the darkness and saw a pin-point of light bouncing around near the woodpile. He had no idea what Vickie was doing, and he told himself he wouldn't walk over there to find out. She had grown up in these mountains and knew how to take care of herself. She didn't need him to look after her. But he felt his feet carrying him in that direction anyway. He felt like a dog being led around on a leash.

Vickie nearly jumped out of her skin when Slade spoke from behind her.

"What the Sam Hill are you doing out here?" he asked.

Using her shirtsleeve, she dashed tears from her cheeks before she turned to face him. *Long in the tooth.* It was a saying to describe horses when they grew old, which hadn't been very flattering to her, either.

"I, um—I'm looking for small pieces of wood to use as kindling." That was a complete lie, but she couldn't very well tell him she'd been searching for two limbs with some branches still on them. When he found them at the edge of camp later, he'd know she'd put them there. "I like shavings and little slivers for starting fires. I thought I could find what I need over here where your foreman did all the woodcutting."

He gestured toward a stack behind her. "There's plenty of kindling. Can't you just use it?"

Thinking quickly, she said, "Of course, but I've learned that smaller bits catch easily and get the kindling arranged on top to burn hot a lot faster."

He shrugged. "Well, you're the camp jack. I guess you can start fires however you want." He rubbed beside his nose, a nervous habit of his that she remembered well. "We haven't really gone over your duties. You want to do that tonight?"

Vickie had plans that talking with him would totally screw up. Nancy was waiting for a play-by-play account of the first practical joke later tonight, and she'd be very disappointed if she didn't get a text. "I'm really tired, Slade. Riding up the mountain zapped my energy." Oh, how it galled her to add, "This business of getting long in the tooth isn't for sissies."

In the darkness and with that hat casting his face into deep shadow, she couldn't read his expression, but she did hear him chuckle. "Ah. That got to you, did it?"

Vickie hugged her waist. "Not really. At this age, I roll with the punches."

"You're not *that* old."

She'd always loved it when he walked right into a good comeuppance. "I like to think that, and as I drove over from the coast this morning, I had myself almost convinced. But then I saw you."

"Ouch."

She smiled sweetly, which might have been lost on him because it was dark. But it felt good, anyway. "Oh!" she cried, lacing her tone with fake concern. "I'm sorry. I didn't mean it *that* way. You're not *old*, Slade. You're just—well seasoned."

He cleared his throat. "Is this how we're going to play this? Every time we see each other, exchange insults? It's sort of juvenile, don't you think?"

"You started it," she said.

"I did not."

"Did, too."

"I did *not*. You took the first shot, implying that I wear a hat to hide my *bald* pate."

"Oh." Vickie did remember saying that. She'd been steamed because he meant to send her away and he'd flatly refused to set aside a tiny bit of his precious time to discuss their son with her. He had to know what the *unfinished business* was that she wanted to hash out with him. "Well, the thought did enter my mind that you might be bald. Apparently that Stetson is affixed to your head with superglue."

"It is not." He swept the hat off, bent forward, and swept his hand back and forth over the top of his head. "See that? *Hair.* It may go white eventually, but it'll never fall out. Wilder men don't go bald."

"Sorry. It's so dark I can't see."

"Your night vision was always great."

"Yes, well, everything starts going to hell at sixty,

and it's all downhill from there. I can't see as well as I once could."

"Well, damn it, reach out and feel, then."

Vickie knotted her hands into fists to stop herself from touching him. And the truth was, she could see just fine. Once her eyes adjusted, she could see pretty well even on a moonless night. "I'll pass and just take your word for it."

He straightened and clamped the Stetson back on his head. "So *there*. I haven't gone bald."

Pistol found them just then. He leaned against Slade's leg for a moment and then crossed over to Vickie and lay down on her feet. Vickie wasn't sure why the canine had taken such a shine to her, but it pleased her, mostly because she could tell that it pissed Slade off.

"He's a treasure," she said. "I really miss having a dog."

"Why don't you get one, then, and leave mine alone?"

He was so easy. She'd almost forgotten how much fun it could be to needle him. "It's the age thing again, I'm afraid. The average life span of a dog is about twelve years. I worry about getting a pup. It might out-live me."

"That's nonsense. You think you might kick the bucket and never reach seventy-four?"

It was comforting to know that he remembered how old she was. "I turn sixty-three in December."

"Seventy-five, then. It's silly not to have a dog if you

want one. You'll still be going strong at that age. Look at your parents. They're still kicking. Besides that, you've got kids. If something happens to you, the dog will have a good home."

Her body stiffened. She had personally informed him of Brody's existence, but she'd said nothing to him about her other two children. Yet he somehow knew she had more than one child. Had he been keeping tabs on her?

"I'm the one who has to worry about that if anybody does," he said. "I've got no kid standing in the wings to look after Pistol if something happens to me. He'll be on his own unless one of my employees takes him."

Vickie's eyes burned with unshed tears. How could he stand there and act as if his own son didn't exist? Never had she wanted so badly to slap a man's face. Not even Matt, at his very worst, had incited such anger within her. Well, she had wanted to kill him the night he'd beaten Brody, but that had been a cold, blood-chilling rage that had come over her then. What she felt now was scalding hot, an anger that made her want to burst into tears, call him names, and rip his eyes out.

"You rotten son of a bitch!" She hurled the words at him. "You rotten, low-down, heartless son of a bitch!"

He gave her an incredulous look. "What?"

"You heard me. You want to play games, Slade? Fine by me. But fair warning. You're *way* out of your league."

Vickie jerked her feet out from under the dog, wheeled

away, and started toward camp. The men had gotten the fire going. It flared bright orange and gold in the darkness, flames leaping toward the sky that created a beacon to guide her, but she didn't really need one. She'd grown up in these mountains and had learned how to find her way in the dark as a small child. In the fall, her father's base camp had been like a second home to her. Her parents had taken her out of school, and she'd done her lessons at the table in the cook-shack after her mother cleared away breakfast. By the time lunch was ready to be served, she'd had all her assignments done, and she'd spent the remainder of every day running wild in the surrounding woods.

Vickie intended to bypass the fire and take up squatting rights in a tent of her choosing, but a young fellow with blond hair saw her and called out, "Ma'am?"

Vickie was shaking, and she really didn't want him to see how upset she was. Unfortunately, she didn't have much choice. She stopped and turned as he walked toward her. "Yes?"

"I got a tin-can stove set up for you in a tent. If you don't mind, I'll show you the way."

Vickie struggled to tamp down her anger. "That's kind of you."

He drew up and stuck out his hand. "Name's Dale."

She grasped his fingers and let him pump her arm up and down. "Victoria Brown. Vickie, for short, if you prefer to call me that."

"Good to meet you."

He motioned for her to follow him and led the way

to a tent. As they grew closer, she saw that the canvas walls were faintly illuminated.

"I lighted a lantern for you. Rex found your duffel bag, so I carried it over. I also brought what I thought was your bedroll. None of us ever bring one. The boss supplies all the cots and bedding. But feel free to use your own if you want."

She wanted. Sleeping bags rarely got taken to a laundry because dry cleaning cost more than they were worth. To her, there was little more disgusting than the thought of using a bag that some man had slept in last year when he hadn't taken a bath in days. Most men reverted back to childhood in a hunting camp and let their hygiene go. Normally their wives stayed at home, and they could get as dirty as they liked. No reminders to shave. No reason to brush their teeth. For a few days, they could pretend to be a mountaineer and were as happy as clams when they began to stink like one. Vickie believed that the primary reason so many wealthy professionals paid so much to rough it in a wilderness area was because the entire experience was a departure from their reality. For a whole week, they could be *real* men who stood around a campfire at night to drink beer, fart, and scratch their balls whenever they wanted.

Dale swept aside the door flap and then stood back so she could enter the enclosure. He'd set up a cot for her. A fire had already been started in the little stove to chase away the chill. Her things had been dumped on the dirt floor along one canvas wall. Dale stepped inside behind her. The lantern hung from an aluminum ceiling support. He reached over her head to turn up the wick so there would be more light.

"This is so thoughtful," she told him, sincerely meaning it. "I figured I'd have to set this all up myself. Thank you so much."

He was a handsome young fellow with blue eyes and a friendly grin. Fair skinned, he had an overabundance of freckles, but he had even features and nice ears that lay flat against his head. Vickie always noticed ears. When her babies had been born, she'd looked at their ears before she even counted their fingers and toes. She hadn't wanted her children to have teacup handles poking out from the sides of their heads.

"You're the cook, the most important person in camp," he said with a smile. "If you need anything else, don't hesitate to ask."

"That's very kind." Vickie stepped closer to the stove. She hadn't gotten her coat out of her duffel, and the cold night air cut through her flannel shirt as if it were tissue thin. She chafed her hands and smiled at him. "And one good turn deserves another. What's your favorite goodie? Are you into cookies, brownies, pies, cobblers, or cakes?"

His eyes widened. "I like it all, but unfortunately, pie is my absolute favorite."

"Why is that unfortunate?"

"Because nobody's going to make pie out here. It'd be—well, a heap of work."

Vickie laughed. "I love to cook, Dale, and I'll be

happy to make you a pie. It may be a challenge to make your favorite kind until I can get the right filling ingredients." She narrowed an eye at him. "Let me guess. You an apple pie man?"

"I've never met a pie I didn't like, so, yeah, but apple's not my favorite."

"What is?"

He leaned a bit closer and lowered his voice to say, "Pecan."

She made a mental note to put pecans and syrup on her list when someone went down the mountain for more supplies. "Once I get my kitchen organized, I'll make some pies. Maybe not pecan right away, but I'll come up with something."

He winked. "I love you already."

Vickie was still smiling when he exited the tent. Then she allowed her anger to ramp up again. Slade had crossed over a line with her tonight. Brody was a handsome, hardworking, and loyal man. Any father would be proud to call him son.

Except, of course, Slade Wilder.

She crouched over her duffel bag and unzipped it. The items she needed lay on top because she'd bought them just that morning. Another smile curved her lips. *Let the games begin.* Nancy had been right all along. Slade might never willingly acknowledge Brody. Her decision to come here would probably accomplish nothing. But revenge could be sweet, and she intended to get some.

Chapter Eight

Slade heated the three gallons of chili right in the cans by setting the metal containers directly on a bed of hot coals and stirring often. The men fanned out circularly on both sides of him where he crouched by the fire. They all sipped a beer while they warmed themselves by the flames and talked with great enthusiasm about nothing all that important. The conversation drifted from one topic to another. Slade pretended to listen. Occasionally he made a comment. But mostly he just stirred the contents of the cans and puzzled over Vickie's outburst by the woodpile. He kept going back over their exchange, and he was still just as bewildered as he'd been when she first started screaming at him. *Women.* He would never understand them. He and Vickie had been talking about dogs, their own longevity, and whether people their age should get a pup. They hadn't been slinging insults at each other. He'd said nothing mean. And all of a sudden, she'd grown so angry that he'd half expected her to physically attack him. What the hell was her problem?

When she showed up at the central fire, she sandwiched herself between two men and stood across the pit from him. She was such a slender slip of a woman that the contrast between her fragility and their bulk made his protective side surface. The top of her head barely cleared Dale's shoulder, and Rex loomed over her on the opposite side, looking as stout as an old-growth stump. Slade trusted his employees. They were all good guys and had been unfailingly respectful around Cheyenne during seasons past. Unfortunately he couldn't say the same about all the paying guests. Sometimes they were pleasures to have around and sometimes not, men who were temporarily out of their own zip code area and seemed to think that gave them license to be wild and woolly for a week. The thought of anyone following Vickie into the woods and getting out of line with her sent Slade's blood pressure rocketing off the charts.

"Hey, boss?"

John's voice. Slade didn't look up. "What?"

"You stirring that chili, or are you fixing to kill it?"

Slade realized he was getting a little too forceful with the damned spoon and was slopping beans over the sides of the cans. *Shit.* All his instincts had told him not to hire Vickie. The whole situation had "trouble" written all over it, and now, when they hadn't even gotten their base camp set up properly, his tail was already tied in a knot.

Pistol pushed in beside Slade and tried to grab a stray bean that had landed on a firebreak rock. Slade thought nothing of it—until the dog yelped and started whirling in circles.

"Aw, *shit*!" Dale cried. "He burned his nose."

Slade dropped the spoon and ran after his dog. Catching said dog was the challenge. Pistol seemed to think something was chasing him—something other than Slade. He whipped. He flipped. He ran in frenzied circles like a pup chasing its tail. Slade had no idea how bad the burn might be, but he knew treating it quickly would be necessary to prevent blisters.

Vickie leaped into the fray, and unlike Slade, who was still on his feet, she executed an admirable version of a home base slide on her knees, which enabled her to grab one of Pistol's back legs. The dog lost his balance and landed on his back.

"Ice!" Vickie yelled. "A wet rag! Hurry!"

Slade knelt across from her, the whining dog between them. Men scattered like ants to respond to Vickie's request. Rex returned first and slapped a wet cloth into her hand. Someone else brought a chunk of ice. She wasted no time in applying the compress to Pistol's burn. In mid-yelp, the dog quieted and began to emit mournful whimpers.

"It's okay, sweetie," Vickie crooned. "That feels good. Doesn't it? Yes, it does. Just lie still. We'll make it all better." She glanced up at Rex. "I need a good burn salve with an analgesic."

Pistol whimpered but didn't try to wiggle away. The ice-cold cloth was numbing the pain. With a shudder, he relaxed, allowing Vickie to keep the compress on his nose. She met Slade's gaze. "In a second, it'll get so cold that it'll start to hurt him. That'll be our cue to stop. We'll know we've drawn out what heat we can. Hopefully it'll keep the burn from going any deeper."

Slade knew all that. Being a full-time rancher and a seasonal outfitter, he had to treat accidental injuries on a fairly frequent basis, and he did a lot of reading to stay abreast of the newest and supposedly best remedies. Recent studies recommended a steady stream of cool water over a burn for twenty minutes as the best treatment, but out in the middle of nowhere, they had no faucet nor an endless supply of stored water. Going with a wet cloth and ice was the next best alternative.

John arrived with an analgesic ointment. Vickie removed the compress and gently applied the petroleum-based medication to Pistol's nose. The dog pushed with his feet to move closer to her and soon had his shoulders and head draped over her lap. Memories drifted through Slade's mind. Vickie had always had a way with animals, domestic or wild, and he could only smile as he watched her now, comforting Pistol with crooning whispers and soothing strokes. The dog had taken an instant liking to her that afternoon, and now he seemed to trust her. It was irksome, and Slade wanted to resent the friendship that Vickie was so quickly forging with his furry friend, but he knew when he could win a battle and when he couldn't. Vickie sent out signals of some kind to creatures, and they were instinctively drawn to her. He could no more stop that than he could the gravitational pull of the moon from controlling the ocean tides.

She lifted her luminous gaze to his again. Maybe it was the flattering cast of the fire shine on her face and hair—or maybe it was a glow that radiated from someplace within her—but in that moment, which seemed much longer than it actually was, she was, hands down, the most beautiful woman he'd ever seen. Her eyes caught the light like a prism, refracting the color of her irises into a fascinating spectrum of green and gold. Her skin shimmered like a pale pink fire opal. His fingertips tingled with an urge to trace the defined angle of her jaw, which was, he knew, so very fragile compared to his own that he'd always wanted to wrap her in cotton batting. Some things, and to him, Vickie was one of them, were too lovely and precious and rare to put them at risk of being broken.

Earlier in the day, he'd been terrified by the thought of spending time with her. Terrified that she would step back into his world, fill it with the magic only she could bring, and then break his heart again by walking away. Only now, gazing at her unforgettable countenance, he understood that his heart had never healed and, judging by the chasm of emptiness he felt inside him, he knew it never would. Over the years, he'd tried to fall in love again. He'd dated, enjoyed some great sex, and even signed on a couple of times for a longterm relationship, but in the end, he'd done the talking and his boots had done the walking, because he could never find that same special feeling of magic with any other woman.

She owned him, heart and soul. She always had, and she always would, and after forty-one years of trying to live without her, he accepted that there was absolutely nothing he could do about that. He'd been only seven years old when he first clapped eyes on her, a tiny little girl in homemade jeans and a T-shirt, the only big things about her being her hair and eyes. Her mother had tried to tame her curls by plaiting them into pigtails, but fiery tendrils had resisted capture and sprung in all directions from her head like dozens of corkscrews. Slade knew he'd been far too young back then to fall in love, but as inexplicable as it was, he somehow had, and he'd been under her spell ever since.

"He's a wonderful dog," she said softly. "What's his breed? If I change my mind about getting a pup, I wouldn't mind having one just like him."

"He's just a mutt," Slade told her. "A little of this and a little of that. Jack Palmer says he's part Rottweiler, part Australian shepherd, and possibly part border collie."

"Jack Palmer? I don't remember him."

"New vet in town. Well, new to you, anyway. He's been here a long time, eight years, maybe ten. Good man, great doctor."

She continued to glide her hands over Pistol's fur, and the canine appeared to be sound asleep. "After losing Renegade, you said you'd never get another dog. I'm glad you didn't keep that vow."

Slade leaned forward to pet the animal, and Pistol whined as if to acknowledge his touch. "I didn't have much to say about it, actually. He appeared on my porch, the skinniest, filthiest, and most matted excuse for a dog that you've ever seen. I didn't want him. Decided I'd call Animal Control. But in the end, I just couldn't do it. Now I wouldn't change that for anything. He's a great dog, one of the best."

"Do you still miss Renny?" she asked.

Slade made another pass with his hand over Pistol's side. "For years, I did. He left a huge hole in my life and hundreds of wonderful memories." He looked into her shimmering green eyes. "I held those memories close. Sometimes that's all we have left, the memories."

She nodded and her eyes grew suspiciously bright. "Has Pistol filled up that huge hole Renny left inside you?"

"No. That would be saying that he replaced Renny, and that isn't true. Dogs are very like people, special in their own way and absolutely unique in looks and personality. No other dog can ever take Renegade's place." He forced a smile. "Pistol took my world by storm, and he's wallowing out his own hole in my heart. If I outlive him, I'll one day bury him next to Renny under the old oak tree, and I'll feel like I'm going to die of grief. But I won't, because life isn't that easy."

"No," she agreed, carefully lifting the dog's head from her knees onto the ground. "Nothing about life is easy." She met and held his gaze. "Nothing about love is easy, either."

* * *

Vickie was so edgy that she could barely eat any of the chili Slade had served her on a paper plate. Less than fifty yards from the central fire, a pair of glowing green eyes stared at them from the woods, but so far, no one had noticed but her. She tried to think how anyone could *not* notice as she chased beans and clumps of beef with a spoon, scooped up a small bite, and then dumped it out.

"You're not eating much."

Vickie glanced up at Dale, who stood beside her. At any other time, she would have been enjoying the food, the company, and the evening. She'd taken her kids camping often as they were growing up, attempting to expose them to some of the same experiences that she'd had as a child, but they were all adults now, and she hadn't been out in the woods in what felt like forever. The scents alone were intoxicating to her and so long missed that she kept taking deep breaths through her nose to savor them. The sharp, clean smell of pine, the minty traces of sage, a faint sweetness from the abundant growth of manzanita on the hillsides, and the wonderful odor of wood smoke. All of them delighted her. With the bouquet of her childhood surrounding her, she felt as if she'd found heaven on earth, but with those glowing orbs staring at them from the undergrowth beneath the ponderosa pines, she was also experiencing a certain measure of hellish suspense.

"I'm just tired," she told Dale. "It was a long ride

up, and I drove over from the coast this morning as well. It wore me out."

"That does make for a long day," Dale replied. "A good night's rest will set you right."

"I'm sure it will, and thanks to you, I should sleep like a bug in a rug. My tent is so warm and cozy. I expected to be sleeping on the ground, so I'm grateful for the cot. I put my gel mattress pad on top of it and lay down to try it out. It's almost as comfortable as my bed at home."

"Awesome! I should get a gel pad."

A voice boomed from somewhere outside of camp, making Vickie jump with a start. "Hello, camp!"

Dale turned to stare into the darkness and reached high with one hand to wave. "That's Wyatt, Slade's foreman."

Half-blinded by the firelight, Vickie squinted to see. "It looks like three riders, maybe more."

"Wyatt's brother, Kennedy, and Tex," Dale told her. "They're bringing in supplies, mostly food. We'll be stepping pretty until bedtime, getting everything put away."

Vickie almost groaned. She truly was tired and didn't want to be on her feet until the wee hours. Unfortunately, she was the cook, and the arrival of food meant that she would have to be involved in its storage. Otherwise she wouldn't be sure where anything was when it came time for her to cook, and that would be a pain in the neck.

Alerted to the arrival of supplies, the men around

her made fast work of shoveling their plates clean. Flares of bright yellow shot up from the fire as paper dinnerware was tossed, Frisbee-style, into the flames. Pistol, who seemed to have recovered from his burn, gave a glad bark, and an instant later, he was rolling over the ground in playful combat with a gorgeous border collie that someone called Domino. Vickie liked the name, which suited the black and white collie perfectly. Unfortunately, in all the confusion, she doubted that anyone was going to notice the *eyes* that she'd planted at the edge of camp. That was a shame, because her daughter waited on tenterhooks to receive texts about how the prank played out with the men. Vickie anticipated that she'd be sending a very *boring* account. Not even Slade, whom she knew was an extraordinary woodsman, had seen those green orbs.

Laughter tried to bubble up in her throat, because the entire situation struck her as being beyond bizarre. She was surrounded by men who claimed to be professional wilderness guides. They led greenhorns, who trusted them with their lives, into rugged and treacherous terrain, and yet not a man among them was watchful enough to be aware that something big and scary stood in the brush, studying them like a hungry diner did a menu.

The three human newcomers stepped into the fire glow, giving her an opportunity to look them over. Wyatt and Kennedy were tall, strapping young men who greatly resembled each other with their chiseled features, burnished skin, and straight golden hair. Tex, a short, wiry man of about seventy, looked like a dwarf standing between them.

"Dinner is meager tonight, only hot chili," Vickie told them. "We've plenty, though. Would you like me to dish you some up?"

Kennedy grinned at her. "I'm so hungry I could eat the south end of a northbound jackass, but we'll wait to eat until we get the horses taken care of."

Vickie took an instant liking to this young fellow. It wasn't often that someone his age put the needs and comfort of animals before his own. With a last glance toward the woods, where those eyes still shone like green marbles, she tossed her still-laden plate into the fire and walked out to join the men, who were already removing packs from the backs of the horses.

Three hours later, Vickie felt like a dishrag that had been wrung out repeatedly by strong hands. She had no idea what time it was. Her nostalgic musings about Slade had faded completely from her mind. She was so exhausted that she no longer cared about the absolute failure of her practical joke or how long a glow stick lasted. She was done, finished, and going straight to bed.

As she trudged toward her tent, she did remember the green eyes, however, and stopped to look out into the woods and at least admire them one more time before she fell onto her cot and passed out. When she drew to a halt, she stood about twenty feet from the doorway of her shelter. Never having expected to be gone so long, she'd only rolled down the wick of her lantern and hadn't extinguished it, so the canvas walls glowed faintly yellow and reached out into the darkness with fingers of light. With little difficulty, she located those eerie glowing eyes. Even though she'd totally failed in her mission, which had been to give all those men the heebie-jeebies, especially Slade, she patted herself on the back for how realistic they looked. The shape as well as the space between the eyes was almost perfect to make someone believe it was a bear. She grinned and sighed, thinking what a shame it was that all her efforts had gone unnoticed. Sadly, it wasn't a joke she could repeat unless she could find another glow stick in Mystic Creek.

She was about to start walking again when she thought she saw one of the eyes blink. She froze in place. Now the green orbs were just staring at her again, as well they should, because they were fake animal eyes, created with a paper towel roll, a knife, and a party stick. But then, even as she stared, the same eye appeared to blink again. An icy shudder crawled up her spine. *Okay, Vickie, don't be a numskull. There's a light breeze. The bushes may be moving, and if leaves get between you and one of the holes, of course it will look more like a real bear.* Amused at herself for feeling nervous, she started to smile, a gesture that she abandoned when it struck her that the location of the eyes seemed to be slightly off. She'd placed them in an almost direct line with the campfire so the men would be sure to see them, and now she was off to one side of the leaping flames.

She shifted her gaze to the left, saw another set of eyes, and nearly wet her pants. *Shit*. There really *was* a bear standing in the trees, and it wasn't that far away from her. Over her lifetime, Vickie had seen countless black bears in the wild. At around the age of nineteen, she'd even bottle-fed an orphaned cub until her father had found a rescue shelter that would take it. So, she wasn't really afraid of bears, but she did have a very healthy respect for them.

And this bear was behaving oddly. It was in way too close to the camp, apparently had no fear of humans, and—she peered into the blackness—now it was moving toward her. A scream welled in her throat, but rather than waste time allowing it to pierce the night air, she broke into a run for her tent. The moment she dashed inside, she turned to secure the flap, and immediately abandoned the task because a chilling realization slipped past the panic she felt. A rectangle of canvas fastened shut with flimsy ties wouldn't keep a chipmunk out, let alone a black bear.

She scrambled across the small enclosure, jerked open her duffel bag, and began rifling through the contents to find her handgun, a trusty nine-millimeter, which could conceivably drop an adult black bear if the shot was well-placed. As she jerked things from the bag, her hand finally located the weapon, which she had unloaded for safety reasons before leaving Coos Bay. A loaded gun bouncing around in a duffel bag was, in her opinion, a recipe for disaster.

She groped frantically for the zip-up sandwich bag

that she'd put the cartridges in that morning. *Oh, God, oh, God.* Had Nancy forgotten to pack it for her? She could hear the animal outside. Where the hell was her ammo? She heard a low rumble. Then there came a swishing sound as something big and hairy brushed against a canvas wall. *Oh, God, oh, God.* Black bears weren't renowned for harming humans, she reminded herself. Most attacks occurred when people got between a sow and her cubs. So it was highly unlikely that this particular bear would try to enter her tent. The scent of food might tempt one into doing something outrageous, but she had nothing in the shelter that a bear would want.

Then she heard it at the door flap. She twisted around on her knees, clasped the useless gun in her violently shaking hands, and took aim, praying this particular bear knew what weapons were and was afraid of them. Her heart nearly stopped when a huge blond paw pushed through the slit and curled over the panel of canvas. *Blond?* The majority of black bears were dark brown or nearly black. She knew blond ones existed, but in all her years of being in these mountains, she'd never seen one. Was it possible that grizzlies had migrated into eastern and central Oregon? Blond or light brown coloring was more prevalent in that species. She'd been living elsewhere for over forty years. Things changed. Wolves now existed in this state. Why not grizzlies? It wasn't as if she exhaustively read outdoor publications to keep herself informed.

Just then, that side of the flap parted from the canvas

wall, and the massive head of a bear poked through the opening. Vickie took aim with the gun, drew a steady bead, and said, in a tremulous squeak, "Go away, bear. Go away!"

In response, the animal opened its mouth, displaying evil-looking teeth, and roared at her. Vickie pulled the trigger, heard the useless click of the firing mechanism, and wet her pants.

Slade had both boots off and one leg halfway out of his jeans when a piercing scream rent the night air. *Vickie.* She was the only female in camp. His heart jerked and shot up into his throat. *Shit.* Vickie wasn't a screamer. Not like other women he'd known, who saw a mouse or shrew and went into shriek mode, stomping their feet in place, grabbing handfuls of their hair, and pretty much just acting crazy. For Vickie to scream like that, something really bad had to be going down.

He cursed under his breath as he jerked up his britches, forgot to point his toes down, and got his foot stuck in the sheath of denim. *Son of a bitch.* The leg of the jeans wouldn't go up without dragging those five digits backward. Wouldn't pull off without bending them double the other way. *Stuck as tight as a hair in a biscuit.* With a mighty pull upward, he got his foot pushed out and winced at the pain. That was his gouty toe, damn it. Now he'd be hobbling for days.

Zip, snap. He hopped to pull on a boot. Heard another scream. He put the second boot on, grabbed his rifle, a seven-millimeter Remington Mag bolt-action, and lurched out of the tent, his big toe joint shooting pain a mile up his shinbone. Breaking into a run, he realized that Dale had chosen the last tent down the line to serve as Vickie's quarters. That put her smack-dab at the edge of camp with nothing and nobody between her and the wilderness. It also put her too far away from him. *Not good.* He'd reacted to her screams faster than a prairie fire with a tailwind while the younger fellows were still fumbling around to get their pants on. *Screw that.* Vickie's tent needed to be next to his, not so far away that he had to grease the wagon twice before he could reach her.

Even though the screaming had stopped, Slade was still frightened for Vickie's safety. The woman hadn't been raised on concrete. There wasn't much in a montane forest that got her knickers in a twist. If she didn't have a gun, a bear or a cougar might scare the bejesus out of her, but not much else would send her into hysterics. *A bear. Oh, Lord. Had Four Toes already found the camp?* Whenever Slade left the ranch to do guided hunts each fall, it normally took Four Toes four or five days to figure out where he'd gone and follow him. But the bear was older now and a little wiser. Since Slade set up his base camp in pretty much the same location every year, Four Toes might have remembered the way and no longer needed a genius IQ to find him.

Slade sent up a silent prayer that it *was* his bear bedeviling Vickie. At least Four Toes wouldn't hurt her. Well, Slade didn't believe the bear would harm a human, but he was a wild animal. Nobody with half a brain ruled out the possibility that a bear could suddenly go loco. He chose a path well away from the tents. The night had turned as black as truck-stop coffee, and he didn't want to trip over a tie-down peg.

Slade reached Vickie's tent, which was illuminated from within and shone golden in the darkness. With a sweep of his left arm, he pushed back the door flap. He wasn't sure what he expected to see. Vickie's torn and bleeding body, he guessed. He only knew he didn't expect to find Four Toes with his broad rump parked on the dirt floor of the tent and a bottle of ketchup held between his front paws. Vickie, whose face had drained of color and looked sort of gray, huddled at the head of her bed, her slender arms hugging her knees. She watched her uninvited guest with eyes that had turned jade green and looked as round as marbles. A handgun lay on the sleeping bag beside her.

"Four Toes, what the Sam Hill do you think you're doing?" Slade yelled. "Get your fat ass out of here!"

Vickie shot a wondering look at him. "You know this bear?"

Slade had jacked a cartridge into the chamber of his rifle as he was racing to reach her. Now that he knew the ruckus had been caused by Four Toes, he reversed the action, popped the copper casing out onto the floor, and bent over to pick it up. "Oh, yeah. Vickie, meet Four Toes. Four Toes, get your sorry self out of her tent."

The bear's response to that order was a slurping

sound. He'd punched a tooth or claw through the squeeze bottle and, suckling like a baby, was now enjoying what appeared to be a much-needed ketchup fix.

Vickie's shoulders visibly relaxed. "Oh, thank God. I thought he was wild."

"Oh, he's wild, and cantankerous, and the biggest pain in the ass I've ever been cursed with. He was orphaned as a tiny cub. His mama got killed in a rockslide up Flotsam Trail."

A hint of color returned to Vickie's cheeks and mouth. She gave Slade a ghost of a smile. "You rescued a bear cub?"

Slade laid the rifle across the center of her cot.

"She all right?" someone yelled from outside.

"Yes, she's fine," Slade called back. "Four Toes came in for a visit."

A rumble of masculine laughter rang out. "Uh-oh. He's a pain in the butt. Maybe you should try to shoot him again tomorrow."

Vickie sent Slade an appalled look. "Shoot him?"

Slade hollered over his shoulder, "I've got this, guys. You can go back to bed now." He shifted his gaze back to the bear, who now had tomato sauce smeared all over his nose. "And, yes," he said to Vickie. "At least once a week, I try to shoot him."

"But you can't," she finished for him. "Because you raised him from a baby, and you don't have it in you to pull the trigger."

Slade sighed. "Yeah, something like that. But sooner or later, maybe I'll do it. Bottle-feeding him was one of the worst mistakes I've ever made." He settled his gaze on the bear. Then he arched an eyebrow in question. "Why do you have a bottle of ketchup in your tent? That might be what brought him in. Maybe he could smell it."

"Maybe." She didn't immediately answer his question. Then she said, "I'm a ketchup fiend. I didn't know if you kept any in camp, so I bought some."

"I always have ketchup and most other condiments on hand. One reason the cookshack is so far away from the tents is because of bears. If one happens to come in, it'll go for the cookshack and not us. We use bear-proof food containers for a lot of stuff, but once you cook, the smell of food is all over everything, and no matter how careful you are with edibles, a bear may catch the scent."

She watched as Four Toes finished off the ketchup and discarded the now-flattened squeeze bottle. "Now what? Is he going to get mad if I don't give him something more?"

Four Toes swiped at his crimson nose with a paw and belched. Slade stepped over to the tent flap and held it off to one side. Sitting on his ample hindquarters with his back legs sprawled for balance, Four Toes looked far too comfortable and content for Slade's peace of mind. "Out," he ordered.

The bear grumbled, which sounded a lot like growling, but if it frightened Vickie, she did a superb job of hiding it. When Four Toes had vacated the shelter, Slade turned to study her. "I'd like to move your tent closer to mine. Dale shouldn't have put you out here at the end of this row."

"I'm fine now that I know he's your pet. If he comes back, he can sleep on the floor. I draw the line at sharing my bed with him." She settled her gaze on his. "I appreciate your concern about where my tent is positioned, but practically speaking, I think right where I am will work well for me. It'll be quieter here. Not so many men talking all around me and keeping me awake."

"If something happens, you're too far away from me here. The boys were a lot slower to respond when you screamed for help."

She swung her legs over the edge of the cot and stood. "I wouldn't have screamed if I could have found my ammo. From now on, I'll keep my sidearm loaded and be perfectly safe."

Slade knew better than to press the point. The Vickie he'd once known had been hardheaded at times and always fiercely independent. She pushed at a curly tendril of hair that had fallen over her eyes.

"I really appreciate that you came," she told him.

Slade knew a dismissal when he heard one. She wanted him out of her tent. He told himself that he didn't want to be there anyway, but he knew he was lying to himself even as he formed the thought.

"You're more than welcome." He leaned over to pick up the empty squeeze bottle, expecting it to be goopy, but Four Toes had licked it clean. "Sleep tight."

He turned to leave. Just as he reached his exit point, she said, "Slade?"

His heart leaped with hope even though he knew it was stupid of him. She'd made it abundantly clear that she had buried that particular hatchet long ago, and he'd be a fool to think she still had feelings for him. He struggled to school his expression as he turned back toward her so she wouldn't be able to read any of his emotions. "Yes?"

Her gaze clinging to his, she just stood there for a moment, and he really thought she might say something important—like maybe apologize for growing angry and calling him names earlier, or that she'd finagled her way into this job just so she could see him again. Finally she said, "Don't forget your rifle."

Vickie felt far less safe in her tent than she'd let on to Slade. Four Toes was out there somewhere, and she had no guarantee that he wouldn't lumber back into her quarters. She had no more foodstuffs in her duffel that would attract him, only some bottles of hot sauce that were reputed to raise blisters on the tongue and a container of baking powder that was the key ingredient for a ketchup bomb that she hoped would go off right in Slade's face. He loved his ketchup and slathered it over everything at breakfast, even his eggs.

Hopefully, the bear wouldn't be back. Using her penlight, she stepped out of the tent to get some more firewood. The little stove did an excellent job of warming the interior of her tent, and she didn't want the fire to go out during the night. Though it had been more years than she cared to count, she could still remember the shuddering morning cold of the mountain air in late September. It was no fun to crawl out of a toasty sleeping bag to put on ice-cold clothing.

After loading the stove belly with as much wood as it would hold, she sat on the edge of her bed to check her phone messages. There were several from Nancy, all related to the glow-stick prank. Feeling weary, Vickie texted her daughter, explaining that no one had noticed the fake eyes and how the trick had been a complete flop. She decided against telling Nancy about Four Toes' invasion of her tent. Her daughter had never been in a real wilderness area, and she might lose sleep worrying about Vickie's safety if she read about something so alarming right before bedtime. Vickie heard a rustle of movement on the other side of the canvas wall, listened for a moment while holding her breath, and then decided that she would probably be the one who lost sleep, fretting about the bear deciding to return. She'd never been all that afraid of wild black bears, because, for the most part, they tried to avoid humans. But Four Toes wasn't really wild in the strictest sense of the word, and he had no fear of people. While that didn't necessarily make him dangerous, he was a large and extremely powerful animal. Something as simple as a toothache might put him in a grumpy mood.

After digging out her nightclothes, a fleece sweatshirt and sweatpants that would keep her warm even if the fire went out overnight, she turned down the lantern wick until the lamp put off barely any light and then peeled out of her garments. Knowing that even faint illumination might cast her shadow upon a wall, she hurried to get her body covered again. She opted to keep her socks on. They'd serve her well as slippers and keep her feet warm.

Before turning the lantern completely off and climbing into bed, she dug through her duffel one more time to find her new solar charger, which she'd set on the sunny dash of her car that morning while driving over from Coos Bay. After hooking her phone up to it, she doused the light, felt her way to the cot, and groaned with exhaustion as the fluffy sleeping bag enveloped her body. *Out like a light,* she assured herself. If she didn't allow herself to think, she'd be asleep before she could count three sheep.

Only how did a woman turn off her thoughts when her heart was breaking? She punched her pillow with her fist, imagining that her target was Slade's midriff. Right in the solar plexus. Her anger began to resurface. She tried to tamp it down. She told herself that she'd already cried a river of tears over Slade Wilder and wasn't about to shed any more. And, *damn it*, she wanted to turn off the voice of that desperate person inside of her who kept whispering, *Maybe he never got those letters. He wishes he'd had children. There's nothing he wants more in the world than an heir. So why would he so stubbornly refuse to acknowledge Brody?*

Vickie had no answers, and her rational self knew, beyond a shadow of a doubt, that all four of her letters to him in regards to Brody couldn't possibly have been lost in the mail. If anything, the United States Postal Service had been even more dependable back then than it was now. Times had been slower. The population had been smaller. People had taken personal pride in their job performance. Slade must have received at least *one* of her letters. How could he have stood there tonight, acting as if he had no idea she'd borne him a child? If she lived to be a hundred, she would never understand it. They'd been so open with each other at one time. No lies, no secrets. Or so she'd believed. But maybe all the honesty had come from her, and she'd never really known him at all.

She pictured Brody, so very much like Slade in both looks and demeanor. But there the similarities between the two men ended. Brody loved his wife, Marissa, and he was a steadfast, affectionate, and responsible father to his three children. He believed that family ties were all-important. In short, he was everything his father wasn't, a man who would never turn his back on one of his kids. Even now, if some young fellow knocked on his door and told Brody that he was his son, Brody wouldn't immediately discount the claim. Brody would undergo DNA testing, if necessary. The only thing he would absolutely never do was tell some kid to get the hell off his porch.

Slade had sent out that message, not with words, but with his failure to respond to her letters in any way, fashion, or form. Nancy had it right. He was a dead-beat dad. Vickie was tempted to have a T-shirt made for him with that title emblazoned across the front and back. Tears welled in her eyes, and they weren't for herself or for Slade or for the shattered dreams of the girl she'd once been. They were for her son, who'd never really gotten a fair shake his entire life. She'd saved any gratuities that the restaurant serving staff had shared with her to buy Brody western-style cloth-ing, enabling him to attain the look he'd wanted, but she'd never been able to afford any of the other things he yearned for. He'd had to wait nearly twenty years to buy himself a patch of land and a good horse. Then, without any formal schooling, he'd learned to train horses and turned that talent into a paying business. By all rights, he should have been well-set at this point in his life, but Marissa's illness was slowly but surely draining him financially. Brody's health insurance company had canceled on him when Marissa was first diagnosed, claiming that her rheumatoid arthritis was a preexisting condition. All the diagnostic testing had cost a small fortune, and the insurance had refused to pay for even that. Marissa needed some kind of special medicine that started with an *m*, a chemo drug of some kind that cost over five hundred a month, to prevent the deformities that her arthritis would eventually cause. The pharmaceutical company that produced it had a giveaway program for patients who couldn't af-ford the shots, but Brody made just enough money to disqualify Marissa. And that didn't count the expenses for her physical therapy, her pain medications, the nutritionist, or all the special foods she needed to strictly follow her diet. Vickie had seen dark circles form under her son's eyes. He'd started working with more and more horses and putting in longer and longer hours. She knew without him saying a word that he was dog-paddling in water way over his head in a desperate attempt to stay afloat. Yet he'd never once complained to Vickie. Never once asked why it had to be his wife who got a horrible disease. Never once cursed the vagaries of fate that were eroding the life he'd worked so hard to build.

Vickie turned her face into her pillow to muffle her sobs. She'd grown so furious with Slade tonight that she'd almost ruined everything by bringing up Brody too soon. If nothing else good came from her taking this job, she could at least work nearly the full month to draw all the wages she could. Maybe when she got back to Coos Bay, she'd put her house up for sale after all. Pay off the equity loan. Get herself a cheap apartment. Draw on her social security. Maybe she'd even quit working entirely. With no job to eat up her time, she could go out to Brody's farm on a daily basis and help out around the place. Marissa had always been a champ about doing her share of the work, but now she was in so much pain most of the time that she couldn't contribute much.

Vickie cried until she felt drained, and then she just lay there in the darkness, with only a faint fire glow coming from the stove to illuminate the enclosure.

Sounds from the surrounding forest drifted to her. The mournful calls of a coyote. The hoot of an owl. A light wind rustling through the boughs of the trees. If she strained her ears, she could even hear the chuffing of the horses. At one time, all those sounds had seemed beautiful to her. Now they just made her feel empty, and she wished that she'd never come home.

Chapter Nine

Bluish light pressed against Vickie's eyelids. As she surfaced from deep sleep, she dreamed that she'd been abducted by aliens, flown through space faster than the speed of light, and enclosed in a sterilization capsule that used infrablue beams to eradicate all communicable germs. Warmth pressed close around her. She felt as if she were drifting on clouds. If this was how it felt to be cleansed, maybe she'd just stay.

"He tore my shitter all to hell!"

The shout, laced with murderous rage, jerked Vickie from slumber. With a backward swing of her arm, she sent the top layer of her sleeping bag flying. A blast of frigid air cut through her fleece sleepwear and raised goose bumps all over her body.

"I'll kill him!" the male voice came again. "I mean it this time! I'll put a bullet right between his eyes!"

Swinging her legs over the side of her bed, Vickie sat up. *Where am I?* That was the first thought that ricocheted around in her foggy brain. *Who in the hell is shouting like that? He'll get a throat rupture.* Fighting to come awake and clear her head, Vickie took in her surroundings, but for at least three seconds, she recognized nothing. Then her gaze landed on her duffel bag, and all of it came rushing back to her. Driving over from the coast. Meeting Slade at the trailhead. Riding up the mountain. Being the ungrateful recipient of a nighttime visit from a blond bear that loved ketchup. The memories, coming to her in short blips, fell so far out of the realm of what she accepted as normal that it might all have been part of her dream. Only she liked the aliens better.

"Son of a *bitch*! He broke my fucking toilet seat! It's in three pieces!"

Vickie leaped to her feet. Pain exploded up the backs of her legs and pooled like molten lava in her butt cheeks. She nearly dropped to her knees. *Saddle sore.* Placed on a horse when she was a toddler, Vickie had grown up riding. She'd never gotten saddle sore, not even after her first day-long ride each spring. Now she felt a lot more sympathy for all the people she'd known who had been nearly unable to walk after a long trail ride.

"Where's my rifle, damn it! He is *so* gone! I'll do it this time! Mark my words, he's a dead son of a bitch."

Vickie hobbled to her duffel bag, started grabbing clothes, and whimpered as muscles in her thighs knotted and sent charley-horse spasms knifing down into her calf muscles. The fire in the woodstove had burned out. It was so cold inside her tent that the ground beneath her stocking feet felt frozen, and in the first, faint streaks of daylight, ice crystals sparkled in the air. She jerked on her jeans from the previous day, shoved her feet into her new boots, and pulled a sweatshirt on. *Jacket.* She needed outerwear. Her fingers grazed something silky and soft. Her puffer coat. She grabbed it and hurried from the tent.

Seven men stood in a huddle about twenty feet from her door. She recognized Dale, Wyatt, and Kennedy, all the blondies that she'd met already, and the wiry Texan, but she didn't know the names of the other three. Not that it mattered. No one seemed to notice her. They were all staring off into the trees with blank looks in their eyes. Vickie followed their gazes and saw Slade, stomping around, tossing things, and just generally throwing a temper tantrum.

"What in the world?"

"Bear," Kennedy told her. "Ongoing war now. Slade started it with a pepper bomb, and I don't think Four Toes will ever forgive him."

Tex sent Vickie a mischievous grin. "Moral of that story is, don't piss off a bear. They got memories like elephants."

Slade strode from the woods, looking dangerous, his normally tanned countenance flushed red with anger. Vickie might have felt afraid of him if he'd held something more lethal in his hand than a roll of toilet paper. He walked right past her toward his tent, located at the opposite end of the row and closest to the cookshack. When he emerged again, he'd ditched the bathroom tissue and replaced it with the rifle she'd seen the night before.

"Yep. Here we go ag'in," Tex muttered. "Same old

rerun. I got ten bucks that says he'll do it this time." He held out a hand, palm turned skyward. "Who's in?"

"Me!" said a cowboy whose face Vickie only vaguely remembered. "And I'm betting he'll do it, too. Law of averages. Right? Sooner or later, the cows always come home."

Alarm coursed through Vickie's body as her sleep-numbed brain started to clear. Eating up the ground with yard-long strides, Slade walked to the edge of the woods, brought the rifle butt to his shoulder, and sighted in on something. And, as if on cue, Four Toes reared up onto his hind legs so she could see him. Forefeet spread wide like a man greeting a crowd before delivering an oratory, the bear swayed on his hind feet, yawned, and emitted a roar so loud it seemed to vibrate the air.

"What in God's name is he *doing*?" Vickie cried. "Don't just stand here, placing bets. Somebody go out there and stop Slade before he docs something stupid!"

Seven pairs of eyes became fixed on Vickie. Seven faces bore the same incredulous expression. Tex was the only one who spoke. "You can have a go if you want. We don't mess with the boss when he's that pissed."

"Why?" she demanded. "Are all of you chicken?"

Tex nodded. "When it comes to him and that damn bear, sure as tootin'. Slade ain't thinkin' past his mad right now. He'll either finish it this time or get over it. That's the fun of it, not knowin' how it'll end every time this happens."

"Oh, for heaven's sake!" Ignoring the white-hot

flares of pain that shot from her butt to her ankles, Vickie took off toward the trees. No matter how mad Slade got, she'd never be afraid of him. Her boots found soft dirt layered with moldering pine needles and then roots that trailed like arthritic arms just beneath the soil to trip her. Rocks, too. There were always rocks in these mountains, mostly lava that had spewed over the area centuries ago during an eruption. *"Men."* Sometimes Vickie wondered if a dozen of them had a full brain between them. Slade couldn't shoot that bear. Especially not over the destruction of an outdoor toilet. It was ludicrous. About fifty feet away from Slade, she stopped to admire the bear, who still stood on his hind legs and loomed against the backdrop of trees like a gigantic stuffed toy. It wasn't often that humans got an opportunity to study a bear out in the wild. They had to visit zoos, sanctuaries, or observatories to even see one.

"He's beautiful," she said to Slade's back. He'd assumed a firing stance, his left foot forward, right one back, his rangy body angled slightly sideways to his target. "I guess it's hard for you right now to appreciate how pretty he is, so golden with those dark markings. It would be such a shame to end his life just because you're in a snit over a toilet seat."

Slade lowered the gun and spun toward her. "Did I ask you for your opinion? No. Do I appreciate your commentary? Another no. Just go away and let me shoot the bastard."

Vickie saw the pain in his eyes and knew he wouldn't be able to shoot that bear even if she helped him pull the trigger. "How did you end up with an orphaned cub, Slade? I would think that you would have remembered the mess I got into with Hershey and thought better of interfering. Good intentions and wild animals mix like oil and water."

"I remembered how it went with Hershey, so I left him on the mountain behind the ranch. He was tiny, injured, hungry, and alone, and I rode away without looking back. One of the hardest things I've ever done in my whole life!" He strode over to a gray boulder that was wide and smooth on top. Taking care with his gun, he laid it on the ground and sat on the rock beside it. If the picture he presented had been a painting, Vickie would have named it *Dejected*. He sat with his limp arms resting on his spread knees and bent his head to stare at the ground. "Damned if he didn't follow me home."

Four Toes bellowed again, as if to tell his side of the story.

Vickie yearned to join Slade on the rock. Just to sit there beside him, as she once would have done without thinking twice. To talk. To listen. To share with each other what they could tell no one else. They'd been such good friends. Best of buddies and soul mates, with a bond that had existed between them since long before their feelings for each other had deepened to a lasting kind of love. Only it *hadn't* lasted. Vickie wondered if the truly magical things in life ever did. Maybe they were more like ice cream cones, to be devoured swiftly before they melted into a horrible mess.

She considered leaning against a pine that grew near him, but at the last moment, she veered toward his rock and lowered herself to sit beside him. She almost moaned with pain. The stone pressed hard against her throbbing butt and legs. She needed to go riding again today. Back in the saddle again, and all that. If she didn't, she might not be able to walk tomorrow.

"I should've shot him then," Slade went on. He didn't seem surprised that she'd sat beside him. "I knew it wasn't a wise idea to feed him. Sure as rain is wet, you always end up with a nuisance bear if you do."

"Yes," she agreed. "Bear rescues rarely go well. I got lucky with Hershey. Daddy found that rescue shelter to take him in. I heard later that Hershey ended up at a wildlife compound, one of those places where wild animals get to live in an environment as close to their natural habitat as possible. He became a favorite with tourists, because he liked people so much." She angled a questioning look at Slade. "Have you checked into that? Four Toes is a perfect candidate for rescue." She looked over Slade's slumped shoulder at the huge animal, which still stood among the trees, waving his front legs like people talked with their hands. It seemed strange to her. "Why is he just standing there?"

"He's waiting."

"For what?"

"*Breakfast!* Damn his rotten hide."

The whole story came pouring out of Slade then, about how Four Toes' mother had been killed, how Slade had ended up bottle-feeding her baby that night, and how Slade had come to love him against all his better judgment. "They're so cute when they're little," he said. "You just can't help yourself. But then they grow up."

Vickie thought of her children and smiled. "Into teenagers, no less, who remind their parents multiple times a day why wild animals eat their young."

He let out a startled laugh. "Come to think of it, I do like bear meat if it's dressed right. Maybe I'll shoot him and make Four Toe burgers."

"With lots of ketchup in honor of his memory."

He sighed. Then he gazed off across the clearing with a distant look in his eyes. "It's always been this way. Even though you hate my guts now and I'm not sure I like you much, either, I can still talk to you like I've never felt inclined to talk to anyone else."

Vickie wanted to remind him that he'd been the one who destroyed their relationship, but she held her tongue. She'd lied to Slade about burying that hatchet, but she was starting to realize now that she needed to start digging the hole. Life went on, and she didn't want to live the rest of hers feeling so many negative emotions.

He resumed speaking. "And to answer your question, no, I haven't tried to find a shelter that might take him. I broke the law when I took Four Toes in, and if I get caught, my ass will be grass." He told her about calling ODFW to get help for Four Toes that long-ago afternoon. "The man—Wilson was his name—didn't mince words. Four Toes needed to stay in his natural habitat. If it comes out now that I ignored the dictates of the state, I could do time. I think the penalties are pretty stiff."

Vickie doubted that Slade would face anything as serious as jail, but occasionally she did wonder if judges didn't get overzealous in their rulings to make an example of people. And messing around with wild creatures, especially making any attempt at all to domesticate them, was a serious offense. "From here on out, it's only going to get worse, Slade. Bears and people don't mix. As he ages, he'll grow bigger, stronger, and bolder. The ending to that story won't be pretty."

"What can I do except shoot him? I tried running him off." He gestured with an extended thumb toward the bear. "Stopped feeding him. Peppered the ground around him with buckshot to scare him away. Nothing worked. He just kept coming back. Now he's on a mission to make my life hell. Two weeks ago, I repaired fences. Had all my men helping me. When I got my section finished, Four Toes tore it all apart that very night. No one else's section, only mine. Last week, I put brand-new tires on my truck for winter. Knobby ones. He punctured every last one of them with his teeth and claws. Fifteen hundred bucks, down the drain. Oh, and he destroyed my grandma's rocker on the porch, too. Bastard saw me sitting in it of an evening. I love to end a day that way in the summer. Relax. Think. Watch the sun go down. He went after that damned chair because he knew it was a favorite possession of mine. My grandma's chair, damn it. I'm paying a furniture guy to fix it, and for the cost, I could buy a half dozen just like it with change to spare."

Vickie joined him in studying the trees. Four Toes was still chuffing behind them. He made her think of a cranky toddler who needed breakfast and a morning nap. "Sounds like a vendetta to me."

"It *is* a vendetta. I broke his trust, and he's out to get me."

She turned to glance at Four Toes again. "He's only a bear, Slade. I wouldn't think he has the mental capacity to reason his way through stuff and hold a grudge for long. What on earth did you do to him?"

"Pepper bomb."

"Tex mentioned that, but I've never heard of one. What, exactly, is it?"

"Jake—he owns and operates a new place in town called the Jake 'n' Bake—called a friend of his, an Alaskan outfitter, who has to deal with problem bears all the time. When he heard about Four Toes coming in every morning and night for food, he said to wrap a can of bear spray in a pound of bacon and put it in Four Toes' pile of food." He sniffed and rubbed his upper lip with the cuff of his shirtsleeve. Vickie wondered if he'd been holding back tears and now had a runny nose. It was one of the things she'd always loved most about Slade, his ability to cry. He was as rugged and strong as any man she'd ever known, but he also had a tender heart. "Every afternoon someone from town brought out two garbage cans of food for Four Toes. That sounds nasty, but the stuff in the cans was fresh stuff, not trash. Jake kept the receptacles clean, set them by the back stoop of his bakery, and every restaurant owner in town brought daily offerings. Leftovers and extra stuff from their kitchens."

"So feeding Four Toes became a community effort?"

"The whole community, no, just a few chosen people we knew we could trust. Well, it was like that at first. But you remember Mystic Creek. There's no such thing as a secret in that town. Almost everyone knows about him, a lot of people donated food while I was still feeding him, and nobody talked about it. It's been way over three years, and there's not a law officer at the department who knows."

"A best-kept secret," Vickie mused. "I'm amazed. In Mystic Creek, everybody knows everything. Maybe more law officers than you realize know about it, and they've just decided to look the other way."

"Maybe."

The sun came up over the treetops, sending triangular beams of diffused yellow through the pine boughs to paint stripes on the wilderness floor. Mist rose around their feet and hovered in cloudlike pillows over the frozen earth. Near the tree line, Vickie spotted a doe and her half-grown fawn. She knew she'd seen things just as beautiful in these mountains countless times, but she couldn't remember when. It was inarguably a Kodak moment, but she'd forgotten her phone in the tent.

"So," she said. "Stop stalling and spit it out. You followed the advice of the Alaskan outfitter and baited Four Toes' meal with bear spray. Right? So what happened then?"

"He punctured the can with his teeth, and it exploded in his mouth. Not like a bomb, where it actually hurt him or anything."

"I'm sure it felt to him as if a bomb had gone off."

He wiped beneath his nose again. The strengthening warmth of the sun bathed their backs. For the first time, she noticed that Slade wasn't wearing his hat. She treated herself to a long study of his gloriously thick hair, which was threaded with silver now, but still had shine, as shimmery and dark as a freshly poured cup of camp coffee. She wanted to tidy it with her fingertips and feel the heat rising from his scalp. Instead she pressed her hands together as if in prayer and clamped them between her knees.

Slade took a deep breath and released it. His voice turned gravelly and tight when he said, "I was his surrogate parent. He loved me, trusted me, and came to me for food. It was a habit I knew I had to break. For his sake. You know? I saw it as the equivalent of booting an eighteen-year-old kid out the door and forcing him to make it on his own. Four Toes likes people. If I persist in not feeding him, he's going to move into town. People will find him on their porches. He'll rob their garbage cans and strew trash all over their yards. Someone will get fed up and shoot him. Or he'll get his feathers ruffled and hurt someone. I had to do something. I prayed the bomb would do the trick."

Vickie knew that was inarguable. Four Toes might hurt someone unless he was discouraged or prevented from going near people. But she wasn't sure a pepper bomb had been the answer. "You should pursue a more permanent solution."

He sighed. "I know, but—" He turned to look at her. "You're a good shot. Will you do it for me, Vick? Every time I get him in my sights, I remember rocking him to sleep at night."

"You rocked a bear to sleep?" She laughed and added, "Oh, Slade, you're such a *softie* sometimes."

"Hey, easy on the ego. I haven't recovered yet from your *bald pate* comment."

She laughed and wondered what it was about Slade Wilder that never failed to disarm her. When she was around him, she felt as if her heart was divided into sections like a department store, one for each of her kids and one for this man, only she couldn't move from aisle to aisle. When she thought about Brody, she got stuck in his section, and so forth. With Slade, all the other sections fell away, and she could focus on only him.

"I'd apologize," she said with a grin, "but I'm long in the tooth and can't remember saying anything about a pate, bald or otherwise."

It was his turn to laugh, but there was no humor in

the sound. "I have to destroy him, Vick. Before he harms someone."

"No. You need to neutralize him, and by that, I don't mean kill him. Four Toes has done nothing wrong. Yet. We need to find him a forever home. Maybe have him tranquilized and moved clear out of this area. So far away that he'll never find his way back. Someplace to hell and gone from people, where he'll be forced to survive the way God intended. He prefers easy. But don't we all? As long as he is near people, he'll seek them out for free meals."

"There are approximately thirty thousand black bears in Oregon alone. The sanctuaries, shelters, observatories, and zoos are already filled. Transplanting him to another area would be the only option, but the state tries to avoid doing that. It costs a small fortune, for one thing, and believe it or not, some bears manage to find their way home again. But the more serious concern is a possible contamination of the black bear gene pool in another wilderness area. Black bear populations have risen. Disease is always a threat. If Four Toes is a carrier of a virus that he's built up an immunity to, he could introduce that viral strain into another population of bears and wipe them out."

Vickie drew her hands from between her knees and chafed her palms. "So . . . before he's transported, a vet needs to run a blood panel on him to rule out that possibility. That's a no-brainer."

"The state won't get on board. I guarantee it."

"Maybe not without some pressure."

He angled her a questioning look. His gray eyes reminded her so much of Brody's. "You got friends in high places or something?"

She smiled and shook her head. "I'm a cook. I prefer the title of chef. It sounds more impressive. I even went to culinary school. But I'm still just a cook. We may serve people who are wealthy and important, but we aren't good enough to socialize with them."

"Don't say that. You could rub elbows with the president and do yourself proud."

Vickie waved her hand to erase all that nonsense from the air between them. "I was thinking more of becoming the proverbial squeaky wheel. Mystic Creek's a small town, but if you get its people all fired up and they start to demonstrate with signs that read SAVE OUR BEAR, the state will have no choice but to pay attention. Squeaky wheels get the oil, Slade. If animal activists got wind of it, our capital city of Salem would be swarming with demonstrators. The upper-ups would be messing their pants. People in governmental positions of power *think* they wield a big stick until the people raise their voices, and then they realize very quickly that they're one election away from losing their jobs."

A thoughtful frown pleated his forehead, deepening the creases between his grizzled eyebrows. "You know? You may be onto something."

Vickie stifled a moan as she struggled back to her feet. "Of course I am. It's me, the rabble-rouser, remember. Back me into a corner, and I come out swinging."

He grinned. It was that fabulous, slightly crooked grin that she remembered so well, just a little bit cocky, but a hundred percent charming, flashing his strong, white teeth and the crevices in his lean cheeks. They'd started out as dimples when he was but a boy. Time had chiseled them deeper, and now they slashed from his cheekbones to each corner of his mouth. She gazed down at him, feeling miffed at herself for noticing how handsome he still was. He hadn't shaved yet this morning, and his whiskers hadn't grayed evenly. He had silver patches bracketing the cleft in his chin. If he grew a tidy mustache and beard, it would undoubtedly look sexy as hell and have women half his age swooning at his feet.

"Where you off to?"

She answered as she walked away. "First I'm going to wash my face and brush my teeth. Then I'm going to deliver breakfast to a bear. Leftover chili, still in the cans. That'll keep him busy for a while."

"The hair, Vick. Don't forget the hair."

Vickie wondered what was wrong with her hair. Three minutes later when she finally located the unbreakable hand mirror in her duffel, she stifled a shriek of dismay. Her mane of kinky curls was always impossible to control, but she'd slept on it wrong last night and had a rooster tail poking up about eight inches from the top of her head. If she'd stiffened it with helmet hair spray, she couldn't have made it stand up straighter.

* * *

Setting up base camp was always a hellish experience for Slade, and this year was no different, except that Vickie was present. Though he tried to resist it, Slade was filled with a feeling of rightness. Even though bitterness and anger simmered between them just beneath the surface, he enjoyed hearing her voice ring out, sometimes grouchy in tone, other times laced with good humor. Vickie had always been an energetic, nononsense person who jumped into a job and did what had to be done. But she wasn't afraid to complain, either, and the unorganized condition of the cookshack and everything that had to go inside it gave her plenty of reason to bitch.

It amused Slade to watch his hired hands scurry around to do her bidding. She was fond of following an order with, "Chop, chop!" And when she did, everyone stepped a little faster. More than once, he heard her yell, "If you hope to put a hot meal in your belly tonight, don't ask me *why*, just *do* it!" And amazingly enough, the work got done in short order. At one point, she advanced on the three new guys that Slade had hired. He still didn't have their names straight, and clearly neither did she, but Vickie didn't let a little thing like that hold her up. She just called them *you* or *hey, you.* The men were sorting and organizing the saddles and tack, something that needed to be done, for sure, but wasn't exactly a priority.

For almost a full minute, Vickie stood with her hands on her hips and watched them work. There was a method to her madness, because when the fellows noticed their audience of one and asked what she wanted, she said, "I'm just wondering if you can brown pancakes and fry eggs on one of those saddles."

The taller guy—Slade thought his name was Ron—decided to field the question. "No, ma'am."

Vickie folded her arms at her waist. "Uh-huh. I see. And what about those canteens? Can you make coffee in them?"

Ron shook his head. "Um, no, ma'am. I've heated water in metal ones, but I don't reckon I could ever make coffee."

Vickie tapped a fingertip on her chin. "I guess I'm just confused," she observed. "You're all over here, busy as bees. As important as it may eventually be to have everything sorted, saddle-soaped, and placed within easy reach, I don't think your efforts will put a hot meal in your bellies."

Ron made the fatal mistake of chuckling. "No, ma'am. That's *your* job."

Vickie smiled and snapped her fingers. "Oh, I understand. I'm getting our job descriptions confused, right?"

"Kind of, I think. We're outfitters, not cooks."

She nodded. "Thanks for getting me straightened out." She started to walk away. Then she stopped, turned back, and flashed a hundred-watt smile. "Just out of curiosity, have you boys ever heard the story called 'The Little Red Hen'?"

"No, ma'am," Ron replied. His two sidekicks mumbled negative responses as well.

"It's such a shame that parents stopped reading to their kids. Stories like 'The Little Red Hen' teach children valuable life lessons. I suggest that you read it. Sooner rather than later, I think. Because I'm really big on the Little Red Hen's philosophy."

"What's her philosophy?"

Her smile turned syrupy sweet. Slade knew that boded ill. "It's simple. She found seeds to plant, but none of the other farm animals would help her. When the seeds produced wheat, none of the other animals would help her harvest it. When it came time to take the wheat to a mill to be ground into flour, none of them would help carry it to town. When she got back to the farm with the flour, she had to make the bread all by herself. And, then, guess what?"

"I dunno," Ron said with a shrug of his shoulders.

The syrupy smile flashed again. "All the other farm animals wanted to help her eat the bread, but she ran them off and ate the bread all . . . by . . . herself."

Vickie waggled her fingers in farewell and walked away. Ron glanced at his buddies. "What the fuck? Did she just threaten not to feed us?"

The shorter of the three men, a stout redhead, said, "I think maybe so."

"Well, shit," Ron said. "She can't do that. Right? We work hard. We have to eat to keep our energy up. The boss will cloud up and rain all over her if she cuts us off from the chow line."

Slade grinned and rested his shoulder against a tree.

Watching Vickie in action was more entertaining than a three-monkey circus act. A powwow ensued between the new boys, the exchanges punctuated with curses and plenty of blackguarding. Slade wouldn't worry about their language unless they spoke that way in front of Vickie, but he doubted they would. Ron seemed to be the leader, and he'd been respectful during his conversation with her.

After a goodly amount of grumbling, the three men abandoned their task of organizing the riding gear and headed for the cookshack. Slade spent a couple more minutes propping up the pine tree with his shoulder and observed all the activity. Men opening boxes to discover the contents. Others assembling racks and more shelving. Slade figured that Vickie would have the kitchen in tiptop shape by late afternoon, which would break all of Cheyenne's records. Not that Cheyenne was a slouch when it came to work, but she hadn't yet acquired the ability to make grown men snap to and salute. Vickie definitely had. Slade could only applaud her.

He nearly parted company with his skin when Wyatt's voice rang out just behind him. "She's really something, boss."

Slade nodded. "Yep. Always has been."

Wyatt stopped on the other side of the tree and volunteered his shoulder to help hold it up. "She's the one. Isn't she?"

Slade shot him a surprised look. "The one, what?"

Wyatt, who stood slightly forward so he could read Slade's lips, merely grinned. "*The* one, the love of your life. I knew it the instant I saw her last night."

Slade didn't like the sound of that. "Was I that obvious?"

With a shake of his head, Wyatt said, "No. Neither of you said or did anything out of the ordinary. I just sensed it. The air between you sizzles. I'm talking high voltage."

Slade sighed. "You could've knocked me over with a feather when she showed up. It was like seeing a ghost. I was going to send her packing, but then I changed my mind."

"What changed it?"

"My need for a cook."

"Now that she's up here, are you sorry you let her stay?"

Slade considered the question. "No," he finally admitted. "I've been waiting over forty years to see her again."

"What caused the two of you to split up?" Wyatt asked. "I know it's a personal question, and you don't have to answer. It's just that you seem so right for each other."

"We are." Slade backed up to rephrase that. "At least we *were*, way back when. Then someone told her I'd been unfaithful. She didn't believe me when I denied it. And she walked."

"Wow. And you just let her go?"

"Yep. I gave her my word that I was innocent. She

thought I was lying." Slade saw Four Toes rolling around at the edge of camp, scratching his back on the grass. He watched for a moment. "The way I saw it then, she either believed me or she didn't. Without trust in a relationship, what the hell do you have but a recipe for misery?"

"What the hell did you have after you let her walk away?" Wyatt countered.

"Nothing." Slade heard the hollow note in his voice and didn't care. Wyatt wouldn't pick up on intonations. "Absolutely nothing."

"If you could go back in time, would you handle the situation differently?"

"Knowing what I know now, I would. With age comes wisdom, and all these years later I realize what I didn't know then. I'd rather be miserable with her than miserable without her."

Chapter Ten

The navigation in Erin's old car had always sucked, but it was especially bad in Mystic Creek. She'd named the woman whose recorded voice issued all the directions Peach, after a female character in *Lonesome Dove* who'd been obnoxious and overbearing with the weak-willed men in her family. Erin had disliked the character in both the book and the film, and she liked her navigation lady even less, mostly because she managed to be thoroughly unpleasant even when her every utterance was polite and sweet.

Erin was seldom polite and sweet in return, mainly because, in Mystic Creek, Peach couldn't find her ass with both hands. And, unfortunately, today was no exception. Noreen lived on Elderberry Lane, and the address to her residence had been properly entered into the nav system, but Peach had been taking Erin up and down the same section of road for over ten minutes, telling her to turn where there was no driveway. It made no sense. Erin finally concluded that road construction must have revamped some of the turnoffs and the maps had never been updated to satellite. She slowed her car to a crawl and started reading the numbers on the mailboxes. She needed to find 3234. When she found that address on one of the roadside receptacles, she almost gave a victory shout, but the urge quickly vanished, because finding the right sequence of numbers on a mailbox didn't tell her which house it belonged to.

Erin decided she'd wasted enough time and called Noreen's cell number. The other woman answered the call with a pop of her bubble gum and, "Hello, this is Noreen."

Erin explained her dilemma. Though Noreen sounded reluctant to have Erin drop by her house, she was much nicer over the phone than she usually was over the department radio. She explained that the county had excavated all the ditches to install new drainage culverts and some of the driveways had been rerouted over easements that crossed other people's land.

Once at Noreen's house, a small blue structure with spotless white trim, Erin got out of her car and took several deep breaths. She wanted this meeting to go well, knew it probably wouldn't, and really wished she could just drive away. But workplace animosity couldn't be dealt with by running from it, and Erin had reached her breaking point. Getting little time off and even less sleep kept her on the brink of losing her temper, and if Noreen woke her up one more time in the middle of the night, Erin feared she might explode. It was time for a talk.

When Noreen answered her knock, Erin expected the exchange to be unpleasant, but Noreen's face was puffy and swollen, either from the worst allergic reaction in history or from crying, and the head of steam Erin had built up for a nasty confrontation lost pressure the moment she stepped over Noreen's threshold. "Are you all right?" Erin asked.

Unfolding a tissue she'd wadded up in her hand, Noreen dabbed at her eyes. "Would you be all right if *you* had kids and knew you were about to lose your job?" Noreen's voice wobbled as she asked that question. "I made cookies last night, and I've got fresh coffee." She gestured at a table that was so large it overwhelmed the small dining area. "When the kids get home from school, the cookies will be history, so please, have a seat, and don't be shy about helping yourself."

Erin felt completely off balance, and a dozen questions zigzagged through her mind, but she expressed none of them. She sat at the table, which was covered with a plastic cloth. With three kids living there, Erin guessed plastic was a smart choice. Spillages would trash a regular tablecloth, and kids tended to be messy eaters. Well, most were, anyway. Erin's mother, whom Erin called Martha Stewart in jest, had insisted that her daughter practice impeccable table manners, and that had left no room for dribbled food or knocked-over glasses of milk.

Given Noreen's lackadaisical approach to dispatching, Erin scanned the living area of the home with a measure of incredulity. The house was about the size of Erin's cottage, and with small children in residence, it could have been a wreck, but instead it was tidy and welcoming. Bookcases lined the television wall and sported organized collections of paperbacks, children's books, and DVDs. The walls were tastefully adorned with hodgepodge, blending trendy accessories with older items, a sure sign that Noreen had decorated on the cheap, possibly picking up stuff at garage sales, but it worked well together. Erin lacked that talent and wished, not for the first time, that she was better at making a house into a home. The living room branched off into a short hallway that Erin guessed led to one bathroom and two bedrooms, a common layout for small homes. What alarmed her was that boxes sat just beyond the archway, two standing with the flaps open and several flats leaning against a tiny closet.

Was Noreen planning to relocate? In the process of moving? With three children, she needed a bigger place, for sure, but it seemed like an odd time for her to uproot her kids. School was in session. The holidays would soon be upon them. And bad weather was on its way. Erin had experienced only one winter in Mystic Creek, but by spring, she'd felt like a lifelong resident. Snow berms higher than her head on Main. Roads that were ice rinks. Absurdly low temperatures that crystalized the air, burned the lungs, and turned hands numb in two-point-five seconds. Many locals wore shirts emblazoned with MYSTIC CREEK AIN'T FOR SISSIES. That was true, and Erin sure wouldn't want to move in the winter.

With a trembling hand, Noreen poured coffee into a

mug for Erin and then sat across from her. She nudged the plate of cookies toward her guest. "Please, help yourself. I can be accused of many things, but I've never been inhospitable."

Leashed anger threaded the comment, which made Erin want to bolt. She glanced at the baked goods, saw that they were chocolate chip, and wondered if Noreen had laced them with chocolate laxatives. She smiled and said, "Only if you'll join me."

Noreen shrugged and reached for a cookie. "Why not? I've blown my diet all to hell anyway."

Only after her hostess had shoved an entire cookie into her mouth did Erin take a bite of her own. The delicious taste rolled over her tongue. "Oh, man. You know just how long to bake them. I love them chewy like this."

Noreen's cheeks turned as pink as the end of her nose, which had apparently been rubbed raw by tissues. "Baking is the one thing that I do really well," was all she said.

Erin's stomach knotted. This woman wasn't the sarcastic, bubble-popping Noreen that she'd come to know. "I'm sure you do lots of things well."

"Not really. Haven't you noticed?"

Okay, that had been a slam, but Erin couldn't take offense because Noreen looked so upset. "What's going on here, Noreen? What have I done to make you dislike me so much?"

Noreen's red-rimmed eyes filled with tears and her chin quivered. "I don't merely dislike you. I *hate* you!"

Erin tried to think what she might have done or said to deserve that, and she came up with nothing. "I don't understand why. Maybe if you level with me, I can try to fix it."

"You're everything I'm not! Everything I'll never be, no matter how hard I try."

Erin couldn't think what to say. "What on earth are you wanting to be?"

"Smart!" Noreen cried. "Self-confident! Pretty!" Her gaze dropped to Erin's upper torso. "And skinny. I'd like to be skinny, just once. Only, unlike *you*, I'll probably have to be dying of cancer."

Erin's heart caught as it began to filter into her brain that Noreen was jealous of her. The realization might have made her laugh if Noreen hadn't looked so pathetic and miserable. "Oh, Noreen. There's nothing special about me, and just for the record, I'm not naturally slender."

"You aren't? What did you do, get one of those bypass surgeries? I've thought about it myself, but the health insurance the county provides doesn't cover stuff like that unless a person is almost dying of obesity. Typical of me, I can't even do *fat* without screwing it up."

Erin took a sip of coffee, which she didn't really want, but the pause gave her time to think before she spoke. "You aren't fat."

"I am so. And I know it, so don't be condescending."

"You're a tiny bit plump," Erin told her. "Drop twenty pounds and you'll be as skinny as a rail. But is that what you really want? I diet constantly to stay trim, but the only reason I do is because I'm a cop, and cops need to stay in shape. If I had a different job, I wouldn't worry about my weight, at least not to the degree I do now."

"I'd give an arm to have your figure."

Erin felt as if she'd walked through that front door into an altered reality. She didn't know this side of Noreen. At all. "I never dreamed you felt that way. Is that why you don't like me?"

A spark of anger flared in Noreen's blue eyes. "I don't hate you because you're skinny!" She leaned slightly forward to jut her chin. "I *hate* you because you stole Hank away from me!" Tears spilled over onto her cheeks. "And you know the worst part? You didn't even *want* him. You're a bitch that comes on to men, gets them hooked, and then moves on to the next victim."

Hank. Erin did a mental scramble. Was she talking about Hank Bentley, a senior deputy at the department? Erin saw the guy in passing a lot. He was a large man with brown hair, ordinary features, and a belly that shrank or swelled, depending on whether he was dieting or not. "I assume you're referring to Deputy Bentley."

Noreen twisted her face into a sneer. " '*I assume you're referring to Deputy Bentley*,' " she echoed in a singsong voice. "Don't treat me like an idiot! He's a handsome, wonderful man. Of *course* that's who I'm talking about!"

Oh, boy. Erin hadn't understood what she was

walking into when she'd asked to come here and talk with her coworker. This went way beyond heavy. Hank Bentley probably was a wonderful man, and he was good-looking in a Dan Blocker sort of way, a big, lumbering fellow with a mild manner. As a girl, Erin had watched *Bonanza* reruns and had loved his character, Hoss. But when she dreamed of Mr. Right, the pictures that formed in her mind weren't very Hoss-like. Hank was too old for her, somewhere in his late forties. She was only thirty-one. She wasn't interested in dating someone nearly twenty years her senior. She hoped to have children someday. A man Hank's age wouldn't wish to start a family, let alone raise one. If he had any kids, they were probably college age by now.

"Noreen, please believe me. I don't have a thing for Hank."

"Well, he has a thing for *you*. He liked me. I know he did. He used to hang out at my station when he had desk duty. We'd have coffee and talk. I'd take baked goods in, not just for him, but for everyone." She shrugged. "Okay, that's a lie. I made them mostly for him, but I made them available to everyone, because I didn't want him to know that I was—well, you know—hoping he'd ask me out." She dabbed under her eyes with the tissue again. "Then you came along, and he didn't hang out at my desk anymore! One night he told me that he was worried what others might think if we kept talking so much. He said he couldn't afford to have Sheriff Adams see us and believe that we were—well, you know."

Erin ran that through her mind twice before she spoke. "And you blame me? Noreen, Hank barely even speaks to me. I'm not sure he even knows I'm alive. Has it ever occurred to you that his decision to cool it with you might have been due to the department rules?"

"What rules?"

"We aren't allowed to date our coworkers. Sheriff Adams tells everyone when they're hired that department romances are taboo. Any hanky-panky whatsoever will result in instant termination."

"Uncle Blake never told me that."

Erin shrugged. "You're not a deputy, and you're also his niece. Maybe he just never thought about it."

"Maybe. But I'm more inclined to think that he never expected me to become a long-term employee. I'd just left my husband, and I think Aunt Marietta talked him into hiring me. It was a mess. I needed a job so I could support my kids. He probably thought I'd hightail it home to my husband the first time he got in touch with me after the breakup. Only I didn't. I couldn't. My ex had a temper, and it was getting worse instead of better. For the sake of my kids, I had to get them away from him."

"I see."

"No, Erin, you don't see. I still need the job to support my kids, and Uncle Blake threatened to fire me yesterday."

Erin almost slopped coffee down the front of her uniform shirt. "He what?"

"Don't pretend you don't know," Noreen said, her

tone accusatory. "He mentioned you by name. He said unidentified individuals have been complaining about the way I treat you. It didn't take a genius IQ for me to figure out who'd complained the loudest."

Horrified, Erin said, "No, no! Back up, please." She held up both hands. "I'm innocent here. I've never spoken to Sheriff Adams about you, negatively or otherwise."

"Give me a break. You'd love to see me go down the river."

"That's not true. I don't want you to lose your job, Noreen. You've got kids to support. If one of us has to go, I'd rather it be me."

Noreen emitted a bitter laugh. "Yeah, right. We can't even talk on the radio without you picking on me."

"Only because you make no attempt whatsoever to learn and use any of the code!" Erin popped back.

Noreen shoved her chair back from the table. "I *can't* learn the codes. I've tried and I can't!" She gestured toward the boxes in her hallway. "Why the hell do you think I'm packing to move? Because it sounded like a fun thing to do? In addition to insisting that I start treating you right, Uncle Blake says I have to learn the codes or I'm out the door!"

"Learning the codes really isn't that difficult. Just take a few each week and memorize them. You're probably trying to get all of them down at once, and hardly anybody can memorize stuff that way."

"Maybe it isn't difficult for *you*," she cried. "But it's *impossible* for me."

"Nothing's impossible."

"Easy for *you* to say. But I'm dyslexic!"

Noreen's voice went shrill on that last word, and Erin's heart felt as if it plummeted to her feet and bounced around on the floor for a full second before it resettled in her chest where it belonged. "Oh, Noreen," she whispered. "Why on earth didn't you say something?"

"I never tell anyone! It's a serious disability! I can barely read. Do you think I want my kids to know that? Or m-my b-boss?"

With that, Noreen burst into tears—not the pretty kind, but the wet, snotty, sobbing ones. Erin jumped up from the table, stepped around the chairs, and caught the redhead in her arms. "Okay, okay," she soothed. "Calm down, Noreen. Dyslexia isn't the end of the world. I can still help you learn the codes. We can do it together. I won't let you lose your job." She rocked from side to side. "You hear me? Together, you and me. You'll learn them. Sheriff Adams won't fire you. We'll just explain this to him. He's not a mean man. He'll feel terrible when he finds out what the problem is."

Noreen shook her head. "Aunt Marietta doesn't even know! My mom never told her. She was ashamed. I guess she thought it might reflect on her, that Aunt Marietta might think she was dumb, too."

Erin felt physically sick to her stomach. She thought of all the times she had complained to Noreen about her failure to use any codes and how that must have made the woman feel.

"Your mother is misinformed," she said. "People with dyslexia aren't dumb. The condition has nothing to do with intelligence."

"Tell it to my mother. She's been calling me dumb all my life."

"God should have made parents returnable." Anger welled within Erin as she thought of her father, and her mother wasn't exactly up for a Mom of the Year award, either. "As a kid, I would have sent both of mine back and picked out new ones."

Erin led Noreen back to her chair. Once she got her seated, she kept a hand on her shoulder, hoping to convey through touch that the overall forecast of Noreen's future wasn't as dismal as it seemed. "I'm so sorry for all the times I bitched at you for refusing to use any code. It was so *wrong* of me."

"I wanted to learn them," Noreen wailed. Then she cupped her shaking hands in front of her as if she held a book. "That *stupid* manual. All gibberish! Tiny print! It gave me a ferocious headache just trying to read it."

Erin remembered how frustrated the manual on noxious weeds had made her feel, and she knew it must be a hundred times worse for Noreen. She gave her another comforting pat on the shoulder and sat back down across from her.

Fresh tears welled in Noreen's eyes. "I'm moving back to Eugene to be close to my mom. I don't *like* living near her. She says shit in front of my kids, always mocking me and putting me down. But I don't see that

I have a choice. I can't study the codes, and Uncle Blake is at the end of his rope. I'm lucky he's kept me on this long."

Erin didn't think a move to Eugene was a stellar idea. Noreen's self-confidence was already trashed, and being near a mother who constantly demeaned her would only worsen the problem. "He's at the end of his rope with you only because you've acted as if police codes are ridiculous and unnecessary."

"If you were dyslexic, how would you handle it? I couldn't act like the codes were important! If I had and then hadn't bothered to learn them, he'd be even madder at me right now."

"I would tell the truth," Erin replied. "Most people will immediately understand the difficulties you face and be far more patient than they would be with someone else. Noreen, are you aware that experts believe Einstein was dyslexic?"

"What?" Noreen's voice came out barely more than a whisper and rang with disbelief. "He was one of the smartest men *ever.*"

"Yes, I believe he was one of the most amazing humans ever born. And Picasso. Are you familiar with his work?"

Noreen nodded. "I love his art. It speaks to me. I went to an art museum once, and other people were bewildered by his painting, said it was all wonky, but to me, it didn't look confusing at all."

"Probably because he was dyslexic," Erin pointed out. "He saw things like you do. You are *not* dumb.

You're probably way smarter than I am. It's sad how a parent can mess with our heads and make us think we're less than what we really are."

"I think my little Brock has the same learning disability." A tortured look entered Noreen's eyes. "Maybe not as bad as me, but he's failing first grade. I know he's trying, but every second at school is a struggle."

Erin pressed her palms flat on the table. "Get him tested. Immediately, Noreen. Don't do to him what your mom has done to you."

"I don't want him to grow up with that label! It marks people."

"When were you diagnosed?"

"I was older."

"And believed you were dumb until you found out?" Erin asked.

"I *still* believe I'm dumb."

"Because you struggled and failed in school, Noreen, and your mother compounded the problem by calling you names. Brilliant people have dyslexia. You didn't know you did, so your inability to excel in some things made you feel dumb. Don't let that happen to Brock."

"How do I get him tested?"

"I'm not a parent yet, but I think the best place to start would be by asking his teacher."

"You mean tell *her* I'm dyslexic? Then she'll know, and she'll tell other people, and then everyone in town will know."

Erin recalled Wyatt Fitzgerald's reluctance to admit to her that he was profoundly deaf. Now here was Noreen, with a different disability but the same refusal to be labeled. In Erin's opinion, there was no such thing as normal or abnormal. People were unique and couldn't be stuffed into categories.

"I want to get you a T-shirt made that reads, 'I'm dyslexic and proud of it.' And you *should* be proud, Noreen. I never guessed. Nobody at the department has a clue! That you've worked with everyone there—for how long? over four years?—without anyone so much as suspecting is absolutely amazing. And except for your failure to memorize the codes, just look at how well you do that job. Dispatching can be demanding."

"Not so much in Mystic Creek. In a city, it would be crazier."

Erin could see she had her job cut out for her with Noreen, if she chose to take it on. The woman couldn't even give herself a pat on the back. "You are amazing. Now that I know what the problem is, I'm in awe of you."

Noreen rolled her eyes. "I'll have trouble finding a job in Eugene, and I honestly don't know how I'll manage. It costs more to live there. My ex gets around paying child support by working under the table. He has a brand-new pickup and just bought a ski boat, but he doesn't send me a dime for the kids."

Erin reached across the table to grasp Noreen's hand. "You won't be fired. I promise. If the sheriff even makes noises about firing you, I'll threaten to quit. I'll even ask other deputies to threaten the same. We won't let you lose your job. Your dyslexia doesn't interfere with your performance."

With her spare hand, Noreen wiped wetness from her cheeks. "Why would you do that for me? I've been nothing but awful to you!"

Erin couldn't help it; she burst out laughing. "You really have been!"

"I'm so sorry. I was really steamed at you about Hank."

"You're already forgiven," Erin assured her. "But from this point forward, can we work on trying to be friends instead of enemies?"

Noreen nodded. "I guess. But if you think you can teach me the codes, you're dreaming."

"What's a code eight?" Erin asked her.

"An officer needs help," Noreen replied. "But I only know that one because you and I were fighting about codes when you told me the meaning, so it stuck in my brain."

Erin nodded. "True, but you now have code eight memorized."

"I do. Don't I?" She smiled through her tears. "Maybe you're right and I really can memorize the rest."

Erin gave her fingers a comforting squeeze. "No maybe to it, Noreen. You're a bright lady. We can work around your dyslexia, and even better, it'll be fun. When I'm working, we can practice on the radio as long as we're careful and everyone on that frequency knows it's only practice." She strengthened her grip on the other woman's fingers. "Let's try it. When I say over the radio that I'm taking a code seven, it means I'm breaking to have lunch. An easy way to remember that is thinking, 'She's taking a code seven *again*? If she keeps that up, she'll be seven times bigger than she already is.'"

Noreen dimpled a tear-streaked cheek. "I'll push you to take lunch breaks. The more you go code seven, the bigger you'll get and the happier I'll be."

"With a friend like you, who needs an enemy?"

"Is that what you think, that we're going to be friends?"

Erin released Noreen's hand. "Well, we haven't done so well being enemies. Why not give friendship a try?"

Noreen nodded. "Yeah, why not? And as my new friend, don't lie to me when you answer this question. I want honesty. Do you really think Hank might like me, and he's just cooled it because he's afraid he might get fired?"

Erin considered the question. "Hank Bentley hardly even looks at me. I bet he's said hello all of a half dozen times in the whole year I've worked there. He definitely didn't put a damper on your friendship because of me. So, yes, I think he backed off because he can't afford to lose his job." Erin sighed. "You really like him a lot, don't you?"

"Oh, yes. He's so nice, and he tells stories that make me laugh. When I found out he's single, I couldn't believe my good luck. I'd really like to find a nice man—someone who would be a good role model for my boys. They need a father figure."

"Well, we'll work on the sheriff," Erin assured her. "I understand his reasons for instituting the no-dating rule. Workplace romances cause trouble. Look at Hank, for instance. He's a senior deputy and an attractive man. But his position is problematic, both for him and his female subordinates. If a woman seems to be attracted to him, how can he be sure she likes him for himself? And on the flip side, if he hits on a subordinate, how can she be sure she won't lose her job if she tells him to hit the road?"

Noreen's eyes clouded. "So even if I get to keep my job, I may as well erase Hank from my list of possibilities."

"I didn't say that. Blake Adams instituted the rule. He can therefore make exceptions. He knows Hank isn't a player. He knows you even better. Sometimes, when two people meet and hit it off, a rule that forbids them from seeing each other is ridiculous. Human nature declares that they'll sneak around to see each other, and Blake would be crazy to want that happening."

"So you think he might lift that taboo for just me and Hank?"

"Maybe." Looking into Noreen's eyes, Erin hoped so. Positive reinforcement from Hank might do wonders for Noreen's self-esteem. "But first, we have to get you up to speed on code. What's it mean if I say I'm taking a code seven?"

"I means you're breaking for lunch, getting fat, and I won't feel jealous of you anymore."

They both burst out laughing, and in that moment, Erin believed the quirky bubble-gum chewer might end up being one of the best friends she'd ever had.

It had been the most chaotic five days of Wyatt's career as a ranch foreman. Getting the base camp set up had gone faster than it ever had in his memory, mostly due to Vickie Brown's incredible talent for organizing and directing people. Her years of working as a chef had definitely honed her ability to keep track of a dozen different activities at once. But otherwise the whole process had been a shit show. Four Toes' mission to get revenge against Slade had not been mitigated by giving him the three partially filled chili cans. Instead he now expected more food, and because Slade had been the person who'd tricked him with a pepper bomb, Slade remained the target of Four Toes' ire. On top of that, some idiot was playing practical jokes. With three new men and Vickie in camp, it was impossible to finger the culprit. Wyatt thought it was Vickie, but that was only a guess and unsubstantiated by any facts.

So far, the pranks had been harmless and even funny. One night Ron, the oldest of the new guys, had seen eyes out in the woods, nearly crapped his pants, and almost opened fire with a high-powered rifle to kill what he believed was a predator. Slade had grabbed the long barrel of the gun to direct it at the ground, and there had followed an angry diatribe from Slade on the follies of shooting at things one couldn't clearly see. *That* had been unpleasant, to say the least, even though Wyatt thought it was a good lesson for Ron to have learned. Then there'd been the spider trick just the previous morning. Slade had walked out to use his special outdoor toilet, the broken seat for which had been replaced when Dale went into town for fresh produce. Wyatt wasn't sure exactly what had transpired behind the shower curtain the boss had hung to give himself privacy, but Slade had let out a caterwaul and come charging from the makeshift enclosure with his Wrangler jeans and boxers down around his ankles. Still caterwauling, he'd proceeded to toe off his boots and the puddle of his clothing, only to stomp on it, yelling with every breath that a spider had dropped into his britches.

Wyatt had one hope, that he eventually would be able to erase that memory from his mind, because there was something downright pathetic about a grown man of Slade's caliber hopping around half-naked in broad daylight with his dingus flopping in the breeze. Okay, yes, it had been funny. Wyatt had known Slade didn't like spiders, but he hadn't realized the boss was phobic about them. Afterward Wyatt had braved the outdoor toilet area to find the huge spider that Slade swore he'd seen as he started to pull off a section of bathroom tissue. And he'd quickly found said spider, which had been artfully drawn onto a square of the paper with a black felt pen. The thing had *looked* three-dimensional, and Wyatt could see why Slade had been fooled. The question was, who had known about his irrational fear of spiders?

Wyatt was back to Vickie again. Only, after watching her, he found it difficult to believe that she'd target Slade so mercilessly. He knew the two of them had an unpleasant history and that Vickie believed Slade had been unfaithful to her all those years ago. But he found it difficult to believe jealousy might still push her to get even with him for the alleged transgression. She seemed like a bright, accomplished, and genuinely sweet person. Not a doormat, by any means. With her dander up, he had a feeling she'd belly up to a logger in cork boots and dare him to try kicking her ass. He'd heard of little man syndrome, and he guessed the slightly built Vickie might have a feminine version of it, but she was also incredibly kind. The dogs both worshipped her. The men were all fond of her already. After Dale's trip into town, she'd made six of the most beautiful and delicious pecan pies that Wyatt had ever seen, one of which became Dale's pie, hands off to everyone else. Even Four Toes was smitten with her and hung out near the cookshack a lot. Wyatt suspected she was slipping the bear treats, but he hadn't caught her at it.

Bottom line, he was tired, and he was glad to be heading into town on a booze run. Paying guests would start arriving at camp the next day, and although Slade forbade any drinking during the day when guests were riding horses and handling weapons, he did allow a happy hour at night. Well, he called it a happy hour, but it normally started with before-dinner drinks and lasted until bedtime. Most people were responsible about their consumption and didn't get sloppy. But sometimes Slade didn't get the luck of the draw, and they had a lush on their hands for a week.

Wyatt was happiest when he worked mostly with horses and cows. Animals of all species were far more predictable than humans. He knew what they liked to eat, how to handle them, what frightened them, and what soothed them. He didn't constantly feel on edge. People were another kettle of fish. They got pissed off over the stupidest things. One time they liked a certain food and the next time they hated it. And their peculiar routines and expectations could drive him right over the edge. Like the guy last year who'd refused to walk out into the woods a little way to brush his teeth and spit. Instead he'd done his spitting right outside the cookshack doorway where everyone might step on bluish globs of toothpaste. By the time that guest left, Wyatt's boots could have been featured in a Crest commercial.

When Wyatt reached the fork in the trail, he saw the old drop box and remembered that Erin had sent up a parcel for him. If he waited to pick it up, he was afraid he'd get distracted in town and forget to collect it when he came back up the mountain.

He told himself that he didn't really care what she'd gotten for him. He was a man with few needs and didn't want for much. For his birthday and Christmas, he asked his family members to just get him socks and boxers, because those were items that he wore out fast. In his line of work, he did a lot of walking. People thought he sat on a horse all day, but that was a romanticized picture. He did spend a lot of time in the saddle, but he couldn't do much of anything from the back of a horse. He went through socks like nobody's business. He was also constantly getting his pants hung up on barbed wire. He covered the cost of replacing his Wrangler jeans, because they could get expensive for his folks if they bought him a couple of pairs twice a year. But boxers and a pair of socks didn't cost that much, so he didn't feel bad about asking for those.

The problem with Wyatt's Christmas and birthday wish lists was that he rarely got a surprise when he opened a present. Socks and boxer shorts ranked way low on the wow factor. He always tried to act excited so his family members would know he really appreciated what they'd gotten for him, but the truth was, undergarments didn't really float his boat. They were necessities.

It was kind of nice to get a package when he had no idea what was inside. He'd be surprised no matter what it was, and that would be kind of nice. When he drew the parcel out of the drop box, he had to smile. She'd wrapped it with cowboy paper. A tiny horse with an equally tiny cowboy on its back was plastered all over it.

He'd told himself that he wouldn't open the gift until he was back at base camp, which wouldn't happen until he rode in way after dark. But now that whole idea seemed silly. If he opened it now, he could stow the contents in his saddlebags and leave the box. Plus he could text Erin while he was in town and thank her for the gift if he knew what it was.

He grinned as he sat down on the sloped lid of the drop box. It groaned under his weight, telling him that he should probably speak to Slade about replacing it soon. It had been in service for years, and everything wore out sooner or later. It had put in its time.

He didn't want to tear the paper. It wasn't often that someone bought special wrapping just for him. In fact, he couldn't remember a single time. He quickly learned that Erin was fond of using tape. Clear lengths of it covered nearly every seam, and when he tried to pull on it, he removed bits of the wrapping design. He finally drew his knife from its sheath and used the razor-sharp blade to slice through the tape.

When he finally got down to the gift, he whistled. He'd guessed right. She hadn't spent a lot, but she'd chosen something he really liked, special kinds of coffee beans. And she'd even gotten him a grinder, which would be useless until he went back to civilization. It was a thoughtful present, though. She'd seen him eyeballing the coffee, he guessed, and had probably asked Julie at the Morning Grind what he particularly liked. He saw an envelope tucked in beside the grinder. He plucked it from the box, opened the card within it, and found a whole letter tucked inside. He wasn't expecting that.

She might be a city girl without a clue about base

camps, horses, or wilderness areas, but he was coming to think that she might be a genuinely nice person.

Erin kept her hand on Johnny Walker's shoulder. He was only six, and the manager of Flagg's Market had scared the devil out of him by calling the cops. The child, dressed in what looked like garage sale specials and a pair of ratty shoes, kept looking at the handcuffs dangling from Erin's belt as if he expected her to clamp them over his wrists. Poor kid. He'd been caught stealing a candy bar, and in her opinion, the manager was handling the situation all wrong. She couldn't argue the point that all children needed to learn that shoplifting was a huge no-no, but she intensely disliked being used as the proverbial boogeyman to frighten the boy half to death. There were other ways to steer a child away from a life of crime, for heaven's sake. Positive ways.

Erin had never met the store manager, but her first impression was less than favorable. She thought he was a pompous ass. Johnny was trembling. He'd wet his pants. He struggled not to cry and kept holding his breath. When he absolutely had to breathe, snot gushed from his nose. The manager saw it, but he didn't offer the child a tissue, and Erin didn't have one on her. Her new purse, which had everything in it, was sitting in the county truck parked outside at the curb.

Luckily she saw a display of Kleenex on a nearby shelf. Leaving Johnny to fend for himself for a second, she walked over, grabbed a box, and returned to the child. Driving a thumbnail through the plastic that covered the top, she worked out a tissue and crouched down in front of the little boy.

"Can you blow for me, Johnny?" When he nodded, she clamped the paper over his button nose to catch the eruption. All the mothers she'd ever watched made this operation look easy, but for Erin it wasn't. She was afraid of squeezing his nose too hard and hurting him, so she ended up smearing mucus over his cheek. When she finally got him cleaned up, she smiled at him. "I'm not a very good nose-blower helper, am I?"

He shook his head no. Erin pushed to her feet and handed the just-opened box of tissues to the manager with the crumpled, soiled one perched on top. He was a tall man with dark hair, regular features, and cold blue eyes. She didn't often take an instant dislike to people, but him, she did.

He held up the Kleenex box. "You do plan to pay for this, I hope."

"You mean it isn't complimentary?" she asked, lacing the question with sugary sweetness when she wanted to call him a jerk instead.

"We are *not* in the habit of allowing customers to open products, use some of them, and then just walk out the door without paying for them," he replied. "Surely you can understand that."

Erin felt her temper rising and made a conscious effort to keep her hand relaxed on Johnny's little shoulder. "What I understand is that Mr. Flagg advertises this as a *neighborhood* market. He wants everyone in

Mystic Creek to feel welcome here. When a little boy needs to blow his nose, I don't think the cost of a tissue is going to make or break him. Do you?"

"It isn't only the cost of one tissue," he said. "It's an entire box that has now been opened and can't be sold."

She made a point of staring at his name badge. He went by Jack, which was all she needed to know when she contacted Mr. Flagg to tell him that his manager's public relations skills totally sucked and that he had no problem with terrifying little boys. "Cold season is on its way. Maybe you can set the box near one of the registers so the clerks can grab one to cover their mouths when they cough."

"That's hardly the point."

Erin stopped trying to smile. "The point, sir, is that I am not a customer at this moment. I'm a county deputy who was called to the scene because a crime was committed. I commandeered the box of tissues to wipe the perpetrator's nose, and I have no intention of buying the entire box when you should have provided a tissue as a common courtesy. Why do you think Mr. Flagg goes out of his way to make this store attractive to locals? Safeway, that's why. It's bigger, better, and the prices are a bit cheaper. If I want to deal with impersonal corporate BS, that's where I go. If I want to be greeted like a friend, I come here. Surely you can understand *that* and realize friendliness and helpfulness are vital to the success of this market."

"He's not my kid. His mother should make sure he

carries tissues with him. Mr. Flagg would go broke if we ran around wiping noses with tissues he's got to pay for."

Erin lifted her eyebrows. "Hmm. Interesting." She looked down at Johnny and resurrected her smile. "Are you about ready to go for a ride in a cop truck?"

He managed a quivery smile and nodded. Erin bent slightly at the waist to take his hand.

As she turned to leave, Jack said, "I cannot allow you to leave without paying for this item, Deputy De Laney."

Erin stopped and half turned to meet his gaze. "What's your plan, Jack? Are you going to call the department again and have me arrested?"

"This is absurd," he said with a huff.

"I agree. But on the other hand, it might be kind of fun. I haven't been cuffed and stuffed since I was seventeen."

"Let me put it this way," he replied. "If you leave without paying, I will call the sheriff and tell him about this incident."

Erin nodded. "I like that plan."

Johnny walked out with her, then he stared for a moment at the truck and his bottom lip began to tremble again. "I can't sit in there. I got so scared I wet my britches, and I'll get pee all over the seat."

Erin hunkered down to get at his eye level. "It's not really my truck. It's a county vehicle. Do you know what that means?"

He waggled his head.

"That means that it's your truck as much as it is mine. It belongs to your mom and dad and to everyone else who lives in Mystic County."

"Why?"

"Because everyone who lives here pays county taxes. We all contribute a little out of the money we make at our jobs. The money goes into a bank. And when the sheriff's department needs a new truck, the taxes are used to buy it."

"But my daddy doesn't have a job, and our car broke, so now my mommy can't get to work, either. I don't think we own part of that truck."

"Yes, you do, because you live in this county. When people don't have jobs and can't pay taxes, other people still pay them. And eventually your daddy and your mommy will be working again to help buy the next truck." Erin could tell that he was a bright child, and she couldn't help but smile. "And you know what's even better? Sheriff Adams always gets trucks with leather seats that wash right off. When I get off work tonight, I'll be sure to wash the upholstery where you sat, so you don't need to worry about your pants being wet."

He looked past her at the truck. "Are you gonna take me to jail?"

"Stealing a candy bar was a very bad thing for you to do. Are you ever going to do it again?"

He shook his head no.

"Then I see no reason to put you in jail. I do need to talk to you about stealing the candy bar, though. Do you mind if I do that?"

"No, except it makes me 'barrassed."

"Well, we can't have that, so I won't talk for long. I think the main thing I want to tell you is that almost everyone gets a powerful craving for a candy bar sometimes. So powerful a craving that we just have to have one."

"Do you crave candy bars?"

"Sometimes. My favorite of all is a Heath bar, and sometimes I want one so bad that I stop at the store to grab one. The difference is that I pay for mine, and you didn't."

"That's cuz I don't got any money."

"I know. And that's what we need to talk about. Just because you don't have any money doesn't mean you won't ever get a really powerful craving for another candy bar. And I never want you to steal again. So, here's the deal. The next time you get a powerful craving for a candy bar, will you call the sheriff's office and ask for me? That way I can drive to where you are and give you some money to buy some candy. How's that sound?"

"But I can't pay you back."

Erin cupped his chin in her hand. "That's where you're wrong. Someday, you'll be a man, and you'll have a job, and you'll always have money for a candy bar. By then, I may be an old lady. When I get old like that and have no money in my pocket, it'd be really nice if I could call my friend John and see if he'd mind buying me a Heath bar."

"Me? I'll be your friend John?"

Erin nodded. "If you want to be my friend, that is."

"I do. And whenever you want a Heath bar really, *really* bad, I'll buy you one."

Erin held out her right hand. "It's a deal. Let's make it official by shaking on it."

Johnny looked expectantly at the truck. Now that he no longer feared incarceration, he was clearly excited about going somewhere in a police vehicle. She could still remember how excited she'd been the first time her father had taken her for a spin in his patrol car.

"Before I take you home, Johnny, do you mind if I stop at Safeway for a couple of things?"

He looked over his shoulder at the neighborhood market. "Why can't you just buy 'em here?"

"I could," Erin confessed. "But I don't think that store manager is very nice."

"Me, neither."

"And," Erin added with a smile, "Safeway has a candy bar special going right now, two for a dollar." That was a lie, but she wanted Johnny to remember that she really would give him money for candy if he was ever tempted to steal again. "I'm getting a Heath bar! What kind is your favorite?"

"Milky Way. They don't got any nuts."

Erin had delivered Johnny to his front door, spoken with his father to hopefully make it clear that Johnny had already been punished enough by the store manager for his mistake, and then told his mother what a wonderful, well-mannered little boy he was. Now she sat in the truck, knowing she had to drive away. That boy, dressed in little better than rags, had captured her heart, and she hated to think that his parents might spank him or yell at him or send him to bed without dinner. The poor tyke hadn't even gotten to eat the candy bar he had swiped. He had gotten to enjoy the one she'd gotten for him, though, so that was something.

Her cell phone notified her of a text. She figured it might be Julie, who sent her pics or jokes or updates on how her day was going. Only when she glanced down, she saw Wyatt Fitzgerald's name instead. She couldn't imagine why he would text her. Then she remembered the gift that Blackie had taken up to the drop box and smiled. She knew he was probably just sending her a quick thank-you, nothing more, but with Johnny and all the hardships children from poor households endured playing on her mind, she welcomed any distraction.

She swiped the screen, went to Messages, and began to read.

"Hi," he wrote. *"I got the package. Plan to have an early dinner at the Straw Hat. Want to join me? My treat."*

Erin grinned. Her shift had officially ended twelve minutes before. She still needed to do her end-of-shift reports, but she could meet Wyatt for dinner and drop by the department afterward to do her paperwork and get her own car. She texted back, *"I'd love to. See you in ten."*

As Erin backed out of Johnny's driveway and got

the truck headed down the road, it suddenly hit her that she had a date. Well, maybe not a *real* date, but it was dinner with a really good-looking guy. She couldn't go dressed in this stupid uniform.

Instead of heading directly to José Hayden's Mexican restaurant, she drove straight to the Mystic Creek Menagerie. When she burst into the Morning Grind, she shouted, "Wyatt Fitzgerald just asked me to meet him for dinner. I've got five minutes to get ready, *tops*, and I can't go looking like this! I just can't!"

Julie got a horrified look on her face. "I don't keep any clothing here, Erin! And I live clear out on Bearberry Loop!"

Erin plopped her purse on the counter. It was a huge, metallic gold thing, and she loved it. "Please, Julie, think of *something*!"

"Switch!" Julie dashed out from behind the counter, grabbed Erin's hand, and took off for the unisex bathroom at the back of her shop. "We'll just trade clothes! Thank God I wore something halfway sexy today."

The bathroom was barely big enough for one person, and as Erin gave Julie the fastest once-over in history to see what she'd be wearing to meet Wyatt, she glanced down and couldn't drag her gaze from Julie's shoes. They were black, strappy things with wedge heels—really *high* heels. "I can't wear those."

"They'll fit. We're the same size."

"No, I mean—they just aren't *me*."

Julie was already peeling off her top, a low-cut burgundy thing with cold-shoulder sleeves. She kicked off the shoes. "Thank God they aren't *you*. Your style is— well, you don't have one."

"*Ouch*. Not nice. I have a style. It's just not one that flips your skirt."

"Shut up and strip!" Julie cried. "And, please, get that stupid hat off. And don't accidentally shoot me with that horrible gun. You're not leaving me with that self-defense arsenal, by the way. I'd have bad dreams all night with that weapon in my house."

"I'll stow my arsenal in the truck. Like I'd let you *touch* my sidearm? You'd end up shooting yourself. As mean as you are to me, you're the only friend I've got. I'd like to keep you."

There followed the fastest exchange of clothing imaginable, with both women asses to elbows trying to get almost naked and trade outfits. Erin stared down at the black skirt, which was a slinky knit with graceful folds and a scalloped hem that had a higher cut in the scallop over her right thigh. "It's a Mexican place, not the Ritz!"

"Oh, come on. It's not fancy." Julie stood back, which put her butt in the corner created by the vanity and the wall. "You'll make his eyes pop out. Get the shoes on."

While Erin struggled with the ankle straps of the shoes, Julie threw on Erin's uniform. When Erin glanced up, she said, "Oh, God, no. You'll get arrested for impersonating an officer!"

Julie's response to that was to take the shirt back

off, turn it inside out, and put it back on. "This will work. Badge hidden. Lettering almost hidden. People who can read inside out and backward may report me, but I'm not too worried about someone like that coming in before I close in fifteen minutes."

She jerked open a cabinet and plucked out a little zipper bag. "My shop makeup so I can freshen up during the day. Come here so I have better light."

Erin moved closer to the vanity and soon felt about Johnny's age as her friend messed with her face. As Julie shadowed Erin's eyes, she said, "You'll have to stop by my place later to get your uniform."

"Tomorrow. Just bring it to the shop. I have three more sets at home."

"Okay. That works." Julie grabbed a fat brush and began highlighting Erin's cheekbones with blush. "Thank the saints that the bruises on your cheek and eye are gone. Be still. Almost there. All we need now is a touch of mascara and some lip gloss."

"What do I look like?" Erin tried to roll her eyes far enough sideways to see herself in the mirror. "Not too heavy. You know how I am about makeup."

"I know how you are about everything that's girly, and trust me, Erin, my way's better."

Erin suffered through getting mascara applied to her lashes, fearing an accidental stab of the wand would render her blind in one eye if she wiggled. "Careful."

"Don't blink! You're smearing it!"

"It's a little hard not to blink when you're poking at my eyes with a black stick."

"Shut up," Julie said as she uncapped a pale pink lip gloss. "I can't hit your lips when they're moving. I hope he likes watermelon."

"It's flavored? My enchiladas will taste weird."

"You're not meeting him to *eat*. Your aim is to turn him on."

"Which may be impossible. You said you didn't think he was attracted to women."

Julie laughed. "Yeah, well, as you very well know, my stud finder is malfunctioning. Maybe he deep-froze me because I'm not his type, and maybe the reason he doesn't date is—heck, I don't know *why* a guy that handsome would willingly be celibate. But go meet him, smile, don't do the cocked-hip thing with your arms akimbo, and give him the benefit of the doubt."

She jerked Erin's shoulder-length hair from its clasp and rubbed styling gel between her hands. The next thing Erin knew, Julie went after her hair as if she were trying to shake out fleas.

"There!" she said. "Magical transformation in three minutes. You look beautiful."

Erin stepped close to see herself in the mirror. Her hair looked like she'd slept restlessly, had a bad case of night sweats, and had just climbed out of bed. "Julie, that's *awful*."

"Don't touch it! It's perfect."

"But it's *messy*."

"It's bed hair. When a guy looks at you, it makes him think about doing things to you. Really *delicious* things. Trust me on this."

Erin sighed and turned from the mirror. "Thank you. It's better than how I looked when I walked in."

"Such gratitude overwhelms me." Julie opened the door. "Now, get your beautiful self and that horrible gun out of here. I've still got to determine how to button a shirt when it's inside out."

Chapter Eleven

Slade sat on a fallen log near the creek, a spot that had become his favorite quiet place many seasons ago. He loved the smells here and always thought about the little net bags his mother had once made to put in all the dresser drawers and closets. Sachets, she'd called them, to make their clothes smell nice, floral scents for her and Slade's sister, woodland smells for him and his dad. Of a morning, he'd liked to press a clean T-shirt to his nose and savor the perfume of pine, cedar, sage, manzanita, and traces of mint. It had filled his mind with images of places just like this, where the massive trunk of a dead ponderosa provided him with a seat while other elements of the forest tantalized his senses. Mother Nature had created a collage of beautiful things to commemorate both new growth and decay, with every stage of life represented in between. The tree upon which he sat was rotting—disintegrating little by little—but its contribution to existence hadn't ended. Worms and insects had burrowed deep into its pulp, turning what had once been wood into dust that fell to the ground and nourished tiny saplings, sprigs of fern, the roots of grass and flowers, wild strawberries, and moss, to name only a few. The mature sheltered the young. The dying leaned against the strong to stay standing as long as possible. Slade was, for this moment, melding physically with a cycle that never ended, and he was as much a part of the process as the moldy carpet of the forest floor.

Huge ponderosa pines stood like sentinels along both banks. A small waterfall, created by a deposit of rocks that had shifted into a bottleneck during high water, sent up a melodious babble that was never the same from one moment to the next. Listening to it soothed and helped center him. He could drink in the beauty of nature or he could close his eyes and just breathe for a few stolen minutes.

He came here when he was troubled. He'd learned over time that if he stayed long enough, he would become aware, heartbeat by heartbeat, of how great and magnificent Creation was and how insignificant he actually was. It followed that his troubles and worries were also insignificant. These majestic old-growth trees would still be standing a century from now, long after he was dead and buried. Life would go on. The earth would keep turning. The sun would continue to go down at night and come up in the morning. When a man considered just how temporary his own existence was and how unnecessary his presence was, he came to understand that he wasn't even one of the cogs that kept the wheel turning. Once he internalized that, he also came to realize that the little frustrations of his daily life weren't all that important to anyone but him.

Normally Slade's worries at base camp were about his guests. When they began coming in, he often had at least two people who took an instant dislike to each other. It became Slade's job to think of creative ways to keep them separated. But it wasn't always easy to manipulate two hardheaded adults, especially not when they sought each other out for another round of bristling and posturing. Other times he'd get a Rambo—some damned fool who'd gone through survival training, pumped his muscles up with steroids and weight lifting, paid a fortune for some mean-looking tattoos, and suddenly believed, beyond any shadow of doubt, that he was the roughest, toughest wilderness guru that had ever walked. The Rambo guys didn't bother Slade that much, unless they tried to guide, advise, or correct the behavior of other guests. If that happened, he had to intervene, and he'd been known to boot an offender out of camp if it became necessary.

But this evening his worry was about Vickie. She was proving to be the best chef and camp jack he'd ever had in his employ, skilled at her job, willing to work the equivalent of three split shifts, never shying away from heavy loads, eager to please palates, and ever cheerful and friendly. Well, mostly cheerful and friendly. When she saw him, her smile vanished and her lips puckered like the top of a drawstring pouch. Sometimes they had a civil exchange, but more often she responded to his questions with monosyllabic answers and he grunted. He wasn't sure *why* he grunted, only that it seemed safer than talking. Around Vickie, he seemed to have a talent for saying the wrong thing. Grunts were left open to interpretation by the giver and the receiver. Slade could be thinking *eff you* when he grunted and the person he grunted at might think he was saying *fantastic*. That worked.

Vickie would tell him that his guttural utterances were a coward's way out, but after nearly a week of tiptoeing around that woman, he would only agree with an emphatic *hell, yes*. She was as mercurial as the red shit inside a thermometer. He could make the most unobjectionable observation ever—like the night he'd told her she wasn't too old to get a pup—and in a twinkling, he was a no-good, rotten, heartless son of a bitch. He'd go before a jury of his peers to plead his case on that one, and he had every confidence that he'd get a unanimous vote of not guilty.

So, he grunted. When she said good morning, he grunted. When she asked how his meal was, he grunted. He grunted so much, in fact, that he wouldn't be surprised to find himself eating bananas and grazing his knuckles over the ground when he walked. He formed words only when she asked direct questions, and he kept his answers brief and to the point. The last thing he needed or wanted was to cross horns constantly with a woman half his size. She didn't fight fair.

And that was why he was out here, sitting on a grubworm nest. He had to talk to Vickie about the practical jokes, and grunting his way through that conversation wasn't going to cut it. First off, he had no proof that

Vickie was the culprit, so he'd be broaching the subject with his hat in his hand and an apology on his lips for suspecting her. Secondly, the pranks had been harmless and funny. *Scary, glowing eyes out in the woods.* That trick was almost as old as the ponderosas that loomed over him and as common in a camp as gnats in the pancake syrup. In the old days, glow sticks hadn't yet existed, so people had stuffed a slender flashlight into a paper towel roll. Same effect, same result: spooked campers.

The spider drawn on the toilet paper had been hilarious, too. For most people, it would have been a harmless instant of startled fright. Only, Slade wasn't most people. He had a bad case of arachnophobia, and only Vickie had known that—until he'd hopped out of the shitter with his pants down around his ankles, screaming like a girl. Vickie had deliberately targeted him. Others used his makeshift toilet on occasion, but ninety percent of the time, Slade was the occupant. He had what he called a "rodeo knee." He'd busted up his kneecap years before, and the joint could no longer handle being bent into a full squat with his weight adding pressure. He could hunker by a fire with his rump resting on one boot heel for hours—a position often called a "cowboy rocking chair"—but squatting in the woods brought tears to his eyes. Thus, his regular use of the shitter he constructed every year.

No doubt about it, Vickie had set him up to make a fool of himself. Slade cringed every time he considered what a picture he must have made. As he'd pulled on the tail of tissue, which hung from the branch of a limb he'd poked in the dirt, the squares had unfurled, making the drawn-on spider appear to be moving toward him. He'd gotten only a glimpse before the arachnid flashed out of sight, and he'd been sure the damned thing had dropped off into his pants. *My bad,* he thought. Vickie couldn't be held to blame for his irrational panic. The prank hadn't been intended to do any harm. But, despite that, Slade felt that he'd been victimized and injured, even if the blow had been dealt only to his pride.

He knew she probably hadn't considered any of the far-reaching results of making a laughingstock out of him. It had been only a joke, something everyone got a kick out of. In a camp, jocularity every once in a while kept the tensions down and embellished the whole experience of roughing it with unforgettable memories that brought a smile to the lips. He got that. Hell, he'd even played a few camp pranks himself, always just for fun and never with malicious intent. But he had to make Vickie understand that he couldn't allow his authority as the outfitter and boss to be compromised. And, hello, if a Rambo dude showed up tomorrow, he'd lose all respect for an outfitter who screamed and ran from spiders. That spelled trouble. Slade couldn't allow some overblown weight lifter to constantly contradict him, disregard camp rules, or usurp his authority in any other way.

Only how could he explain all that to Vickie? He guessed he could come right out with it. *Don't embar-*

rass me like that again and make me look like an idiot.
But that pretty much placed the blame entirely on
Vickie, and the truth was, it had been Slade's reaction to
a harmless trick that had actually caused the problem.

He went back to staring at the trees, and after about
twenty minutes, he finally found that peaceful place
within himself where the little frustrations of daily life
weren't all that important. His wisest course of action,
he decided, would be to leave it alone. Chances were
good that Vickie would target someone else with her
next prank. And even if he took the brunt again, he
needed to remember it was all in good fun. In camps,
it was almost a rite of passage for people to learn how
to be a good sport when the joke was on them.

Yep, he just needed to chill, as Kennedy was fond of
saying. Why risk getting Vickie's back up when her
next prank might be something as silly as putting salt
in the sugar bowl? Even if Vickie was deliberately trying to bedevil Slade, she would soon run out of pho-
bias, because he had only two, the second one being an
irrational fear of snakes.

Wyatt got back to base camp at around nine thirty that
night. Domino came charging out to greet him with
happy barks, which Wyatt couldn't hear, but even in
the gloaming, he could see each jerk of the canine's
body. He swung out of the saddle and bent over to pet
his dog. Domino hated when Wyatt went places without him, but sometimes it was necessary. Today had
been one of those times. Having to stay in the truck

most of the afternoon wouldn't have been fun for an animal who was happiest when he could run and play.

Wyatt was surprised to see the central fire still blazing. And what a welcome sight it was, not only because the leaping orange and yellow flames looked beautiful against the sooty backdrop of the forest, but because he was cold and tired. He led Shanghai to the tack area, removed the pack of booze from where it was draped over his rump, and then set himself to the task of seeing to the horse's well-being and comfort.

Before walking into camp, where the guys were all congregated by the fire to stay warm while they talked and drank beer, Wyatt stopped to collect two bottles of whiskey, which he'd bought in Mystic Creek for himself. Once guests arrived, Wyatt would make a polite appearance by the fire at night, but then he'd escape to the privacy of his tent and enjoy a couple of drinks in blissful solitude. He avoided groups of people as much as he could. It was too draining to attempt to read lips fast enough to keep up with all the conversations. So he socialized for only a short while before he escaped. Sometimes he read. Other times he *listened* to music; the habit drove his brother, Kennedy, nuts, but contrary to what hearing people believed, Wyatt could, in his own special way, *listen* to music. Nothing relaxed him more than to plug his headphones into his phone and play songs with the volume up as far as it would go. Then he'd just lie back on his bed with the phone on his chest and his palm pressed over it. He could feel the music that way, and he could entertain himself for hours trying to imagine the tunes. What he created in his mind probably wasn't anything like what other people heard, but that didn't matter. He enjoyed music in his own way, and after two drinks, he could almost dance to the beat.

Wyatt circled around the central fire to reach his quarters. He rarely took bottles of his own liquor to the common area. Slade bought everything the guests needed, and Wyatt wasn't about to provide an open bar for strangers. He was happy to share with Slade or other camp employees when they visited his tent, but his generosity ended there. He'd learned the hard way that paying guests came into this situation believing that everything was complimentary. He got that. They paid big bucks to have fun at camp, and they tended to help themselves to everything in sight without thinking much about it. Wyatt's private stash of pricey sipping whiskey was not up for grabs.

Once inside his tent, he put his saddlebags under the cot, set his whiskey in a corner, and was about to connect his cell phone to the solar charger when he thought of Erin. *Again.* He'd thought of little else as he'd come up the mountain after enjoying such a nice time over dinner together.

He wrote, *"I'm back at camp. Didn't get lost in the dark. Didn't go to sleep and fall off my horse. Safe and sound. Thanks for joining me for dinner. It was nice getting better acquainted with you."*

There, he thought. He'd done the polite thing by texting her, and nothing in the message hinted that being with her tonight had fired up all his jets. That was his business and only his business. He would never act upon it. He had sworn off women, and he meant to keep it that way.

He was trying to get the USB cord inserted into the bottom of his phone when it vibrated in his hand. On the screen, a notification told him that Erin had texted back. He smiled slightly and opened the screen to her message.

"So glad you made it. Dinner was wonderful. Good food. Good company. I enjoyed getting better acquainted with you, too. It's so awesome that you taught yourself to speak so clearly. I'm impressed by your determination and all the time you invested to reach that goal."

Wyatt's smile deepened. Having worked with deaf children, Erin probably understood almost as well as he did how hard he'd worked to accomplish what he had. Most people failed to understand that he'd done something truly remarkable.

His phone vibrated again and a second text from her popped up. *"We aren't really right for each other, but I think we have a shot at being great friends."*

Wyatt's smile vanished. Why in the hell did she think they weren't right for each other? That bugged him. He wasn't interested in a relationship with her, but she *was* attractive, and he liked to think he still had what it took to turn a woman's head.

He messaged back. *"You're a beautiful woman, and when you start getting some time off, you'll meet more men, and you will be asked out. I guarantee it."*

"Thank you for the compliment," she said in reply. *"Sleep well. Have sweet dreams."*

"Sweet dreams."

Wyatt had just gotten his phone connected to the charger when the shadow of a passerby was cast against the front of his tent. His attention wouldn't have been drawn to it except for the speed of movement, which was inexplicably slow. Whoever was out there crept forward and was hunched over at the waist as if trying to keep a low profile.

Curiosity piqued, Wyatt pushed aside the door flap and leaned his head out the opening to see who it was. *Vickie.* Her tent was at the end of the row, so in order to reach the cookshack she had to walk by his. Only she wasn't walking; she was skulking. And her behavior told him she was up to no good. *The wronged woman.* He didn't quite understand her reasoning. According to Slade, she'd been the one to take another woman's word over Slade's. She'd been the one who ended their relationship. She'd been the one who'd married, had children, raised them to adulthood, and never once notified Slade of her whereabouts. Now she was back and as pissed off as if he'd screwed around on her only yesterday. How in the hell did that make sense?

His skin pebbled with apprehension when she halted outside Slade's tent, glanced back over her shoulder at the central fire, and then slipped inside the shelter. He almost groaned. *Not another spider prank.* Slade's reaction had been one that Wyatt would never forget. It wasn't often that he got to see a strong, normally fearless man get so frightened that he danced around in broad daylight half-naked. Wyatt had never witnessed anything like it, at any rate. But enough was enough. He could understand why Vickie might harbor some residual bitterness toward the boss, but after so many years, she shouldn't be obsessed with getting back at him. Someone needed to make her memorize the old maxim *Let bygones be bygones*.

He gave himself a stern mental lecture to keep his nose out of other people's business. He believed in freedom of choice. That didn't mean he always agreed with what people chose to do, but oh, well. They still had a God-given right to make their own choices. So if Vickie and Slade wanted to play games and end up killing each other, he guessed he should pretend he was both deaf *and* blind.

Vickie knelt by Slade's cot and reached inside her zipped-up vest to pull out the rubber snake she'd hidden under her clothes. *Party time. Again.* She drew back the top fold of his sleeping bag to reveal his pillow, encased in white, and the plaid flannel lining. She curled the snake into a coil as if it were about to strike. It was a gorgeous replica of a rattlesnake with some kind of bendable wire running the length of the body, which enabled her to position it realistically. It was getting late in the year for snakes to be out, but Vickie knew from experience that sunny days could bring them aboveground until hard freezes became the norm at night. It wasn't beyond the realm of possibility that one might have wandered into camp. There weren't many rattlers in this part of central Oregon, but Slade wouldn't think of that. He'd just freak out when he started to get into bed.

Hurry, hurry. She knew he might decide to hit the sack at any moment. He rarely stayed by the fire for more than one beer. She couldn't fuss with this for long. She managed to position the snake low on the flannel, with its tail loosely coiled, its head elevated to strike. The replica had its mouth open and its fangs bared. It even spooked her, and she knew it was fake.

When satisfied with how the serpent looked, she drew the top fold of the sleeping bag back up to hide it. *Perfect.* If she studied the top of the bedding, she could tell something was hidden under it. But Slade wouldn't notice. He'd be tired when he came in. After tossing some wood into the stove to keep his small fire going for most of the night, he'd strip down to his boxers, lower the wick of his lantern, and start to climb in bed. In the dimming lamplight, the snake would look even more realistic. *Easy-peasy.*

"For Brody," she whispered as she pushed to her feet. "I won't let you ignore the fact that you have a son any longer. Either we'll come to a meeting of the minds on that or I'll never let up on you for the rest of your life."

Vickie escaped from the tent and retraced her steps to the end of the row where her own shelter sat. She whistled softly, wanting to appear relaxed. *Bad move.*

She couldn't whistle a tune to save her soul. She sounded like a sick cat.

When she was safely inside her quarters again, she curled up on her sleeping bag and drew her phone from her pocket to text Nancy. *"I did it! There's a rattlesnake in his bed. I'm so nervous I'm about to get the giggles. Talk to me! I can't be laughing when he finds it."*

Nancy was apparently carrying her phone around with her because she messaged back almost immediately. *"You'll be okay. You used to keep a totally blank look on your face when I lied to you, and then you lowered the boom."*

"I hope you're right," Vickie typed. *"I'll be his number one suspect. I'm okay with that. I just don't want him to know for sure that I did it."*

"Sooner or later, he'll be really, REALLY eager to discuss Brody with you. You're not just sending him letters that he can ignore now. You're right in his face."

Vickie grinned. *"Yes, I am, and he'll play hell trying to make me back off."* Her mirth waned. *"How's Brody tonight? Any better? I'm worried sick."*

The previous afternoon, Brody had agreed to work with a crazy mare because he needed the money. The mare had started bucking the instant Brody got on her, and according to Nancy, Brody's only comment on the matter was, "I didn't last for eight seconds." It was a rodeo term for outlasting the clock. If a rider stayed on a bronc for eight seconds, he'd gone the distance and could dismount.

"He went to the ER today. Doc thinks he tore a muscle in his lower back. In a brace. Bed rest for seven days. Wait-and-see game."

Vickie groaned. *"He can't lie around for a week! He'll get behind on the bills."*

"He's hurt, Mom. He's got no choice."

"He'll be back out there tomorrow on that damned horse!" Frustration welled within Vickie. She loved her son, but he was just as stubborn and bullheaded as his father was. *"His back won't heal if he doesn't do as he's told. He's going to wind up a crippled old man without a dime to his name."*

"Tell him that. He may go down, but he never stays down."

Vickie pushed at her hair. *"I'll update you when the snake show is over. I have to put on my pj's. It'll look funny if I go to see what all the commotion is about when I'm still fully dressed."*

"Dead giveaway. Hurry. Text me when it's over."

Slade took a page out of Wyatt's book and bade everyone who stood by the fire a friendly good night. Pistol often chose to linger with the guys. They frequently had bedtime snacks and shared them with the dog. Pistol didn't want to miss out on the goodies. Slade was fine with that. Pistol took his job as the camp watchdog seriously and guarded all the tents, not just Slade's. As a result, he rarely slept inside Slade's shelter, choosing instead to snooze wherever the mood took him. When Slade woke up of a morning, he sometimes found his dog curled up on the ground just outside his tent. Other times he wouldn't see Pistol until everyone gathered at the cookshack for breakfast.

He was tired, and all he wanted to do now was crawl into bed and listen to an audiobook on his phone until he fell asleep. His solar charger was a blessing up here in the back of beyond. Listening to a story drained his phone battery, but the solar device recharged it while he slept.

He carried an armful of wood into the tent to stoke up his fire. Then he shed his Carhartt jacket and kicked off his boots. He got his phone hooked up to the charger before he stripped off his clothes, leaving on only his boxers. *Life is good,* he thought. He was enjoying the sci-fi novel he'd downloaded. Slade liked being transported into a fictional world where he could forget about this one. He didn't feel lonely. He didn't feel frustrated. His mind didn't race in circles to keep him awake. And in that other world, Vickie didn't exist, so his heart didn't ache, either.

Shivering in only his boxers, he started the play function on his phone, turned off the lantern, and then swung toward the cot to jerk back the top fold of his sleeping bag. The male narrator's voice came over the speakers. Klieg, a male character in the story, hovered his finger over a button that would annihilate another planet. Slade was about to flop down on the bed, but in the fading glow of the lamplight, he saw a rattlesnake coiled to strike. Almost before he could register that, the lantern sputtered and everything went black.

Snake. He jumped backward. Turned to run. But he couldn't see. Just as Klieg blew the planet of his enemies to kingdom come, Slade plowed into the woodstove. The piping hot metal caught him across the shins. The next thing he knew, flames, burning wood, and embers spilled out onto the dirt floor, blocking his way to the door. *Sweet Christ.* Fire licked up the front wall of the tent, blocking Slade's only path of escape.

The flames at least gave him some light. He couldn't see the snake, but he knew it had to be near him. A rattler. He was trapped in a tiny enclosure with one of his worst nightmares.

"Snake!" he screamed. "Snake!"

And then he faced the real danger. The flames had reached the ceiling. He had no way out. He grabbed his pants, the loops still threaded by his belt. He felt the leather scabbard, unsnapped the flap, and jerked out his hunting knife.

"Fire!" he yelled. "Wake up! *Fire!*"

Slade's fear doubled. The tents weren't that far apart. Unless they got this fire under control, most of the camp could go up in flames and possibly the forest along with it. He slashed at the canvas wall with the sharp blade. The blistering heat of the fire closed in on him. The instant Slade had created a path of escape, he plunged through the hole to get the hell out before the entire structure collapsed on top of him.

Vickie giggled when she heard Slade scream, "Snake!" Then her heart tumbled when she heard him yell,

"Fire!" In her stocking feet, she ran from her tent and cast a horrified gaze at the flames stretching toward the sky. *Oh, dear God.* She burst into a run, her brain barely able to assimilate what she was seeing. She'd done nothing to start a fire, but there was Slade's tent ablaze. She didn't hear him shouting now. Had he gotten out? Been hurt? What if he was still inside?

Vaguely aware of the others who were racing in from the central fire and running in the same direction she was, Vickie sent up a mindless litany of prayer. *Don't let him be hurt. Please, God, don't let him be hurt.* By the time she reached the flaming tent, her lungs felt as if they might burst. "Slade!" she screamed.

He was in there. Oh, dear God. She had to help him. Had to. Not allowing herself to hesitate, Vickie hunched her shoulders, tightened all her muscles, and burst into a run. If she hit the flaming canvas going fast enough, maybe she could get through the fire so quickly it wouldn't burn her. Slade would do it for her. She knew he would.

"Whoa!"

A hard arm came around Vickie's waist, vising her belly so hard that it slammed some of the breath out of her. She managed to scream anyway. "Let me go! He's in there. Let me *go*, damn you!"

Using her fingernails and all her strength, she clawed at the arm that held her back. Slade might be overcome by the smoke. Possibly the heat. She could still save him. He wouldn't be dead yet. Not yet. *Please, God, not yet.*

"Vickie, stop it! It's me. I'm here. I'm okay."

She went limp within the circle of his arm. "Slade?"

When he loosened his hold on her, she whirled around and then bounced on her tiptoes to throw her arms around his neck. "Oh, God, thank you, God! I thought you were still in there!"

His solid embrace closed around her, and for the first time in over forty-one years, she was pressed full-length against his body again. A feeling like she'd just rediscovered where she truly belonged swamped her. A sob tore up from her chest. He ran a big hand up and down her spine. She was so grateful that he was *there*, that he was okay, that he wasn't in that tent.

He set her away from him. "I've got to help. If this fire gets away from us, all the tents will go. It could also catch some of the trees."

Vickie staggered and almost fell as he walked away. Dazed, feeling numb, she caught her balance. *Men, all around her, half of them naked from the waist up.* They fought the fire with anything they'd been able to get their hands on, swinging their shirts, blankets, and shower towels to stamp out the flames. Vickie saw the next tent catch fire. She crossed her arms over her waist to grab the hem of her fleece sweatshirt and peeled it off over her head. Then she was on it, beating out the flames licking up the side of Dale's shelter. To her relief, she stopped the fire there from spreading and was able to smother it with repeated swats of her shirt.

But behind her, the other tent continued to burn. A

pine bough above what was left of Slade's tent caught. Within seconds, Rex was jerking the starting rope of a chain saw. When the motor roared to life, he reached over his head to cut through the tree limb and leaped out of the way when it crashed to the earth. Men descended on it to extinguish the flames.

It seemed to Vickie that an eternity passed. She grew so exhausted that she could barely move her arms to continue swinging her blackened shirt. Her legs felt rubbery. Her lungs rasped from breathing in so much smoke, but she wouldn't allow herself to stop and rest. Not until every last trace of fire had been obliterated.

Finally silence fell all around her. Vickie swayed on her feet as she glanced at the soot-streaked faces of the men. They looked like oversize raccoons. Her arms went limp and dangled at her sides. Her fleece shirt, barely recognizable now as a garment, slipped from her fingers to puddle on the ground. Trailing her gaze over each male countenance, she searched for Slade, needing to see him again so she'd know he was all right.

He came around the end of what had recently been his tent but was now only a blackened framework of aluminum poles with ragged and charred strips of canvas dangling from them. "Everything," he said hollowly. "All gone, even my phone. That damned snake got to die listening to my bedtime story."

"I thought I heard you yell snake," Kennedy said. "But that was what woke me, and then you started yelling fire, so I thought I dreamed it."

"Nope," Slade assured him. "I opened my sleeping bag to crawl in, and there it was, a rattlesnake coiled to strike. I'd turned off the lantern, so I got only a glimpse before everything went black. I *hate* snakes. Garter snakes, bull snakes, racers, you name it. But nothing terrifies me more than a rattler." He shuddered and rubbed his bare arms. "Son of a bitch, I'm damned near naked, and all my clothes are gone. Even my boots."

Vickie ran her gaze from his face down his rangy body. Someone had brought lighted lanterns, and the glow illuminated his skin, which had always been dark, even where the sun didn't touch. But cast against the inky blackness of the night, he looked as white as a ghost except for the streaks of soot all over him. She registered a bit dimly that age hadn't changed his physique. He was still a powerfully built man, and looking at him, remembering making love with him, made her heart hurt.

"Where's Wyatt?" someone asked.

"Probably asleep," Kennedy replied. "He could have slept through all that commotion. Should I go wake him?"

"Might better," Slade said. "He's the only man in camp as tall as I am. With any luck, he may have a pair of pants that'll fit me."

"I'm tall," Kennedy pointed out.

"And skinny as a beanpole," Slade noted.

As Kennedy turned to advance on his brother's tent, Rex stepped through what had once been the doorway to Slade's shelter. "Stove's on its side. What the hell happened?"

"I ran into it," Slade explained. "It was as black as smut in there. I couldn't see. Caught it with my legs and knocked it over."

"So that's what started the fire," John said. "Please don't tell me you were running to get away from the snake."

"What the hell else would I run from?" Slade retorted. "Of course I ran. It was poisonous, and I couldn't see where the hell it went."

Vickie's chest felt as if it were imploding. Collapsing in on itself. Flattening her lungs. She found it difficult to breathe. *The snake.* What she had intended to be a practical joke had sent Slade into such a panic that he'd tipped over the woodstove. He could have been badly burned. He might have died. And it would have been her fault. Suddenly she felt sick to her stomach. The lemony puckering of her mouth that always preceded vomiting made her try to swallow spit she no longer had.

"Huh," Rex said. "Only got half your sleeping bag."

"Be careful," Slade warned. "I didn't imagine the rattler. If the bag isn't toast, the snake could still be alive."

Rex leaned forward, grabbed an edge of the sleeping bag, and flipped it back. "Yep," he said. "It's still here. Not really what I'd call alive, though. It's halfway melted."

"What?" There was a sharp edge to Slade's voice.

"I said it melted. It's—well, it *was*—a rubber snake, not a real one."

"It sure as hell looked real," Slade shot back. A glitter of anger entered his eyes. "Rubber? You mean someone put it in my bed as a fucking *joke*?"

Slade sliced his gaze through the darkness to settle it on Vickie. She flinched as if he'd slugged her, and when she looked into his eyes, she knew that he knew. She'd been prepared to be his primary suspect earlier. But that had been when she'd seen all of this as a harmless prank. Now she stood next to the rubble of what might have been Slade's crematory, and nothing about any of it seemed funny anymore.

And then Slade grabbed his chest as if with sudden pain, moaned, and crashed to his knees. Rex leaped clear of the charred debris to reach his boss's side. He curled a big hand over Slade's upper arm. "Talk to me, boss. Is it your heart?"

Slade then slumped sideways against Rex's leg. Three more men converged on them. In the blur of motion, all Vickie could focus on was the man she'd loved nearly all her life. Wyatt arrived, his straight hair in a stir from his pillow. He went immediately to Slade, felt for a pulse in his wrist, and shouted for someone to lend him a watch. Vickie couldn't move. A heart attack. She'd believed for a few brief minutes that God had given her a pass and somehow worked things out so her prank hadn't done any lasting harm. Only Slade held a splayed hand over the center of his chest, and his face twisted into a grimace from the pain.

"Get a spare cot into the cookshack!" Wyatt yelled. "Hurry. We need to lay him down!"

Vickie whirled to do his bidding. Dale outdistanced her to reach the nearest guest tent, but she was on his heels as he stepped inside. "I'll get the bedding," she told him. "You get the cot."

Dale did as she said, and within a minute, they were both racing toward the cookshack. Vickie entered first. This was her bailiwick, and she knew her way around by heart. By patting her palms over the table, she located a lantern and matches. Within seconds, the phosphorous sulfide tip of a match ignited, and she lighted the lantern with violently trembling hands while Dale moved behind her to unfold the cot and set it up in front of the prep table. She grabbed the bedding she'd tossed on a bench and quickly made up a comfortable place for Slade to lie down. Her brain ran in circles. They needed to call for help. Was there a helicopter pad anywhere close to them? If Slade was having a heart attack, they had to get him medical care, ASAP.

"Is there a hospital in Mystic Creek yet?" she asked Dale.

"No, ma'am. Only urgent care. They do a good job, though. Get people stabilized for transport. There's a great hospital in Bend. We'll have to get him to a heart center."

Vickie covered her face with her hands, which were smeared with black grime and stank of smoke. "Oh, God. This can't be happening."

"He'll be okay." Dale curled a hand over her shoulder. "Regroup, Ms. Vickie. He's a tough old coot. He'll make it through this."

Oh, how Vickie wished she were still as young and naive as Dale was. But she wasn't. She'd had friends younger than she was keel over dead from heart attacks. It didn't matter how tough Slade was—or how strong he might be. When the heart blipped to a stop, not even the strongest of the strong could survive without intervention, and Slade was hours away from any kind of help.

A cold knot of fear took up residence in her stomach, crowding out the nausea that had plagued her only moments before. Slade couldn't die. Not now, when she'd only just found him again. Not now, when there was so much unsettled between them. She'd do anything God asked—*anything*—if only He'd let Slade live.

But there was no time to pray, no time to bargain with God. Four men entered the tent, carrying Slade between them, two walking backward, their denim-clad rumps poked out behind them. Wyatt and Kennedy each held one of Slade's feet. With a shuffling of boots and a good deal of cursing, they finally got their boss onto the cot. Vickie hurried forward with a blanket, which they used to cover him. He moaned. Nudging the males aside, she stepped in closer to take Slade's hand.

"I'm here, Slade," she said shakily. "I'm right here."

"Vickie?"

"Yes, it's me, sweetheart. I won't leave you. I promise."

"Never?" he asked, his voice sounding fainter.

Tears sprang to her eyes, nearly blinding her. Why had it taken something like this to make her realize how very much she loved him? Why, oh, why hadn't she come home years ago with Brody in her arms so Slade could have seen his only son at least once? Now it might be too late. Too late for Slade. Too late for Brody. Too late for her.

"Never," she pushed out. "I'm right here with you. Wild horses couldn't drag me away."

His hand went limp in hers. Terror, icy and cold, washed through her in waves. She gripped his lax fingers with all her strength. "Slade? Slade!"

He stirred and fixed a twinkling gaze on her. "Gotcha."

Vickie jerked and loosened her grip. She shot him a bewildered look, and he gave her one of his trademark grins. "What?" she said stupidly.

"You heard me." His voice didn't sound weak at all now. "Gotcha. Or maybe I should say, Gotcha back."

Wyatt, who stood at the foot of the cot, said, "Okay. We're out of here. Guests are coming tomorrow. While these two kill each other, let's grab some shut-eye, boys."

Kennedy's voice rang out. "But it's just now getting interesting!"

"We-are-out-of-here," Wyatt said. "*We* means everybody."

Vickie heard boots shuffling over the plywood to the door. Wafts of cold air came in as the tent flap lifted again and again to provide egress for the men. Her senses began to clear. She focused on Slade's chiseled features and then on the twinkle of mischief in his gray eyes. She'd seen that look so many times, mostly after he'd done something playfully ornery. After shoving a snowball down her shirt, his eyes had always twinkled in just that way. When she ran from him and he caught her, he'd looked at her just the way he was now.

"You son of a bitch," she whispered.

He laughed and sat up, looking as muscular and fit as a man half his age. "Yep, that's me, and I have to tell you, it feels really good. I could get into this practical joke stuff. It's kind of fun."

Vickie had dropped to her knees to grieve at his side. Now she felt like a complete idiot. It all came clear to her then. How Slade had grabbed his chest and pretended to be in pain right after Rex told him the rattlesnake in his bed had melted. He'd instantly known that she had been responsible, and he had decided just as quickly to teach her a lesson she would probably never forget.

"How could you?" she asked in a voice that sounded more like her own. "I thought I'd killed you! That I'd caused you to have a heart attack. How *could* you?"

"How could *you*?" he volleyed back. "You know I'm phobic about snakes. That they terrify me. But you planted one in my bed. All in good fun. Right? Well, maybe now you have an inkling of how it feels when you're on the receiving end of a vicious prank."

Vickie pushed to her feet. He ran his gaze over her with insolent slowness. "Nice bra."

She dropped her chin to look down, just then remembering that she'd jerked her shirt off to help fight the fire. Her first urge was to cover herself with her arms. But she refused to do any such thing. She'd seen bikini tops that made her bra look modest. "Luckily, I kept it on under my sleepwear." She forced herself to smile, a sugary smile that she hoped would irk him. "I knew you'd start screaming like a little girl when you saw the snake, and I'd have to race to your tent, acting as surprised as everyone else. Running without a bra is . . . not fun."

He pushed away the blanket and swung his legs over the edge of the cot. Bracing his hands on the metal frame, he gazed up at her with an expression that was suddenly solemn. "I love you, too," he said. He held up a hand when she started to speak. "Don't deny that you love me, Vickie. You were terrified when you thought I might die, not just in here, but out by the tent. If I hadn't stopped you, you would have leaped through a wall of fire to reach me."

He was right; she couldn't deny that she had feelings for him. "So what? I've loved you since I was a little girl. You threw that love back in my face."

"No. You *think* I did that, but I *didn't*."

Vickie was so tired of the lies and she was fed up with his refusal to acknowledge his son's existence. She folded her arms at her waist, which made her feel less vulnerable. "You're so full of it your eyes should be brown. And just for the record, I no longer care if you slept with April or not. That was your choice."

Shadows darkened his gray eyes, revealing pain and yearning but absolutely no regret. "I didn't make that choice, though. I told you then and I'm telling you now, I never touched her. And if you no longer care whether I did it or not, why in the hell do you still hold such a grudge against me?"

"I sent you *four* letters, Slade. One might have been lost in the mail. Hell, I'll cut you even more slack than that and say *two* might have gotten lost. But all *four*, Slade? How dumb do you think I am?"

He frowned and rubbed his forehead, leaving a black smudge just above his nose. "Letters. I don't know what you're talking about, and I'd really appreciate if we could stay on topic."

"That *is* the topic. It's the *only* topic. I still love you. Why, I don't know. You don't deserve it. But those feelings have been buried for so long, Slade, that they can just stay buried now. The important thing at this point, the *only* important thing, is that you step up to the plate like a man and finally acknowledge our son!" Tears filled her eyes, the blur of them almost blinding her. "I won't allow you to pretend he doesn't exist anymore."

"What?"

The incredulous, stunned expression on his face grabbed at her heart, and she wanted to believe in him so badly that she almost wavered. But no. She'd learned long ago that Slade could be a very convincing liar when he chose to be. "You heard me. I will no longer allow you to deny our son's existence. Game over!"

The stunned look turned to outrage so quickly that Vickie fell back a step as he sprang to his feet. The muscles in his face tightened, contorting his features. A flush crept up his neck and flooded into his cheeks. *"What?"* he said again.

"Stop it!" she cried. "I know you got those letters, damn it! I know you saw the snapshot of Brody! How could you look at that baby and tell yourself he wasn't *yours*?" She no longer cared how angry he might be and took a step toward him. "Were you afraid Brody and I were a package deal? That you'd get tied down with a wife you didn't want and a passel of kids that would cramp your style? Think again! You'd already made me eat my pride! I wasn't about to crawl back here and spit it out at your feet so you could walk all over it again!"

He bent his head and held up both hands as if to silence her. "Give me a minute. I need a time-out."

"You've had a forty-one-year time-out!"

He raised his head, and he shot out a hand so fast to grab her arm that she barely saw him move. His fingers bit into her flesh. "God forgive you," he said raggedly. "I have a *son*? I have a son, and you never *told* me?"

She tried to jerk her arm free from his grasp, but the clamp of his hand was like an iron manacle. "I did tell you! Four different letters, Slade! Don't you get all self-righteous on me! I did my part! You never wrote back. I included my address on each envelope, and you never once showed up on my doorstep wanting to see that little boy! The *least* you could have done was stick a check in the mail every year to contribute to his support." She jerked away from him, surprised when he relaxed his hold and let her go. "You didn't even do *that* much."

"You need to leave," he said, his voice gone flat and expressionless. "I need some space. Please, go. I've never struck a woman in my life, but God help me, I'm tempted to now."

Her feet felt stuck to the plywood. "I'm not afraid of you, Slade Wilder."

"Right now, you should be."

"Fine! I'll leave. But know this! He's *your* son, and if you try to deny that any longer, I'll steal some of your DNA to prove it."

She whirled to storm out the doorway and stopped right at the edge of the flooring. "One other thing." She turned to face him again. "Don't think for a minute that I'm after your money, if you even have any. That's not why I came here. Your son needs help right now that I can't give him. I came here, hoping against hope, that you might finally step up to the plate and act like a father instead of a deadbeat jerk."

When Vickie burst out of the tent, she almost ran

into Wyatt, who stood with his shoulder braced against a tree. "I didn't stay to eavesdrop. That's impossible for me. I just had to be sure everything was okay."

"He isn't in any danger of dying from a heart attack. You can safely go back to bed."

"It's dark. You're too far away. I can't read your lips."

Vickie closed the distance between them and repeated herself. Wyatt said, "I figured as much, but I had to be positive. He was pretty convincing."

"When he's lying, he's always convincing."

From inside the cookshack, Slade yelled, "I heard that! Just go to bed, Vickie. I'll find you when I think I can discuss this without throttling you."

As if Slade hadn't just filled the night with an angry male roar, Wyatt said, "I needed to make sure you were okay, too."

Vickie touched his shirtsleeve. "His bark is worse than his bite," she said, barely above a whisper. Volume of speech wasn't necessary for Wyatt to understand her. "You shouldn't have worried about me."

She patted the younger man's arm and stepped around him.

Wyatt went inside to check on Slade. The boss was as hard to take down as a gnarly old oak tree, but that didn't mean he was invincible. And it had been a rough night, stressful for everyone in camp.

"I'm fine," Slade told him. "Sorry if I gave you a

scare. I didn't think about frightening all of you. I just wanted to teach her a lesson about practical jokes by scaring the bejesus out of her."

Wyatt bit back a smile. He guessed even people past retirement age were entitled to act like children every once in a while. "I think you succeeded. Now you're even. She scared you just as badly."

"Yeah, the score was even for all of a minute. Not now, though. She got in the last punch."

Wyatt had no idea what to say, so he kept quiet. After a moment, he said, "If you need to talk, I'll be happy to stay. If not, I'll head to bed."

"I couldn't carry on an intelligent conversation right now if I tried. Go ahead and get a good night's sleep."

Wyatt left the tent. He'd never seen the boss look so devastated or defeated. He didn't know what had passed between him and Vickie, but it had shaken Slade up. As he walked to his tent, he stared at Vickie's. Her light was still on. Her shadow danced against the golden walls. It looked as if she were pacing in tight circles. He glimpsed a light-colored blur moving toward her shelter. *Four Toes*. Wyatt stopped in his tracks. Was the bear about to go inside? If so, the third scare of the evening was about to occur. Vickie's screams would rattle the nerves of every man in camp except his.

Just as Wyatt feared, the bear stopped in front of her doorway and pawed the flap aside as if he did so often. Seconds later, in he went. Muscles snapping

taut, Wyatt glanced around, expecting men to pop
from their quarters like peas from a shooter. *Nothing.*
That meant Vickie hadn't shrieked in terror. He swung
his gaze back to the illuminated wall of her tent and
saw her shadow drop to its knees. The next instant,
Four Toes' silhouette was cast against the canvas, and
the two shapes blended together.

Wyatt closed the distance between him and her
shelter. City folks tended to have romantic notions
about wild animals and believed they could be domes-
ticated with enough love and understanding. Vickie
seemed to have a vast knowledge of the wilderness and
its inhabitants, but maybe she'd lived in town for so
long that she'd forgotten some of the things she'd
learned as a kid. Tamed bears could be friendly and
harmless most of the time, but if any little thing set
them off, they could kill a person with one swat. And
Four Toes was *not* tame. He'd spent most of his life out
in the forest, coming in to his feeding station at the
ranch in the morning and at night so Slade could feed
him. Slade had stopped providing Four Toes with food
the previous summer, after serving him the pepper
bomb, and the bear had been out for revenge ever
since. Slade wasn't afraid of him. No one who'd been
around Four Toes in his infancy was. But nobody was
stupid enough to hug him, either. Vickie was putting
her life at risk.

Wyatt almost tried to knock on her door flap but
caught himself. His knuckles rapping against canvas
would make no sound that Vickie would notice. He

cleared his throat. "Vickie, this is Wyatt. Can I speak to you for a second?"

From this angle, her shadow didn't show, so he was mildly startled when she swept back the canvas partition and stepped outside. With the night temperatures plunging as they were, most people would have invited him inside. He decided she must be trying to hide her furry visitor.

"I saw Four Toes going into your tent," Wyatt told her. "I couldn't turn a blind eye. It's dangerous for you to be chummy with that bear."

Shivering from the cold, she hugged her middle. Then she spoke, but with the illumination of the tent behind her to play heck with his night vision, he couldn't read her lips. He held up a hand. "Sorry. I can't hear you, Vickie, and it's dark."

As soon as the bear slipped past the two of them and lumbered back out into the words, Wyatt bade Vickie good night and sought out his quarters, removed his phone from his pocket, and started texting Erin before he even reached the bed to sit down. He could only hope she was awake. *"Things are a mess here."*

His phone vibrated almost instantly. Her reply popped up. *"Is Uncle Slade okay?"*

"Physically, he's okay. Emotionally, I think he's a wreck."

"What happened?"

Wyatt tried to think how he might explain without typing a whole manuscript. Texting was his only means of communicating over a phone, so he could light up a keyboard and overwhelm people with long texts. *"It's a long story."*

"Hit me."

Wyatt pressed the microphone symbol and just started talking. He was tired, and he didn't relish the thought of tapping out everything he had to say. *"There's this woman named Vickie Brown in camp. Years ago, she and your uncle were in love and about to be married. Before the wedding, some girl told Vickie that your uncle had sex with her at a beer party. He says he never touched the girl, but Vickie broke their engagement and vanished. I think he cried to find her."* Wyatt stared down at the words. *Damn.* He'd been lazy and allowed his speech to slur. He manually corrected the errors and moved on, speaking more deliberately. *"He still loves her. Never stopped."* Okay, he was being lazy again, but she'd be able to make sense of the incomplete sentences. *"I think she's the reason he never got married."*

"Uncle Slade, in love? OMG!"

"I get the feeling from Slade that a part of him died when she walked out. Anyway, she popped back into his life without warning, and it's like she's got a vendetta against him. Playing stupid practical jokes that target him. Tonight she went too far. Don't think she meant anything bad to happen. Put a fake rattlesnake in his sleeping bag."

Wyatt went on to tell Erin the rest of the story, ending with, *"I guess Slade decided to show her just how awful it sometimes is to be on the receiving end of a joke. He pretended to have a heart attack. Scared me so bad that I almost had one myself. I'm pretty sure it ended with them having a huge fight. Being deaf, I can't eavesdrop, but it sure looked like things got ugly."*

"I'm coming up. I need to make sure he's okay. He never married. It sounds like this Vickie gal was his one and only. He must be devastated."

"I thought you couldn't get time off."

"I made friends with the dispatcher who had it in for me. It's my weekend off, and she won't call me in. She's promised to pick on someone else for a while when there's an emergency."

Wyatt's heart lifted at the thought of seeing Erin again so soon. But the feeling of gladness was another warning sign to him that she was dangerous. He'd vowed never to mess with another woman, and he'd kept that promise to himself for years. Most of the time, he could look at females to his heart's content and just walk on by, but Erin De Laney was different somehow. Despite that tough-gal, kick-ass-and-take-names image she tried to project, he sensed something vulnerable and fragile in her that attracted him. Everything within him felt frozen at the very thought of starting anything with her. He had learned that women were bad news.

"No need to come up. I've got this," he texted. *"Take the weekend to rest. You deserve the downtime."*

"No way am I staying home. I'm coming. If nothing else, I'll have a one-on-one talk with her and tell her how the cow ate the cabbage."

The last thing Wyatt wanted was two pissed-off women in Slade's camp. Slade might have a *real* heart attack if the two women he loved tore into each other like she-cats.

"I don't think confronting her is a good idea," he typed. *"They aren't kids. We need to butt out of their personal relationship."*

"You can butt out. But if she's hurting my uncle, she'll do it again only if she goes through me."

Wyatt politely concluded the texting session. *Shit.* Maybe he shouldn't have told Erin about the fake heart attack episode. He'd just been worried, not so much about the older man's ticker, but about his mental state. Slade's behavior tonight had been totally out of character for him. He was normally levelheaded and calm. He never grew impulsive and did stupid stuff, but faking a coronary was plain-ass stupid. At Slade's insistence, Wyatt had gotten first-responder medical training and knew better than to perform CPR on anyone whose heart was still beating, but the rest of the hired hands hadn't taken classes. If Wyatt hadn't been there, the dopes might have done Slade serious harm.

Weary beyond words, Wyatt decided to hit the sack and "listen" to some music on his phone. It always soothed him. He got settled on his cot, pressed his cellular device to his chest, and was starting to relax when he remembered that damned bear. How were he and

Slade going to explain the presence of Four Toes in their camp when Erin showed up? Slade had taken full responsibility for rescuing the bear when he was a cub, but Wyatt and Kennedy had been his partners in crime. The three of them had broken the law nine ways to hell. Erin was honor bound to uphold those laws. If she realized that Four Toes had been habituated to humans, which was clearly the case, she'd have to turn Slade in. It was more than just a part of her job; she'd taken an oath when she was sworn in to uphold the law, and that meant she couldn't turn a blind eye when she loved someone who had done or was doing something illegal.

Chapter Twelve

Slade jerked awake when Vickie entered the cook-shack before the crack of dawn. He could normally see well in the dark, but not in a tent with all its walls lined with stocked shelves. Even so, he knew it was her by the light tread of her boots. Men walked differently, taking longer strides and making louder thuds with the soles of their shoes. He heard her groping for the lantern that sat on the table and then the rustling of stick matches in the box. He angled an arm over his eyes to shield them from the sudden glare of light.

"You can look now," she bit out. "No modeling of underwear this morning. I'm fully clothed."

Okay, she was still in a snit. Under any other circumstances, Slade might have offered her an olive branch, but he was too damned pissed off himself to give a shit how mad she was. "What the *fuck* were you thinking to name my kid Brody?" He snarled the question as he lowered his arm to glare at her. "What kind of name is *that*?"

She flashed him a stiff smile, more like baring her pretty little teeth than making a friendly gesture. "Oh, jeez, sorry if you don't like it. In the first letter, I did ask what name you'd like if it was a boy. No answer, so I just went with what *I* liked. It seemed fair at the time. I *was* the one who had to work while puking my guts up with morning sickness. I *was* the one who spent three months of my life unable to see my toes. And I *was* the one who went through three days of labor without my child's sorry-ass father in attendance to so much as hold my hand. How inconsiderate of me."

"I never got a fucking letter!" he yelled. "I didn't know I knocked you up! How could you do this to me, Vickie?" He sat up and thumped his chest with a knotted fist. "My *son*, my very own flesh-and-blood, and you never bothered yourself to even so much as call my folks' house? They would've told me. I would have been banging on your door in a fucking heartbeat!"

"If you use that word one more time, you may wear your breakfast, you son of a bitch! Unless you've changed, you never use the *F* word around ladies."

"I'm not so sure you qualify as a lady anymore," he shot back.

When she rounded on him, Slade had a flashback to their younger years when she'd been such a beauty that she'd taken his breath away. And, *damn* her, she was still beautiful even though she'd pulled her wildly curly hair back into a rubber band and it poked out at the nape of her graceful neck like the prickly fur of a hedgehog. He knew how soft it would actually feel, though. And he'd always loved the scent of her hair.

How it tickled his lips. And her body. She still had the slender figure of a woman half her age. And those eyes. It broke his heart just to look at her.

"I'm no longer a lady," she agreed. "I'm one *hell* of a woman. Shall we exchange insults, Slade? I'm ready."

"You used to say you wanted to name our first boy Slade. What happened to *that* plan?"

"That plan flew out the window when I was forced to marry a logger who could support me while I was pregnant and too sick to work, and then later support your son." She sent him one of those angry looks that always had made her eyes look like emeralds shot through with sunlight. Some things never changed. "Fool that I was, I still loved you, but my husband wouldn't have tolerated it if I had named our son after you. So I did the next best thing."

Slade didn't want to hear that she had still loved him. She'd thrown her diamond engagement ring at his feet and walked away from him, damn it. And she hadn't trusted him at his word. And then, to make all that even worse, she hadn't made sure that he knew he had a kid. What if he *had* gotten drunk and screwed April Pierce that night? If Slade had been guilty of the most horrible mistake of his life—which he wasn't—it wouldn't have diminished his love for Vickie one bit.

"So where did 'Brody' come from? It's Irish, isn't it?"

"It's American slang for making a car or motorcycle spin in circles. About that time, you were doing rodeo and spinning in circles on a bull or a bronc." She bent to shove wood into the stove and crouched to light the fire. When she slammed the door, the sound of cold metal striking metal rang out so loudly that he thought it probably woke every man in camp except Wyatt. She stood and dusted her hands clean on her jeans. "Pretty much the same thing. Don't you think? Slade Wilder, the rodeo champ, doing his damnedest to get himself killed."

"And I damned near succeeded a few times."

"I know." He heard her voice break. She tried to cover it up with a cough, but he wasn't fooled. "Marilyn and Mary Alice wrote me letters and kept me updated on you. I burned them so Matt wouldn't find them." She shot him another sparkling look, beautiful but lethal. "Stupid fool."

"And why do you think I didn't give a shit if I lived or died, Vickie? Because I loved you. The rodeo was all that kept me sane."

"I'm sure the buckle bunnies and booze helped a bit."

Slade bent his head. He wasn't proud of what he'd done during that period of his life. "Yep, there was a long string of women and a lot of hangovers, Vickie. And maybe all that helped, too. Bottom line is, if you loved me, why in the hell couldn't you trust in my word when I told you I didn't get drunk that night and have sex with April?"

She walked past him. "Get your ass up and fold that cot. I'm going to need that prep table to start breakfast."

"I asked you a question!" he shot back, putting more volume into his words than he intended.

She turned from the sink with a butcher knife clenched in a white-knuckled fist. For an instant, Slade thought she might come after him with it. "Because you must have had sex with April! She was at the party! You never denied that! And she described that birthmark on your right butt cheek perfectly." She laid the knife across the edge of the sink with exaggerated care. "Hmm, let me see. Maybe April had X-ray vision and could see through a pair of Wrangler jeans. Nope. Mere humans aren't gifted with that superpower. So I guess that must mean at some point during the evening, your britches were down around your ankles."

Slade couldn't have been more bewildered if she'd told him that he'd spelled his name on April's neck with hickeys. *"What?"*

"Give it up, Slade. You're guilty. Why can't you just admit it? She saw the birthmark."

"She *couldn't* have seen the birthmark! She wasn't even there the whole time. Her brother got too smashed to drive and she came late to give him a ride home. Somebody had his truck radio on. I did dance with her, Vickie, but even that didn't include touching. It was fast music, not the snuggle-up-and-cop-feels kind."

"She described your birthmark in detail. It has that little jag on one side that makes it look like a pie somebody took a slice out of."

Slade felt so agitated that he wanted to get up and pace, but he'd be damned if he'd do that in front of her when he wore nothing but soot-streaked boxers. "I never dropped my trousers in front of that woman! Why in the hell can't you believe that?"

"You say you weren't drunk, but you'd been drinking when you came by my parents' house to see me. We made love in our hayloft that night." Tears gathered in her eyes. "Did you even shower her off of you before you buried yourself inside me?"

Slade was getting one hell of a headache. And he decided he didn't give a shit if he was wearing only dirty shorts. He sprang to his feet. He was no longer so angry that he feared he might harm her, but his hands did itch to grab her by the shoulders and shake her until her perfect teeth rattled. "I-did-not-have-sex-with-that-woman! And you can paint it any way you like, but the bottom line is, you kept my son from me! My *son*, Vickie. I never got any damned letters! I never saw a picture of him when he was a baby! Even if you believed that I'd screwed every girl in Mystic Creek that night, did that obliterate everything you knew I stood for? Everything you knew I believed in? Did it alter your feelings so damned much that you couldn't trouble yourself to climb in your damned car and drive home to make *sure* I knew you were pregnant? Or later, if you were too sick to drive during the pregnancy, why didn't you come home then?"

"My car broke down!" she screamed back at him. "Not long after I got to Coos Bay, before I even realized I was pregnant! I had no money to get it fixed. I walked to work, stopping to puke in the gutters. For

months, I could hold nothing down until late afternoon, not even water!"

"And later?"

"I was married! He was jealous! I'd told Matt I
couldn't love him, because I still loved you! He said he
loved me enough for both of us. And, hello, Mr. Judg-
mental, Matt was my surefire bet. You *weren't*! Four
letters went unacknowledged. Well, explain where four
letters wandered off to, Slade. I sure as hell didn't get
your name wrong!"

Slade mentally circled her argument. As angry as he
was with Vickie, he'd never known her to look him in
the eye and tell a bald-faced lie. A white lie, maybe, or
a little fib. But even then, she hadn't been able to maintain visual contact with him. He distinctly recalled one
time when his parents were throwing a surprise birthday party for him, and she'd had to lie in order to get
him home in time for the shindig. Even then, she'd had
to look away as she told him some story she'd made up,
and he'd known she was telling him a whopper.

So it followed that she truly had written to him. Letters that he'd never received. In a town where everyone
knew him. A memory flashed in his mind, and his
blood ran cold. Only a couple of weeks after Vickie
had fled Mystic Creek, April Pierce had gotten a job at
the post office as a mail sorter. Rage roiled within him.
It was inconceivable to him that any young woman
could be so besotted with a man who barely even knew
she was alive that she'd fabricate a tale to break up an
engaged couple a week before their wedding. It was

even more of a stretch for him to believe that April would have been so vicious that she might have seen Vickie's letters and somehow prevented them from ever reaching him. All his life, he'd heard people use the quote "Hell hath no fury like a woman scorned," but he'd never rejected April. It made no sense that she might have done something so horrible. And yet, what other explanation was there? His mind raced with questions, but of one thing he was certain. He couldn't so much as hint to Vickie the possibility that had just occurred to him, not until he knew for sure. He assumed a stony expression, because this woman that he loved so well knew him better than anyone else on earth.

Chapter Thirteen

Still ranting, Vickie advanced on Slade, her small fists doubled as if she might take him on. "How *dare* you ask me why I didn't do this or I didn't do that? While you were out bonking little blondes with no brains, I was big and pregnant and hobbling around on swollen ankles, and we were so broke we could barely pay the rent. It was a year before we could even afford a phone. And by the time we got one, when I could have called you collect, Matt had turned into a mean drunk! If he had seen that I had placed a phone call to someone in Mystic Creek, he would have known. And trust me, I might not have lived through the consequences."

Seeing the pain in Vickie's expression, Slade felt his heart clench in his chest, and for an instant, he thought he might have a coronary for real. He struggled to modulate his voice before he spoke. "Don't tell me he beat on you. I swear to God, I'll hunt him down and kill him with my bare hands."

"You can't. He's already dead." Her eyelid twitched, and then her mouth quivered. "But, yes, he was violent. I didn't need you to play hero and take care of the problem, though. I'm a Granger, and I was a big girl. I took care of it myself. He beat the hell out of me only once."

"Please tell me you divorced the son of a bitch."

"Not then. It wasn't long after I'd given birth to Brody, and I hadn't gone back to work yet. I had to think of my baby. What would happen to him if I couldn't put a roof over his head?"

"Your folks were here! They had a roof. Why in the hell didn't you just come home?"

"I still didn't have a home phone to even call them. It was spring, and the weather was horrible. I worried over exposing a tiny baby to the cold wind and driving rain to walk to a phone booth. I had to step up and act like a grown-up for my child. So I took care of it. Matt backed off and never struck me again."

"I'm sorry you went through so much, Vick. If I could go back and change it, I would. Please know that. I am so very sorry."

Her hands relaxed, and he knew her anger was ebbing. He glanced down at himself. Half-naked and covered with soot and dirt, he was surprised she still cared enough to be standing there to argue with him.

"I, um, need to find some clothes," he said. That was true. He couldn't go down the mountain on a horse without at least a pair of boots on his feet. He also had guests he'd have to meet at the trailhead late in the afternoon. But maybe, just maybe, he could replenish his wardrobe, whistle up another rifle, see about getting his hunting license replaced, and still have time to pay April a short visit. If he was wrong about her, so be it. But everything seemed to circle straight back to her.

"And so that's it?" Vickie's hands clenched into fists again. "You haven't asked me one real question about our son."

Slade wanted to ask her a thousand different things, and when the time was right, he would. But right now, he had far more pressing matters to think about. "Today's Saturday. Guests arrive late this afternoon. Buck season opens tomorrow and runs until Friday. In the fire last night, I lost everything I need to guide a hunt, even my saddlebags." Slade knew he was driving another wedge between them. She undoubtedly wanted him to ask what color Brody's hair was, how tall he was, what he did for a living. She needed to know that he cared. But right at that moment, he had other important questions to ask, and she wasn't the woman who could answer them. "I love you, Vick. I'll carve out some time this evening to talk with you. I promise."

He saw her expression grow shuttered. "That's fine. Business is business. I get that."

Only Slade knew that she didn't get it at all, and she wouldn't until he got some answers. He raked a hand through his hair and realized he'd just rubbed more soot through it, not that it mattered. Even though the fire she'd built now snapped and crackled behind him to warm the tent, he pretended to shiver. "I need to roust Wyatt out of his bedroll and see if he has some threads I can borrow. I'm freezing."

"Go." She said the word as if she were telling him

goodbye. "I need to get breakfast started, anyway. If I don't, I'll have a bunch of starving men breathing down my neck."

Slade turned to walk away, but then an awful thought struck him. She'd obviously come back mainly to confront him about the son he hadn't known he had. Now that she'd done that, there was nothing more to hold her in Mystic Creek. He faced her again. "Promise me something."

"What?" she asked woodenly.

"Promise me you'll still be here when I get back, Vickie. You said Brody's in a jam and you can't help him out of it. If there's any way I can, I will. I swear it. But we do need to talk."

She hugged her waist and gave him a deadpan look. "I'll be here. You owe me money. So if your checkbook went up in that fire, get another one while you're gathering stuff up. I won't leave until I'm paid."

As Slade left the cookshack, he decided then and there that he might not cut her a check until her month of employment ran out. Even if his suspicions were correct about what had happened to the letters, even if he could prove to Vickie beyond a shadow of a doubt that he'd never been unfaithful or lied to her, they would still need hour upon hour to simply talk. He knew she still loved him just as much as he loved her, but forty-one years was a very long time, and they'd changed. Maybe not in huge ways, but they still needed to bridge that chasm of separation and get to know each other again.

As he gimped over the icy ground, hopping when he stepped on rocks and made his gouty toe send stabs of pain up his leg, he promised himself that no matter what happened, he'd never just let her walk away from him again. Maybe they couldn't change all the miserable things about their story up until this moment, but damn it, they could make sure the ending was beautiful.

He'd make that happen or die trying.

Slade was exhausted by three o'clock that afternoon when he knocked on April's front door. Her last name was Jones now. A few years after Vickie left town, April had married a stocky fellow named Harley. He seemed like a nice guy, and when Slade had seen them together around town, Harley seemed to adore his wife. Slade wasn't a revenge seeker by nature. After Vickie broke their engagement, he had confronted April. Yelled at her, actually, for telling the woman he loved such a vicious lie. But once he'd vented his rage, he'd walked away and never looked back. April hadn't been worth any more of his time. At that point, she couldn't change what she'd already done. He hadn't been able to find Vickie so he could drag her home and make April tell her the truth. What was the point? Slade was a great believer in karma. Or maybe it was more accurate to say that he believed every bad thing people did was noted and written down somewhere in the sky. God eventually dealt with individuals like April. It wasn't Slade's job to punish her.

Now, as he waited for her to answer the door, he could only hope her husband wasn't home. Harley would step in if Slade raised his voice. He also might overhear everything Slade said. Not a good situation. Rumor had it that Harley was extremely protective of April, and Slade had also heard that the big man had a jealous streak. This meeting would go smoother without his interference, not that Slade was in any mood to play nice if it got rough. While he didn't believe in retaliation or getting even, he wasn't above utilizing someone else's lies against them.

The door finally opened. In Mystic Creek, people didn't normally use the peephole to identify a caller or have a chain guard latched to prevent a sudden entry. Totally unsuspecting, April drew the portal wide and smiled in greeting. Slade had seen her only from a distance for more years than he could recall, and he was a little shocked by how well preserved she looked. Like Vickie, she was younger than he was, but only by a year or two, and that still put her at well over sixty. Her once-slim figure had grown a little heavier, but she appeared to be fairly trim. Gravity sure as hell hadn't yet won the war. She still bleached her hair and slathered on makeup, he noticed. At a certain age, most women couldn't get away with that. The application of too much foundation and eye shadow highlighted the wrinkles. But April didn't seem to have that many. Surgical intervention, he guessed. She'd always been a little obsessed with her appearance. Big hair. Lots of mascara. Heavy on the lipstick and glittery stuff. Slade preferred Vickie's natural look. He supposed she probably wore touches of makeup when she wasn't camping, but he doubted she would ever go heavy, not even for a night on the town.

"Slade!" April said, her tone conveying that she couldn't be happier to see him if he were a treat-filled basket from the Easter bunny.

He had no doubt that her surprise at seeing him was genuine. "April," he replied, keeping his voice even.

She pushed at her hair and tugged on the hem of her knit top, which hung fairly loose but still molded snugly to her generous bosom. She wore black leggings that revealed nicely toned thighs and calves.

"To what do I owe this honor?" she asked.

Slade rested a shoulder against her door frame and cocked one hip. "I'm just in the mood for a little walk down memory lane."

"A what?"

"You heard me." He let that float on the air between them for a moment. "Vickie's back in town."

He saw the shock register on her face, but she quickly rearranged her expression into a smile. "Oh, how lovely. How is she doing?"

"Pretty good. The same old Vickie, still mad as a wet hen because I allegedly got drunk and fucked you at a beer party over forty-one years ago." Slade recalled Vickie's comment that morning about his choice not to use the *F* word in the presence of ladies, and she'd called it right. His father had raised him to hold women in high regard. But April wasn't, in his opinion, a lady. In fact, he suspected that she was a malicious, self-serving bitch. "Crazy, huh?"

"It certainly is," she agreed with a nervous twitter. "It's hard to believe she's still fussing about something that happened so long ago."

Slade kicked his relaxed-cowboy stance up a notch by slipping his hands into the front pockets of his jeans. "Don't you mean what *didn't* happen so long ago?"

Bright spots of color suddenly flagged her cheeks. "Why are you here, Slade?"

He gave her points for catching on fast. "Oh, I don't know. Guess I've been thinking too much. I paid dearly for what *didn't* happen that night. Lost the woman I loved, just for starters. Never found anyone else. Never tied the knot with anyone else and had kids. I'll be honest, April. I've lived a lonely life. The hottest bed partner I've had in the last ten years was a panting dog. I never stopped loving Vickie, and now that she's back, the way I see it, I've got one more chance to set things right between us. One more chance to maybe fix things so we can be together in our golden years. One more chance to convince her how much I love her and that I never cheated on her or lied to her." He met and held April's wary gaze. "You following me?"

"I wish you well, Slade. You deserve to be happy."

"Thanks for saying that, April. And I think you're right; I do deserve to be happy, and so does Vickie. Which is what led me here. Being the wonderful old friend that you are, I thought I'd ask you real nice if you'd help me out."

"How can I possibly do that?" She rolled her heavily lashed blue eyes and planted her hands on her hips, showcasing inch-long, bright red fingernails. Like everything else about her, they were fake. "If Vickie can't grow up and get over it, nobody can make her."

Slade crossed one boot over the other and leaned just a bit more heavily against the wood frame to make sure she couldn't slam the door in his face. He had a feeling they would quickly reach that moment. "Well, you know, it's not really about Vickie's maturity level. Come to find out, she was pregnant with my baby when she broke our engagement and left town. And what's *really* mind-boggling is that she tried to notify me by letter, four times, only I never received the correspondence. That is odd. Don't you think? How could the United States Post Office lose *four* letters? One, maybe. By a big stretch of the imagination, maybe two. But *four*? How could that conceivably occur?"

She reached for the interior door lever. "Beats me. I'm sorry, Slade, but I have a hair appointment this morning and need to get going."

He held up a hand. "Not so fast, April. It occurred to me this morning that shortly after Vickie blew out of this little burg, you got hired on at the local post office. As a mail sorter, if I recollect it right." He drew one hand from his pocket to touch the brim of his Stetson. "I have to salute you on moving up the ladder and turning that into a lifelong occupation, by the way. When are you going to break through the glass ceiling and become our postmistress?"

Her chin came up. "I think it's time for you to leave."

Slade gifted her with a slow grin. "You and what army plan to make me?"

She straightened her shoulders. Studying her, Slade sincerely hoped she and Vickie never tied it up physically, because April weighed at least thirty pounds more and that muscle tone she'd undoubtedly worked hard to maintain at the Crash and Burn would give her a big advantage.

"If you don't leave, I'll just holler for Harley," she threatened. "He'll make short work of tossing you off our porch."

Slade chuckled. "I don't doubt that. He's a big boy. I hear he loves you like no tomorrow. How long you been hitched now?"

"Thirty-eight years."

"That's awesome, April. I love when I hear happily-ever-after stories. But it does make me feel sad for Vickie and myself, because somehow we got dealt a really rotten hand of cards. So here's my idea, and I think it's a good one. I thought maybe you could meet us tomorrow evening, say about seven, at the Witch's Brew. I hear JJ did extensive remodeling to draw in a classier crowd." He chuckled. "Of course, we all know JJ's idea of *classy* may differ from ours. But it might be fun to check it out."

"Tomorrow is opening day of buck season. Harley will be tired tomorrow night. Besides, we got religion a few months back, and we've pretty much given up drinking."

"Good on you!" Slade hooked the thumb of his free hand over his belt. "Have you given up lying, too?"

She acted as if she might shut the door, but she knew as well as he did that it wasn't going to happen. He'd have to move first, and for the moment, the soles of his boots had pretty much put down taproots.

"If you don't get your ass off my porch, I'm going to call the cops!"

Slade released a theatrical sigh. "Oh, April, please don't do that. I'd like to settle this peaceably without it getting messy. If you dial nine-one-one, it may be my niece who shows up, and she'll be all over me about minding my manners and not getting off a lady's porch when I'm asked."

"That'll be your problem."

"Yeah, but she loves me, you know, and if I defend myself by explaining why I'm here, I might slip and say something about a mail sorter at our post office intercepting and destroying someone else's mail years ago. That could get ugly. Isn't it a federal offense? I don't even know if there's a statute of limitations. Do you?"

"Are you threatening to have me *prosecuted*?"

"Oh, hell, no." Slade gave an exaggerated shake of his head. "That'd be just plain old mean. You've worked hard to get where you are, and I'd never want you to lose your job and possibly even your retirement. So I'm more inclined to give back only as good as I got. You know what I'm saying?" He flashed her another smile. "Way back when, the Mystic Creek grapevine was abuzz about us on the riverbank the night of the beer party. You remember all that. Vickie breaking our engagement. Then leaving town. Practically everyone knew we'd been getting it on. So I was thinking about resurrecting our affair. Two star-crossed lovers who denied themselves the pleasure of sneaking around to be together for almost forty years and finally gave in to temptation. You following me?"

Her face blanched. "If you do such a horrific and conscienceless thing, it will destroy my marriage."

"Turnabout's fair play, or so I've always heard. You destroyed mine. If not for your malicious interference, Vickie and I would soon be celebrating our forty-second anniversary." Slade shifted his weight to the opposite leg, getting more comfortable. "But you know what, April? The real clincher for me is that I've got a son I didn't know existed until last night. He was just a seedling when Vickie took off. The fourth letter to me included a picture of him, according to Vickie. Now, hell, he must be going on forty-two. I've never met him. Can you imagine how I felt when I learned about him?"

April thinned her lips. "You know what, Slade. You and Vickie are grown-ups now. Seems to me the two of you are responsible for ironing out your differences and mending your own relationship. There's not a reason on earth that I need to be involved in that."

"You were sure as hell involved when we broke up. And you were sure as hell involved when you pitched those letters in the trash bin. And that's where you totally stepped over the bounds of common decency,

April. You didn't just screw Vickie over. You didn't just screw me over. You messed up an innocent baby's whole life. He's a Wilder. By all rights, he should have grown up on my family's ranch, if not full-time, at least for regular visitations. He should have been supported financially and emotionally by his father. He should have known when he looked in a mirror where he got his nose or the cleft in his chin. Not that I know for sure if he looks like me, but I'm just saying."

"There's no way in fucking hell I can fix that *now*."

Slade winked at her. "It's so good to see the real April coming out of her churchgoer closet."

"What do you want from me, Slade?"

"The truth. Be at the Witch's Brew tomorrow evening. Buy Vickie a drink and tell her exactly what went down."

She cackled. There was no humor in the sound. "That'll happen when ice cubes won't melt in hell. Using your words, you and whose army are going to make me?"

Slade shrugged and straightened away from her door frame. "Okay, fine. I know stubborn when I see it. I reckon I'll just pay Harley a visit and tell him how sorry I am for sneaking around behind his back with his beautiful wife."

As Slade sauntered across the porch, she shrieked, "You get your sorry ass back here!"

Slade started down the steps. "Nope. I said my piece. Now it's entirely up to you. If you hope to celebrate your thirty-ninth anniversary, you'll be at that bar tomorrow night. Seven, sharp. Be sure to ask what Vickie likes to drink. Because of you, I haven't been around her enough to know."

Vickie was surprised when a lone rider approached camp around four that afternoon. The dogs barked loudly in greeting. For a moment, Vickie surmised it was one of Slade's paying guests who'd ridden up from the trailhead alone. But when she stepped closer to the central fire, she saw that it was a young woman with dark hair and a slender build. It wasn't inconceivable that a female might pay the steep fees for a guided buck hunt, but it was odd that she would come up the mountain alone. Women who were unfamiliar with a wilderness area normally chose to travel with companions. Men, too, as far as that went. On some level, most greenhorns realized they were out of their element here and sought safety in numbers.

As the woman dismounted and bent to pet the dogs, Vickie saw that she wore a sidearm. The holster it rode in looked like police-issue, and something about the way its wearer moved hinted strongly to Vickie of military training. *This is great, just great.* All Slade's certifications and licenses to guide had been destroyed the night before, along with his saddlebags. If that woman was a USFS agent out of uniform, Slade could be cited and fined. *What a mess.* That thought no sooner crossed Vickie's mind than she remembered Four Toes. He didn't hang around camp constantly, and she could only pray he wasn't nearby right now.

There truly would be hell to pay if a forest ranger saw what appeared to be a tame bear in Slade's camp.

Vickie started to walk out, thankful that no one had set to work on cleaning up the rubble from the previous night's fire. If their visitor was a law officer, she would see evidence that Slade's documentation had indeed been destroyed, and if any questions lingered in her mind, she could check on the Internet to be sure Slade's licenses and permits were all current.

To Vickie's surprise, Wyatt appeared from out of nowhere and reached the woman before she did. As Vickie approached, she heard the woman say, "I know, but I just had to come. He's my uncle, and I love him."

Wondering if the woman might be related to Tex, the only other older man in camp, Vickie mulled over that possibility until she got close enough to clearly see the gal's face. Her heart missed a beat, for there was no mistaking her resemblance to Slade. But what messed with Vickie's emotions even more was that she also resembled Brody and his younger son, Austin. Slade's niece, then: His sister must have finally bitten the bullet and decided to have a kid.

Vickie stepped forward with her right hand extended. "Welcome to camp," she said. "My name's Victoria Brown."

"Erin De Laney," the younger woman replied.

She had a firm grip, Vickie noted as they shook hands. Vickie appreciated strength in another woman. "I'm pleased to meet you," Vickie said. "I knew your mother when we were younger." It felt strange to be meeting a young lady who might have been her niece by marriage, even stranger to meet her son's first cousin. The age difference would have made the two kids unlikely playmates, but as adults they could have become close friends. "How is she doing? I haven't seen her in a coon's age."

"She's great," Erin replied. "Enjoying life as a Bellevueite."

Vickie thought she detected a hint of resentment in Erin's voice. "I'm glad she's happy." Vickie had always liked Slade's slightly younger sister just fine, but she'd always been a little prissy, making it difficult for Vickie to feel a true connection. "Bellevue is a beautiful city."

"It truly is," Erin agreed. "But after living here for a year, I think all the traffic would drive me crazy now."

Vickie didn't care for driving in heavy traffic herself. "I just put on a fresh pot of coffee," she told the younger woman. "Won't you please join me in the cookshack for a snack? I have a selection of tea as well and some fresh-from-the-oven cookies."

Wyatt stepped closer to Erin and grasped her arm. "Can she join you in just a moment, Vickie? I need to get her settled in a tent and show her around."

"Sure." As Vickie walked away, she wondered if the foreman had a thing going with the younger woman. Vickie hoped so. Wyatt wasn't merely handsome; he was a genuinely decent fellow. "No need to knock!" Vickie called over her shoulder. "The cookshack is open twenty-four/seven."

* * *

Erin tipped her head back to study Wyatt's sun-burnished countenance. Something was up. She could only stay tonight, so she hadn't packed all that much by way of clothing and toiletries. Getting her *settled* would be a simple matter of tossing her small satchel into a tent and calling it good.

"Okay," she said, holding his gaze. "Out with it. You're stewing about something."

Wyatt removed his hat and raked his fingers through his hair. Erin wished she could run her own through it. She imagined it would feel silky, but it could be coarse. She loved the way it drifted over his shoulders when he turned his head or the breeze caught it just right.

"I, um . . . I just don't want any trouble, Erin. Slade's been looking out for himself for a lot of years. He really doesn't need you to step in now and take up for him."

"I can't argue that point," Erin replied. "I came up the mountain with a bit of an attitude. I admit that. But Vickie isn't what I expected."

"What did you expect?"

Erin frowned as she tried to find words to explain. "She's definitely pretty. Striking. But she's not a femme fatale. All natural, and she seems very down-to-earth. The worst part is, I can see what drew Uncle Slade to her. She's sort of—well, charming isn't the word. Straight-forward, definitely. And the instant we shook hands, I felt kind of like I'd met a kindred soul."

"She definitely isn't girly," Wyatt agreed.

Erin struggled not to react to that comment with bruised feelings, but apparently her expression gave her away, because Wyatt quickly added, "Not that you aren't. Girly, I mean."

She waved his apology away. "No worries. I'm a tomboy, and I know it."

"But that isn't a bad thing, Erin. Not to guys, anyway. Well, not *all* guys, I guess."

Erin watched him search his mind for something else he might say, and the slightly injured part of her felt almost instantly better. He was scrambling to take his foot out of his mouth, and that told her he might actually prefer women who didn't fuss too much about appearance. "Wyatt?" She waved her hand in front of his nose so he would look at her. "I'm good. Really. I know I'm not a fashion plate."

He smiled and gazed off into the trees for a moment. "I worked hard to learn how to speak normally, but sometimes when I'm talking, I'm searching my mind so hard for the words that I don't think about how they'll sound when I say them."

She playfully slugged his shoulder. "You're amazing, and I'm fine. Now let's get my stuff in a tent so I can go to the cookshack. I'm starving!"

"Horse first. He's not a motorcycle that you can just park and forget about."

Erin glanced over her shoulder at Butterscotch, and as much as she hated to admit it, even to herself, she'd forgotten all about him. That was *not* okay. "Right. Horse first, me second." She remembered her first ride up the mountain on Butterscotch, and to her credit, she had seen to his needs before her own that day. There was just something about Wyatt that rattled her, that was all. As they grew better acquainted, she felt sure she would get over that. The last thing she envisioned for herself was to hook up with a cowboy, and he probably preferred genuine cowgirls, not a gun-toting deputy who couldn't quite come to grips with her own femininity. She turned toward the horse. "Poor Butterscotch," she crooned. "I'll bet you're even hungrier and thirstier than I am. I'm so sorry." Knowing that Wyatt couldn't see her lips with her back to him, she gathered the horse's reins and said, "If it hadn't been for him, I'd have forgotten all about you."

Vickie took an almost instant liking to Slade's niece. She was a straight shooter who had an engaging laugh and an energetic air about her. Because guests would arrive tonight at an undetermined time, Vickie had Irish stew simmering in huge pots, and she'd made authentic Irish soda bread, a family recipe from her grandmother, who'd been born in the old country. Vickie's mom had increased the ingredients to feed a large crowd, and in Vickie's experience, it was often a favorite with campers, whose appetites were stimulated by the fresh mountain air. For dessert, she'd made brownies, lemon bars, and chocolate chip cookies. Given that she had everything prepared and covered with flour-sack towels, she could sit at the table with Erin, visit to her heart's content, and consume calories that would add width to her hips if she didn't get plenty of exercise the next day.

She discovered that Erin was quite the athlete and had earned the distinguished honor of being an Ironman, or Ironwoman, a term that Vickie felt certain would one day become the norm as more and more females entered into the competition. Erin also shared with Vickie her dissatisfaction with her profession, which struck Vickie as being sad. She couldn't imagine being pushed into attending college to become something she didn't wish to be. It wasn't only a waste of years and money, but to feel trapped in an occupation that was unfulfilling had to be a daily trial.

"Anyway," Erin said with a smile. "Enough about me. I understand that you and my uncle Slade nearly got married many years ago, and Wyatt tells me that my uncle never stopped loving you."

Vickie hadn't expected Erin to broach this topic or to even know about her and Slade's history. "True. But that was a lot of years back, Erin."

The younger woman nodded. "Right. But you broke his heart. He's a good man, and in every way that counts, loving you that deeply destroyed his life. He never remarried or had kids, and I know he wanted them. He was amazing with me when I was little. So relaxed and fun to be with. I love him a lot, and because I do, I really didn't want to like you."

Vickie nodded, and her throat went tight. She met Erin's gaze. "Do you really think the heartbreak was one-sided? I won't say that loving Slade Wilder destroyed my life, Erin, but it did send me down a path that I never would have chosen for myself. I was deeply unhappy much of the time, and living from day to day, week to week, and month to month was always a struggle, both financially and otherwise. I had three children. I married a man who turned out to be a violent drunk. After I divorced him, he never paid a penny in child support. I would never wish that things had happened differently, because my children have been the greatest gifts of my life. To alter the past would mean they never would have been born. I can't bear the thought of that. But my life after leaving Mystic Creek wasn't easy. I didn't walk away from this place and forget what I left behind."

"So you never stopped loving him, either."

Vickie released a taut breath. "No, I never did."

"Is that why you came back? Why you're here now? Why you put a fake snake in his bed last night and scared him so badly that he knocked over a woodstove and could have burned to death as a result? I've been told you believe Uncle Slade cheated on you right before your wedding. Even if he was guilty of doing that, don't you think it's a little over the top to still bear him so much animosity? Can you explain any of that to me?"

Vickie met and held Erin's gaze. She refused to look away. "I can't even explain any of it to myself," she finally offered. "When I look back on all of it, what he did and what I did, or the decisions I made afterward, none of it really makes sense. I can't think of any one reason that pushed me to make all the choices I ended up making. There were always dozens of reasons. Pressures. Financial hardships. Hurt. Anger. A bone-deep sense of betrayal. Desperation. Stung pride. Fear. I could go on and on. But to go into detail about all those things with you, and maybe even with Slade, is impossible. I simply can't put all of it into words. So if your loyalty lies with your uncle and you can't like me because you feel I ruined his life, I won't blame you for that. There have been times over the years that I haven't liked myself very much, either."

Erin nodded. "Fair enough. And I kind of get it. When I look back, I can't understand why I did half the stuff I did, either. You know why I entered the first Ironman competition? To make my father proud of me. Why did I turn around and train for another year to do it again? To make my father proud of me, because the first time didn't quite take. Why did I become a law enforcement officer instead of a speech therapist? Your guess is as good as mine. At thirty-one, I look back and wonder what the hell I was thinking. So I do understand that we can't always make sense of stuff, and if we can't, we certainly can't explain it to someone else."

Vickie felt a burning sensation in her eyes. "Thank you for that."

Erin nodded, her lips curved in a slight smile. "You're welcome. But from here on out, can you stop with the practical jokes? It's like you have a vendetta against him. Given how much you loved him, I guess I can understand you feeling bitter, but maybe if you ask him to explain what made him make all the choices he did, he'll give you the same answer you just gave me. That he isn't clear on all of it himself and can't really explain it to anyone else."

"Maybe so," Vickie conceded. "Maybe so."

Slade arrived around seven that evening with five men on horseback. Vickie wondered where all the horses had come from, because Slade hadn't taken any from camp. She assumed that he must have trailered them from his ranch to the trailhead. That told her that he'd had a very tiring day, and she mentally kissed away her hope that he'd find time to talk with her that night. She wanted to be angry with him for making her play second fiddle, but in all fairness, she couldn't. Outfitting in the autumn was a business, *his* business, and he was responsible for every person in the camp. She had no idea how much money he made over a season, but she knew her dad had done quite well. If Slade counted on the income, he couldn't afford to shirk his duties as the camp host, and a reasonable person wouldn't expect that of him.

Vickie just wasn't feeling very reasonable. She dove into the dinner hour, which was a misnomer, because before it was all over, she'd worked three times that long. The cookshack table easily accommodated Slade and the five men who'd ridden in for a week-long adventure. It was Vickie's job to feed them, entertain them with conversation, and clear away their dishes, and then Slade's employees took their places at the table. By the time she had all the cleanup done, she was exhausted, but she was still too wired to contemplate sleep. So instead of going to her tent, she grabbed her flashlight and made her way down to the creek. A half-moon bathed the woodland with silvery light. Once she found a log to sit on and turned off the torch, she took a deep breath and then exhaled, letting the tension in her body drain away. She texted Brody, but he didn't reply, so she messaged Nancy, knowing that her daughter could give her an update on her son's physical well-being. Nancy repeated what she'd said the previous night, the only difference being that Brody now had only six more days of bed rest before he saw the doctor again. Vickie told Nancy how the rattlesnake prank had blown up in her face, but she left out the part about Slade faking a heart attack and that she'd finally told him he had a son. All of that was so thickly laced with emotion that she simply didn't have the energy to deal with the explanations just then. To complicate matters, things were still up in the air between her and Slade. She was sorely tempted to swipe a jug of Slade's whiskey and have her own private tent party. At least the liquor might relax her so she could drift off to sleep.

"You found my thinking place."

The sound of Slade's voice coming from the darkness

made her jump with such a start that her rump parted company with the log. "Damn it, Slade. You shouldn't sneak up on people like that. Why not act like a normal person and use a flashlight?"

"Don't need one. I could find my way down here blindfolded. It's my special place. Trust you to find it and take up squatting rights. First you tried to steal my dog and then my bear. Now you've taken over my private spot."

Vickie sighed. "I can see why it's special to you. The sound of the little waterfall adds the perfect touch. It's so beautiful and peaceful among these trees, the vastness of the wilderness all around me. Being here makes me realize how insignificant I really am."

He said nothing for a moment while he sat down beside her. "You stole the words right out of my mouth." He echoed her weary sigh. "That's why I fell in love with you, you know. Because you've always understood me better than anyone else."

"Huh. All these years, and I always thought it was because I was such a damned good lay."

He chuckled. "That, too. The best of the best, Vickie mine. I've never felt the same way about any other woman."

A slab of bark was poking her in the buttock and she shifted to get a more comfortable seat. "So is this how our *talk* will go?" In Vickie's estimation, their feelings for each other and the quality of their long-ago lovemaking were low on the list of importance when their son was in such desperate circumstances. Nancy had driven out to check on Brody, and she'd found him in bed, but she didn't rule out the possibility that he'd disobeyed doctor's orders. "I'm postmenopausal. I doubt I'd even like sex now. It's no longer important to me, that's for sure. It's been so many years that I'm not even sure I can remember how it all goes."

He laughed. "Yeah? Well, anytime you want a refresher course, you just let me know." He straightened his legs and crossed his ankles. "But we can drop that topic for now. I know we have a lot to hash out, but if my son is in a jam, he should be our first priority."

Resentment welled within Vickie when he referred to Brody as *his* son. He'd never done one thing to deserve the title except to donate his sperm. "Yes," she said tightly. "He's injured and in a financial jam. The doctor has ordered bed rest for a week, just for starters. No indication of how long it will be before he can work, and if he doesn't work, he'll lose everything."

"He got a family?"

"Yes, a sick wife and three sons. His wife has rheumatoid arthritis. That's the crippling kind, in case you don't know. She's a registered nurse, earned a good income until it struck, and now she can't work. Brody has nearly gone broke trying to take care of her. His son Marcus is brilliant. He earned a scholarship to attend Oregon State, but his dream university was Harvard. Nobody but me believed he'd get accepted there, but he did. I ended up getting an equity loan against my house to help him follow that dream, which is why I decided to get a job as a camp cook with an outfitter.

I can't pay my mortgage by working in the depressed economy along the coast right now. I could lose my place. You know the rest of that story."

"Kind of, sort of. But what didn't make sense to me the first day is making more sense now. I didn't know about Brody then. I had no idea." He clamped a big hand over her knee. "And don't go getting all pissed at me for saying that. I truly never got your letters. The night you broke our engagement, I begged you to trust in my word, and you couldn't. I'm asking you to do that again, Vick. From where you're standing, I know it appears that I'm lying. But I swear to you I'm not. I never got them."

"All right. *Fine.* Somehow four letters went astray in the mail. That makes perfect sense."

"I know it doesn't make sense. But will you look at me?"

Vickie couldn't. When she did and he stuck to his same old lies, she got an unholy urge to slap his mouth. "I'm not going there, Slade. You say you never got the letters. The pity of it is, that story doesn't hold water. You're asking me to believe in the incredible. I quit believing in fairy tales a very long time ago."

"Please, just look at me, Vickie. Straight into my eyes as I repeat it one more time."

"You're impossible. I looked into your eyes when you lied to me once. I prefer not to do it again. So, here's the deal." She finally forced herself to meet his gaze. "If you'll step up to the plate now and acknowledge your son, I'll pretend from this moment on that I believe you. If that's what it takes for us to move forward from here and help Brody, it'll be a small price for me to pay. You did a good job of breaking my heart the first time. You shattered it into a thousand pieces, and I could never glue it back together again. You can't break things twice. You can only grind the fragments to dust under the heels of your boots. I'll ask you to resist that urge. I've learned to cope. I moved forward. At least leave me with the fragments so that when I leave here, I'll still have what I came here with."

"The last thing I've ever wanted to do is hurt you, Vickie. I loved my dad. I loved my mom. I even love my sister, even though she's a bitter pill to swallow sometimes. But you're the only person I've ever loved more than I love myself."

"Oh, Slade." Vickie wanted to tell him that she wished she could believe that, but she knew that would be the wrong thing to say. "Thank you for that."

He grunted. It was sort of a huff under his breath, and he'd been doing it a lot lately. He gazed off into the moon-silvered darkness for a while. She suspected that he knew she hadn't bought into his profession of love for her. But there was very little she could do to change the truth.

"Okay," he finally said. "Brody. Let's stick to that. How much money do you think he needs right now to keep him afloat? I'll send him a check."

Vickie's heart caught, because that couldn't happen, not yet, and she knew when she told Slade, he'd be as angry with her as he'd been the night before. It was going to get ugly. But she saw no way to avoid it. "I'm sorry, but I'm afraid you'll have to make the check out to me, Slade. I'll have to send Brody the money."

"Why?" he asked. "Does he think my money is tainted or something?"

"No." The words she needed to say clogged in her throat. She had to knot her hands into tight fists and force herself to speak. "I haven't told Brody you're his father yet. He doesn't even know you exist."

Chapter Fourteen

Slade could scarcely believe his ears—he stared at Vickie for at least five full seconds, trying to make sense of the words she'd just uttered. What the hell? If the man had three kids, he sure as hell knew how babies were made, namely, that it took two people to get the job done, one of them a woman and one of them a man. He shot to his feet.

"How can that be possible?" He knew his voice had gone up in volume, but he couldn't for the life of him speak calmly. "What does the boy think, that you found him in your garden under a cabbage leaf?"

Even in the faint moonlight, Slade saw Vickie's face drain of color. She looked up at him with those big green eyes, only right then they didn't look green, but shimmery like the silver light that gilded the forest around them.

"Please, Slade, don't yell at me, not over this. I think I was a pretty good mom in most ways, but this one thing—well, it's haunted me for years. I made a bad decision. I understand how wrong it was. I lied to my children about it for *years* and only told my daughter, Nancy, the truth right before I left to come here."

Slade took three paces away from her, then turned and walked back. *Self-control.* He'd prided himself for years on his ability to hold his temper, and he could surely do that now. He made himself sit back down on the log. "Okay," he pushed out. "For you, Vick, I'm going to stay calm and not yell."

"Do you promise? Because I'm not entirely sure my nerves can take this conversation."

"I *promise*!" It irked him beyond measure that she might cling to a promise he made to her, but she couldn't trust in his word. "Just spit it out."

She nodded. In the shadows he saw her dainty larynx bob up and down. She was digging her nails into her knees, and watching her do that almost made him wince. Even through denim, she would gouge her skin if she bore down any harder.

"For God's sake, nothing can be *that* bad. Just tell me. Then we'll talk it over. It'll be okay, and I promise I won't yell."

She nodded. Then she closed her eyes, her lashes casting fringed shadows onto her pale cheeks. "I, um—I let Brody believe Matt Brown is his real dad."

As the words hit the air, they didn't sound so bad. Slade was halfway through nodding his head when their meaning sank into his brain. "You *what*?"

She leaned toward him. "Please try to understand. I had sound reasons, Slade. Matt said he would love Brody as if he were his own. He said if we told Brody that he wasn't Matt's, he would always feel like the odd child out when we had more kids."

Slade bit down so hard on his back teeth that he was afraid he had cracked a molar. "Let me get this straight," he said in what he felt was a normal voice. "You allowed a violent, drunk, woman-beating son of a bitch to decide if my son should be told who his real father is? And now, as Brody approaches middle age, he still believes another man's blood flows in his veins?"

"Slade, you're starting to raise your voice."

"I am *not* raising my voice, and even if I was, raising my voice is *not* yelling. When I yell, the veins pop out in my neck and on my forehead! Do you see any popping out?"

"Yes. It makes me worry you're going to have a stroke."

"I am *not* going to have a stroke. What I'm going to have is a jug of whiskey. I'm going to take it to my new tent, build myself a fire, and pretend you didn't tell me this while I drink the whole damned thing!"

"That sounds like a really good plan. Maybe it will—I don't know—give you a different perspective on things."

Slade got up and walked back toward camp, but with every step he kept seeing Vickie dig her nails into her knees. He finally stopped and looked back, hoping to find her following him. But in the glimmer of moonlight, he could still see the blurry shape of her sitting on the log. He slumped his shoulders, stood there for a moment, and then retraced his steps to her.

She jumped with a start again when he circled the log. "Why are you back? Did you forget something?"

"Yeah," he said as he sat beside her again. "I forgot to say I'm sorry for raising my voice at you." He took off his hat, thrust his fingers through his hair, and put it back on. "And I need to say I'm sorry for not being more understanding about what you went through."

She looked up at him, and in the moonlight, tears shimmered in her eyes like quicksilver. Slade had never been able to stand it when she cried. Maybe it was because she so rarely let go and wept. "Don't cry, Vick." He scooted closer to her and curled his arm around her shoulders. "No funny business. Just as your friend."

"Yeah, right," she said in a choked voice. "If this is friendship, who needs enemies?" He heard her gulp. "I'm so sorry, Slade. I should have told Brody the truth after I divorced Matt. Well, maybe not right away. He was only five, almost six. But I should have done it as soon as he was old enough to understand and deal with it."

"It's done," he told her. "We can't go back and re-write the script, Vickie. Once we mess up, we can't undo it. I wasn't there, so I can't say if you handled it wrong or perfectly right. You knew our son, what he could handle and what he couldn't. I'm sure you made what you believed was the right decision at the time. None of us should expect more from ourselves than that, and we shouldn't allow anyone else to."

She'd turned her face against his coat, and her voice was muffled. "The truth is, I was scared to tell him when he got older. He's so much like you, Slade."

"He is?" That revelation made Slade smile. "Really. Tell me about him."

"Well, he looks almost exactly like you. The day I told Nancy the truth, I was going through old pictures, and I'd found one of you. It was taken near where we are now, right here on Strawberry Hill. You were standing under a ponderosa pine and wearing that red shirt I made you for your twentieth birthday."

"I remember that day," he said, and his smile deepened, because his memories of that time in their lives seemed almost magical to him now. "So what possessed you to finally tell Nancy about me?"

"She thought it was a snapshot of Brody. I won't get into all the rest. What's important is that she looked very closely at the photograph, marveling over how young Brody looked, and she honestly believed it was her brother until she noticed that you were wearing a championship buckle. Brody placed in a few competitions later, when he was older than you were in that picture, but he didn't have the money for rodeo events at that age."

Slade tried to imagine how it might feel to meet his son and recognize familiar features on the young man's face. "You know what, Vick? By coming here to tell me about Brody, you've given me something I yearned for and believed I would never have after all of these years." He pressed a kiss to the top of her head and breathed in the scent of her hair. "For that alone, I'll be grateful to you until the day I die. When you talk about the pregnancy—well, I wish I'd known so I could have been there." He felt her try to pull away and tightened his hold on her. "Nope. You promised to pretend you believe me about the letters if I'll step up to the plate. Remember? I'm doing that, so you have to keep your end of the bargain. And if you believed me, you'd want to hear this."

"Okay. Fine. Say what you want."

He bent his head sideways to rest his cheek against her hair. She hadn't drawn it back into a band, so her curls wisped against his skin like watch springs made of silk. "At my age, a single man who never had children starts to face his own mortality. I have that ranch. It's been in my family for generations, it brings in a damned good income, and the land alone is worth millions. Sometimes I'd be out working and sweating my ass off, and I'd look out across the green pastures and wonder how it could be that I'd have no one to leave all of it to when I died. That's an awful feeling. It made me wonder why I kept working so hard. Why I didn't just quit and let the forest encroach upon it, little by little."

"Oh, Slade."

"I know it sounds morose, but I'm only telling you so you can understand how learning of Brody's existence is like a dream come true for me. You say he needs help. Well, I do, too. Do you think there's any possibility that he might be interested in ranching?"

She laughed softly. "Any possibility? Slade, your son isn't only an apple that didn't fall far from the tree.

I'm not sure if he ever parted company with the branch."

"What's that mean?"

"It means he's like you in so many other ways that raising him brought tears to my eyes sometimes. I think horses and ranching and cows run in his blood. As a toddler, he saw a horse out the car window and fell in love. A few weeks later, he saw a magazine with horses in it. He got so excited. His first three words were *mama*, *daddy*, and *horse*.

"By the time he was a teen, his love of horses had become a passion. I couldn't afford to get him one. He wanted nothing to do with soccer or football or basketball. He wasn't interested in playing baseball with the neighborhood kids. It was always only about horses for him. I set back as much money as I could for the kids to attend college. Nancy and Randall—Randall is my middle child—both attended college. Brody took his money to buy a horse and a dilapidated old farmhouse on ten acres. He lives there to this day."

Slade loved the thought that his son was a lot like him. It was a gift that he wished had come to him sooner, but he couldn't quibble over the time lost. Meeting his boy, getting to know him, maybe even working side by side with him on the Wilder land. *That* was like a miracle to Slade.

"What's he do for a living?"

"He's a horse trainer. Self-taught. There are colleges that offer that kind of coursework now, but Brody wouldn't have gone even if it had been available. He wanted land and a horse, and he took that meager start and built a career out of it. He has an affinity with equines. Most of them take to him immediately. It's an incredible thing to watch. When you meet him, you'll be astounded, because he couldn't be more like you if you'd raised him yourself."

"I can't wait. You've got to tell him soon, Vickie. Now that I know about him, it'll be hard for me to stay away. It'll be less of a shock for him if you pave my way."

"I'll tell him. It won't be easy. He'll probably get angry and yell at me, just like you."

He chuckled. "I raised my voice. I didn't yell. There's a difference." He jostled her with his arm. "You said something I'd like to back up to, that you were scared to tell Brody the truth about his father when he got older. Were you afraid he'd be angry with you?"

"No, not then. I'm afraid of that possibility now, but not when he was still a kid. What scared me was that he yearned for so many things I couldn't give him, and I knew you could. Only what if I told him and he went looking for you? Once he turned fifteen, he could drive. Not legally, but teenagers don't always let a little thing like that stop them. I could have awakened some morning and found my car gone. I didn't know how you'd react if he knocked on your door. I won't get into it tonight, but Brody had already endured a lot of hurt in his relationship with Matt. Even though Matt had promised to love Brody like his own child, he couldn't in the end. He resented him. I couldn't take a chance that you might reject him, too."

Slade got tears in his eyes. "I never would have done that. I swear to you, Vickie, I would have welcomed that boy with open arms and slaughtered the fatted calf." He tightened his arm around her. "Aw, Vick, what the hell happened to us? We had it all, and we let it slip through our fingers."

"April happened," she whispered.

Slade agreed. April had happened, all right, but not in the way Vickie believed. He could only pray the woman would show up at the Witch's Brew the next evening and put his and Vickie's world back on its axis. He toyed with the idea of telling Vickie about his visit to April's that day and his belief that the woman had intercepted Vickie's letters to him. But he held back. Maybe he was wrong, but he thought it might mean more to Vickie if she finally heard the truth straight from April's lips.

"I need to get you back to your tent." His voice sounded like a frog's, deep and gruff. "Morning will come early, and we're both going to have a long day tomorrow."

Slade clasped her elbow as they made their way out of the forest. She carried her flashlight, but she hadn't turned it on. Even though Slade knew she had fairly good night vision, hers wasn't as sharp as his, and he didn't want her to trip and fall.

They'd just reached Vickie's tent when a woman's scream rent the night air. Since Vickie stood right beside him, Slade knew it had to be his niece, Erin, and it sounded as if she was in the cookshack. Heart pounding, he broke into a run. He heard Vickie fall in behind him. Seconds later, as Slade closed the distance to the large tent, he heard Kennedy yelling.

"No, don't shoot! He won't hurt you! Don't kill him!"

Slade burst into the cookshack to see Erin standing on top of the prep table. She was trembling violently, the gun in her hands shaking as badly as she was. Kennedy had hold of the scruff of Four Toes' neck.

"He's Slade's bear, Erin. He won't hurt you."

As Slade stepped inside the shelter, his heart sank. This was the moment he'd been dreading ever since that day three and a half years ago when he'd rescued Four Toes from starving to death. He hurried over to the prep table and reached out to his niece. "Give me the gun, honey. Kennedy has it right. This is Four Toes. He's been around people so much that he's really not a danger to you."

Slade heard the footsteps of other men hurrying toward the tent. All the previous summer, he'd worried about the eventual fate of his bear and had tried to keep Four Toes' existence under wraps. But he'd always known it was only a matter of time before Four Toes showed himself to the wrong person. Now it had happened. Some of the men he heard gathering outside the entrance were bound to be paying guests. They were strangers who would return home and tell everyone they knew about the crazy outfitter with a pet bear. Anyone who knew anything about the wilderness and wildlife knew that it was against the law for wild animals to be kept in captivity or for someone to try to tame a bear. Slade's secret was definitely out.

He shoved Erin's sidearm under the waistband of his jeans and then grasped her by the waist to swing her down from the table just as Vickie stepped into the tent. She hurried over to a shelf and grabbed a bottle of ketchup. Kennedy stepped out of the way as she handed the condiment to Four Toes. The bear rumbled, making Erin jump. Slade slipped an arm around her shoulders. Everyone in the room observed the blond bear as he punctured the squeeze bottle and started sucking out the ketchup. Four Toes was oblivious to the peril of his situation. Slade wasn't, and knowing what the bear's fate might be nearly broke his heart.

Vickie met Slade's gaze. "Remember what we talked about? I think it's time to get people in town behind us and become a squeaky wheel."

"It won't work, Vickie. I talked with the state the day I found him. There's a lot to consider when a bear is transplanted, and it's a costly endeavor. They don't make the decision lightly."

Erin looked up at Slade, her blue eyes aching with sadness. "Oh, Uncle Slade, what have you done?"

"His mama was killed in a rockslide. He was just tiny. He got scared and ran." Slade turned his gaze on the bear. "At least that's how I think it went down. He stepped in a coyote trap, the old-fashioned kind with teeth. It cut his foot up, and he lost a toe. I should have shot him. I knew there was no way he could survive on his own, but I got him out of the trap and doctored his foot, instead. I tried to leave him up on the mountain. I figured that at least would give him a fighting chance. But he followed me back to the ranch. I couldn't just ignore him and let him die of starvation. So I fed him. And as a result, I've created a problem bear. I'm sorry he gave you such a fright."

"What happens now?" Erin asked.

"I guess I'll have to call the state."

"But, Uncle Slade, rescuing him was against the law. Feeding him anything is against the law. You're likely to get in big trouble."

"I knew that when I did it, and I know that now."

Slade stepped outside. Three of his five guests stood with all of his hired hands, including Wyatt, who couldn't possibly have heard the commotion. Slade had noticed over time, though, that his foreman sometimes had an uncanny knack of sensing when something wasn't right, even though he couldn't hear the audible warnings as everyone else could.

For the benefit of his guests, Slade said, "As you all saw, we've got a blond black bear in the cookshack. If you've never seen a blondie, try to get a good look at him tomorrow and treasure the memory. Chances are you'll never see one again."

"What's gonna happen now, boss?" Rex asked. "He's never hurt anybody, and maybe he never will."

"I don't know exactly how the state destroys problem bears, whether they're shot or tranquilized for a euthanasia procedure. I do know that many of the people who work at ODFW are often individuals who became game biologists because they love the wild animals as much as we do. They work their butts off, studying the animals and doing research. Their aim in life is to protect our wildlife. They must also work within the framework of our laws, so sometimes they seem like heartless bureaucrats to us, because we don't understand what they're up against."

"If they destroy Four Toes, they *are* heartless bureaucrats!" Kennedy cried. "And we're stupid for allowing laws to be passed that leave bears like Four Toes hanging out to dry!"

Slade could almost feel the young man's pain and sense of injustice, but Kennedy wasn't a kid anymore. Slade didn't want him to go off half-cocked and do something harebrained. "It's a hard, cruel world sometimes, Kennedy, and life is rarely fair. You have to trust that the state employees who decide Four Toes' fate will make the very best choice for him that they can. And I will remind you that *you* are the public they must protect. I'm the public they must protect. So is your brother. So are your parents. So is everyone in Mystic Creek and in this camp. How will you feel if a bear like Four Toes isn't properly dealt with, and it happens upon your mother when she's out working in her garden and it kills her? I can almost guarantee that you would be asking why that bear wasn't destroyed, why it was allowed to remain in the forest near your family's ranch. And the answer would be that someone didn't do his job."

Slade scanned the small sea of faces in front of him. "I'm sorry everyone's sleep was interrupted. We'll be heading out early in the morning, so if you want to be well rested, you should consider returning to your tents."

With that, Slade cut through the cluster of men and walked to his own shelter.

Vickie waited for Four Toes to finish his ketchup, and she tried to keep her attention fixed on the bear, but she was concerned about Erin, who still stood where Slade had left her. She had a stunned expression on her face, and she looked alarmingly pale. Vickie wasn't sure if the young woman had gotten such a fright that she was in a mild state of shock or if something else was troubling her. She was trying to think of a way she might ask when Erin suddenly swung away and plunged out the doorway of the shelter.

Vickie remained with Four Toes until he drained the ketchup bottle and tossed it on the wood floor. As always, he belched and licked his chops, his expression one of complete satisfaction. Vickie had put extra bottles of ketchup on her list of needed supplies, just so she could offer Four Toes treats. He'd gotten into the habit of enjoying his ketchup once a day, usually in the evening. Heart heavy, Vickie bent to pick up the condiment container and tossed it in the trash.

"Nothing can happen to you until Monday," she told the bear. "Maybe not even then. It's more likely that the state won't get around to dealing with you for the better part of a week, if not longer. We've got some time, Four Toes, and I promise you, I'll do everything I can to get you moved to another area where you can do without your ketchup fixes and just be a normal bear."

But for right now she had a more immediate concern. She shooed Four Toes out of her cookshack, tied down the door flap, and went in search of Erin's tent. She hadn't paid attention earlier to see where Wyatt had chosen to put Erin up. Using her flashlight, she spotlighted the ground, finally saw the imprint of smaller boots, and followed them to a tent three spaces from the end on the left side of the shelter alley.

"Erin?" she called softly. "It's Vickie. Can I come in?"

A lantern still glowed inside the canvas structure, but Erin gave no response. Vickie drew back the flap, saw Erin huddled on her cot, and was glad that she'd come. The younger woman didn't appear to be aware of Vickie entering her quarters. Something was wrong, really wrong. Vickie turned off her flashlight and set it by the doorway. Then she went to sit on the edge of Erin's cot.

"You need to talk about it?" she asked.

No answer. So Vickie decided to stoke up the fire while she gave the deputy a chance to collect herself. As she hauled in wood and crouched down to shove pieces into the belly of the little stove, she started talking.

"I know Four Toes scared the daylights out of you when he entered the cookshack. The first time I saw him, he came into my tent, and I tried to shoot him. I screamed, too, and trust me, I'm not given to screaming over any little thing."

Vickie bent to blow on the bed of embers to catch the kindling. Then she sat back on her heels to leave the door open until the fire was going strong.

"You're very pale, Erin. I'm worried that you may be in shock. That's normal. You won't die of it or anything." She chuckled. "Well, it's not likely at your age to get scared to death, anyway. At my age, maybe." She sighed and rubbed her hands together. The enclosure was chilly. It would take a few minutes for the space to grow warmer. She saw Erin's jacket lying across a small satchel and went to get it. As gently as she could, she draped the outerwear over the younger woman's shoulders. "There you go. It's cold in here."

"I don't know what to do," Erin suddenly said, fixing Vickie with an imploring gaze. "Is this how it ends, Vickie?"

"Is this how what ends, sweetheart?"

"My career in law enforcement. Is this how it's going to end?"

Vickie wasn't sure she was following Erin's train of thought. She resumed her perch on the edge of the cot.

Erin looked directly into Vickie's eyes. "When I go back to town tomorrow, I have to turn Uncle Slade in for breaking the law. It doesn't matter why. It doesn't matter if it's right for him to be fined and have to serve time in jail. Some judge will decide what happens next."

Vickie's heart squeezed. It seemed to be a night for young people to run face-first into the brick wall of reality. First it had been Kennedy; now Erin. "Oh, sweetie." Vickie couldn't think what to say. "You're in an awful pickle, aren't you?"

Erin drew her knees to her chest and clenched her arms over her shins. An almost frantic look entered her lovely eyes. "I can't do it, Vickie. During law enforcement training, they teach you that you must be prepared to arrest your own mother if she breaks the law. We're not supposed to treat loved ones any different than we would a stranger. I thought"—she broke off and swallowed—"I felt pretty confident that nobody I loved would *ever* break the law." She lifted her shoulders in a shrug. "And Uncle Slade? He's a law-abiding citizen and an honest man. I know you believe he lied to you about screwing that girl way back when, and I can understand how your faith in him got shaken. But I don't think he lied to you. I just can't picture it."

Vickie wished Slade hadn't been factored into this conversation. She liked Erin, and she felt awful for her. The young woman had been pushed into a career she wasn't cut out for, and now she was being forced to make a choice between her job and being loyal to her uncle. Vickie wanted to be her sounding board. If possible, she might offer some worthwhile advice. But she couldn't discuss Slade's transgression with April Pierce, especially not with Erin.

"I believe your uncle is a wonderful man."

That was true, as far as it went. Vickie really did think Slade was a good guy. He just wasn't good husband material, because he couldn't keep his jeans zipped up, and after he committed a transgression, he tried to lie his way out of trouble. Maybe there wasn't a man alive who wouldn't do the same. Vickie didn't know. The only certainty in her mind was that she'd struck out twice, and she was done.

Still deathly pale, Erin said, "I have to surrender my badge, Vickie. I can't turn my uncle in. I think I'm supposed to arrest him, actually. I never really expected to work on federal land, and I haven't retained all the information I studied about that. I may be required to make an arrest if I see a crime being committed here."

Vickie scratched at a dried blob of cookie dough on her jeans. Her mind swam with things she might say to Erin, but she wasn't sure any of them would be a comfort or provide her with solutions to the underlying issue, which was her unhappiness in her current profession.

"I don't really know about any of that," Vickie finally said. "But I think if you talk to your uncle, he will tell you to do your job, Erin. I'm sure he's very proud of you. He understands that you've sworn to uphold the law. The whole mess with Four Toes is just that, a mess that happened. Slade didn't go looking for trouble that day, and Four Toes sure as heck didn't. Life often has a domino effect. There's no way to change that."

Erin stared at something behind Vickie on the wall of her tent. After a long silence, she said, "It's not only about Four Toes and Uncle Slade, though. It's about me, Vickie. When push comes to shove, will I be able to arrest someone I care about? When I was an idealistic rookie, I believed I could. But tonight what I thought would never happen *did* happen."

Vickie could see Erin's dilemma. Sadly, she had no pearls of wisdom to offer her. "I'm sorry it's come down to this for you, honey. Maybe it's God's way of tapping you on the shoulder."

"To tell me what?"

"That maybe—just maybe, mind you—you'd be happier helping a child to overcome a lisp or a stuttering problem. Speech therapy, the profession of your heart."

"I'd have to go back to school! It's too late for that."

Vickie pushed to her feet. "Nonsense. You're thirty?"

"Thirty-one."

The tone in Erin's voice almost made Vickie laugh. "As old as all *that*? I still call nonsense. I went to culinary school in my forties. I met people there who were getting their degrees in their fifties and sixties."

"I have bills to pay. Rent, utilities, a car payment."

Vickie bent over to hug her. "Move in with your uncle. He's got plenty of room in that big old ranch house. The two of you could wander around in there for a day and never bump into each other, and he'd probably love to have you. That would get rid of everything but your car payment and insurance. You could commute to Crystal Falls or Bend for your coursework. I don't know if either college offers degrees in speech therapy, but if not, maybe there's something they do offer that you'd find rewarding."

Erin nodded. "I'll think about it."

"Good," Vickie said. "That'll take your mind off the more immediate question, whether or not you should turn in your badge. For now, just try to get some sleep. Everything will look better in the morning. It always does to me."

The following day began well before daylight, and Vickie felt as if she'd gotten no sleep. It was Sunday, the traditional day of rest for most people, but she was up at three in the morning and making drop biscuits by half past the hour. On the stove, she had a huge mound of diced potatoes and six pounds of bacon frying in two overlarge skillets. She had sixteen mouths to feed, plus her own. She hadn't fed the guests a breakfast yet, and she wasn't sure how much bacon they might devour. Cooking for a group was often a guessing game, and she might miss the mark this morning. Bacon was always a favorite, but her yield would theoretically give each person over a third of a pound. Not everyone would want that much, leftovers were a waste, and she had to take her chances.

A guest came in for coffee. He was a short fellow

with a spectacular mustache that he fiddled with almost constantly as he talked, but Vickie couldn't recall his name. "Good morning," she said. "How'd you sleep?"

"Not worth a damn. Every time I drifted off, I thought I heard that bear coming into my tent."

Vickie couldn't stop herself and laughed. "Do you have food of any kind in there?"

"Hell, no. I'm not stupid."

"Then you really shouldn't worry tonight. You aren't on Four Toes' menu. Cream and sugar are right there by the coffeepot. Stir sticks off to the side. Help yourself and grab a seat. Chat with me while I work."

Seconds later, Slade came in. He gave Vickie a long look. "I meant to ask you to go into town with me tonight. Then everything got exciting around here last night, and now I can't remember if I remembered to ask you."

Vickie glanced over her shoulder at him. "Is your memory going, Slade?"

"Is yours?"

"Oh, no. It already went south without me."

"So will you?" Slade asked.

"Will I what?"

"Go with me into town tonight?"

Vickie considered her options. "Business or pleasure? Business, yes, pleasure, no."

"Business."

"When the boss says jump, I jump. What time are we leaving?"

"Three."

She shot him a questioning look. "Who'll feed everybody?"

"I'm sending everybody down the mountain. I do it once with every group. I think it's a nice addition to the wilderness experience for guests to see our town and get acquainted with its people. You ever done a bus tour of Europe?"

"No, can't say that I have," Vickie replied. "I can tour the world on television, and that's cheaper."

He did his grunting thing as he stirred what had to be a quarter cup of sugar into his coffee. "My point is, all those people who go on bus tours see less of the people in a foreign country than you do on television. The bus stops at points of interest. To me, the points of interest are the little bakeries where only locals buy their bread. Or a neighborhood church instead of a famous cathedral. I want off the beaten path."

"If I were to tour a country, I'd be with you on that." Vickie sighed. "My dream is to win the lottery and visit Italy. Not on a tour bus. I'd rent a beautiful villa and stay right there for at least a month. I'd shop in the little fresh produce markets and walk home with my food to cook my meals. I'd *try* to create authentic Italian cuisine, just for the fun of it."

Slade winked at her. "When you win the lottery, let me know. I'll go along to carry your groceries." He started out the door. "Don't forget, three o'clock."

"Dress code?"

"You always look great. Nothing fancy."

Vickie wondered why Slade needed her to accompany him into town. Supplies, maybe? In the next minute, three more guests and two employees stormed the cookshack, and she didn't have time to worry about it. She was too busy making an extra pot of coffee and dishing up plates of food.

Chapter Fifteen

Vickie enjoyed the horseback ride down the mountain with Slade. It took her back in time to happier days when they'd been young and crazy in love with each other. When the mountain breeze whispered in the boughs of the ponderosa pines, she could almost hear their voices drifting on the air, and she found herself wishing that she really could go back to that period of her life for just one day. One fabulous, lighthearted day. She'd want to know she was there on borrowed time, though, because she would make the most of every single second. Riding, joking, laughing, and making love. She would turn it into the most fabulous twenty-four hours of her life.

"What are you thinking about?" Slade asked.

They'd come to a wide section of trail, so he rode abreast of her. Looking over at him, so relaxed and competent in the saddle, stimulated her imagination, and she could almost believe her wish had been granted. Slade looked older now, of course, but she couldn't honestly say that the extra mileage detracted from his handsomeness. If anything, he was sexier now than he'd ever been in his early twenties. He exuded confidence. In his visage, she saw the lines etched there by the passage of time, but she also glimpsed power, decisiveness, and strength that came only from facing life's many challenges.

"I'm supposed to ask *you* that question," she informed him. "Women are renowned for it. It forces the attention of men back onto them and puts men in the unenviable position of having to fabricate something fast, because most of the time, their thoughts would probably piss women off."

He chuckled. "You think you have us all figured out, huh? Careful, Vickie. Too much confidence in the war between the sexes can set you up for defeat."

"Is that what we're doing, Slade? Engaging in a war between the sexes?"

"You're female, I'm male. What do you think?"

"That I'll win."

He threw back his head and laughed. "I outweigh you by a good eighty pounds."

"Oh, you're referring to a physical battle. I'm sorry. I thought it was a war of wit, not physical strength. But, of course, you'd prefer physical, because women can outthink men with one side of their brain fried."

She sent him a smile that she knew was sassy, and a part of her realized that she was trying to recapture just a few seconds of how it had once been between them, because wishing for a whole day would never make it happen.

"Which side of your brain would you sacrifice to a frying pan?"

"The left, because it's mostly useless."

He chuckled, and then he made that little throat-clearing sound with *humph* at the end. She was starting to wonder if he made that grunting noise because he couldn't think what to say. But Slade had always been quick with comebacks. So it was far more likely that he was holding back, afraid that his rejoinder would irritate her.

"Do you remember that tree?" He drew his horse to a stop and pointed. "That lone pine with the low-hanging limb."

Vickie followed the line of his finger, saw the tree, and felt heat rising up her neck to burn like fire in her cheeks.

Slade glanced over, saw her expression, and winked at her. "You *do* remember. You challenged me to do more chin-ups than you could, if I recollect right, and while you were pumping them out, I started removing your garments. My plan was to make sure you would get distracted and quit before you did so many I'd have to wear myself out trying to beat you. As it happened, I got worn out anyway. Damn, girl, but you were hot."

"You lie like a rug, Slade Wilder. You took advantage of my determination to outdo you and introduced me to a whole new way of"—she broke off and glared at him—"doing chin-ups."

"No, sir. My aim was to make you stop and drape those beautiful legs over my shoulders. Which you did. Want to give it another go, just for old time's sake?"

Way deep in her belly, where she hadn't felt much

going on for at least twenty years, her muscles bunched, started to twitch, and sent out little shocks of sensation to parts of her body that she'd been convinced had long since atrophied. Dead from the neck down, that was she, only Slade was making her body come back to life, even if her mind refused to go there.

She didn't want him to see how flustered he'd made her. "For old time's sake, it's your turn to do chin-ups first. I'll be the one on the ground, jerking your clothes off." She wiggled her eyebrows at him. "Role reversal. My favorite thing."

"Oh, *hell*, no. About the time I let go of the limb like you did, we'd both go down. You couldn't stand up under my weight. I'd probably break my back, and possibly yours along with it."

Vickie nudged her mount into a trot. She needed to put that damned tree behind her. Slade was like a foxtail that stuck to her clothes and then burrowed in to get under her skin. She had allowed him to do that once, and she couldn't let him do it again. He would destroy her if she gave him a second chance.

He caught up with her at the bend in the trail. She slowed her horse, because there was a drop-off on one side. He drew up to ride abreast of her again. Her journey down memory lane was over, she assured herself. It was too dangerous for her to relive those moments. He'd been an inventive lover, blending laughter with sex, and she knew beyond a shadow of a doubt that she'd never meet another man like him. Not that she wanted to. Once had been enough.

When they reached the trailhead, they put their horses into the holding pen, and then fed and watered them before they got into Slade's truck and he drove them into Mystic Creek. Slade left the town center and hung a right onto Dewdrop Lane. When he pulled off into the parking lot of the Witch's Brew, she sent him an inquiring glance.

"I thought you said this was a business thing."

"It is. Any guests who don't opt to dine on sandwiches tonight were told to meet us here. I'm buying the food and drinks. You're my pretty little sidekick. Normally I have to go it alone. It'll be a relief to have a partner to help me chat up the guests."

Vickie relaxed slightly and then she looked at the building again. "This place was a ramshackle dump even back when we were kids."

"JJ has remodeled recently. I'm looking forward to seeing what he did."

Ever the gentleman in public places, Slade lightly grasped her elbow as they walked the length of the sagging boardwalk. "Well," he observed, "the outside hasn't changed any. One of these days, somebody's going to crash through these rotten boards."

"Just not one of us, I hope."

Once inside the bar and grill, Slade looked around before he released his hold on her arm. Vickie remembered that about him, too. He'd always been alert for trouble and protective. It had always been a pleasant feeling to have him look after her, as if she were a special treasure, and she enjoyed experiencing it again.

He led her down the length of the bar to a tall pub table along one wall, and then raised a hand at the bartender, a pencil-thin little guy with black hair, who moved so swiftly from place to place that he reminded Vickie of a frantic gerbil.

Someone had just plunked money into the jukebox, and "Ring of Fire" came over the speakers, forcing Slade to holler. "Where's JJ?"

The bartender yelled back. "He don't work on Sundays. Claims it's a sin. Never stepped inside a church in his whole life, I don't think, but he gets religion on the Sabbath."

Slade chuckled and drew back a stool for her. Vickie climbed up onto the elevated seat and then squeaked when Slade picked up both her and the chair to get her closer to the table. She'd forgotten how strong he was, and it was a little unnerving to remember while he held her on a stool in midair.

He swung a denim-sheathed leg over his seat as if he were mounting a horse, and he did it with just as much masculine grace. "What's your poison these days?" he asked.

Vickie considered ordering a girly drink, but she enjoyed the strong stuff a little too much to settle for something sugary. "Whiskey, straight up."

Slade shot her a questioning glance. "Whoa! My girl grew up while my back was turned." He winked at her. "I'm with you, though. I like a nice whiskey. What brand do you like?"

Vickie rarely drank, and when she did, she did it on

the cheap. "What's the best in the house?" She dimpled a cheek at him. "You are paying, right?"

He laughed and winked at her. Then he strode to the bar, rested his arms on its edge, and cocked one hip. It was a purely masculine stance, one lean leg bent, the other straight and angled out slightly behind him. Vickie couldn't help herself. She ogled his butt. Not that he had much of one. He was narrow at the hip. But in that moment, she thought he looked good enough to eat.

"Not literally," she muttered to herself. "You need to cool your jets, girlfriend, or you'll get yourself in more trouble than you can handle. Slade Wilder isn't a pussycat. Keep your head on straight."

Only her body wasn't listening. It had started back at that damned pine tree, and forgotten places inside of her felt as if they were tingling back to life. Slade returned with two tumblers filled to the halfway mark. Vickie normally limited herself to two fingers. Well, except when she drank with her daughter, which had only happened once.

"You didn't bring me here to get me drunk, did you?"

He grinned and winked at her, all at once, and Vickie totally understood why April Pierce had crushed so hard on him. He wore nothing special, just his usual blue chambray shirt and a pair of faded Wrangler jeans. But with the gold and silver belt buckle to add a touch of sparkle and the Stetson cocked just so over his gray eyes, he looked hot enough to fry eggs. She studied his face and decided she liked the way his dimples had been carved deep into long creases. She even liked the little fan of wrinkles at the outside corners of his eyes. His lashes were still thick and dark, the touches of silver in his thick brows striking an attractive contrast.

She forced herself to stop ogling him. He wasn't a damned homework assignment she had to memorize, and the way he was making her feel might make her forget that he'd gotten her pregnant, broken her heart, and never come riding into Coos Bay on a white steed to rescue her when she'd been a damsel in distress. *Asshole*. She'd never count on a man for anything again.

Besides, she was no longer a damsel at almost sixty-three. She was an old lady with breasts that looked like slightly deflated balloons and little white stretchmarks on her hips. She also had a slight case of baby gut after bearing three children, only age had removed the batting so her skin there felt loose when she touched it. Moving on down to consider her thighs, she decided she'd have to be three sheets to the wind to ever get naked with him again, and if she ever got stupid enough to do that, she'd feel embarrassed and humiliated as soon as she sobered up. Not happening.

"What are you thinking about?" he asked with that mischievous twinkle in his eyes that she remembered so well.

"I'm not saying. But if you show me another pine tree tonight, I'll hang you from a lower limb with your own belt until dead."

He laughed and took a sip of his drink. "Oh, darlin', this is the good stuff. You have to try it."

Vickie followed his advice, and the honeyed flavor

of the liquor almost made her moan with delight. She swallowed and said, "That's like sipping sunshine. It goes down so smooth it should be illegal."

Someone entered the bar behind her. She felt a waft of cool evening air and heard the overhead bell jangle. Slade glanced over her head. Then he put down his glass, pushed it over by the napkin holder, and said, "Excuse me for a couple of minutes. I need to see a man about a dog."

Vickie had almost forgotten the saying that meant he needed to use the restroom. She nodded and watched him walk away. He'd no sooner pushed through a door at the far end of the room when a woman climbed up onto his stool. Vickie smiled politely at her. "I'm sorry, ma'am. That place is taken."

"Yep, I'm sitting on it."

Vickie felt an odd sense of recognition. The lady had dyed blond hair and would be considered attractive if you appreciated a heavy application of cosmetics. She wore fake eyelashes and her bright red acrylic nails matched her lipstick.

"You don't recognize me, do you?"

Vickie stared harder at her. "I'm so sorry. I don't mean to be rude. I haven't been home in over forty years."

She shrugged, then commandeered Slade's drink. "My feelings don't get hurt that easily, Vickie. I intended to buy you a drink, but if I double you up on that one, Sparky will have to roll you out of here." She flashed a smile. "I'm going to make this short and sweet. No point in reminding you of who I am, because you'll remember as soon as I start talking. Slade never touched me the night of that stupid party."

"April?" Vickie said in a half whisper.

"Who else supposedly fucked Slade that night? Anyway, I lied."

"Why?"

"Let me talk, and you just listen. I got my speech all memorized, you know, and I didn't account for any interruptions. I'll forget what I want to say next." She took a huge gulp of Slade's expensive whiskey. "Damn, but that man has class. Way back when, I would have licked him up one side and down the other like he was a melting ice cream cone, but he didn't want any part of me. He only had eyes for you. You may not believe this, Vickie, but I'm sorry for what I did now. I was just a goofy girl back then, and I thought I'd shrivel up and die if I couldn't make Slade Wilder fall in love with me. For almost a year after you took off, I was heartsick. He came by my parents' house and read me the riot act about lying to you and ruining his life. I got five minutes of his attention, and then when he walked away, he never glanced in my direction again."

Vickie's stomach had wound into knots, and she started to shake. She grabbed her still barely touched drink, tipped back her head, and gulped it down. All of it. Right at that moment, she would have taken that whiskey straight into a vein. With more force that she intended to, she slammed the tumbler back down on the table. "April, I understand how silly all of us girls could be back then, but do you comprehend that you destroyed my life?"

Her eyes took on a suspicious shimmer. "I'm sorry. But you need to stop interrupting me so I can finish. Slade got four letters from you. I'd just gotten hired on at the post office as a mail sorter. I knew it was wrong to tamper with the mail, that I could lose my new job if I got caught, but I was so infatuated with him, I didn't care. When I saw letters from you come in, I stuck them in my purse and took them home so I could read them. Mama sent me to counseling a couple of years later, but she climbed on that idea a little too late. I know now that I was messed up in my head, but I didn't then, and it gave me a thrill to read what you wrote to him."

Vickie gaped at her. April waved at the bartender and yelled, "Sparky, bring us each another round! The lady has drained her well dry! Harley's paying!" She made eye contact with Vickie again. "Anyway, after I got counseling, I wished sometimes that I could tell you Slade had never screwed around on you. And maybe I would have if anyone could have found you. Not even your mama would tell me where you went, and I finally figured that if Slade couldn't find you, nobody could."

"My return address was on every envelope, April. You could have found me."

Sparky arrived with their drinks. Vickie's hands were still shaking, and Sparky no sooner set down the glass than she grabbed it and took a couple more slugs.

"Easy, honey. That'll knock you flat on your ass."

Vickie took a deep breath and was grateful for the

sudden infusion of heat that flowed from her belly to warm her whole body. She took another gulp. When the alcohol finally started to make her feel calmer, she sighed and set the glass on the table. *Better now*. She was no longer shaking so hard that she might tumble off the barstool.

"Anyhow, now that I've got that puked up, can we finish our drinks and try to let bygones be bygones?"

"Bygones? If you read my letters to Slade, April, you knew that I was pregnant with his baby. I wrote to him in desperation, hoping against hope that he'd help me out somehow. Do you have any inkling how much heartache and suffering you caused?"

"Like I said, I'm truly sorry. That's all I came to say. Harley doesn't know about this, and I'm counting on you to keep it under your hat. I don't want thirty-eight years of marriage to get flushed down the john over some foolish prank I played on you over forty years ago. I hope you can accept my apology and we can both get on with our lives."

"I haven't had a life, April, and neither has my son. *Slade's* son. I just want to clarify something before you leave to get on with your life. Did you open the fourth letter?"

"Oh, yeah. That'd be the one with a picture of the baby in it. Right? Cute little guy. He sure looked a lot like his daddy."

Vickie picked up her drink and downed the rest of it. In some distant part of her mind, she realized that she'd had too much when liquor dribbled down her chin, and she bypassed the napkins to wipe her face with her arm. "April, your lies deprived my son of ever knowing his daddy. Your lies deprived him of his father's support, and he went without so many things because I couldn't afford to buy them for him. Right now, he's injured and he can't work, and unless he can earn an income soon, he'll end up going bankrupt. He's got one son in college, and two more close to being that age, so your *prank* and the damage it caused has trickled clear down to the next generation. Those boys may not get college educations because of what you did."

April sighed and shrugged. "Hey. You're not the only woman who ever got herself knocked up and ended up paying the price."

Vickie stood up on her barstool, her fists knotted on the tabletop like hardballs. "How could you *look* at the picture of that precious baby boy and not do *something* to make sure it got into Slade's hands? You could have put the letter and picture into a fresh envelope and dropped it into the Wilders' roadside mailbox if nothing else. Nobody would have known who put it there! And Slade would have known where to find his child!"

"Vickie, I get that you blame me for a lot of stuff, and like I said, he was a cute little guy, but he wasn't *my* kid. If anybody at that house had seen my car pull to a stop on the road, I could have lost my job and faced criminal charges. Do you honestly think anybody would put her ass on the line like that for some kid that didn't mean diddly-squat to her? You made your choices way back then. You could have taken Slade's word about what happened, but you didn't."

"Because you described his birthmark to me. I knew for you to have seen it, he had to have been bare-ass naked!"

April slapped the table and laughed. "Oh, shit! I'd forgotten all about that. I did see him naked, only I was watching all the guys skinny-dip through Daddy's binoculars. He forgot them in the pickup, and it was too good an opportunity to pass up. You know?" She shook her head. "God, I had more balls than my brother did." She laughed again. "If you've got Slade nibbling at your bait again, sweetie, give the line a hard jerk and hook him on the lip. That boy had a build on him like a wet dream, and he had more hanging than any other guy there."

Slade glanced at his watch, decided that he'd given April enough time to spill her guts, and stepped out of the bathroom. He couldn't wait to talk to Vickie now that she'd gotten the true story straight from the horse's mouth. As the door swung shut behind him, Slade shifted his gaze to the table where he'd seated Vickie. He was just in time to see her standing up on her barstool with both doubled fists planted on the table. Then April laughed and said something more, and the next thing Slade saw was a blur of red hair, a green top, and blue denim as Vickie launched herself across the table at April.

Oh, shit. Slade lurched into a run. He heard somebody

yell, "Catfight! Catfight!" And then he heard wolf whistles and hands clapping in a steady beat. When he reached the spot where he'd last seen Vickie, she wasn't there. He turned, frantically searching for another flash of green, and saw her rolling across the floor with her legs locked around April's waist. *Oh, shit.* This was bad. Really bad. Vickie was going to get her ass kicked. He ran toward the women just as April grabbed Vickie by her hair and twisted her head at such a sharp angle that Slade was afraid it would snap her neck.

"Okay," he yelled. "Break it up! Come on, ladies. Time to let the tempers cool down."

That normally worked with men unless they intended to kill each other. But these two females didn't seem to even hear him. He made a grab for April's arm. And just as he almost caught her wrist, which was attached to the hand that was about to break Vickie's slender neck, a huge, beefy paw clamped over his arm. Slade looked up. And then he lifted his gaze higher. Harley Jones loomed over him like a giant out of a children's storybook. The man didn't look quite so large from a distance. But he was built like a refrigerator, only taller.

"Don't you go layin' a hand on my wife!" he roared.

"I wasn't going to hurt her, Harley! I was just going to break it up."

"Ain't no need!" Harley bellowed. "Your woman started it! My April can take care of herself."

"Look, you stupid son of a bitch, it isn't about who's going to win! She's about to break my woman's neck!"

Harley's grip tightened on Slade's arm with such

crushing force that Slade feared he'd break his radius and ulna bones both at once. The man's chest swelled, and his broad face turned scarlet. "Ain't nobody calls Harley *stupid*!"

And the next thing Slade knew, he was flying backward through a plate-glass window. Stunned almost senseless, it took him a few seconds to realize where he was. As he gingerly sat up, he remembered that shards of glass lay everywhere beneath him. He was going to take his time standing up, but through the now pane-free window, he heard a man yell. "She's gonna kill her. The cops better get here quick!"

Vickie. Slade forgot about the danger of cutting himself up and sprang to his feet. He hit the push-through front doors of the bar at a dead run, spilled inside at such a speed that he couldn't stop, and slid into the bar. He whirled, searching the space for the woman he loved. But she wasn't anywhere to be seen. He panned the interior of the establishment again more slowly and finally spotted a splotch of green through a gap between the shoulders of two men.

Slade ran in that direction. To save her. Even if he had to face off with Harley again, he had to protect Vickie. Both men and women had formed a circle around the combatants. Slade tried to push and shove his way through the spectators, but the circle around the fighting females was two bodies deep. One man yelled, "Look at that woman go! Knockout!" Someone else yelled, "Nope. She's gettin' back up! Hit her again, honey! Hit her again!"

Slade finally gained the inner circle so he could clearly see the two women. He expected it to be Vickie on the floor, but it was April on her hands and knees, struggling to stand back up. Vickie bounced around her like a boxer, both her small fists doubled. Blood trickled from April's nose. Her bottom lip was split. And to Slade's horror, he saw a bald spot on the side of her head where Vickie had ripped strands of hair out by the roots.

April seemed unable to regain her feet. Slade was about to yell to Vickie that the other woman had had enough, but without any prompting from him, Vickie suddenly stopped circling and pumping her fists. For a second she stood there, gazing down at April. And then she stepped toward the other woman with her right hand outstretched.

"Let me help you," she said to April.

Slade had seen this trick before, and he yelled, "No, Vickie! Let someone else help her up!"

But he was too late. Vickie clasped April's hand, and the instant April got a firm grip, she jerked Vickie off her feet. Vickie landed on her back. April scrambled forward and sprawled on top of her, landing so hard on Vickie's torso that Slade almost felt the breath-expelling jolt in his own chest.

"Unfair!" Slade yelled.

And the onlookers took up the word as a chant. "Unfair! Unfair! Unfair!"

Just as Slade surged forward to get the blonde off Vickie, some other woman burst through the crowd.

She was a short, stout woman in baggy jeans and a gray T-shirt. She dived at April, plowing into her broadside with one shoulder. April went rolling, and the stout woman sprang after her, her arms flailing like windmill blades. Just then Slade heard a roar and saw Harley lumbering forward to rescue his wife. *Good,* Slade thought as he ran to collect Vickie and get her the hell out of there. Only things didn't play out as Slade expected. Harley grabbed the stout woman and flung her away from April with one mighty sweep of his arm.

Slade wasn't sure exactly what happened next, except that some man took exception to the stout woman being thrown aside, and he raced over to accost Harley. A rumble of rage came up from Harley's chest and he swung the other man from his back like he was a baby ape clinging to its mother. Before Slade could reach Vickie, some other man leaped into the fray. Almost as if some invisible hand had flipped a switch, people all around Slade were swinging at each other.

Slade had witnessed his share of barroom brawls during his misspent youth when he'd been grieving for his loss of Vickie, but he'd never in his life seen a building full of people go so nuts. It was like a contagion swept through, affecting everyone it touched. His original intention had been to pick Vickie up and carry her out of there, but two men had started swinging barstools. He grabbed Vickie's arms, hunched forward to shield her upper body as much as he could, and dragged her toward a sturdy-looking table, minus all its chairs, which he suspected were being used as weapons. He stuffed Vickie under the table and crawled under there with her. To hell with these fools and their mindless fighting.

Finally Slade heard sirens. He'd never been so glad in his life to know the cops were coming. Other patrons of the bar didn't seem to share that sentiment. They vacated the building so fast someone might have yelled "Fire!" Some of them leaped out the broken front window. Others went out through the kitchen to the rear exit. Before Slade knew it, Harley and April were the only two people, besides him and Vickie, who remained inside the building. Even Sparky, the bartender, had vanished.

Vickie gave him a bleary-eyed study for a moment once the commotion had ceased, as if she didn't recognize him, and then she smiled despite the pain it must have caused her with that badly split lip.

"Why are we under a table?" she asked.

"I put you under here to keep you safe, and you looked so damned comfortable, I decided to hide with you."

She giggled. "You don't have a cowardly bone in your whole body."

He narrowed an eye at her. "Put another snake in my bed, and I'll prove you wrong on that count."

She giggled again. Then she heard the police sirens and that seemed to strike her as being even funnier. "Are we going to get arrested?"

Slade considered the question. "Probably," he finally replied. "Vickie, are you drunk?"

She pinched her forefinger and thumb together, swayed sideways as she lifted her arm, and said, "Maybe just an itty-bitty bit."

Slade couldn't help himself. He burst out laughing. Then he shot out an arm to keep her from toppling over just an itty-bitty bit. "I sure was proud of you when you offered April a hand up. You fought fair and square."

She shrugged. "Not the whole time. I think she really hated it when I jammed my pinkie up her nostril." She grinned again. "I don't care. I got even with her for all of us. For what she did to you. For what she did to me. But most of all, I made her pay for what she did to Brody. I'll never regret a single second. That woman will never forget the name Wilder."

Concern welled within Slade. "Honey, did you get hit on the head?"

"No. Why?"

"Because your last name is Brown."

She bent forward to smooth his hair. "Brown is such a *common* name. I like Wilder a heck of a lot better. It's got some pizzazz."

Slade tried to tamp down the surge of hope that filled his chest. "Yeah, well, I hate to bring up the *m* word, but that's what would have to happen for you to take my last name."

"Well, of course that's what'll have to happen." She reached down and playfully grabbed his cheek to give it a light shake. "My Slade, true blue, and you never lied to me. I think I'm falling in love with you all over again."

"I thought you never stopped."

"I didn't. But I'm starting over fresh. When we ride back up the mountain, let's stop at our pine tree. I wanna whip you at chin-ups. I'll go first, and you have to beat me, or I'll call you a loser for the rest of your life."

"If you stick around for the rest of my life, I really don't care what you call me."

"That's good, because I want to call you my husband. We have to get married, Slade. Otherwise April wins."

"Well, we can't let that happen," he said.

And despite her split lip, Slade kissed her with all the passion he felt for her. Right there in a destroyed bar, with deputies swarming through the front doors like a country-bumpkin SWAT team, he claimed her mouth, dove deep to find the never-forgotten taste of her again, and then drew up for air when he heard a very familiar voice start to read him his rights.

"Erin, is that you?"

"Yes, and this is likely my last act as a law enforcement officer. As soon as I can figure out what I want to be when I finally grow up, I'm turning in my badge. I can't be a deputy with an uncle who has a criminal record."

Epilogue

Nothing outshines a central Oregon day in the late spring. As Vickie gazed up at the powder blue sky, laced with the filigree of pine boughs, limned in golden sunshine, she refused to close her eyes in gratitude. Instead she gazed out the partially opened window at the beautiful wilderness and breathed in the air perfumed with all the scents of home. This was where she belonged. She'd left for a long while, but she'd been born here and she hoped, if she was lucky, she would die here, if possible at home on the Wilder Ranch in Slade Wilder's arms. *No, that can't happen,* she reconsidered. *I need to outlast Slade by at least one day. Otherwise the silly man will try to drown his sorrow in booze, women, and rodeo. And that will happen over my dead body.*

She jumped with a start when a voice resounded behind her, one that had been imprinted forever on her mind and heart from the time she was six years old.

"What are you thinking about?"

Vickie smiled and turned to gaze up at her cowboy. Other women had coveted him, and for a time, through no fault of hers or his, as she now knew, they'd lost each other. But life had a funny way of setting every-thing right in the end, if only two hearts could with-stand the storms. They'd mourned for each other and moved through the days living a kind of half-life, merely existing because they'd been separated. Now, in the autumn of their lives, they would finish what remained of their journey together, facing whatever came. Vickie knew she would never stop feeling grate-ful for this second chance that they'd been granted, to enjoy the last few chapters of their lives, side by side.

"Slade Wilder, how many times have I told you that it's generally women who ask that question?"

He bent to press his sun-burnished forehead against hers and grasped each of her hands in his. "I'm letting my feminine side come out," he said. "I want to know what the other half of my heart is thinking."

She'd always loved his big, firm hands. Warm, strong, and yet undeniably gentle. "I was thinking that we made it," she said, hearing the tremor that weak-ened her voice, not with sorrow but with joy. "I was thinking that I'm almost glad now that things hap-pened the way they did." She looked up into his gray eyes, which she'd become lost in on her first day of school nearly sixty years ago. "I was thinking that if we hadn't had April to interfere, we'd have been married forever by now, and that today, such a beautiful day, might not mean as much to me as it does now."

"Not to me, either, Vickie mine. Not to say I don't regret all the years we weren't together. We could have had a lot more fun on that pine tree with the low-hung limb."

He caught her by surprise with the lewd comment and made her laugh. But that had always been the most priceless part of her relationship with Slade Wilder. Laughter when she least expected it. "Always thinking about sex, aren't you?"

"Not *always*. If a calf is coming breech, I don't give it a thought."

"How about when we're mad at each other?"

He leaned down to settle his lips over hers for an instant, a tantalizing promise for later when they could be truly alone for an uninterrupted period of time. "Yep, I think about it then. I get singed by the green sparks shooting from your eyes, and all I can think about is how I'll make you pay when you're over being pissed."

At any other time, Vickie might have gone up on her tiptoes and looped her arms around his neck, because she definitely wasn't angry with him right now. But she'd just looked out the window of the Wilder ranch house and knew the backyard below was filled to the brim with wedding guests, the minister, her parents, and their children. In less than a year, she and Slade had accomplished a complete melding of their pasts, the present, and the future. Their son Brody would serve as Slade's best man, and she'd spotted him standing near a makeshift altar, waiting for the nuptial celebration to begin that would finally bind his father and mother together. Brody's wife, sitting with their grandsons on the groom's side, was feeling well enough now under new, expensive yet effective medication to work four shifts a week at the Mystic Creek Urgent Care as a registered nurse. Nancy, along with all her family, sat beside Randall, with all of his, on the bride's side. There was a festive air to the gathering that Vickie could appreciate even from her vantage point inside the house.

Vickie tugged Slade over to the window. "Before we go down, I want to stand here with you for a minute to admire that picture."

She tilted her chin to gesture at the crowd below, everyone seated expectantly, with Four Toes, now that Slade had secured the necessary permits to keep an indigenous black bear on the wildlife grounds surrounding his isolated ranch, held in check behind the winged sections of seating by Kennedy Fitzgerald. The residents of Mystic Creek had been instrumental in lobbying behind Slade and lending their support to his permit application. Vickie recognized that Four Toes had earned his place both in Slade's heart and at his wedding.

"Isn't that a beautiful sight?"

Slade nibbled on her ear. "It sure is. Even the dogs get to be present."

Vickie gave him a playful shove. "You aren't even looking. Just think of it, Slade! How much things have changed for us. Our son has a place in your life, and he's standing down there to be your best man. You have a special license now to keep Four Toes on the ranch—if only you had applied for one sooner, you could have saved yourself a lot of grief! When that little female black bear comes to us for permanent shelter on your land, Four Toes will be beside himself, having a companion of his species for the first time."

"Yeah. In a way he's just like me. I waited for years for you to grow up."

Vickie elbowed him in the ribs. "Can you be serious? It's important to me to acknowledge how much we have to celebrate, beyond you and me getting married. We aren't the only ones in love. Even if we were, I'd still be so very happy. But Kennedy starts college in the fall for game biology after finding some direction in his life, and there's your sweet niece Erin down there, studiously ignoring Wyatt, while he does just as good a job of ignoring her. Tex is here with that lady from Flagg's Market with the black beehive hairdo."

Slade stepped behind her and looped his arms around her waist. "You're right. It's pretty amazing. It's not about just you and me, living our own separate lives anymore."

Vickie leaned back against him, absorbing his strength and warmth. "It never was," she told him softly. "It never is. The kind of love we feel for each other affects everyone around us. We never lost that, Slade, even all those years we were apart and I wished that I could stop loving you. I look down there and see an affirmation of our commitment to each other in the faces of everyone present. We did it, Slade. We *are*. It's such a beautiful way to celebrate our wedding day."

He rested his chin atop her head. She felt a slight tension slip into his rangy body. "Vick?"

"What?" she asked, her voice thick with emotion.

"I think Four Toes is getting impatient for his ketchup. If we don't hurry down there and tie the knot, he may eat the minister."

Vickie giggled and grabbed his hand. "You're right! Let's hurry, Slade Wilder. Bears are unpredictable, you know."

Together they navigated the staircase, neither of them needing to use the banister for support, but both of them aware that each day together was a beautiful gift and nothing lasted forever.

Except love.

Dear Reader,

I am so excited to present you with *Strawberry Hill*, a story that speaks to me on so many levels and that I hope will touch your hearts. If you've read my work before, you already know how much I love domestic animals and our wildlife. It is always a heartbreak for me when I know a certain species is in trouble, as our American black bear is today. All across the country, black bear rescue organizations have facilities that are becoming overcrowded. This doesn't mean that I'm saying the black bear populations are out of hand, only that, for one reason or another, there are not enough zoos, observatories, and shelters to permanently house and care for those bears in custody.

So how can we help? First and foremost, small donations might work wonders. More importantly, though, please speak up if you're ever with individuals who find a black bear cub and believe it should be rescued. No matter what the circumstances may be, those people should call the pertinent state's fish and game offices before anything is done. If a black bear cub is alone, that doesn't necessarily mean its mother has abandoned it. She may be trying to find her baby, or she may have gone hunting for food. Baby bears can also be much like toddlers in shopping malls, wandering away from their mothers to become temporarily lost. Removing a baby from an area where the sow may be searching for it is normally a mistake and often ends up being a tragic story for the baby.

Also, in order to pen a novel with a happy resolution for Four Toes, I've exercised poetic license in creating a lovely ending for this bear. In many instances, black bears who are fed by humans, accidentally or purposefully, meet with sad endings. Please don't feed black bears! Also make sure that you store your kitchen trash in bear-proof bins if you live in an area that black bears frequent.

It sounds fun to raise a black bear cub, but after reading *Strawberry Hill*, please keep in mind that rescuing a black bear may end with the death of the bear—or with you being seriously injured or killed. We should respect their habitat and try to keep them where they belong.

When I was a child and my father picked me up for visitation, we always stopped at a little diner for lunch where a roadside zoo existed. For a small fee, I could walk around and look at the wild animals while my meal was prepared. As I grew older, I realized that the animals, though fairly well cared for, existed in tiny pens and weren't happy. It made me very sad.

I was about eleven when we stopped at the diner, as we always did, and the building looked as if it had been attacked during a battle. The black bear at the zoo had gotten loose. Always a friendly and seemingly harmless creature, it had gone on a rampage, seriously injuring a man (I can't recall if he died) and wreaking havoc on the building. Shutters and screens had been ripped off. There were claw marks gouged into the siding. It was as if that poor, imprisoned bear had tried to seek revenge on the people who had used its presence there for financial gain.

Never forget that black bears are wild creatures and shouldn't, in most instances, be adopted as pets. You can never completely train them to be harmless. They are strong beyond our comprehension, and any little thing can set them off. They have even been known to open unlocked doors, so they are clever as well. Let's all endeavor to do the kind thing and keep them in their natural environment where they, too, can be reasonably safe and happy.

All best,
Catherine Anderson
facebook.com/catherineandersonbooks
catherineanderson.com

Don't miss the previous book in the
Mystic Creek series by Catherine Anderson

SPRING FORWARD

Available now!

Wind whistled into the big black van, whipping Tanner Richards' hair across his forehead as he drove. Squinting at the gravel road through the brown strands drifting over his eyes, he hauled in a deep breath of pine-scented air. Five years ago he'd agonized over his decision to sell his accounting firm and move to Crystal Falls, Oregon. He'd given up a six-figure annual income with no assurance that he could even find a job in this area. Crazy, really. Looking back on it now, though, he was glad that he'd come. Being a delivery-man wasn't as prestigious as working in his former chosen profession, but he made enough money to provide a good life for his kids, and he truly enjoyed the occupation. Having a rural route suited him. He was required to make fewer stops than he would have been in town, which equated to shorter workdays and more time in the evening to be with his children. And he'd made a lot of friends. Folks around here were more congenial than they were in larger towns.

As he rounded a curve in the country road, Tanner saw Tuck Malloy's house. Sadness punched into him. For three years running, he'd often stopped there to visit at the end of his workday, and he'd enjoyed a lot of cold ones on the porch with his elderly friend. Now the windows reflected the darkness of an empty structure. A For Sale sign rode high on the front gate. It had appeared nearly a month ago.

Tanner had considered calling the Realtor to learn what had happened to the property owner after his calls to Tuck went unanswered, but he really didn't want to know. Tuck had been a crusty old codger and eighty years young, as he'd been fond of saying. Unexpected things could happen to people that age. A heart attack, maybe, or a stroke. Tuck liked that piece of ground, and he would never have left voluntarily. He'd said so more than once. Tanner figured the old fellow was dead. Otherwise why would his place be up for sale?

Tanner pulled over and stopped outside the hurricane fence for a moment, a habit he had developed since the home had been vacated. He trailed his gaze over the front porch, now devoid of the comfortable Adirondack chairs where he had once sat with Tuck to chat. Recalling the old man's recalcitrant dog, he smiled. *Rip.* Tanner hoped the blue heeler had found a good home. He'd been a handful and was probably difficult to place.

Damn, he missed them both. With a sigh Tanner eased the van back onto the road. He had only one more delivery before he could call it a day. Maybe he could mow the lawn and do some weeding before his kids got home. Tori, now eight, had dance class after school today, and Michael, eleven and getting gangly, had baseball practice. Since his wife's death, Tanner had been a single dad, and not a day went by that he wasn't grateful for his mom's help. She got his kids off to the bus stop each morning and chauffeured them to most of their activities, which took a huge load of responsibility off his shoulders.

Tanner delivered the last parcel of the day. After he dropped the van off at Courier Express, he needed to pick up some groceries. Milk, for one thing. Tori wouldn't eat breakfast without it. And if he didn't get bread, he'd have no fixings for his lunch tomorrow.

His cell phone, which rode atop a sticky mat on the dash, chimed with a message notification. Tanner grabbed the device and glanced at the screen to make sure the text wasn't from his mother. She never contacted him during work hours unless it was urgent. When he read the name of the sender, his hand froze on the steering wheel. *Tuck Malloy?* He almost went off the road into a ditch. How could that be? The old coot was dead. Wasn't he?

Tanner pulled over onto a wide spot, shifted into PARK, and stared at his phone. The message was definitely from Tuck. They had exchanged cell numbers months ago, and Tuck had occasionally texted to ask Tanner to pick up items he needed from the store. It hadn't been a bother for Tanner. There was a mom-and-pop grocery not that far away, and Tuck's house was on the road he always took back to town.

He swiped the screen. A smile curved his lips as he

read the message. *"I fell off the damned porch. Busted my arm, some ribs, and had to get a hip replacement. Now I'm doing time in assisted living, and the bitch that runs the place won't let me have my beer or chew. Can you buy me some of both and sneak it in to me? I'll pay you back."*

Tanner had been picturing the old fart in heaven, sitting on an Adirondack chair with a six-pack of Pabst Blue Ribbon and a spittoon within easy reach. It was unsettling to think someone was dead and then receive a text from him.

He tapped out a response. *"I don't mind bringing you things. My kids have activities this afternoon, so I'm not pressed for time. But I don't want to get in trouble for delivering forbidden substances. My job could be on the line."*

Tuck replied, *"No trouble. Just put it inside a box and pretend it's something I ordered. If I get caught, I'll never tell who brought me the stuff. Sorry I can't just call, but these nurses have sharp ears and I got no privacy."*

Tanner grinned. He trusted the old man not to reveal his name if it came down to that. And he truly did sympathize with Tuck's feelings of deprivation. Just because a man was eighty shouldn't mean he no longer had a right to indulge his habits. Staying at an assisted living facility was costly, and in Tanner's estimation, the residents should be able to do whatever they liked in their apartments as long as their physicians didn't object.

He texted, *"Do you have your doctor's permission to drink and chew?"*

Tuck replied, *"Well, he ain't said I shouldn't. I been drinking and chewing my whole life. I'm eighty. What can he say, that my pleasures might kill me?"*

Tanner chuckled. He agreed to deliver the requested items and asked Tuck for the address. He was surprised to learn the facility was in Mystic Creek. Tanner didn't cover that area, and it was a thirty-minute drive to get there. He mulled over the fact that he would be driving for more than an hour round-trip in a Courier Express van to run a personal errand. He'd also be using company fuel, which didn't seem right, but he supposed he could top off the tank to make up for that. He could also adjust his time sheet so he wouldn't be paid for an hour he hadn't actually worked.

Whistling tunelessly, Tanner made the drive to Mystic Creek. He hadn't yet gotten over this way. The curvy two-lane highway offered beautiful scenery, tree-covered mountain peaks, craggy buttes, and silvery flashes of a river beyond the stands of ponderosa pine. To his surprise, he saw a turnoff to Crystal Falls—the actual waterfall, not the town—and he made a mental note to bring the kids up sometime to see it. They'd get a kick out of that. Maybe they could spread a blanket on the riverbank and have a picnic.

Once in Mystic Creek, a quaint and well-kept little town, he found a grocery store on East Main called Flagg's Market, where he purchased two six-packs of beer and a whole roll of Copenhagen for his elderly friend. In the van he always carried extra box flats. He assembled a medium-size one, stuck what he now thought of as the contraband into it, and taped the flaps closed. With a ballpoint pen, he wrote Tuck's full name, the address, and the apartment number on a Courier Express mailing slip, which he affixed to the cardboard. *Done.* Now he'd just drive to the facility and make the delivery. The rest would be up to Tuck.

Mystic Creek Retirement Living was in a large brick building with two wings that angled out toward the front parking lot. The back of the facility bordered Mystic Creek, which bubbled and chattered cheerfully between banks lined with greenery, weeping willows, and pines. He suspected the residents spent a lot of time on the rear lawns, enjoying the sounds of rushing water and birdsong. If he were living there, that's what he would do.

Striding across the parking area with the box in his arms, Tanner began to feel nervous. What if someone questioned him? Pausing outside the double glass doors, he took a calming breath and then pushed inside. A middle-aged woman with red hair sat at the front desk. She fixed her friendly-looking blue gaze on Tanner's face and smiled.

"You're new," she observed. "Brian usually delivers our Courier Express packages."

Tanner nodded. "Uh, yeah. Just helping out today. I've got a package for Tucker Malloy, apartment twenty-three."

She pointed to a wide hallway to the left of the counter. "About halfway down on the right."

Tanner circled her workstation and moved past her. When he reached Tuck's room, he knocked on the door and called, "Delivery. Courier Express."

He heard a shuffling sound, and seconds later, Tuck opened the door, flashing a broad grin. "Come in, come in," he said in a booming voice. "Must be those shoes and pants I ordered."

Tanner winked at his old friend as he made his way through the doorway. As he set the box on the living room floor, he noticed that Tuck held a walking cane in his left hand. After closing the door, he walked with a limp as he crossed the tiny kitchen. Tanner guessed the old fellow's hip still pained him. Otherwise he looked the same, tall and lean with slightly stooped shoulders. His blue eyes held the same merry twinkle. Deep smile creases bracketed his mouth. His hair, still thick, was mostly silver, but a few streaks of brown remained to indicate its original color.

"It's good to see you," Tanner told him. "When your place went up for sale, I tried to call you several times and left you voice mails. Then I couldn't get through anymore. I figured you'd passed away and your phone had been retired to a drawer."

"Hell, no. I'm too ornery to kick the bucket just yet. Not to say it's an outlandish thing for you to think. At eighty, I don't buy green bananas anymore. They're a risky investment."

Tanner laughed. Tuck bent to open the box, plucked

a can of beer from one six-pack yoke, and offered it up. With regret, Tanner declined. "I can't stay, Tuck. My kids will be getting home in a couple of hours."

Tuck straightened slowly, as if stiffness had settled into his spine. On his right arm he wore a red elbow-high cast that extended down over the back of his hand to his knuckles and encircled his thumb. "That's a shame. I miss our bullshit sessions."

"Me, too," Tanner confessed. "I'll try to come back for a visit when I have more time." He bent to lift the six-packs from the box. "Where you planning to hide these?"

"In my boots and coat pockets. My beer'll be warm, but that's better'n nothin'."

Tanner carried the twelve-ounce containers to the closet, opened the doors, and began slipping cans into the old man's footwear. Tuck hobbled in with the roll of Copenhagen, which Tanner broke open before stuffing the rounds into shirt and jacket pockets. He couldn't help but grin when everything was hidden. With a wink at Tuck, he whispered, "They'll never know."

"Damn, I hope not," Tuck said. "My Pabst Blue Ribbon helps me relax at night. Without it I toss and turn. When I complain, the damned administrator just scowls at me and says to ask my doctor for sleeping pills. Like that'd be any better for my health? Hell, no. I like my beer."

Tanner stared at him. "What are you going to do with the empties?"

Tuck winked. "They got a resident laundry room down the hall with two tall trash cans. I'll sneak 'em down there and bury 'em real deep under other garbage."

"I see no harm in you enjoying your beer of an evening unless your doctor has forbidden it," Tanner said. "You'd tell me if that were the case. Right?"

"Wouldn't have asked you if he had. I don't have a death wish. I just want my damn beers and chew. The doc knows I have three beers a night and he never said nothin'. Of course, it's a different fella here. Their Dr. Fancy Pants might not make allowances for a man's personal pleasures."

"That sucks." Tanner had never stopped to consider how many liberties people could lose when they grew old. "But it's temporary. Right? Once you've healed, you can live somewhere else again." Tanner remembered the real estate sign on Tuck's front gate. "You *do* get to leave here, I hope."

"The doctors are sayin' that I shouldn't live alone again." He shrugged. "At my age, that's how it goes, with other people decidin' what's best for you."

"I'm sorry to hear you can't live alone anymore." Tanner sincerely meant that. "Maybe you can make arrangements for some kind of in-home care. If you can afford that, of course."

"I'm workin' on it. I got plenty of money saved back, so I had Crystal get me another house here in Mystic Creek. She found a nice little place on ten acres just outside town. It's a short drive from her salon, and she's already livin' there. The house was made over for an old lady in a wheelchair, but she passed away. Crystal thinks it'll suit my needs, and she's willin' to stay there to look after me."

Tanner nodded. "That sounds ideal. Ten acres isn't quite as much land as you had in Crystal Falls, but at least you'll still have elbow room." For most of his life, Tuck had been a rancher. Tanner doubted he would be happy living inside the city limits on a small lot. "You're blessed to have a granddaughter who loves you so much."

"I am, for certain. She's a sweet girl."

"Where's Bolt? At the new place?"

"Nope. Crystal has enough to do without fussin' over a horse. I had her find a place to board him. When I'm able, I'll bring him home and take care of him."

Tanner walked back into the living room, stabbing his fingers under his belt to neaten the tuck of his brown uniform shirt. "I sure wish I could stay for a while, but I've got to run."

"I understand. It'll soon be suppertime, and you've got kiddos to feed. Next time we'll enjoy a beer together and get caught up. You drive safe on that curlicue highway gettin' home. You're all your kids have left."

Tanner paused at the door. An urge came over him to hug the old fart goodbye. He wasn't sure when he'd come to care so much about Tuck, but after believing him to be dead for nearly a month, he found the feelings were there inside him. The old man had some crazy notions that Tanner didn't agree with, and sometimes he told stories so far-fetched that no sane person could believe them. But he also had a big heart, an indomitable spirit, and a way of looking at life that brought everything into perspective for Tanner sometimes. Still, Tanner wasn't sure the older man would appreciate being hugged.

"I'll be seeing you," he said.

Then he let himself out and softly closed the door.

Crystal Malloy's feet ached as if she'd run barefoot on concrete for eight hours. When she glanced in the styling mirror and saw her reflection, she yearned to wash her long red hair. Pink spray-on highlights had been a poor choice. The clash of color was nauseating, and she looked awful. But she had no time to spare for herself. She hadn't even found time to eat lunch or visit the bathroom.

Prom night. It was normally her favorite spring event, the school year's grand finale that always filled her salon to the brim with customers. She had girls sitting double in the chairs lining one wall and all four stations were filled with more teenagers. They wanted updos, wash-out streaks, metallic highlights, straight hair, curly hair, or crimped hair. And all of them wanted their makeup done.

The sulfuric smell of permanent-wave solution burned Crystal's nostrils, her skin felt sticky from the clouds of hair spray inside the building, and her nerves were shot. Her technicians had been trained never to overbook appointments, so half these kids must have been walk-ins. With only four stations, how would they get to all of them? There were drawbacks to owning the most popular salon in town.

Relax, she told herself. *Just roll with it. By six thirty, they'll all look gorgeous and be going home to put on their gowns.* Only, she was so tired. It had been a long day, and everything that could go wrong had gone wrong. At noon she'd gotten a call from a neighbor that Rip, her grandfather's dog, was running loose again. In order to find the animal, she'd had to hand over a tint job to Shannon Monroe, a tall, slender brunette who'd had a cancellation and was able to finish the customer's hair. Then, after two hours of driving the gravel roads surrounding Tuck's new house, she had missed two more appointments and she *still* hadn't found the dog. Where was he? Had he been struck by a car? Her grandfather loved that heeler like no tomorrow and would be inconsolable if anything happened to him. Even worse, Rip's escapes were becoming a daily occurrence. How could she make a living when she spent half of what should have been her workdays looking for a runaway canine? Locking him up inside the house was out. He was destructive when he was confined indoors alone.

Glancing around the salon, Crystal remembered a time when this place had been only a dream. Instead of being in a foul mood, she should have felt proud of her accomplishments and thankful that she'd met her goals. The shop was high-end and classy. The hair and nail techs were dressed in designer uniforms. The waiting room was packed with paying customers who hoped to look beautiful when they left. Soft Hawaiian music played on the sound system, enabling people to imagine they were in a tropical paradise. The thought made Crystal smile. Mystic Creek was anything but tropical. City plows sometimes left berms of winter snow in the middle of the street that were higher than her head.

The phone rang just as Crystal had finished applying temporary color to a strand of a girl's blond hair. "I can't get it! Does anyone have a hand free?"

Nadine Judge, a half-Cherokee woman with thick black hair and almond-shaped brown eyes, yelled back, "I'll get it!" Then Crystal heard her say, "I'm sorry. Is this an emergency, Patricia? She's really busy." Then, in a louder voice, she cried, "You've got to take it, Crystal. It's Patricia from the assisted living facility. Tuck has done something wrong, and she's threatening to evict him."

Pain bulleted into Crystal's temples. For a dizzying moment, bright spots danced before her eyes. When her vision cleared, she grabbed a piece of foil, laid a still-wet strand of her young client's lavender hair on it, and said, "Sorry, Megan. I'll be right back."

Crystal walked over to the front desk. Nadine cupped her hand over the mouthpiece and said in a stage whisper, "God, she can't kick him out! You don't even have neighbors near the house who can check on him during the day, and according to what you've said, he's still not steady on his feet."

Crystal didn't need anyone to outline the reasons she couldn't take her grandfather home yet. She tried to smile at Nadine and knew she failed miserably. She took the phone and pressed it to her ear. "This is Crystal."

"Hello, Crystal. This is Patricia Flintlock. *Again.* Your grandfather has really done it this time."

Crystal clenched her teeth and counted to five. She didn't have time to go clear to ten. "Hi, Patricia. I know Tuck is having a hard time adjusting to his new surroundings, but surely he's done nothing so bad that he should be evicted."

"Think again." Patricia didn't handle a position of authority well. As administrator of the assisted living center, she reigned like a female Hitler. "I have rules in this facility, and they're nonnegotiable."

The pain in Crystal's temples stabbed deeper. "What rule has Tuck broken?"

"Make that *rules.* We caught him drinking beer and chewing tobacco in his apartment. I will not countenance drunkenness in my building, and chewing tobacco is messy and thoroughly disgusting. I won't have it, I'm telling you!"

Crystal had to bite her tongue. She'd gone to live with Tuck when she was eleven; she was now thirty-two, and in all those years she'd never seen her grandfather drunk. "How could Tuck get his hands on beer and chew? He can't drive yet, and even if he could, his truck is at the house."

"Well, now," Patricia replied in a snarky tone,

"that's a good question, and the only answer I can think of is that *you* brought it to him. I know you're aware of the facility rules. Your flagrant disregard of them is infuriating, to say the least."

Crystal struggled to control her temper. "That's a preposterous accusation. You know Tuck isn't recovered enough to come home. I haven't even found a daytime caregiver for him yet. Why would I take him beer and tobacco when I'm fully aware that you might evict him from the only place he has to stay right now?"

"Another good question. Tuck is new to Mystic Creek. Nobody but you comes to visit him. Do you expect me to believe those substances appeared out of thin air?"

"I expect you to believe me when I tell you straight-out that I did not supply my grandfather with beer and chew."

"You complained early on about the rules here being too strict."

"But I agreed to abide by them," Crystal argued. "And I have. I don't know how Tuck got his hands on beer, but I can assure you I'll find out and it'll never happen again."

"You need to come to the facility. We'll discuss the matter further. Your grandfather is upset and yelling obscenities. If you don't get him calmed down, I'm calling the police."

Crystal scanned the crowded salon. She couldn't leave her techs to deal with all this by themselves. But she knew the facility administrator meant what she said. She'd evict Tuck without hesitation. "It's prom night, Patricia, one of my busiest days of the year. I've got a girl half-finished at my station. I can't drop everything and leave her with only one side of her head streaked."

"We all have our problems. Mine is an angry old man who is disturbing other residents."

Crystal started to reply, but Patricia hung up before she could. She stared stupidly at the phone and then returned it to the charging base.

"What did Tuck do this time?" Nadine, putting the finishing touches on a girl's layered bob, flashed a worried look over her shoulder. "What'll you do if she kicks him out?"

Crystal jerked off her salon jacket, a dark brown tunic-length garment patterned with palm fronds. "They caught him with beer and chewing tobacco. Patricia says he's yelling obscenities and being disruptive."

"Patricia Flintlock is an uptight pain in the butt," Nadine retorted. "Why can't Tuck have a couple of beers? Better question, what is her definition of an obscenity?"

Crystal tossed the jacket in the laundry basket. "Regardless, I have to drive over there and get Tuck settled down. Then I need to defuse the situation so he doesn't get kicked out." Glancing toward her station, she said, "I'm sorry for abandoning all of you, but I see no way around it."

Jules Wilson, a slightly plump blonde with twinkly

blue eyes, said, "I can finish Megan. You have an emergency on your hands. And, Crystal, recommend to Patricia that she come to see me. I'll color her hair and accidently make it green."

Crystal grabbed her purse and left the building. The moment she stepped out onto the back porch, she dragged in a deep breath of fresh air and took a moment to appreciate the sunlight angling through the pine boughs to splash the needle-covered ground with butter yellow. *Everything will be okay,* she assured herself. *Patricia will get over her snit, and Tuck will start behaving himself. All I need is a couple more weeks to make arrangements. Then I'll be able to take care of him.*